18

D1437032

GOODBYE TO DREAMS

GOODBYE TO DREAMS

GRACE THOMPSON

First published in Great Britain 2011
by
Robert Hale Limited

Published in Large Print 2011 by ISIS Publishing Ltd.,
7 Centremead, Osney Mead, Oxford OX2 0ES
by arrangement with
Johnson & Alcock Ltd.

British Library Cataloguing in Publication Data
Thompson, Grace.
    Goodbye to dreams.
    1. Sisters - - Fiction.
    2. Family-owned business enterprises - - Fiction.
    3. Large type books.
    I. Title
    823.9'14–dc22

ISBN 978–0–7531–8906–1 (hb)
ISBN 978–0–7531–8907–8 (pb)

Printed and bound in Great Britain by
T. J. International Ltd., Padstow, Cornwall

CHAPTER
ONE

As the last minutes of 1929 slipped away, the music in the dance hall seemed to become more and more frantic. Even when the eight-piece orchestra was playing a waltz, the figures on the floor moved at a rapid pace, jigging up and down in the excitement of the occasion, laughing breathlessly as they gave up trying to keep to the beat of the music. It was unlikely that anyone, even the most accomplished and enthusiastic ballroom dancer, could have performed much of a dance: there was no room to move their feet more than a few inches at each step.

Cecily Owen watched the clock on the furthest wall and tried to keep her eye on it until the minute hand jerked and clicked forward, marking the passing of another minute. She was always excited at the prospect of a new year, although she shuddered at the reminder of how her youth was slipping away. For a moment the thought took hold of her, isolating her from the hilarity around her. The waltz finished and the band began the lively strains of "Oh Johnny". Around her dancers and watchers began singing and Cecily heard many changing the name to one of their own favourite love. She began to follow the words in her mind, substituting the name for Gareth, in a secret prayer that 1930 would be the year in which Gareth Price-Jones thought of her as more than a dancing partner. She looked around the room for him and saw he was dancing with her sister, Ada. She only caught a glimpse of them through the bobbing and swirling crowd, laughing and talking, their heads thrown back in relaxed abandon. She felt a surge of jealousy and willed him to come back to her for the next dance.

The Owen sisters were alike, although Ada, the younger by two years, was a less vibrant version of her twenty-five-year-old sister. Her hair was brown rather than golden and was inclined to frizz from the permanent waves they both suffered from time to time. Ada's eyes were grey and Cecily's were blue but apart from the colouring differences they were very alike and were often mistaken for twins.

The music stopped and the red-faced musicians took out their handkerchiefs to wipe their brows. It was like a band of people at a railway station waving goodbye to friends, Cecily thought, as the white plumes rose in the air and were shaken backwards and forwards in the vicinity of each sweating face. She smiled at the thought.

Even in the uncomfortably hot dance hall, Cecily had no more than an attractive glow in her cheeks. Her blonde hair was set in waves as rigid as the ripples in wet sand on the local beach down each side of her head, ending in kiss-curls which framed her pretty face.

She jumped up and down to see over the heads of the dancers who waited for the Master of Ceremonies to announce the next dance in case a friend she had not yet seen had arrived later. She pretended not to notice Gareth asking one of the other girls in their crowd to dance with him as the conductor raised his baton and the first chord sounded. A young man asked her to dance and she took to the floor, passing her sister, who grabbed her arm and shouted, "Make for the windows at five to twelve — we've got to be together at New Year!"

"You bet!" Cecily shouted back as she was whisked away.

When the dance ended she thanked her partner and, standing on one of the chairs arranged around the edge of the dance floor, searched the crowd. She saw Ada's neatly waved head and, close to it, very close, Gareth's dark one. She willed him to look for her and ask for a dance. He was an excellent dancer as well as someone she was beginning to find more and more attractive.

When the Master of Ceremonies announced a foxtrot she crossed her fingers and looked hopefully towards him but he was soon lost from her sight as some struggled to leave the floor and others fought for a place to attempt the dance. The musicians were wearily sorting out their music. She watched and smiled at the efforts of the women to pat their shiny faces with lacy, scent-sprayed handkerchiefs, and the men, running fingers around their collars to ease their hot, sticky necks. The heat didn't worry Cecily, it was all part of the fun: the heat, the crowd, the noise.

She wondered how many the room held. The ticket sellers had told her there were 250 tickets sold but she felt certain there were more. Extra tickets printed and sold on the side, maybe? It wouldn't be the first time the printer, Phil Spencer, had earned himself a little extra in that way. She had never trusted Phil Spencer, not since he had been found out in the chicken raffle swindle. She remembered now Phil Spencer's name had been in the paper accused of printing extra tickets and pocketing the money.

The orchestra started up again and the babble of chattering lessened. Gareth pushed his way through the crowd that was pairing off for the next dance and Cecily managed to avoid the man approaching her, obviously intent on asking her to partner him. She smiled at Gareth and slipped into his arms.

His straight brown hair fell wetly over his forehead now, and his rather prominent ears were shiny and red. It was when he smiled that his attraction was revealed. His full mouth opened slightly and his even white teeth glistened. Eyes which were really a nondescript light brown sparkled when he smiled and his whole face lit up and made Cecily feel wonderful for being the cause of the transformation. How could she have once thought him unattractive?

They began to dance, but the crush of people who were becoming more and more giggly and foolish as midnight approached defeated any attempt to follow the correct steps or even the rhythm so determinedly adhered to by the metronomic arms of the conductor. They settled for just moving to the music and enjoying the excitement of the hour.

"We'd better try to get near the windows," Cecily said. "Ada will be there and I don't want to be on the other side of the room when midnight strikes."

"Get behind me and I'll push us a path through. We'll tread on a few toes but no one will care." Gareth took her hand and wove his way through the dancers, pulling her behind him.

Reaching the window, he didn't let go of her hand and she smiled at him. He really was rather nice, and clearly interested in her as more than a dance partner. If only his mam would leave him alone, she sighed inwardly, then he would surely invite her out.

Her musings on Gareth, and Mrs Price-Jones, his possessive mother, were cut short by the musicians playing a loud chord. The drummer began a roll which increased in volume until everyone was standing silently, waiting for the announcement to come.

The Master of Ceremonies stepped up beside the conductor and said, "Ladies and gentlemen, I know you will forgive my interruption of the dancing a little before time when I tell you about the surprise we have arranged for you. In exactly four minutes we will be tuning the wireless to 2LO to hear the broadcast sound of Big Ben, in London, chiming in the new year." He held up his hand to quell the applause and the burst of excited chatter. "So, if you open the windows and join us to the millions doing the same, we will listen to the new year begin. Ladies and gentlemen, 1930 is about to be welcomed in and may it hold nothing but good fortune for us all!"

Gareth pulled Cecily closer. "He isn't expecting to hear Big Ben through the window, is he?" he joked. "South Wales we are, not the great metropolis!" Cecily laughed and they were both hushed. A few people in the closely packed revellers moved closer to their special friends and lovers and Cecily felt Ada's arms touch hers as she pressed close to her sister and whispered, "May it be a good one for us both, eh?"

"Yes. With our dad leaving us alone to get on with running the shop the way we want to run it!" Cecily whispered back. "That's one wish for the new year." She looked up at Gareth but kept that other more fervent wish to herself.

Through the loudspeaker set up on the far wall, peals of bells came loud, adding to the excitement in the room. Cecily felt a lump swell in her throat. New Year was one of the many occasions that made her want to weep although she would be hard pushed to explain why. She felt Gareth's hand touch hers and their fingers joined. On her other side, Ada's hand reached for hers and she hoped that the three of them would be together a year's hence but with Gareth more than a dancing partner. She was unaware that her sister was looking at Gareth and wishing the same.

The bells ceased and others could be heard, this time through the open windows. A silence followed when everyone seemed to be holding their breath. Then the sound of Big Ben was heard reverberating around them, chiming out the beginning of the new and sending the old year on its way. Forget the past, the chimes seemed to say, this is a new year, a new decade and a new beginning.

It had been a bad decade for many in the small, Welsh seaside town where employment was at a low ebb and hundreds queued for even a single day's work at the factories and timber yards and docks. Women helped family finances by accepting poorly paid, menial tasks. Some found seasonal work serving teas on the beach, carrying trays to families of summer visitors and thankful for the few shillings the tiring work brought them. Men stood on street corners beside boarded up shops. The lacklustre of their defeated spirits showing in their eyes and in the slouched shoulders.

Allotments flourished and it was there that many spent the days, digging, hoeing and coaxing a crop from the earth, or standing in groups leaning on their spades and discussing other, more buoyant times and the good years that would surely come. They would return home burnt by the sun on their faces and necks down as far as the respectable collars they wore. The sun was never allowed to touch their skin lower than that most uncomfortable garment, making their heads and upper neck look incongruously contrasted with their pale bodies when shirt and collar finally came off in the privacy of their darkened bedrooms. Winter or summer, respectability was worn like a jewel.

Cecily and Ada were protected from the worst of the poverty by their shop. That, and the work their father found on the docks where cargo ships were unloaded and reloaded with goods as varied as Welsh coal and awkward pig iron to the carefully handled bananas. Old

7

bones, collected hundreds of miles away in some distant desert, arrived to be ground down to make bone-meal to feed those essential fields and allotments. Another ship might bring undreamed-of luxuries like furs and silks for the backs of the very rich.

Cecily wanted to be rich. She had talked of her dreams to their mother frequently until the day she had left them to start a new life with a man who offered her more than Owen Owen and his small shop.

Cecily missed her mother dreadfully and frustration grew as month after month their father persistently refused to allow them to run the shop as they wanted. He was deaf to their entreaties to increase stock to encourage more customers. Most weeks the takings hardly did more than cover their expenses. She and Ada frequently talked long into the night about their dream of complete ownership. But what chance was there of that?

On this New Year, she closed her eyes and wished for some change of their fortune that would bring about the chance she and Ada needed. Some change of heart on their father's part to allow them to manage the shop in their own way. She opened her eyes and saw Gareth smiling at her.

"What are you wishing for, then?"

"Never you mind, Gareth Price-Jones," she teased, "but a kiss will do for a start."

"Bold you are, Cecily Owen." He kissed her briefly, in an embarrassed way, hoping no one would notice and report back to his mam — she did go on, so.

Through the windows, where people leaned out as if to join the rest of the world in their celebrating, the chorus of ships' hooters continued, some deep and some shrill, in a crazy symphony. Steam engines whistled, car horns sounded and sirens wailed into the night. As the cacophony faded, the band began to play Auld Lang Syne and the dancers organized themselves into two concentric circles, linked arms and sang with gusto.

The music stopped and all around them couples were kissing, changing partners and kissing again. Shyness and inhibitions were lost as the excitement of the hour bewitched them all. Cecily turned first to hug her sister then to Gareth. Before the orchestra could begin to play again, Gareth put an arm around both sisters and began to perform a polka, shouting the tunes unmelodiously. Seeing them, others did the same. This time, the band, instead of being the instigator of the dance, followed them, joining in gradually to the despair of the conductor.

In a corner of the hall, hidden by the few people not joining in the impromptu polka and by the shadow of the balcony above him, a man stood watching the crowd. He stepped back sometimes and to the keen observer it would have been plain that he wanted to watch someone without being seen himself. His dark eyes never left Cecily.

He was tall but stood stooped, perhaps as a disguise against recognition. His black hair curled around his face and helped him to fade into the shadows and it was only his eyes catching the light that made some aware of his silent, non-participating presence. He looked foreign or maybe a gypsy; there was even an earring in one ear to add to that impression. Dark, dark eyes and a skin bronzed, even now in the middle of winter, made others look pale and sickly beside him, although few noticed him enough to comment, except for a young prostitute looking for someone to take home for the night.

He had paid for a ticket but had not once stepped out to dance. Two shillings wasted really, he thought, but he knew this was the one place where he could be certain of seeing Cecily. His teeth clenched as he watched her hugging Gareth and showering others with hand-blown kisses with a few real ones for some of the young men who showed eagerness to be so saluted.

"Tart!" he muttered angrily.

He had seen enough. Leaving the crowded room where the last hour of dancing was well underway, he moved through the doors and made for the exit into the cold night.

"Dance, sailor?" The young girl stopped and faced him, pert face looking up into his, a hand spread on the opposite wall, her arm a slender barrier.

"I don't dance. I just came to see someone."

"Won't I do instead, sailor?" She put her head on one side appealingly.

"I'm not a sailor and no, you won't!" He was so angry with himself for bothering to reply, repulsed by the expression in the young/old face. She succeeded in delaying his departure and he backed away and

10

re-entered the hall. He continued to stand amid the revellers, thinking his own angry thoughts, oblivious to the merriment around him, hating himself for being there but unable to leave. In his distressed mind, Cecily and the young prostitute were alike. He watched, feasting his eyes and his anger on the sight of Cecily dancing as close to Gareth as ivy to an oak tree.

The dancing was little more than a blatant excuse for cuddling; clear to see now the crowd had thinned a little. Their cheeks were touching and he felt the familiar jerk of pain when he saw the glazed and dreamy expression in Cecily's eyes, a look he remembered so well. Good luck, Gareth, he thought bitterly, you'll need it! The sight produced the deep agony of jealousy, but still he stayed.

At one o'clock the Master of Ceremonies announced the last waltz. The lights were lowered and partners chosen. To the surprise of the man watching, Cecily and Ada left the floor. He searched the heads of the dancers as they drifted past his shadowed corner but there was no sign of Gareth. He must have slipped away to avoid the dance which tacitly asked to escort a girl home. "Best for him too," he muttered with mild satisfaction.

People dawdled out, reluctant to end the evening, a contented tiredness slowing their steps, and he began to push his way through. Reaching the door, the cold hit him and he tightened his navy coat more tightly around him, pulling up the collar against the icy night air. He had left his motorbike propped against a tree but when he reached the place it had gone.

★　★　★

Gareth felt guilty about hurrying away before the end of the dance but he did not want to take Cecily home, not with Ada there too — it would have been embarrassing. Besides, Willie would be waiting for them with the horse and trap. He knew how close the sisters were and how difficult it was going to be to get between them. If he tried, that is. Mam was against him taking Cecily out. "No prospect there," she repeatedly told him. "With two sisters-in-law to argue about the shop when Owen Owen goes, those girls will have nothing."

Gareth didn't consider that a disadvantage. Better to have a wife dependent upon a man; there was less likely to be any trouble that way. No, with his barber's shop doing very nicely, he thought he and Cecily would manage very well. But it was best to listen to Mam, for a while yet anyway.

He broke into a run, the tunes he and Cecily had danced to ringing in his head. It had been a good night. Pity not to end it by walking Cecily home though. Perhaps if he invited her home for tea one day, he mused. Mam might soften towards her if she talked to her a bit more. He walked past the barber's shop where he earned the money to keep himself and his mother. The adjoining shop was a tobacconist, both shops sharing the same triangular-shaped entrance. Now if he could buy that as well as his own he'd be comfortably off. He wondered idly how much old man Owen would leave to Cecily. If Mam thought her prospects were good she would be more tolerant.

He removed his shoes before going into the house. Light sleeper was Mam. No need for her to know just

12

how late he got home. He ate some bread and jam and went to bed to dream about Cecily.

The man who had watched Cecily and Gareth dancing cursed when he failed to find his motorbike in the vicinity of the dance hall. He went back to the doors which were spilling out the last of the laughing, happy revellers and listened to the shouts of friends arranging other venues and calling affectionate goodbyes. The doorman shook his head when questioned. He didn't remember hearing a motorbike start up.

"Not a chance in the rowdiness of the past hours," he grumbled. "Young people today, never happy unless they're making a row. A real suck-in this job is. Told me I'd finish at twelve and here it is gone half past one and me still trying to get them off the premises." He turned and shouted for the stragglers to hurry.

The man left the doorman still complaining and went to begin a search of the streets. Outside he bumped into the girl he had been watching but had hoped to avoid meeting.

"Danny!" Cecily gasped.

"Hello, Cecily, Ada." He nodded at the surprised sisters. "Someone has stolen my motorbike," he said foolishly, as an explanation of his presence there at that time.

"Willie's waiting for us with the trap if you'd like a lift?" Cecily spoke nervously, quickly. She didn't know whether to stop and talk or run away.

Danny shook his head. "No, I'd better search for the bike."

"No, come on, Danny," Ada said, taking his arm, "come with us. Willie won't mind driving around. Better chance of finding it then."

Cecily was in a daze. She stood, silent, as Danny approached the trap, and it was Ada who explained to Willie what had happened. The young stable boy nodded and jumped down to help Cecily and Ada up to their seats.

"Come on, Cecily," Ada said with a laugh. "Don't fall asleep yet!"

"I'm sorry." Danny belatedly offered his arm to help her.

His arm was something long lost and recently found. The others were talking, discussing where they should look for the bike, but to Cecily their voices sounded far off, as if she were in the strange state when sleep had almost claimed her yet allowed her to eavesdrop on what was going on around her. Ada poked her cheerfully. "Budge up, sis, make room for me." And Cecily shook off the disbelief of seeing Danny so unexpectedly, and smiled at her sister.

"I can't remember seeing a bike, or hearing one start," young Willie was saying. "Fell asleep I did. Damn me, someone could have stolen the horse and I wouldn't have noticed." He clicked at the horse and they began to pull away. "Leave it to me, I'll go round the locality in a pattern. Find it for you we will, no trouble."

Cecily sat next to Danny, her heart pounding painfully, unable to start a conversation, unable to believe that after seven years she was sitting beside

Danny Preston. He too seemed unable to speak. It was Ada who filled the air with her chatter. Cecily shrugged herself deeper into her fur-collared coat and listened as Ada began to talk about the dance.

"There's a pity you don't like dancing, Danny. Great fun it was, all crowded together and sharing the celebration."

"More for the out-of-doors, me," Danny replied, his voice deep and strong, making Cecily start. She had been telling herself he was a ghost, an unreal image, dragged out of her heart by thoughts of being married to Gareth. She saw his head move slightly and knew the remark was for her. Dancing versus the great outdoors, that had been their constant problem. Dancing was the one subject she needed to avoid, and Ada, bless her, had jumped straight into it.

"You always did prefer walks to dancing, didn't you, Danny?" Ada was saying. "Just as well, you taking a job as a postman! Still a postman, are you? Haven't heard of you for years, Danny Preston."

"Still a postman."

"And we're still helping Dadda in the shop. Doing most everything now, mind. With our mam not with us any more."

"I heard about her going off with some man and leaving you all." A brief embarrassed silence and he added, "Your father, still on the docks, is he?"

"Yes, but he helps us with the heavy stuff. Young Willie too. He does a lot to help us. Couldn't manage without Willie, could we, Cecily? But it's me and Cecily running things, ever since Mam . . . left."

Cecily felt the blush heat her face despite the freezing air. The second worst subject to discuss with Danny was their mother running off with the coalman and apart from a scrappy note written on the back of a used envelope, no explanation or a word telling them she was sorry.

"What about trying up round the park?" she suggested, hoping to change the subject. "Aren't we supposed to be looking for a bike?"

"I'm heading there now," Willie said. "Keep a good lookout." He showed no embarrassment at listening to their conversation. He was sixteen and had worked for the Owens in one capacity or another since he was nine.

"Where are you living now, Danny?" Ada asked.

Why doesn't she be quiet, give him a chance to say something? Cecily thought irritably. Tell us what he was doing outside the dance hall for a start.

"I'm back home with Mam, for the present, that is."

Cecily's breath shortened. She waited for the next words. Was he about to say he was married? Living at home with his wife? Or soon to be married and expecting to change accommodation? She had heard nothing of him since they parted when she was eighteen.

Willie called for the horse to "whoa" and stopped near a lamppost. "Come on, Miss Ada. You walk around one side of the park with me and these two can walk round the other. Save us time, that will."

They all obediently stepped down and Danny walked beside Cecily, leaving the other two to walk in the opposite direction and circle the small park. He didn't touch her and only an occasional cough revealed his nervousness. Cecily still failed to think of a word to say to him. Questions abounded in her head. She wanted to know what he had been doing, whether there was someone else in his life, if marriage was on his mind, or whether he had found it impossible to let another New Year pass without seeing her and finding a way back to what they'd had all those years ago. His unreasonable jealously had ruined their love and she wondered if he would remain her only love. Guilt brought Gareth to mind. Gareth was different. She would have married him and cared for him, but there would never have been the excitement and passion she'd known with Danny Preston. Perhaps, she thought with a brief moment of understanding, perhaps that was how it had been for her mother.

"What have you been doing since we parted, Danny?" she asked at last. "None of the crowd have seen you and no news of you has filtered back. You might as well have gone to Australia."

"I did leave, I went to sea. For five years I travelled in cargo ships in and out of a hundred ports. Then I grew tired of it all. I lived in Spain for a while but politics made things difficult so I came home. Went back to delivering letters."

"I'm glad," she whispered, but he appeared not to hear.

"I came home, got a job and found myself a girl and now I'm going to be married. Next month my wife and I will be moving into rooms in Foxhole Street." He said the words fast, as if to prevent her from commenting.

"Foxhole Street. That's over the far side of the docks, near the Pleasure Beach, isn't it? Very nice over there." She was amazed at how calm she sounded, coming so soon after his unexpected reappearance had hurled her back into a dream of his returning to her. All thoughts of Gareth had fled. He was here, walking beside her in the darkness, then the foolish, fanciful, golden dream had been shattered.

"Sudden, wasn't it?" she forced herself to ask. "Meeting this girl and planning to marry her?"

Why did you come? she asked silently and, as if she had spoken the words aloud, he said, "I came to the dance to look for you."

"Why?"

"I've thought about you a lot during the last seven years, Cecily. I've wondered, in the dark loneliness of nights in foreign places, whether we'd made a mistake all those years ago. When I came back and heard you weren't married I wondered, for a while, if I should come back into your life."

"Supposing of course that I wanted you to!" she couldn't help blurting out. "But you didn't."

"I didn't. I met Jessie and she seems to suit me, want the same things and we, well, we're getting married."

"Love match, is it?" Her voice was sweet but the sarcasm was clear.

"I wouldn't marry her if I didn't love her," he defended.

18

"Then why did you come and find me tonight? That was what you were doing, wasn't it? Probably watching me dancing and having a good time and even though you no longer love me, you still felt the old jealousy writhing inside you like an evil snake." She fought down the temptation to hit him for his stupidity. After seven years she still wanted to hit out at the foolish jealously that had forced them to separate. "Danny Preston, with all your world travel and vast experiences, you're still a fool."

Voices came then. Willie and Ada in muted voices, conscious of the lateness of the hour and of people sleeping in the nearby houses. "Danny! We've found it!" Ada called.

"Not damaged so far as I can see," Willie added.

"Not even hidden. It's just by the wall over by there!"

Cecily couldn't decide whether she was glad the painful interlude was over, or sorry they couldn't have worked through the anger and recriminations to something approaching harmony. After seven years it was unbelievable that they were at once on the defensive and even attack, after just moments in each other's company.

Willie and Ada didn't approach them but walked away waiting for Danny to follow to where they had found his motorbike.

Danny reached for her. "Cecily, why do we fight so?" He pulled her close and his lips touched hers, gentle at first but then with ever growing hunger. His touch, his arms enfolding her, the very scent of him were so familiar she sobbed as he released her. In the dim light of a distant street lamp, his eyes were moist too.

"Danny, it's been so long," she whispered. "I hoped you would no longer make me feel this way."

"I was a fool to come." He walked away, calling to Ada and Willie. "Where are you? Thanks for finding the bike. It's a long walk home."

Cecily didn't move to join them. She heard the sound of his feet running on the gravel road, the muffled talk and laughter. Then the sound of the bike starting up and moving away put an end to her anticipation of his returning to her. She wiped her eyes and called in a firm voice, "Come on, Ada, I'm frozen. Let's get home."

When he had settled them in the trap, Willie said, "We're so late anyway, what say we go around the beach road. It's a clear night and you're both well wrapped up."

"What a lovely idea, Willie," Ada said. She sat close to Cecily and put an arm around her, comforting, reliable and concerned. Sensitive to her sister's unease after seeing Danny. "We need to unwind a bit, don't we?"

The hoofs clopped and echoed, an impertinence in the solemn silence of the early hour. As they skirted the wide curving bay and saw the silver-tipped waves on a leaden sea, the only lights were from the few houses where some families still celebrated the beginning of a new year, a new decade.

The sea was separated from the sky by the thinnest pale line, but as they watched, morning came, borne reluctantly in on pink-tinged mist, rolling over eastern point until the lights in the houses were dimmed in its wake.

"Beautiful," Ada breathed.

"Melancholy," Cecily murmured.

"Late!" Willie announced firmly. He clicked to the weary horse and they trotted home through the empty streets.

Danny Preston rode home in the early morning, furious that he had wasted time coming to see Cecily. She hadn't changed. She was still a flirt, laughing and looking up into every man's face, widening her dazzling eyes, not able to keep her charms for one person. He opened the throttle, uncaring of the people he disturbed, remembering how she had hugged and kissed everyone within reach, her dress offering a generous view of her body. Why had he wasted even a moment imagining how she would welcome him back after the lonely years? Lonely years? She wasn't the type to be lonely!

His mind built images of her outgoing personality, her familiarity with strangers that showed her for what she really was: a tease and a flirt. How could he ever have contemplated marrying her and spending half his life wondering how friendly she was being while he wasn't with her? Her mother had left them to live with another man — it must be in the blood — and he'd been a fool to believe Cecily would change.

Jessie was far from exciting but at least she would give him peace of mind. He forced himself to think of quiet, gentle Jessie as he rode the last few yards to his home. Tomorrow he and Jessie would name the day for their wedding. Tonight had not been a waste of time; it had exorcised the obsession of Cecily Owen for good. But it was of Cecily he dreamed and whose face troubled his sleep that night and for many nights to come.

To Cecily the early morning ride was unreal. The wild dancing and the excitement of the New Year, the tentative hand-holding of Gareth, all seemed more like a play she had seen long ago, not recent moments in the darkness. Seeing Danny, sitting beside him, feeling his lips on hers, had distorted everything into a fantasy. Even the shop for which they were heading was not the home she had left only hours before but a place not seen for a long time. It was as if she were the one who had been away for seven years, not Danny, who had popped back into her life to rouse the flames still flickering there, only to fight and depart once more.

As they trotted along the main road she wondered vaguely about the time. If the town hall clock had chimed she had not heard it. The streets were not completely empty even now. When Willie turned the trap from the main road down the hill to the shop, a slow trickle of men were on the way to the docks, their hard boots joining the sound of the horse, who was hurrying now he was close to the stable and food. Shopkeepers were already at work washing pavements outside their premises and carrying out their wares to attract passers-by. Paper boys were off on their rounds, whistling cheerfully.

The shop bell tinkled as they opened the door. Willie waited until they were safely inside then walked the horse around to the back lane and the stable entrance. Cecily walked in first and their father stood up out of the large armchair.

"Been joy-riding, have you?" he asked disapprovingly. "Disgusting behaviour I call that, keeping that young lad out all night. Willie waits until all hours to see you two home safe — you could at least consider him a bit."

Owen Owen was a tall, thin man and as he rose to greet them, ash from the cigarette he had been smoking fell from his clothes. He was in stockinged feet: the heavy work boots were where he always put them, on the fender of the dying fire ready for the morning. Beside them the pipe he occasionally smoked lay fallen on its side, spent ash in an untidy heap. His eyes were red-rimmed with tiredness and the effect of the smoke drifting up to sting them, and held their customary sadness.

"I'll go and help Willie with the horse," he muttered. "Luckily I don't start till two o'clock today. Not that you worried about that!" Continuing his grumbles he stumbled across the room, down the passage and through the back kitchen to the yard.

"Been drinking bad by the look of him," Ada whispered.

"I'll go up and see that Myfanwy is all right." Cecily ran up the stairs and opened the door of the little girl's room. The covers were thrown back and she carefully tucked them around the sleeping child, the little girl so precious to them all, whom they had adopted when she was only weeks old. Cecily kissed her and ran back down to Ada, who was laughing and pointing at the shop door.

"Just look at them!" Ada said and Cecily joined in her laughter. Passers-by, seeing the light shining through the shop from the back room, were knocking on the door in the hope of being served. "You make the tea," Cecily said, unlocking the shop door, "and I'll see to this lot." Still wearing her fur-trimmed coat, she served the opportunist customers.

Owen Owen came back, took the cup of tea Ada offered and sank into his chair. Since Mam had gone, he was like a cushion with the stuffing leaked out, Cecily thought sadly. Poor Dadda. He had been so shocked by their mother's departure he would never get over it.

It hadn't been the first time she had left them to chase a man whom she thought would offer her more than Owen and the small shop. For a long time Owen thought she would walk back into their lives. He didn't even know where she was: all attempts at finding her had failed and apart from a couple of letters to tell them she was safe and happy and hoped they were, she was lost to them completely.

He complained as he drank his tea, about having to spend the night in the chair waiting for them to come in, but the girls knew it was not uncommon for him to fail to reach his bed. He would often be found early in the morning, dazed with drink, slumped, still dressed, in the armchair close to the fire.

He had never behaved like this before their mother ran off and seeing him now, empty, hollow, without any emotion except occasional anger, Cecily and Ada felt pity and love for the man. Wordlessly they both bent to kiss him. Still fuddled with drink as he frequently was, he had always looked after Myfanwy for them to go out.

"Did Van wake at all?" Ada asked.

"No, not a sound from her. I went up a few times and covered her up. There's a fidget that girl is." He went up to the bathroom to wash and change and Ada looked at the big wall-clock. "There's no chance of a sleep but I think I'll bath when Dadda's finished."

Cecily yawned and stretched luxuriously. "Me too."

Ada looked at her sister, elder by two years, her closest friend. "Want to talk about Danny?" she asked softly. "Seeing him again like that, it must have been a shock."

"He only came to see me to make sure he wasn't making a mistake by marrying someone else," Cecily said bitterly. "How could he be so unfeeling? Even after seven years I felt insulted. More like a cow in a market, not a human being."

"After seven years he couldn't know he would still affect you so much."

"He does now," Cecily said with a harsh laugh. "Left him in no doubt. He touched me and I felt the same as I did all those years ago. How could he stay away without a word all this time then come back and casually tell me he's marrying someone called Jessie?"

"Give me your coat and hat, I'll take them upstairs."

Ada went to the back bedroom where six-year-old Myfanwy slept. The little girl was again out of the covers, her rosy cheeks fanned by long eyelashes blinking as Ada stepped into the room. The white counterpane had been folded back and had slipped to the floor. "Still too early to rise, lovey," Ada whispered. She re-covered the child and tiptoed from the room.

"Tell me about the dancing, Auntie Ada," the sleeping voice pleaded.

"Later, lovey, when the shop closes, we'll both tell you all about it." She blew a kiss. "Cecily," she said when she re-joined her sister, "I know we'll be tired, not sleeping last night, but shall we go out again this evening, just for an hour or two? There's a dance at the Regal Rooms. What d'you say?" She watched her sister, hoping she would agree. It would be better than her staying home thinking about Danny's reappearance.

"If I can stay awake past teatime I say yes, we go. If we can get someone to stay with Van. Dadda's working, remember."

There was no time for more than another cup of tea and some toast made in front of the revived fire before they began their day.

"Mad we were, wasting all that time wandering around over the beach instead of coming home to sleep," Ada grumbled as she dragged barrels of goods into the shop porch. It was New Year's Day but they would open for half of the day. Cecily hung up strings

26

of onions and carried baskets of fruit to the window. Oval dishes containing the stiff, board-like salt-fish were placed in the other window on the marble slab. It was heavy work but they were accustomed to dealing with it, had done so for so long that, as Cecily put it, the jobs were only worth two groans now instead of a dozen. It was something that had to be done.

Inside the shop they displayed dishes of brawn, cooked pigs' trotters, chitterlings and black pudding, all protected by muslin dipped in vinegar to discourage flies. The shop also had barrels of corn, pigeon food, dog biscuits, lentils, dried peas and rice, a freshly washed scoop in each one. They hung paper bags in bunches in various places around the shop, patted their hair and stood, ready to serve. Owen's Grocery and Fish was open for business.

Lots of shelves around the shop were empty, wooden boards with their surfaces knobbly and white with constant scrubbing. If only Dadda would let us expand, Cecily thought each morning as she gazed around the wasted spaces, then we could really show what this shop could do. Stubborn he is and won't even listen to our ideas.

Willie returned and was standing by, waiting to deliver orders and deal with anything heavy. They had told him to stay home and get some sleep but he had refused. Miss Cecily and Miss Ada were his responsibility and he took that very seriously.

"Willie, what would we do without you?" Ada smiled at him.

Cecily laughed a lot that day. Determined not to allow the unexpected reunion with Danny to disturb her, she sang and joked and seemed in very high spirits and only Ada noticed how frequently she glanced at the door and how her face fell in disappointment every time it was not Danny who walked in.

When the shop was quiet, which happened too frequently to please Cecily, they went into the living room and watched for customers through the window between the living room and the shop.

"Sinking for a cuppa I am," Ada said, and Cecily turned the kettle on its swivel over the fire where it at once began to murmur. They were both achingly tired but remembering the fun of the previous evening and discussing some of the happy moments, they decided it was worth it. Neither mentioned Danny again.

The clock went slowly: the day seemed neverending. They didn't close the shop; a few customers might need a few things. It all helped, with business so poor. At five o'clock when Van had been given her tea and was playing "shops" with her dolls under the big table — made into a tent with a blanket — Willie came in from the stables.

"Finished the orders. D'you think I can leave a bit early today?"

"Of course you can. We told you to finish at midday, didn't we?"

"Well, there were a few customers hanging about and the stables needed cleaning."

"Thanks for staying," Cecily said. "And thank you for waiting for us last night. The drive around the beach made a perfect end to the evening. Did your mam mind? You being so late?"

"No trouble." He nodded in the direction of the stables. "The horses are fed and everything is put away for the night. See you tomorrow."

"Wait," Ada called after him. "There's some fresh plaice left. Take it for your mam, will you? Loves a bit of plaice, doesn't she?"

Willie thanked them and left — to face a situation he had been dreading for more than a week.

The house where Willie lived was a poor one, with a holed, badly leaking roof. The walls were of earth which had once been whitewashed but were now a dirty brown, coloured with lichen and mosses and patches of strong-smelling mildew.

It was damp inside and far too small for Willie's family, but with only the few shillings earned from his job at Owen's shop and the odd extras from running errands or cleaning stables and grooming horses for the brewery, he couldn't see the possibility of ever improving their situation. Now, from the gossip he had picked up, it appeared that his mother was planning to change things.

It was one of the delivery boys from the large and prosperous Waldo Watkins' grocery store on the main road who had been first to warn him of what was going on at home.

"Don't rush home on Wednesdays, Willie Morgan," Jack Simmons had jeered. "Wednesday's her busy day. Curtains drawn, door shut tight and never answering a knock. Wouldn't hear if the fire bell rang next to her gate, she wouldn't, not on Wednesdays!"

"What d'you mean?" Willie had jumped from the cart and grabbed the head of the boy's horse to stop him then he leaped on Jack and pulled him off his cart and rolled him on the ground.

"It's true, Willie Morgan! Your mam's no better than she should be!" The hateful words stopped as Willie's powerful fist hit Jack's face. Then there were few words, just grunts and shouts of pain as the two young men battered each other almost senseless. A crowd had quickly gathered and formed a ring, calling encouragement to first one then the other as the fight wavered to and fro between the boys.

Phil Spencer, who ran a small printing business, began to take money on the outcome and, seeing the fight going in favour of Jack Simmons for a while, began to get anxious and looked around wondering whether to make a run for it. But then Willie revived and the fight was his again. Jack was the favourite and to make a profit Phil Spencer needed soft Willie to surprise them.

When a policeman rode up on his bicycle to see the cause of the uproar, he had to push his way through almost fifty people to reach the now weakly flaying arms of Willie and Jack. He pulled them apart but neither could stand; the battering had made jelly of their muscles.

The crowd quickly moved away and gathered around the weasel-faced Phil Spencer. He insisted that the result was a draw and there was no payout. It was only the presence of the constable that prevented another, more vicious fight taking place. Both boys were helped back to their respective carts and the horses led the bruised and bloody participants away.

As Willie, lolling back in his seat, moved past Jack Simmons, he leaned up a little, pretending not to be in pain, and whispered in a voice distorted by a blocked nose, "Say another word about my mam and I'll hammer you proper. Right?"

"Don't go home early, not on Wednesdays. That's all I'm sayin'. Hate for you to find them all tucked up in bed. It's her who needs a hammerin', not me! Gettin' talked about like that ACH Y FIE!" he shouted as his horse moved on.

Willie moved as though to pull him out of the cart again and Jack clicked to move his horse faster and hurried away, laughing.

That had been the first time. Since then, several others had hinted at what went on at home on Wednesdays. Today was the first time he had been able to face going home early to see for himself. There had been several times when he had been close enough to call, delivering groceries not far from home, but he hadn't been ready to face the confrontation and its aftermath.

He had been trying — not very hard — to ask the sisters for an early finish for quite a while. He wanted to know but hadn't the nerve to find out. Today, after bringing the sisters home so late, he had no excuse for not leaving early.

He walked home, forcing each foot forward, his heavy boots like lead weights. To stop at the park on the way home was a strong temptation. From what he'd heard, the man left at six o'clock, long before he, Willie, was due home. It was rarely earlier than eight before work at the shop and seeing to the horses was done. He dragged himself on. He was sixteen, a man: he had to face the situation and deal with it.

CHAPTER
TWO

Willie was just sixteen and a tall, rather handsome young man, sure of himself and confident in a way that was unusual in the area and conditions in which he had been brought up. Since his father had died of consumption two years before, he had been the man of the house, caring for his mother and his three younger sisters. Now, things were happening that needed his urgent attention.

His long legs took him home through the streets and across the fields to the older part of the town where he and his family lived. His face showed a tenseness unusual for him and his hands, swinging to match his strides, were tightly clenched.

He normally walked down Green Hill, with the house in view for the last few minutes but now, although the darkness of the winter evening prevented anyone from seeing his approach, he turned past the bridge and along Nightingale Lane and reached the house by passing behind the row of willow trees along the meandering brook.

The door was closed and the curtains drawn. He crept to the window and heard soft voices, one his mother's, the other that of a man. So Jack Simmons had been right, damn him! He wondered where his sisters were. The door didn't lock and the bolt across the bottom had long since fallen away from the rotting wood. He pushed against it and the voices stopped. Holding back his temper, but tense with the prospect of a fight, he walked past the peeling walls of the passage and into the small living room.

The visitor stood up to greet him, and Willie stared. He didn't know what he'd expected but it wasn't this. He saw a portly and rather elegantly dressed middle-aged man with his hair combed forward with rather old-fashioned neatness onto his forehead, almost touching his thick dark eyebrows. His clothes were well fitting and he looked successful and assured.

Willie was conscious of his own shabby hand-me-down trousers and the jacket with torn pockets and buttons missing. He was aware of the shirt, patched and thin, and the white scarf that was an attempt to hide it. They stared at each other for a moment then the man smiled and offered his hand — which Willie ignored.

"Who are you and what do you want?" Willie demanded.

"I'm a friend of your mother. My name is Derek Camborne. You must be Willie," he added as a frightened-looking Mrs Morgan failed to introduce them.

Belatedly, Mrs Morgan smiled at her son and explained, agitation showing in her blue eyes as she watched Willie's fists tighten and his stance begin to stiffen.

34

"Mr Camborne is a dear friend, Willie, and I want him to be your friend too. Sit and talk to him while I get you something to eat, is it? I know you and he will get on, once the ice is broken." She edged out of the room and into the smaller room at the back where she hastily prepared a piece of fish ready for the pan waiting near the fire. The anxiety didn't leave her face as she cooked the food and listened for the dreaded sound of fighting to reach her from the other room.

When she returned to the living room, both men were seated on the edge of chairs, studying each other, and the air between them prickled.

"Tell him, Derek, dear," she urged. "There's no sense in delaying any longer."

"Your dear mother has consented to marry me," Derek said baldly, and he at once moved back as Willie stood and glowered at him.

"Now, Willie," his mother said nervously. "It's all decided and there's nothing you can say that will alter things." Her voice was still nervous as she watched her son's face. "It's happy you should be. Derek will give me and your sisters a good comfortable home in Cardiff and we'll see you often. Now, what's there to be upset about that, eh?"

"What about me?" he asked. "You needn't think I'm moving to Cardiff! I have the Misses Owen to look after. Need me they do."

"That's what we thought, Willie." Derek smiled, unable to hide his relief. "Best you stay here. There's this house with the rent paid up for a month after we leave. We thought that's what you'd prefer."

"Gladys Davies will help if you need her," Mrs Morgan added. She sat beside Derek Camborne, calmer now Willie had relaxed from the threatening posture he had shown from the moment he had walked in.

"What sort of house will it be?" Willie demanded. He tried to think of all the questions he should ask, feeling the need to remind this interloper that he was the head of the family and its guardian. "Can you look after them proper? I want to see for myself before they go, mind!"

"Quite right too. I'm impressed with the way you look after your family, Willie. Your father would have been proud of you. Yes, of course come and see where we'll live. I have a small but well-furnished house and a job in the railway offices so there's no fear that I won't take proper care of them. Come often and if there's anything you can suggest I can do to make things better for them, well, you won't find me a sluggard in doing it."

When the man had gone and the girls were back from their weekly music lesson, paid for by Derek, the family sat and discussed the future. It was clear to Willie that his sisters welcomed the change. His mother's eyes showed excitement and joy and he knew that however lonely the prospects were for himself, he couldn't spoil things for them.

"All right, then, I'll stay in this house, for a while at least, to see how I get on. If it's too much of an effort to shift for myself I'll find a room where the landlady will cook for me and do my washing." Willie was cheerful as they discussed plans, forcing himself to put aside fear of the empty life ahead of him. "But," he added, waving a warning finger, "I'm going to Cardiff to have a look-see at this man's house and to ask a lot more questions before you say for definite that you'll marry him. Right?"

"Of course, Willie, but you'll find nothing bad about him." She patted his arm and added wistfully, "Lonely I've been since your dad died. I couldn't miss this chance, now could I? Not with him being such a kind man an' all."

"No, Mam. I don't begrudge you a chance of happiness."

"Be getting married yourself before long. Everyone remarks on how handsome and clever you are." She patted his arm again, then went to rescue the dried-up fish from the oven, chatting as she went. Willie felt a lump fill his throat, aware of how much he would miss her fussing and her chatter. And losing his sisters too. How would he bear not seeing them growing up and becoming prettier and prettier? Proud of his family he was and now he'd have to find something to fill the empty hours in his days and the hollowness in his heart.

It was nearly ten o'clock and the three girls and his mother settled to sleep on the mattress on the floor of the one bedroom. Willie pulled the couch on which he slept closer to the fire. He longed to rest but he couldn't. He was painfully tired, every bone a dull ache, but his brain needed stimulation and refused to allow him to sleep.

He pulled on his shabby jacket, wrapped the long white scarf around his neck and went out, boots ringing on the cold roads in the old, almost silent, part of the town. He ran until he reached the house where Jack Simmons lived, the boy who worked for Waldo Watkins in the town's largest grocery store. He called him out and fought him again for being the first to tell him about his mother. This time Jack won but both boys went home satisfied.

A few weeks into 1930, Willie arrived home to see a horse and cart outside his house. In the light of a lantern held by one of his sisters and another on the cart, people were in and out of the doorway, loading up the few valuables his mother possessed. He turned away and, instead of going home, went to the pictures, walking to each picture house and studying the advertisements outside, marked T for talking, S for silent and T S for part talking. He decided on Sophie Tucker in *Honky Tonk*, but spent the time thinking not of the story unfolding before him but of the empty house awaiting him. He was hungry and wished he'd spent the money on fish and chips.

It was strange stepping into the dark house. The smell of dampness seemed intensified by the absence of his family. Moving out their possessions had disturbed its dankness. The fire was almost out and he knew that was going to be a problem. He came home so late and to light a fire before he could even boil a kettle — he'd ask a neighbour to feed it for him during the day. Beside the practicalities, the house would seem more welcoming if there was warmth. The silence was absolute. He wished his mam hadn't taken the cat's whisker wireless he'd made.

He lay on the horsehair mattress on the floor of the bedroom and stared up at the calico-rag ceiling. He would make himself a bed. That was what he needed most: a proper bed to put the mattress on and, after that, he'd make a table and a chair. Short-term plans established, he slept.

He hadn't told Cecily and Ada about his family leaving. Ashamed somehow, even though Derek Camborne had married his mother and was taking good care of his sisters. He thought about telling them but somehow the words wouldn't come. Then a week passed, and several more, and he became accustomed to his solitary existence and let the situation slip away into acceptance without a word to anyone.

He had an occasional letter from his mother and he visited the grey-stone terraced house in Cardiff a few times, so, when Cecily or Ada asked, he could truthfully say, "Fine, thank you, Miss, they're all fine."

Accustomed to their own mother's absence, Cecily and Ada continued with the routine of the shop. Owen Owen worked at the docks when there was work. Sometimes the place was busy with ships alongside each other almost filling the docks but it was more and more the norm for there to be no work and he would spend days just hanging around, between going down to the docks office twice a day to "blob" the local name for adding their name to the list of men available for work. Men were grateful for even a few hours' work. Women begged to have food "on the book", promising to pay when their men earned a few shillings.

It seemed to Ada, during those weeks when winter exacerbated the scarcity of jobs, that Cecily was constantly watching the door for Danny Preston to appear. Her sister's eyes looked up every time someone walked in and even when the shop was closed for the night she was still reluctant to move away from the sound of the shop's doorbell.

In the evening, after preparing and eating a meal, and spending time getting ready for the following day, they usually went out. To the pictures or a dance, where again Cecily's attention was on the door, or searching the crowd for a sight of Danny's dark head. Gareth Price-Jones they did see, and each girl thought he had called to see her.

It was Cecily Gareth wanted to invite out but, because he was embarrassed by her forthrightness and confident manner, it was Ada he looked at when he was talking. He closed his barber's shop earlier than Owen's and he developed the habit of calling once or twice each week to buy some fruit to take home to his mam. He didn't tell Mam he bought it from the Owen girls, she did go on so about the unsuitability of a match with Cecily or Ada — more so since their mother had gone off with another man. So, she presumed he had bought it at Waldo Watkins' on the main road.

Clutching the bag of fruit, he would hang around trying to think of interesting stories to make the girls laugh, while they, anxious to close the shop, laughed at his jokes and made him feel a great wit. He was always reluctant to leave but never managed to invite either of them out. He intended to. Every evening he planned what he would say but when the moment came and he had to speak or leave, he always left.

Each morning the girls were up early to attend to their chores while their father set about the tasks he habitually performed. Fitting the work around his hours on the docks it was he who went to the wholesaler to fetch the sacks of potatoes and the greens and carrots and whatever else the girls needed. He brought boxes of fresh fish from the market and prepared it for sale, and efficiently boned the sides of bacon and the occasional ham. The bones were put in a bowl and offered for sale to make soup and were quickly sold. The work was done efficiently and he helped to clear the mess of the day's preparations but he showed no joy in anything he did. He dealt with the work like an automaton, without satisfaction or pleasure.

He'd had two sons, both of whom had died at sea during the 1914–18 war. Their widows were constant visitors to the shop and they worried about the man's health and state of mind as did his daughters. Victor's wife, Dorothy, was the most dominant of his daughters-in-law and she frequently bustled in criticizing Cecily and Ada, and presuming that, as the widow of the oldest son and having a son, Owen Owen, named for his grandfather, that she should have priority when there was ever a slight hint of the other daughter-in-law being favoured. Rhonwen, the widow of the younger son, John, was gentle and inclined to praise the sisters and assure them they were doing everything they could to help their father back to happiness. Rhonwen was Owen's favourite, as his son John had been.

Ada and Cecily discussed their father's health several times with the doctor but they had been told there was no cure for a broken heart. Their mother, leaving as she had, had ruined the man's life completely.

"Coming to the dance tomorrow night?" Gareth asked one Friday evening when he called for his usual bag of fruit. "I — I was wondering, like, if you'd fancy a trip to Cardiff instead and see what's on at the Variety? Good shows they have there." He had chosen a moment when Ada was out, collecting Myfanwy from family friends, Beryl and Bertie Richards, where she was having tea with their son Edwin.

Cecily was so surprised that she stared at him for a long moment and Gareth blushed and stammered out an excuse for her.

"No, no, of course not. I expect you're too tired to travel all that way and on a Friday too. I'll ask again sometime." He began to back out of the shop, clutching his bag of fruit like a shield.

"Gareth, I'd love to come," she said at last. Smiling, she added, "Thank you for asking me."

When Ada and Myfanwy returned, Cecily said in a dazed voice, "He's done it. Gareth has actually invited me out."

Ada felt the bitter taste of jealousy and for the first time ever found it hard to wish her sister well. "There's nice," she said with a stiff smile.

Cecily noticed nothing wrong. She ran upstairs and began pulling clothes out of the big wardrobe. "Van, Van lovey, come and help me choose." Myfanwy went into the big bedroom shared by Cecily and Ada and watched as Cecily tried on dress after dress, coat after coat, until between them they had decided on the outfit for the theatre visit with Gareth.

"Are you going to marry him, Auntie Cecily?" Van asked, her head on one side, hair streaming down in a golden curtain. "If you do, can I be bridesmaid and wear a blue dress?"

Cecily laughed. "Too early to say, Van, lovey. But when I do marry and whoever I marry, you'll be my beautiful bridesmaid and have the loveliest dress we can find, I promise." She hugged the serious-faced girl and they continued selecting, discussing shoes and hats and gloves before declaring themselves satisfied.

Cecily was excited at the prospect of being taken out by Gareth. She still found her dreams disturbed by thoughts of Danny but forced herself to remember that, by now, he would be married to Jessie and living in bliss in Foxhole Street. Better second best than living an empty dream, she thought. Then guilt flooded her face with colour at the idea of considering Gareth in that way. She made a silent promise that should he ask her to be his wife, she would be a good one and push all thoughts of Danny and what might have been out of her mind for ever. She almost believed she could.

It wasn't that she didn't find Gareth attractive or feel the beginnings of love for him, but she had to admit that the way he allowed his mother to manipulate him caused her concern. If their incipient romance ever blossomed, she would persuade Gareth their best chance lay in putting distance between themselves and Mrs Price-Jones — as long as they didn't go to live in Foxhole Street!

Ada was quiet that evening. She was hurt, having convinced herself that it was she whom Gareth had wanted to take out. Perhaps Cecily had pushed him into inviting her; she could be very forward at times. That had been the trouble between her and Danny Preston. Men didn't really like forward women.

The following evening, Ada had arranged to go to the dance with Beryl and Bertie Richards, whose son, Edwin, was a friend of Myfanwy. The Richards lived in a big house that needed three servants to keep it the way Beryl Richards liked it. They had a car and would call for Ada at eight o'clock. Gareth was calling for Cecily at half past six.

Both sisters spent some time away from the shop getting ready, pressing clothes, shining shoes and brushing suede gloves. Willie stood in at the shop between their various appearances although he wasn't confident at serving; he just kept an eye on anyone likely to help themselves and run for it.

Ada was convinced that without Cecily she would stand a better chance of finding partners. Cecily thought that a few hours alone with Gareth would show her how much happier he'd make her than Danny ever could with his touchiness and unreasonable jealousy.

At four o'clock they began to look out for their father. There was a grain boat in the dock and he had been working on her since early that morning. It was surprising he had not yet returned.

"I hope he hasn't gone off drinking," Ada whispered. "He can shift for himself so far as his meal goes if it's spoilt, but we can't leave him in charge of Van if he isn't sober."

"I'll stay if he doesn't come in time," Cecily said at once. "You go with Beryl and Bertie." It might not be a bad thing if she and Gareth stayed home to talk.

"No, it's my turn to wait. You missed the Boxing Day party because Dadda was going out, remember?" They both cared for Van equally. There was never any question of her being one sister's responsibility over the other.

"It's a sailing ship he's working on, isn't it? Perhaps we can go for a walk on Sunday, take Myfanwy to have a look at her."

"Yes, yes, yes, please!" Van frowned with the intensity of her pleading. "I think sailing ships are beautiful."

There was still no sign of Owen when seven o'clock came. Gareth had called and stood nervously waiting near the shop door. Cecily realized it was too late for their planned theatre trip. "I can't go, Gareth. I'm sorry but Dadda isn't back and we're getting a bit worried." She looked for disappointment on Gareth's face but saw only relief.

"Sorry I am, too, but perhaps it's just as well. Mam isn't too good and I'd be worried about her too. Fine pair we'd be up in Cardiff wishing we were home, isn't it?" He hurried off, refusing Cecily's invitation to stay. Like a scared rabbit, Cecily thought irritably, covering her disappointment with anger. If there is a problem, he won't be the one to help.

Ada explained to Bertie when he called at a quarter to eight, filling the darkened shop with his large and prosperous presence and insisting they stopped worrying, saying Owen would turn up unharmed and feeling sheepish any moment now.

"I can't leave Cecily in case there is something wrong," Ada explained. "We always face things together, even a father a bit worse for wear. Apologize to Beryl for me, will you? I hope you both have a lovely time."

Behind her, Van clapped her hands in delight. "Good, now we can play Ludo!"

"You can play climbing the wooden hill!" Ada said and, protesting, the little girl was put to bed and the sisters watched the hands of the clock move around to nine o'clock.

"Perhaps it's a quick turnaround for the ship," Ada suggested. "They might be hoping to reload her and get her off fast. One of the men working on her said they're in a hurry to get over to Avonmouth as a storm is brewing in the channel. They want to get her across before it comes."

"Unusual for Dadda to work overtime and not let us know. He'll be very tired. He isn't well, is he? Dear sister-in-law Dorothy was right about that."

The rabbit stew had dried up and Cecily put it on one side. "I expect he'll have fish and chips when he gets home. They'll be open until eleven o'clock. He surely won't be later than that?"

Ten o'clock passed, then eleven.

"I'm going round to see Sam Small the foreman. He'll know what's happening. Never known him to work this long before, not on an early shift. And not without a message." Ada slipped on her coat and Cecily went with her to the door. Ada ran back a few minutes later.

"The men in Dadda's gang finished long ago. Sam doesn't know where he can be."

"Drinking? Not at this time. We'd best go to the police. I'll stay here and if I see anyone to ask, I'll send them to the club in case he's there and too legless to walk home."

Cecily stood in the shop porch tearful and afraid. People passed whom she knew and were sent first to her sisters-in-law, Dorothy and Rhonwen, then their mother's brother, Uncle Ben Prothero. She wished that by some miracle Danny would appear and was angry with Gareth for not waiting. She needed someone. She was frightened by the prospect of dealing with an accident or worse with only Ada to support her. She was always looked upon as the stronger one but right now she felt as weak and helpless as a baby.

Lights had gone out in the Greek restaurant down the road and the fish and chip shop opposite. The cinema up near the main road had closed its doors and few lights showed anywhere and still he hadn't appeared.

Couples drifted past, sailors with girls, hugging each other and walking an erratic path, sometimes on the pavement, sometimes on the road, stumbling, laughing, oblivious to her and her fears.

Most of the night had gone before the sisters moved indoors. They were stiff with cold but they moved only to make tea for the policemen and others helping in the search. No one remembered seeing him after the men of the grain boat changed shifts. He had not been to any of his usual pubs and clubs.

At eight o'clock the shop opened as usual, with Willie stepping in to do the things usually managed by Owen. People flocked in asking for news and offering help. It was ten o'clock before there was anything to tell. Owen had been found in one of the holds of the ship, drowned in the grain. Apparently, he had fallen and been covered without anyone seeing him or hearing his brief cry.

The next forty-eight hours were a blur. Cecily or Ada took Van to school as usual, although Dorothy, the eldest of their sisters-in-law and the most outspoken, protested, insisting she should stay home.

"Plenty of time for grieving," Cecily insisted. "We don't want her hearing displays of hysterics and getting frightened and upset. Ada and I have spoken to the teachers and they agree it's best for her to be kept out of the worst of it."

48

"Talking to her about it we are, mind," Ada added. "Talking as much as she wants, but seeing Uncle Ben's new wife wailing and driving us all demented won't help her to accept the loss, now will it? Best she's out of it. The shop is full with tearful friends and relations from the moment we open. And," she added later to Cecily, "as we might have guessed, Dorothy was the loudest and the most irritating!"

Dorothy, the widow of their eldest brother, presumed she was heir to the property. Her son Owen Owen, named for his grandfather — as she reminded them frequently over the days following their father's death — was automatically the one to inherit his grandfather's money and business.

"My dear husband, God rest his soul, was the first born and my Owen-Owen-named-for-his-grandfather will of course take over the shop."

"Owen is thirteen, Dorothy. How d'you expect him to manage a business? Shut the shop while he goes to school, will he?" Ada asked sarcastically.

"I'll support him and keep it going for him until he finishes school, of course. And," she added grandly, "you can both stay until you find somewhere to live."

Cecily and Ada looked at each other and shrugged. Dorothy was unstoppable.

Cecily raised a hand to stop the flow of words. "If you've had your twopennorth, Dorothy, will you please go. Ada and I are worn out and we need some rest."

The sisters stood together when the crowded room emptied. Coats and hats, which had been thrown across the shop counters, were shrugged on and the murmur of Dorothy's voice carried to them comments about their stubbornness to see the obvious and how simple it really was.

"We were wise not to tell them Dadda made a will," Cecily whispered. "They'd have been here all night!"

They went in together to see that Van was safely tucked in for the night and found the little girl crying. "Will we be moving from here?" she asked tearfully. "Will all our furniture go on the back of a cart and —"

"No, lovey, there'll be no shifting us, I promise that," Ada assured her.

"Yes, Myfanwy Owen," Cecily added. "Belong here we do, the three of us. It's our home so don't you worry about a thing."

"But Auntie Dorothy said —"

"Don't mention Auntie Dorothy or I'll be saying a swear!" Ada said and the little girl giggled.

There was little sleep for either of the sisters that night, each silently grieving for the father they had loved and twinned with that grief was a longing for their mother to walk back into their lives. Cecily determined once more to try and find her. If she knew about Dadda's death, surely she would come and see them, share their loss and perhaps accept a place in their lives once more?

The need for her mother was a childlike craving to be cuddled and comforted and in her memory Cecily felt the caring arms squeeze her shoulders and the soft cheek pressed against her own. She could almost hear the soothing voice that had gentled away a thousand hurts in her childhood. The child in her longed to dissolve her distress in tears but she determinedly held them back. She had to be strong. Ada and Myfanwy would depend on her, especially during the next few days.

Beside her, Ada lay thinking her own private thoughts that were similar to those of her sister. Neither girl spoke her thoughts aloud, each hoping the other was getting some badly needed sleep.

In the room nearby, Van was also awake, wondering what she had done for God to punish her so. Gran was a faded memory suffused by time into an angelic figure, always smiling and always there to talk to and to read to her and join in her games. But she was gone, and now Granddad had been taken from her. What if the aunties went too? The thought made her heart beat in fright and tears squeezed under her eyelids and moistened the pillow. In all her memory there had only been Gran and Granddad and the aunties. No Mam or Dad, like most of her friends.

She decided she would be very good and make sure she did nothing more to justify further punishment. To be completely alone — or having to live with Auntie Dorothy! — was the very worst thing. She jumped out of bed and tiptoed to the aunties' room. Climbing onto the pillows she slithered down in between Cecily and Ada and felt arms wrap around her and make her feel safe.

CHAPTER
THREE

The shop blinds were pulled right down and the shop was dark in the early morning. It was not empty although it showed a closed sign on the glass door. Women in black coats reaching almost to their ankles, their faces covered with veils and shadowed by shawls, stood silently waiting for the funeral procession of Owen Owen, proprietor, to reach the door.

Cecily and Ada stood with the rest, although without a coat. They were close together, shivering slightly, partly because of the coldness of the winter air and partly because of the uneasy mood of the occasion. Today was a turning point in their lives: the death of their father and the news just confirmed by the solicitor.

Their faces were stiff with the effort of holding in their excitement, fearing the criticism from the mourning relatives gathered around them if the light of exhilaration showed in their eyes on this day, when sobriety was all.

Outside, all was quiet and when the horses eventually turned into the steep street, everyone fidgeted and prepared themselves. Ada opened the shop door and the bell tinkled merrily, incongruous in the awe-filled silence.

"Should have hushed that bell," someone muttered and Cecily thought she recognized the disapproving one of Uncle Ben's new wife, Auntie Maggie Prothero. The remark was echoed by Dorothy.

Oddly, it was the smells that Cecily and Ada remembered when they discussed the gathering later. A thousand shop-scents, from the obstinate fish and fruit to the more subtle spices and teas and coffees were there, a background to their everyday life, but over them all, intrusive and alien, was the powerful smell of mothballs and heavy perfumes.

As the hearse clattered to a stop outside, Ada whispered to her sister, "I'll be glad when this lot have all gone home!"

Cecily nodded agreement. "It'll be hours yet, mind."

The shop filled as more people came through from the room behind to see Owen on his way. Dorothy came to stand near them with a hand on their shoulders. Her son Owen was in the car following the horse-drawn hearse but her daughter, the shy sixteen-year-old Annette, was nowhere to be seen.

"Where's Annette?" Ada asked.

"Oh, probably hiding in a corner! When is she not?" Dorothy said in mild despair. "Such a trial, that daughter of mine. Thank goodness Owen is more sensible."

Marged, the daughter of the other sister-in-law, Rhonwen, giggled nervously and Myfanwy hushed her with all the authority of her six years. "Hush," she warned, "or Auntie Dorothy will give us a wallop!" She handed Marged a handkerchief. "Chew on this," she said, stifling her own laughter.

"Girls are such a trial, aren't they?" Dorothy smiled at Rhonwen. "My Annette so shy and your Marged such a giggler, I don't know which is the worst."

The gentle Rhonwen gave her still-giggling daughter a hug. "Van will keep them in order, for sure," she whispered.

The cortege had stopped outside and the women crowded onto the pavement, hugging themselves against the biting wind that came in from the sea. They stood, some bending their heads in prayer, others just staring at the carriage with its four black horses bedecked with black feathered plumes and wearing black covers over their ears. Four men walked solemnly in and through the shop and returned a few minutes later, moving slowly along the orderly path made for them through the group of grieving women, under the burden of Owen Owen's coffin.

The four men were distant cousins of the Owen family, all in their twenties and all pale-faced beneath the tall black hats they wore. Johnny Fowler was unable to manage his hat and it fell and rolled into the gutter, from where Van promptly retrieved it and held it against her like a shield.

Johnny's thin hair was plastered to his head with grease, the hairs bonded together and trying to escape the curve of his head, sticking up along the side in a frozen fringe. Marged giggled again and suffered a dig in the ribs from Van.

54

The crowd in the shop emptied onto the pavement as the women stood to see the funeral procession turn to go back up the hill and onto the main road. Flowers were placed around the coffin and there were so many that some had to go in the following cars.

"Dadda hated flowers," Cecily sniffed, her voice sounding loud in the silence broken only by the shuffling of the men's feet and the metallic percussion of the horses' feet on the road.

In a corner of the room behind the shop, Annette sat watching Willie, who had stayed with her until the last moment, before leaving to join the rest of the men.

"I'll be back soon," he promised. "Don't worry, I'll see you're all right."

Willie had come across Annette, the shy daughter of the anything-but-shy Dorothy, in the stable with the horses. The prospect of sitting among the relatives and almost certainly being criticized by her mother was too much for her. Willie had coaxed her into the house, found her a chair behind a door where few would see her and had stood there, shielding her from the rest, encouraging her not to be afraid.

He knew it wasn't just people, or her mother, that had made her run and hide between the warm living softness of the two horses where Willie had found her, but also the thought of the coffin and its contents. He boldly gave her hand a squeeze and hurried out to join the others.

At a signal from Johnny Fowler, who had been appointed to walk in front of the cortege of carriage, cars and carts, it moved slowly off, the horses' hoofs slipping briefly on the frosty surface. The plumes on the horses' heads swayed backwards and forwards as if in an attempt to help them up the steep hill to the main road. Then they were on their way, up and out of sight, along the main road where cars and horse-drawn traffic and pedestrians stopped to watch them pass, men removing hats and women reaching for handkerchiefs as they grieved for the man on his last journey.

In the shop, the door closed and the weeping slowly subsided. Some mourners went home and a few comments were heard as they passed through the shop porch.

"Waldo Watkins from the big grocer's shop looked bad, didn't he? Pale as a corpse himself."

"Did you see the way those girls were grinning? Trying to hide it, mind, but I saw them. There's wicked with their father dead and gone."

"They don't realize it yet but they'll miss him, old drunk that he was. Who's going to look after that little girl while they go gallivanting night after night now? Tell me that."

It was mostly the female members of the family who were left and they found seats in the room behind the shop to sit and wait for the men to return from the cemetery. Cecily and Ada went through the passage to the back kitchen where they had already prepared the food. They shuddered at the strong smell of flowers that pervaded the room and opened the back door to help it escape.

On the gas stove stood the large soot-blackened kettle humming gently. Its usual place was beside the fire in the room behind the shop but just for today, Cecily had insisted on doing it "proper". Ada thought it was wrong to show off on the day of their father's funeral but Cecily had insisted and Ada finally agreed. She guessed it was the presence of the critical Dorothy that made Cecily so extra fussy, with tray cloths and the best tablecloths on display.

"Thank goodness that part is over." Cecily threw off the hat she had been wearing and sent it winging across the room and out through the open door.

"Cecily!" Ada glanced at the door passage. "Don't let those in there hear you talking like that!"

"Oh, Ada, he was our dadda and I loved him, but all that moaning and groaning in there is nothing to do with our grief that he's gone."

Ada shushed her and pointed to the door. Myfanwy stood there, her eyes large, her small face bewildered by the strange events of the day, having been brought back from a visit to Beryl and Bertie's home.

"Can I go to school now, Auntie Cecily?" she asked in a low, wavering voice.

"No, indeed! You're having the day off." Both sisters bent down to comfort her. "Go now and talk to your aunties and cousins. The uncles will be back soon and you can help us serve the food. Glad of your help we'll be." Cecily gently patted the blonde head and watched her walk back to the room behind the shop.

"She can sleep with us tonight, can't she?" Ada suggested.

"Good idea. Come on," she said briskly, "you cut the cakes and I'll arrange the sandwiches. You do the cakes much neater than me." They both bustled about setting out the food on large meat-plates that were usually used only at Christmas and special occasions, to be carried into the living room.

"I'll do both if you'll serve the teas," Ada said. "I hate pouring teas. Dorothy only has to look at me and it all goes into the saucers."

They worked swiftly and in unison as always, each able to take over what the other had started, agreeing wordlessly on how things should be done. They had always been close and rarely disagreed about anything.

"He didn't come then," Ada stated after a pause.

"Who? Gareth? I expect his mam was ill again." They sighed and shared a look of impatience.

Gareth Price-Jones owned the barber's shop which had been his father's. It had kept him and his mother in moderate comfort all his life. When Evan Price-Jones died, Gareth had taken over the business and after a few disasters, was now a competent hairdresser with a regular clientele who called once a fortnight for a trim or twice a week for shaves.

He was not an unattractive man and he had charm, but he was rather shy. He showed his reserve in the way he walked, head forward, and it was only on the dance floor that he held himself proudly and shone with confidence, especially when he partnered Cecily or Ada, who were such excellent performers like himself.

On the day of Owen Owen's funeral, he didn't close his shop. He wanted to, he felt ashamed at not doing so, but his mam had insisted he did not.

"Your father built that business up by being reliable, Gareth," she had warned. "Go on, then! Shut the place and send all your customers somewhere else to get their shaves and haircuts! That is, if you want to see the place close completely and watch all your poor dear father's efforts to provide us with a meagre living go down the drain!" She puffed angrily. "Go on, then. Shut the shop and go to the funeral with them two girls. Oh, yes," she added quickly before he could answer, "I know it's them girls you want to see, not show respect for that disgusting old drunk who was their father."

"Mam, that's not fair on him! He was a local businessman and everyone will close for an hour or so. People won't be disappointed at seeing the shop shut; it's what they'll expect."

"If the shop's too much for you and you need a flimsy excuse for a few hours' rest, then say. We'll see about selling it, although what you expect us to live on I don't know." She lifted a perfumed handkerchief to her rather prominent nose and sniffed quietly as if holding back tears. Gareth knew when he was beaten.

"All right, Mam, I'll stay open. But I bet there'll be some talk."

"If someone had bothered to tell us what was happening and if we'd been asked to visit and stay for the funeral, it would have been different," she muttered to herself. "Above themselves the Owens, always have been, and her running off with the coalman!"

So the funeral cortege passed the shop while Gareth was shaving old Busby Morris and, seeing the crowd gathering outside raising their hats or sniffing into elegant handkerchiefs, Gareth left the old man soaped and half shaved and stood in the wedge-shaped porch of his shop as the procession made its way through the main road, his face red with embarrassment.

The funeral was a large one, Owen being a well-known tradesman, but with so many of his family lost during the war, most of the younger men filling the cavalcade of assorted vehicles were not relations but friends and fellow shopkeepers. Beside the vehicles, a considerable number were walking.

Gareth caught the eye of the wealthy Waldo Watkins, a rival in a friendly way to the grocer now carried in the oak coffin behind the plumed black horses. Gareth looked down guiltily. Mam was wrong and he should have gone. Damn me, you don't wait to be invited to a funeral! Why wasn't he strong enough to defy Mam and do what he knew was right? he wondered angrily. But the anger was towards himself, not his mam.

In the car following the horse and carriage sat Bertie Richards, the prosperous landlord who had always been a close friend of the Owen family. Again, Gareth lowered his head in shame.

Traffic had pulled into the side to allow the funeral free passage and in the distance, Gareth could still see the thin figure of Johnny Fowler walking ahead, setting the pace for the rest. As the last of the walkers passed the shop, he went back inside to where a slightly impatient Busby Morris — so called because he had once been in the guards — was beginning to shout his complaints. He collected fresh hot water and, apologizing earnestly, finished the shave.

60

As he worked he only half listened to his customer's chatter. His mind was at the grocery shop where friends and relations would be gathered to learn the fate of the business. He knew it was impossible for Cecily and Ada to run it themselves. Two young women without a man there? Not possible. They would need a man and there was only Willie Morgan and a fat lot of use he'd be, him only a skinny lad of sixteen.

He wondered how soon he might go and see the sisters and ask them how things would be arranged. He wished he'd gone to the funeral. Mam was difficult at times. Now he'd be uneasy going there, expecting a coolness at his apparent indifference.

He closed the shop early — a small defiance — but walked home the long way round so Mam wouldn't know.

At Owen's shop, with everything ready for the meal, Cecily and Ada stood among the black-coated women waiting for the shop bell to ring and tell them the men were back. They went into the back kitchen occasionally to reassure themselves that everything was done. Holding hands with them both, Van went with them.

"Where will we go if we have to leave here?" Van asked.

"Don't worry, lovey." Ada smiled. "We can't talk about it yet but as soon as we're on our own, we'll talk about everything that's happened today. Right?"

The men returned and Cecily poured water into the waiting teapots, four of them. That should be enough for a start. The murmur of conversations filled the air and the sound of people running up and down to the bathroom. The house had a fullness that at any other time would have been pleasing, but today was alien and unwelcome, an intrusion into their grief.

"All ready, love?" Beryl Richards called as she went up with Myfanwy's coat over her arm. "Coming with us, you are, just for a while. Coming to play with our Edwin." Beryl and Bertie had been friends of Cecily and Ada all their lives and Myfanwy and Edwin were used to spending time in each other's home. Beryl and Bertie lived in a large house with servants to keep it the way they wanted it and Van loved spending time there with Edwin.

Beryl went off, Myfanwy holding one hand, her eight-year old son Edwin holding the other. She was a large woman but today she looked larger than usual in a fur coat which, like so many others, left the smell of mothballs in its wake.

"I hope there's plenty to eat," Waldo Watkins called through the passage. "I'm starving."

"That's no surprise," Cecily laughed. "When are you not?"

Carrying food and teas on trays, they went upstairs to the large living room above the shop. There was a piano there, draped with black material in deference to the occasion. Black crepe bows were fastened to the curtains with ends hanging almost to the floor. Two bows hung over the mantelpiece, and the wall gas-lights were lit. A fire burned cheerfully in the hearth, yet inside, the drawn curtains and the darkly dressed figures filling the room gave the impression of night time and defied the clock telling them it was the middle of the day.

The wallpaper in the heavily furnished room was dark, with cherries and roses interspersed with dull green leaves on a black background. The ladies had lifted their veils but hadn't removed their hats. The men in suits were like white-breasted blackbirds with the white shirts picked out by the flickering gas-lights. An elderly man entered and sat in a corner. Several recognized him as the local solicitor.

Cecily and Ada greeted him, then continued walking through the few people still there, offering food and drinks. A few stood to leave.

"No, please stay, all of you," Cecily and Ada pleaded.

The two sisters-in-law, Dorothy and Rhonwen, sat together with their children huddled near them. In their different way they had prepared themselves for what was to come, Rhonwen with little interest, and Dorothy smiling in confidence. Cecily felt a shiver of apprehension.

"Shall we begin, Mr Grainger?" Ada asked the thin, elderly solicitor. Cecily looked at her sister then down at her hands. What would they say when they knew?

"Would you prefer that I go?" Waldo asked. As he was not a relative he had no right to be present at the reading of the will. But he and Melanie were their closest friends and they were asked again to stay.

Mr Grainger stood up, producing a fold of papers. He placed them on the piano, straightened his wire-framed glasses and coughed to gain attention.

"On this sad day," he began, "it is my duty to bring to your notice the will and last wishes of my dear friend, Owen Owen, who had lived in this house since his birth. As the vicar said in his sermon 'he wearied of life and God took him for rest'."

"It was an accident not a disease," Johnny muttered.

"But God's will," the solicitor admonished gently. "God's will."

"What happens now?" Dorothy asked.

"You have helped Cecily and Ada through the difficult weeks since Mrs Owen . . . er left us," he went on. "Family meetings to discuss every change in the running of the shop have been an enormous help to the sisters left holding the reins, as it were, of the family business. Now, with the death of their father, things must change."

"Right too," Uncle Ben's booming voice agreed. "Can't expect two young women to handle a shop like this on their own." His voice was deep and slow and with an air of importance that hinted at his solo work with the choir.

"On the contrary," Mr Grainger replied. He swallowed nervously glancing around at the faces staring at him and felt a strong urge to throw the papers in the air and run for it. "On the contrary," he said, looking at Dorothy in terror. "The two sisters are to be in sole possession of the shop, house and the business."

"Sole possession? You mean a temporary responsibility, surely?" She yanked her fat son to his feet. "I'm the widow of Victor, the eldest son. *My* son should be the one to inherit. Owen Owen he's called, named for his grandfather. The shop is his by right!"

Voices murmured then rose as opinions varied. The room was soon humming with attacks, counter attacks and general disapproval. Only Cecily and Ada sat in silence, not even defending themselves against the abuse that came their way. It was Waldo who succeeded in silencing the irate family. He stood up and thumped a few chords on the piano.

"Ladies and gentlemen, let's have some hush, shall we?" Uncle Ben helped by using the same words, only singing them in a voice so powerful it all but deafened those sitting close to him.

"It was Owen Owen's wish," the solicitor continued after rubbing his ear, "his wish, that his daughters, Cecily and Ada, should jointly own all he had to leave with the exception of a few personal items which I will now list." He read to a silent room a list of the man's treasures: a stamp collection, a couple of watches, walking sticks, his bicycle. There was something for every member of the family but the gifts did not please.

In the discussion that followed, Cecily saw Dorothy's shy daughter slip out and run down the stairs. Dorothy was too involved in protests on behalf of her son to notice her daughter's disappearance.

Dorothy insisted, and threatened, and warned that she would go to the law if necessary to regain her son's inheritance.

"Mrs Owen, I represent the law," Mr Grainger said mildly. "I can tell you there is nothing wrong with the will, and no ambiguity about Mr Owen's intentions. We discussed it just a few weeks ago to make sure there would be no such doubts." He sighed and added, "As if the poor man had a premonition of his demise."

"God works in mysterious ways," boomed Uncle Ben.

"There is something wrong with it!" Dorothy insisted. "My son is the son of the eldest son and named for his grandfather. It smacks of coercion and undue influence to me. Someone put pressure on him."

Rhonwen looked at the sisters, smiled sympathetically and gave a shrug as if telling them to shake off the abuse.

"Come on, Ada," Cecily said. "We'll go down and make another pot of tea while the relatives hear the rest of the will."

"There's more?"

The sisters linked arms and left the babble of voices behind them and went downstairs to the back kitchen. Once inside the cold room Ada closed the door and they both danced around, laughing with joy.

"It's over! The news is out! Once Mr Grainger has told them firmly that the shop is not their business, we'll be free to do with it what we want."

The kettle had been simmering on a low jet and they quickly made tea, washing the cups while the tea steeped. Then, completely serious-faced, they returned to where the family now sat in subdued silence. Mr Grainger had finished speaking and the silence his words had invoked remained almost intact when the tea was drunk. Then people began to rise and Ada went downstairs to hand out coats and assist their guests to depart.

Waldo and Melanie Watkins stayed, obviously wanting to discuss something with the sisters. Dorothy also delayed leaving.

"Where's Annette?" she demanded. "I don't know what's the matter with the girl but she's never where I want her to be. Never doing what I want her to do."

"She's in the stables with Willie, Auntie Dorothy," Ada told her.

"What?"

"Feeding the horses. I went with them but I came back in because they were talking to each other not to me."

Dorothy bustled down the stairs and as she opened the back door, Annette and Willie came in. "What have you been doing?" she demanded. "I've been waiting this ages for you to come home."

"You needn't have waited, Mam. I can find my own way, I am sixteen, remember." The girl spoke quietly with no intention of giving offence. Made anxious by the disapproval on her mother's face, she added, "Sorry if you waited." She lowered her head and followed her mother back upstairs.

Willie hesitated, wondering whether to stay and ask if he was needed any more that day, or sit in the stables until everyone had gone. The decision was taken from him.

"Wait there a minute, will you, Willie?" Waldo called. "I want a word when Dorothy has gone."

Willie waited, clutching his cap in nervous fingers as Dorothy and Annette came down again and out through the shop. Ada and Cecily beckoned him to go upstairs as they closed the door after them with relief.

Waldo sat in the wide leather armchair near the fire. Melanie was adding coals and stirring the ashes with a brass-topped poker. "You young ladies will be needing some assistance," Waldo said, gesturing for Willie to sit. Willie remained standing against the wall just inside the door.

"Yes, it'll be difficult for a while but we'll manage. With Willie to help with the heavy work." Ada smiled at the boy. "We couldn't manage without Willie and that's a fact."

Willie relaxed; he had been expecting the sack. "I'll do anything you want me to do. Just tell me."

Ada motioned for him to sit and this time he moved forward and sat on the edge of a chair, ill at ease in such comfortable surroundings, and angry with himself for feeling so. He was jangled after the time spent with Annette, who had spoken to him with admiration and a respect for his skills and knowledge as she questioned him about the care of the two horses and the trap and the cart. He wanted to go home and lie on the bed and think about her.

"First of all," Waldo began, "I think you should learn how to bone and joint bacon, if you're going to continue selling it?" He looked at Cecily for confirmation.

"Yes. We want to increase our lines not lose some. If you could teach us to bone and prepare bacon we'd be grateful, wouldn't we, Ada?"

"I'll come on Wednesday afternoon when the shop is shut."

"Sir," Willie interrupted. "Can I learn too? I mean, if I'm to help, the more I know the better."

"Thank you, Willie." Cecily and Ada smiled.

"There'll be plenty for you to do besides boning bacon," Waldo warned. "There'll be the wholesalers early in the morning, lifting the bins in and out and other heavy stuff, besides deliveries. But I'm sure you'll sort out a scheme between you on hours and wages." He again looked at the sisters.

"You'll be paid extra, of course," Ada said after a nod of agreement from Cecily. "We won't put on you too much. I'm capable of bringing sacks of potatoes and boxes of fish from the wholesalers."

Cecily chuckled. "I can remember having a ride on the sack truck, sitting on the potatoes on the way back, laughing as we bumped over the cobbles in the yard." The memory saddened her. Their childhood had been a happy one. Now Dadda was gone and Mam hadn't even come to say goodbye.

How could Mam have not known? They had placed notices in all the local papers asking her to get in touch and had even gone to Cardiff and put postcards in several shops. Perhaps she was no longer living in Cardiff? It seemed unlikely they would ever see her again. If she had not even come to her husband's funeral to support her daughters, there was no hope of any future contact.

When Waldo and Melanie left, promising to do anything they could to help the sisters over the first difficult weeks, Willie left too. He went via the back door and the stables, where he paused and stared through the darkness at the place where he and Annette had stood and stroked the smooth warm coats of the horses.

Ada locked the door when Van was safely home. She looked at Cecily and gave a sigh of relief but Cecily was crying.

"I know it sounds ridiculous, Ada, but I am overwhelmed with guilt."

"About what?

"People say that it isn't wise to want something really, really badly as you might get your wish. We'd wished so hard for Dadda to leave us alone and let us get on with running the shop our way, and now we've got our wish, but Dadda had to die for us to get it."

"I think there's always guilt when someone dies so suddenly and unexpectedly," Ada said. She talked about their father, remembering all the happy years of their childhood and soon Cecily felt better. As they talked about the will and the reaction of Dorothy, excitement returned.

"What's wrong with me?" she said, hugging Myfanwy who was listening in silence. "Tears and remorse for wanting so much one minute and the next I feel so excited I could dance."

"There's a dance at the Royalty," Ada said wickedly.

"We daren't!"

"No, but there's a lovely thought." Ada began to sing, moving in time with an imaginary partner. She was joined by Cecily dancing with Van. "Come on and hear, come on and hear, Alexander's ragtime band . . ."

When they fell back into chairs, hot and laughing, Cecily said, "Dancing's out for a while, at least for us to go together. There's no one to mind you, little Van."

"I hadn't thought of that!" Ada gasped. "It all happened so quick! Four days ago we were getting ready to go out, me to the dance with Beryl and Bertie and you to Cardiff with Gareth. Dadda was here to stay with Van and now —"

"We'll take it in turns to go dancing but everywhere else —" Cecily hugged Van, who was solemnly listening to them. "Everywhere else, Van will come with us!"

"Best for you too," Van said primly, "or I'll sulk like silly cousin Owen-Owen-named-for-his-grandfather." She was hugged again.

"We'll have such fun, the three of us," Cecily said.

"D'you think any of the family will help?" Ada wondered.

"Remembering their faces as they left, I don't think we'd better ask, do you?"

Ada began cooking dinner. Lamb chops, tinned peas and potch, she announced a while later. Mixing mashed potatoes and swede together was a favourite meal. It was still early and when they had stacked the dishes away, Ada said firmly, "It's no good, I can't stay in tonight. How would you like to go for a walk instead of going to bed, Myfanwy?"

They put on the coats they had bought for mourning and, covering their heads with large hats, they set off, the heavy shop door key in Ada's pocket, Van's hands in a fur muff. They walked along the dock road in a sedate manner. Only the most observant would have noticed the suppressed excitement in two pairs of blue eyes.

CHAPTER
FOUR

Bertie and Beryl Richards' house was not far from the town end of the docks. It was a double-fronted, impressive, grey-stoned building and the imposing front door and generously proportioned windows seemed to invite passers-by to stop and admire and be dazzled by the obvious success of its occupants.

Bertie had begun buying property when he was hardly more than a boy, beginning in a small way in the long terraces of the older part of the town not far from where Willie now lived. He had worked at three jobs, survived on scraps and paid twelve shillings a week to buy the almost derelict property for his mother when they were threatened with eviction from their shabby rooms.

It had been hard finding the sum of money that was a wage for many, but somehow every week the payment was met. He would eat what he could find cheap, and sleep in snatches in between jobs which included a few night shifts in a hospital and labouring on a building site. Luck had been with him and he soon began to make payment on two more small, mean properties for which his mother found tenants. She also took in a lodger to help pay for them. They rented the shabby places to people whom they trusted and who even helped with some repairs. Now, at forty-one, he was a rich man with property all over the town, a comfortable home with a wife he adored and eight-year-old Edwin to share it.

He had been helped in a small way by Owen Owen offering him work for which he paid generously and had been a friend of the Owens ever since, treating Cecily, Ada and Van as part of his own family.

When Ada and Cecily knocked on the door that evening, it was answered by Gaynor Rees, the young maid, who invited them to wait in the drawing room while the master was told of their arrival. But as the sisters stepped into the hall, Bertie came out of the study to greet them. He spread his arms wide and picked up Van and swung her around, giving her a noisy, wet kiss.

"Beryl," he shouted. "Van's back! We've only just taken you home and you couldn't wait to see us again, eh? Edwin," he shouted, "our Van's back so you can stay up a bit longer!" The two children scampered off to the family room at the back of the house, overlooking the garden, and Beryl joined the others, ushering them into the drawing room.

"Everyone's gone then," Bertie said rhetorically.

"Gone with a lot of resentment, I'm afraid, Bertie," Cecily said. "Dorothy especially had a flea in her ear. She thought her son was sure to have the shop."

"Where she thought we'd go I can't think!" Ada added.

74

"Things will settle. Any straight talking to do I'll do if for you, remember."

"Thanks, Bertie." Ada patted his arm affectionately. "But I expect the shouting will subside to a mumble in a day or so."

"So," Beryl said with a smile, "you are now the proprietors of a shop. Does the prospect frighten you?"

The sisters looked at each other and laughed. "A bit," Ada admitted, "but more because of sleeping in that big house without Dadda being on call than fear of not managing."

"And, to be honest, not being able to go out together because Dadda isn't there to mind Van," Cecily admitted.

"There's no worry there. Van can stay with us any time, day or night," Beryl promised. "If Bertie and I go out there's Gaynor and her sister to watch them. No trouble to us having Van for company for our Edwin. You go out and enjoy yourselves."

While Bertie poured drinks and Beryl fussed with sweets and small biscuits, Cecily watched them with an affectionate smile. Everything about Bertie was large, she mused. His figure certainly, his house, his wife and son, the cigar which was habitually clenched between his teeth. Even his suit was loose and generously cut. His ears were fleshy, his nose broad and his mouth full, hanging wetly around the cigar. His thoughtfulness and his generosity towards them were equally large.

The sisters didn't stay long, for all the inviting warmth of the welcome and the entreaties to settle for the evening near the roaring fire in the carpeted comfort of the over-furnished room. They set off back along the dock road with Myfanwy skipping along between them.

The little girl asked a lot of questions about the funeral and the changes the death of her grandfather would bring. Cecily guessed she had been talking things through with Edwin. They answered her questions as fully and clearly as they could.

"Granddad has gone from us, but nothing else will change, lovey," Ada assured her. "Tomorrow you'll go to school and come home at dinner time with either me or Auntie Cecily. You'll see, everything will be just the same."

When Myfanwy was settled in bed, Cecily said, "Funny Gareth didn't come. Bertie saw him standing outside his shop with a razor in his hand, would you believe? He couldn't spare time from shaving a customer to even put down his razor."

"His mam's instructions no doubt." Ada hesitated then added, "Danny was at the cemetery according to Willie."

"Danny? I didn't see him among the mourners."

"Me neither. But he was there. Went on his motorbike he did and waited for them, then left after the others had gone." Ada watched Cecily's face. "Still want him, do you? Or has Gareth taken his place? Not fair to Gareth if you still want Danny Preston, yet accept invitations to go to Cardiff with him, is it?"

"Fat chance I have of going anywhere with Gareth. How long will it take him to pluck up courage and ask me out again now?" Cecily built up the fire then stretched and gave a yawn. "This inheriting lark is very exhausting, Ada. I'm going to bed."

"Go on, you." Ada smiled. "I'll follow in a little while. I feel the need to let things settle." She reached into the cupboard and brought out two candlesticks and, taking a taper of folded paper from the hearth, lit one and handed it to Cecily.

"Check all the doors before you come up," Cecily said, as she did every evening before going upstairs.

Ada didn't bother to answer. Didn't she always make sure everything was as it should be? Lost without me, Cecily would be, she thought contentedly.

Cecily climbed the dark stairs and pausing only to look in on Van, who had elected to stay in her own bed and not share theirs, went up a third flight to the top landing where she and Ada slept. The room next to Van's that her mother and father had used was empty now but she had no inclination to sleep there. With its white counterpane and white covers on the chest of drawers and the old luggage trunk, which had held Mam's bedding for years, it was a cold, unappealing room. Perhaps it would be improved by adding a few colours, but she thought that even then it was not a room she wanted to use.

Ghosts, she thought whimsically. Ghosts are what we invent from past experiences. Mam running off like that and Dadda's sad accident, they were reasons for not liking the room. She thought of her mother lying beside her father, everything normal, and all the time Mam had been planning her escape with her lover. Mam, who had not acknowledged the news of Dadda's death.

Yet she still felt Mam's presence in that room; ghostly, ethereal, like a whiff of perfume on opening a drawer, there but not easily defined.

It would always be there, Mam's presence. She would always half expect to see her sitting up in the big white bed, her grey hair loose around her shoulders, demanding breakfast and complaining about the hot-water bottle being cold. Cecily looked down over the curving banister to where a light showed faintly. It was all theirs now, hers and Ada's. Tomorrow they would begin to build up the business and make a good life for themselves.

Whether Gareth would have a part in it only time would tell. His non-appearance at the funeral, or even to offer condolences, suggested that, having asked her out, he had been thankful something had intervened and given him a chance to reconsider.

She went to the bedroom she shared with Ada and hurriedly undressed in the icy chill. The sheets were cold and stiff against her body and she enjoyed the punishment for a moment before sliding her feet down to reach the warmth of the stone hot-water bottle.

She thought of their father and how kind and loving he had been. A constant source of security, utterly reliable whatever problem they faced. Now he was gone and she thought again about the saying: "Be careful what you wish for, or you might get it." She and Ada used to wish Dadda would leave them to get on with running the shop the way they wanted to and his death had given them their wish. She was crying when Ada came up and they hugged each other and allowed the grief to find release in tears.

The day following the funeral was busy. Everyone stopped as they passed or called in to buy and stayed to offer their sympathy, and to ask questions about what would happen to the shop now there was no man about.

Willie set about his extra chores with an eagerness that delighted them. He watched and saw what was needed before being told.

"Your mam pleased with the extra money?" Ada asked.

"Yes, thank you," Willie said, thinking of the empty house waiting for him. "Grateful she is and to thank you very much," he said as though he were repeating his mother's words.

Whenever she was free, Cecily left the shop and in the back kitchen busily prepared the cooked meats for the weekend trade. The room still smelled strongly of the funeral flowers and for once she didn't curl up her nose at the assorted smells coming from the cooking. At twelve o'clock everything except the faggots were finished and she went to help Ada clean up for lunchtime closing.

"Thank goodness it's Wednesday and half-day closing," Ada grumbled as she scrubbed the marble counter. "Worn out I am and sinking for a cuppa. I thought this morning would never end."

"Want any help in here?" Willie asked, coming from the passage. "The trap is ready for this afternoon. The deliveries and the stable work is all done."

"Willie, you're a marvel." Ada told him. "Stay and have a bit of food with us then we'll go straight off. We shouldn't be long."

"I found this in the stables, miss," Willie said hesitantly, showing them a grey leather glove. "I think it belongs to Miss Annette. Call with it, shall I?"

"We'll drop it in on the way," Ada said. Willie put it back in his pocket, where it had been since the previous day.

Ada had already pulled the blind on the window where fresh fish was sold from a cold marble slab. She had scrubbed it, first with sawdust, then with hot water containing soda and soap. Now she rubbed the surface briskly with a piece of clean sacking until it was spotless and she smiled her satisfaction at the result.

"The pigs' trotters and tails are cooked," Cecily reported. "I'll bring them in here to cool." As she returned with the steaming dish, Ada said warningly, "Cover them up, quick. Here's Ali."

Taking the freshly washed muslin, Cecily managed to cover the offending sight as the proprietor of the Arab boarding house entered, smiling as he greeted them both.

"Just the gentleman I want to see," Cecily said. "Look down this list of spices, will you, and tell me what we need to stock to save you walking up to the high street." She handed him the list and as he called out the names she noted them in her order book and smiled her thanks.

His dark intelligent eyes met hers. "You are after bigger business, Miss Cecily?"

"Much bigger," she replied. "If there's anything you think we should stock, please tell us."

"The eyes of sheep?" he teased.

"Everything except sheep's eyes."

When they were washing up after lunch, Ada frowned as she looked at the order book. "We'll be spending a lot of money this month."

"Yes," Cecily agreed, "and it will be a long time before we benefit. It will take time for the news to get around that we're increasing our lines."

"Perhaps we could send young Willie around with some hand-bills? We could get them printed cheaply enough at Phil Spencer's print shop."

"Good idea. We'll make Owen's shop the largest shop in the town!"

"Bigger than Waldo Watkins's?"

"Why not? Waldo has made his money, now it's our turn. Besides, I think Waldo and Melanie are falling into the trap of concentrating more on their wealthy friends up around the park. There's more to be made here, among the small streets, where people fill their tables with plenty of good, honest food and not expensive luxuries spread thinly. No, I think we'll do well here if we get the stock right and give a service people want."

They collected their black coats and their hats covered with artificial flowers in sombre colours, then locked the shop and walked through to the stable where Willie Morgan waited to take them to the shops at the beach.

Willie had changed into a newly bought, albeit second-hand, jacket. He usually kept a spare in the stable but since the increase in his wages had been promised and the new duties, which he translated as looking after Cecily and Ada, he was determined to look after himself too. His long, curling black hair had been washed and brushed, and the shirt he wore had been repaired and laundered by his neighbour, Gladys Davies, who looked after his fire. The coat had been sponged and pressed by that same lady. In between his work during the morning, he had polished the trap and washed the wheels until everything was as clean as he could make it.

As the trap climbed the hill and turned into the main road, one of their customers, Gertie Dill, stared at them, disapproval on her thin face, and when she was sure they had noted her expression, turned away, her small mouth tight in disgust. Cecily and Ada waved as they passed her and she glared again before shouting, "All that show at the funeral! It was nothing but a suck-in. The poor dab's hardly cold in his grave before you two go off gallivanting!"

Ada looked upset but Cecily turned and waved again, smiling as if the words hadn't reached them. "Don't worry about her, Ada. Any excuse to give us a slating and she grabs it with enthusiasm. Jealous old witch."

"Yes, she sold all her husband's clothes and his pigeons before he was dead, that one," Willie reminded them with a chuckle.

There were others who showed their disapproval as they rode along, laughing at Willie's remark. Once past the town and heading along the quieter roads leading to the Pleasure Beach, there were few to worry them and they began to sing, Willie joining in the choruses.

Someone who did see them without their being aware was Mrs Price-Jones, who stared in disbelief before hurrying to tell her son Gareth.

They called on several cafes and stalls which, although not open for business, had groups of people working on them, busily cleaning and painting fresh signs to tempt the hordes to come, to enter and to buy. At each place they visited they introduced themselves and left details of the stock they carried and the services they offered regarding deliveries. Willie removed his cap and nodded politely as he was mentioned and described as reliable and conscientious.

"Damn me, you're coming early to talk about the summer trade," one man said with a huge laugh. "How the 'ell do I know what I'll want in June when it's only January?"

"We just want you to know about us," Ada explained. "We'll call again a bit nearer the time, but we were told this was the weekend when many of you come here to plan work on repairs and decoration, so we thought we'd come and introduce ourselves."

Cecily tactfully asked for the addresses of other rival stall-holders and made notes in her book.

"Whitsun, that's the traditional time for us to start," one man reminded them, after introducing himself as Peter Marshall. He gestured to the wooden cafe he was painting a cheerful green. "For the rest of the year this is just a useless responsibility."

"They'd come on bright days if you offered cups of tea," Ada suggested.

"Council wouldn't allow it."

"You could try asking for a short licence," Ada offered.

"And we do a good line in teas, Mr Marshall." Cecily thumbed through her notes and handed him a price list, offering a better price for larger quantities.

"I do think it's a pity you're just out of sight from the approach road, Mr Marshall," Ada said, her head on one side, tilting her hat provocatively. "Now, if this was my cafe, I'd find some tall, strong men to lift it and move it further over so it can be seen by new arrivals walking from the station."

"Council won't allow that either. Sites are given and rules are firm."

"No floor on the building, is there? No trouble getting a few tall men to go inside and take the weight and budge it over a few steps. I noticed how low it is, made for girls, not tall men. Once it was moved, a little at a time, no one would believe it hadn't always been there."

"Specially if, when you moved it, a bit of paint got spilt around the base. Look as though it had been there for years, it would."

Willie was chuckling. The sisters certainly had plenty of daring ideas. Mr Marshall caught the boy's eye and he too began to laugh, a full belly laugh, his head thrown back.

"Damn me if I don't try!"

Willie patted his pocket where he had put the watch the girls had lent him. He pulled it out and said importantly, "We're behind schedule, ladies. We have to be back to meet Myfanwy, remember."

They set off again, waving cheerfully at the cafe owner, then studied their list of proposed calls. Before they left the beach they had forged links with seven more cafe owners who might be interested in the services they offered. But it was Mr Marshall who remained in their mind at the end of their journey.

They stopped at the school and waited until Van emerged, looking around to see which of her aunties was meeting her that day. She gave a whoop of delight on seeing the pony and trap and stopped to fondle the head of the animal before climbing in and settling herself between them to ride home in style.

A stew was simmering on the hob and they invited Willie to share their meal. He politely refused to enter the living room and carried the bowl of stew and a plateful of bread out into the stable to eat in the light of the lantern and a guttering candle.

Before the sisters and Myfanwy ate, they set out a calendar of dates on which to revisit the people they had spoken to that afternoon. They also wrote the addresses of cafe owners they had not managed to see.

"We'll go next Wednesday and visit them all," Cecily said excitedly. "It's going so well, Ada. I think 1930 is going to be a busy summer."

"That Mr Marshall was nice, wasn't he?" Ada mused.

"Too old!"

"And talking about men —"

"Which we weren't."

"Talking about men, he didn't come, did he? Gareth I mean. Funny he didn't come to the funeral and didn't call today either."

"Gareth Price-Jones can't do anything unless his mother gives permission!" Cecily snapped. "Marvellous dancer he might be, but friend he is not!"

Ada ladled the beef stew out of the fire-blackened pan and set the table for their meal. Van came from the kitchen where she had been playing washing her doll's clothes and they all began to eat. They had hardly started on the tasty meal when there was a knock on the shop door and they all looked at each other.

"Who can that be?" Cecily sighed. "Someone run out of sugar or something no doubt."

"I'll go." Ada went through the dark shop and opened the outer door, the bell tinkling cheerfully. "Hello, Dorothy, we didn't expect —" Her politenesses halted as Dorothy rudely pushed past her.

"You won't get away with this, Cecily Owen," Dorothy shouted.

"What are you on about?" Cecily put an arm around Van's shoulders and stared at her sister-in-law in amazement. Dorothy's usual superior expression had been replaced by sheer rage.

"You two. Stealing the shop and everything else from my son! Your eldest brother would have inherited if he'd lived, so his son should have it all. And if you hadn't asserted undue influence on your father —"

"What book did you get that from, Dorothy?" Ada asked sweetly. She also went to stand beside Van, who seemed upset by the angry outburst.

"Never mind what book! Just understand that I have taken advice and intend to get back for my son what is rightly his."

"Sit down." Cecily stood up and her voice was raised. Dorothy began to stare her out but instead sank into a chair beside the table.

"Want some stew?" Ada asked.

"No I do not," Dorothy retorted.

"I wasn't talking to you," Ada replied calmly. For the first time Cecily noticed that, hanging back, afraid to come into the room where her mother's fury was filling the air, was Dorothy's sixteen-year-old daughter, Annette. Ada coaxed her in.

"Go and sit by there," Dorothy snapped, pointing to a chair in the corner. Annette obeyed. Ada went to a drawer and took out some sweets. "Here you are, fach, I know Winter Mixtures are your favourite. You and our Van." Silently the two youngsters helped themselves to the sweets.

Dorothy was shedding her coat and hat and seemed to be prepared to entrench for battle.

"Ada and I are tired," Cecily said. "We don't want a long discussion, so what is it you have to say?"

"I'm warning you that you've broken the rules of honesty and family loyalty, and I won't accept it. This shop —" She waved her arms about vaguely "— it all belongs to my son, Owen Owen, named for his grandfather."

"What about your daughter?"

"Annette is a *girl*!" Dorothy looked surprised at being asked such a stupid question. "Owen it is who belongs here, to carry on the family name. Owen Owen. You've cheated him."

"He's thirteen, for heaven's sake." Cecily was becoming angry. "He can't look over the counter let alone run a business!"

"All I want is your word, written up legal and proper, that it belongs to him and you'll hand over what's his by right."

Ada was taking no part in the argument at this point. She was hugging Van and Annette, reassuring them there was nothing to be frightened of by stupid adults arguing and shouting.

In a low voice, Annette said, "Auntie Ada, I left one of my gloves in the stable and Mam will be cross if she finds out. Can I go and look for it?"

"Pitch black out there it is but, yes, we'll come and help you."

Van pulled the curtain and looked out to where a light shone in the stable, "There's a light. Willie's still there, and he'll help you find it, for sure."

Annette slid off the chair and scuttled around the door into the passage hoping her mother wouldn't stop her. The gas-light in the back kitchen had been lowered but the glow was sufficient for her to see her way. Walking up the yard she called, and Willie came out to meet her.

"Left my glove I did."

"Yes, and I found it." They both smiled and he led her inside and found her a seat on a sack of sweet-scented hay, which he covered with his coat. A shiver

88

shook her shoulders and he took off the coat he was wearing and put it around her.

"What's going on in there then?" he asked, sitting beside her.

"You can guess," Annette told him with a wry smile. "More shouting about how the aunties robbed poor Owen-Owen-named-for-his-grandfather!"

"How does Owen feel about it?"

"He thinks it funny, the thought of him at thirteen owning a shop. Daft they are, the lot of them. How can they expect Auntie Cecily and Auntie Ada to just get out and leave everything to my brother? They have to have a home and the business is theirs. I think so anyway."

"They'll make a real success of it too, now the old man isn't here to stop them," Willie told her. "And I'm going to learn all I can. One day," he said hesitantly, "one day, I won't be Willie Morgan stable boy and odd-job boy, I'll be a man with a place of my own and a position in the town."

"And I hope I'll be there to be the first to congratulate you, Willie."

"Friends we are. Friends we'll always be." He stood up and held out a hand to help her rise. She gripped it and they hesitantly leaned closer until their faces touched, cheek against cheek. A slow movement and lips met in a shy, delicate kiss.

Willie walked with her to the back door where the faint yellow light spilled onto the yard. At the door she whispered "Good night" and he called her back.

"Annette, don't forget this." He took her glove from his pocket and kissed it before handing it to her.

When she went back to her chair behind the door, it seemed her mother hadn't missed her and the argument was continuing the same as when she had left.

"Dadda left the shop to Cecily and me," Ada was saying wearily. "It's legal and there's no argument about it."

"But it's what *you* do!" Dorothy shouted in exasperation. "All right, if the shop is yours legally, it's your duty to see it comes back to my Owen."

Cecily pointedly handed Dorothy the black, fur-trimmed coat and matching hat. Annette stood up from her chair.

"Sorry we are for all the shouting," Cecily said to the anxious-looking girl. She put an arm around Van to include her and said, "Come and see us tomorrow. Why not meet at the school and come home with Van? We'll all love to see you and you can eat with us and Willie will take you home. Right?"

"Lovely. Thank you." Annette had shed the relaxed manner she showed with Willie and returned to the nervous voice she used when her mother was around. "Can I, Mam?"

"No, you're needed at home!"

The sisters escorted their visitors through the shop, Cecily carrying Van, and opened the door. But Dorothy wasn't finished.

"It isn't very likely," she said loudly, "but *should* you two marry, I want it written down that my son has precedence over any children you might have."

"Not likely?" Ada queried.

"Without your poor dear father to mind Myfanwy, when will you be able to get out? Unless you fancy courting with Myfanwy on your arm!" She clutched Annette's shoulder and hurried her out into the cold, dark street. She didn't reply to the sisters' cheerful "good night".

"Phew! I hope that gale's blown itself out."

"I doubt it." Cecily frowned as she put Van down and pushed the bolt on the door. "But she's right about one thing. When are we going to get out and have some fun?"

"I'll stay with Edwin," Van said. "Uncle Bertie and Auntie Beryl say I'm as welcome as the flowers in spring!"

Hugging her, Ada said, "We won't be able to go out as often as before." She kissed the little girl. "And we don't mind one little bit, love."

"Come on, let's warm up that stew. I'm starving. There's nothing like a blast of Dorothy to whet the appetite!" Cecily poked a blaze from the fire. "Let's sit and eat and forget all about Dorothy and her Owen Owen for today."

But the remarks about them being unlikely to marry gave a sombre end to the evening, both sisters reminded that they were of an age when most of their friends were married and had children.

"If you and Auntie Ada marry," Van said solemnly, "will that mean I have two fathers? I get teased in school for not having one."

CHAPTER
FIVE

It was a week after the funeral when Danny Preston called. He came into the shop as the sisters were about to close and introduced the young woman accompanying him.

"Cecily, Ada, this is Jessie." The small, shy young woman offered a limp hand hesitantly, giving a brief smile.

Jessie had thick, rich auburn hair tucked apologetically into a tight bun as though she were ashamed of its beauty. She wore a brown coat out of which thin wrists showed and slender hands revealed her unease by their twisting. She followed Danny into the room where they were invited to sit, and found the chair in the corner behind the door which Annette always chose.

Danny talked loudly of their plans, but when a question was asked of Jessie, her hazel eyes would flutter anxiously to Danny. Asking permission to speak, Cecily thought with contempt. She was determined to dislike this girl whom Danny preferred to herself, yet as they sat and drank tea and made small talk, she found a glimmer of sympathy for her. Why had Danny made her face such an unpleasant interview? Surely not to impress me with his good fortune. Her pity for the girl grew.

"I'm Cecily, my sister is Ada," she said, "In case Danny's casual introduction confused you."

"It didn't," Jessie said with another brief smile. "Danny talks about you so much I knew at once which was which."

"We came to see how you're managing," Danny said.

"We're all right. Why? Are you offering to help us? You and Jessie?"

"If there's anything we can do —" The words sounded as false coming from his lips, the lips she had once known so well, as they would coming from a stranger.

"No thanks. We're managing fine." She spoke the words emphatically, the final word on the subject. "Now, it's getting late and unless you want something from the shop, Ada and I are just about to close the door."

"Best we're off, then." Danny glared at Cecily. "We'd hate to bother you."

"We could do with some tinned plums," Jessie said. "I thought I'd make a plum pie."

"Forget it." Danny took her arm and led her through the shop into the street. "Don't forget to call us when you need help," he shouted back, but he was looking at Ada not Cecily.

Another week passed before Gareth visited them. Both girls had almost despaired of seeing him again. Cecily thought about him, deliberately trying to force his image over one of Danny. Danny Preston, whose dark, powerful presence seemed to surround her with longing.

In the rush of extra business the funeral had caused, with people calling to eulogize over the dead man, and the curious stopping to make small purchases and see how they were managing without a man to look after things, it was rarely that the sisters mentioned either Danny or Gareth. All their time was spent either dealing with customers or planning how to serve them better.

It was late on a Friday evening in February when the gas-lights in the shop spluttered and outside was nothing but blackness when Gareth walked in. He came through the shop door bent slightly forward as usual but with added reluctance making his nervous stoop more pronounced. He coughed to make his presence known. Ada was alone in the shop; Cecily was in the back kitchen with Van, preparing their meal for when they closed the shop.

Ada was startled to see him. She had been thinking about him, wondering how he felt at the date with Cecily being so dramatically cancelled, and whether he might now change his mind and invite *her* to Cardiff instead. She was remembering how well she fitted into his arms when they danced and suddenly seeing him was as if he had materialized out of her dream.

She bent down to hide her blushes, pretending to rearrange some slabs of soap under the counter. He didn't speak or repeat his cough but stood patiently waiting for her to reappear. She stood up when she was in control and asked brightly, "Gareth. What can we do

94

for you?" Both girls used the "we". Everything they did was a shared responsibility and when either spoke it was as one of the co-ordinated pair. "We haven't seen you for ages. Been ill, have you?"

"No, no, not ill, though Mam hasn't been strong this winter. No, no. It's busy I've been. The business, you know."

He always referred to the barber's shop as "the business", giving it an air of importance it didn't deserve, being a small one-chair establishment. It wasn't even a complete shop but a rented half, owned by the man who kept the other half, which was a tobacconist called The Wedge, owing to its oddly shaped front.

"We thought to see you at Dadda's funeral," Ada couldn't help saying.

"No, no. I couldn't shut the business, see. As Mam pointed out to me, let people down and they'll go somewhere else so fast, before you know it there's no business left. Got to be careful in times like these you have. I know you and Cecily would understand, you being seen laughing on the way to the beach only the day after your father's funeral, God rest him."

"Who told you we went to the beach?" Ada asked with a frown.

"Mam happened to see you as she was coming out of a flower shop. Loves flowers, Mam does."

Cecily came in, wiping her floury hands on her apron. "She'd have loved the funeral then, Gareth. Plenty of flowers there." Gareth began to splutter a reply but Cecily went on with a laugh, "Thought you'd moved and not told us, didn't we, Ada?"

"No, no, couldn't do that." Gulping in embarrassment, he explained that he wanted some apples for his mother. His eyes followed Ada as she went to the window display and put some apples in a brown bag. "I'll call again when you aren't too busy," he said, handing them the money. "Pity you won't be coming to the dances for a while."

"Respect for Dadda," Ada said solemnly.

"No, no, I was thinking you've got no one to mind Myfanwy." He swallowed nervously. "That too, of course."

"Why, are you offering, Gareth?" Cecily smiled brightly.

"I wouldn't be able to dance with you then, would I?"

"Well, Happy Christmas, in case we don't see you before then." Cecily leaned on the counter, offering a glimpse of the swell of her breasts. He swallowed again and hurriedly said good night.

"Cecily," Ada scolded with a grin. "You'll ruin his sleep!"

"Honestly, you'd never believe he invited me out just weeks ago!"

"That mother of his has put in a word no doubt. Warned him about two predatory females."

"You could be right, about us being predatory females," Cecily said thoughtfully. "We've had a few strange remarks since Dadda died. We're getting a reputation for being women ready to pounce on the first unsuspecting male to come near us. Dangerous, that's what we've become, Ada. Dangerous women."

"There's lovely." Ada's grey eyes glistened with held back laughter. "Put it on my tombstone. Ada Owen was a dangerous woman!"

Gareth's visits to the shop became regular but not frequent. He called once a week to buy fruit. He was still attracted to the vivacious Cecily but it was at Ada he looked when he spoke, unable to meet the blue eyes of the bolder sister who was the object of his dreams.

Willie appointed himself the sisters' protector. Whenever they had to go out he insisted quietly but firmly that he would take them and wait to bring them home in the trap. One evening they had been to Bertie and Beryl's for a meal. Van and Edwin had been allowed to stay up late and it was almost twelve when they came out of the big house, the door being held by young Gaynor, who rarely seemed to be off duty.

Willie was leaning against the lamppost outside. He wore a Welsh flannel shirt ending at the neck with a band of white cotton, the usual shiny white collar not worn on this late-night duty. Its absence was hidden by a long, knitted scarf wound several times around his neck and with its ends tucked inside the too large waistcoat and jacket.

He held a cigarette between the tips of his finger and thumb, its glowing end within his cupped hand. Cecily wondered how many he had smoked as he had patiently stood there, always arriving early rather than allow them to wait. He leaned against the softly hissing gas lamp, one leg straight, the other bent, with one heavy boot tilted on its toe. He changed feet occasionally to ease the chill. The horse pointed its feet in a similar way, the gesture like a mock curtsey.

When the three passengers were settled into their seats, Bertie went to where the young stable lad was holding the horse's head. "I'm very grateful to you, young Willie," he said, puffing on his large cigar.

"Grateful? What for, Mr Richards?" Willie was surprised.

"For the way you take care of the Misses Owen. I know you get extra pay but you do a lot more than most would." He touched the boy's shoulder. "This is too late for you, though, so in future when they come here you needn't wait. I'll take them home in the car. All right?" He pressed a pound note into the boy's hand. "Just a little extra to show my appreciation."

"Thank you, Mr Richards!" Willie felt self-conscious as he tucked the rug around his passengers, although it was something he always did. Now, with a crisp pound note in his hand, he hoped Mr Richards didn't think it was done to impress.

"There's something about that boy. He deserves to get on," Bertie said to Beryl as they watched the trap disappear into the night. He threw his cigar butt into the gutter. "Yes, a good boy that one."

Over the next weeks as days grew warmer and lighter, Cecily and Ada used their spare time visiting as many of the beach traders as possible. With them all they left a list of prices and the promise of a first-class delivery service. Ada left them a card printed by Phil Spencer, with a drawing of their shop and their name and address, in case others approached them, making it easy for them to forget the promise of reliable business from the sisters.

Waldo Watkins came often to the shop during the months following their inheritance and helped sort out any problems that arose. He was a small, neat man in his early forties but with hair as fair as a young boy. His small hands were deft in their basic skills of preparing food, boning fish and bacon with a speed that made the tasks look easy.

On the day he demonstrated the way of dealing with a side of bacon, Willie was invited in and he listened and watched carefully, questioning Waldo until he was sure he could deal with the job. He boned a carcase while Waldo watched and smiled proudly when the proprietor of the large grocery store on the main road complimented him on how little flesh he'd left on the bones.

"Damn it all, I thought you'd have trouble with the oyster bone but it's out as clean as I could get it, boy."

Patiently a shoulder was boned and Willie declared himself satisfied. "That's another thing I can take off their hands," he said. "Got enough to do with selling, they have. Best I do the back-room jobs."

"Lucky they are to have you, Willie Morgan."

As the days lengthened, the sisters' world widened. They weren't as free as when their father was alive but they found time for a little fun: life had to be more than work and sleep. Bertie and Beryl met Myfanwy from school at least once a week and they were able to go dancing again. Through the dancing, Gareth became more relaxed with them and after many false starts invited Cecily to go to Cardiff for a meal. Ada hid her disappointment and promised to wait up.

"No need," Cecily laughed. "I'm a big girl now!"

"I couldn't sleep, knowing the big front door wasn't bolted. Best I wait and make sure everything is safe before we go to bed."

They planned to go on the bus. Gareth chose the route that wandered through several small villages rather than the direct service most people preferred. "Nice to have a leisurely drive," he explained vaguely. The bus went via the beach in one direction, further inland on its return. Cecily was curious but accepted Gareth's plan.

She suspected, though, that the bus into Cardiff and the meal so far away was partly so they wouldn't be seen by anyone who knew them, saving him the embarrassment of people knowing about their date. He really was a shy man. She wondered whether his mother knew, or if he had concocted some tale about an appointment with a business friend, to save her destroying his confidence by warning him about taking out one of the Owen girls.

Cecily did not love Gareth. She hardly knew him apart from as a dancing partner and occasional customer, but there was something appealing about him, and when they danced she wanted nothing more than to spend the hours with him. He was a different person on the dance floor. He lost his shyness and talked amusingly and with confidence. Yet, when they met outside the world of the shimmy, the Charleston, the polka and the foxtrot, he was hardly able to string a few words together.

After weeks of being so involved with building the business, the thought of a bus ride and a meal were something to look forward to and she chose her dress with care. She decided on a slim-fitting, button-up coat reaching to mid-calf, the buttons threatening to bruise her knees as she walked, but so fashionable it was worth the risk. She chose Cuban heeled shoes, a cloche hat, and a handbag in the same dark green as the shoes. The coat was mauve and had buttons in the same green as the accessories. Ada was impressed when she saw her ready to go out.

"I'd never have chosen green to go with that mauve coat but it looks very smart."

"Auntie Cecily, you are beautiful!" Van said in awe. Then she added cheekily, "Except for the hat, mind. It looks like a bucket for coal!"

Gareth was due at seven, but it was almost eight when he knocked the shop door. Ada went to let him in and the bell jangled its disapproval. Cecily had removed her hat and was sitting, her feet free of shoes, on a stool close to the fire. Gareth puffed in, his face red with embarrassment, bending forward in his anxiety at being so late.

"Mam had a turn," he blurted out. "Sorry I am. But we still have time, if you haven't changed your mind."

"If you hadn't turned up, Gareth, I would never, ever have considered accepting an invitation again."

"Sorry."

Ada walked to the door, a wide smile disguising her dismay at seeing her sister and Gareth walking side by side up the hill to the bus stop.

"Come on, Van," she said to the little girl who had been allowed to stay up to see Cecily in her new clothes. "We'll have a game of Snap before I tuck you in."

When Van was in bed, Ada picked up some knitting and turned on the wireless for entertainment from Savoy Hill. She hoped to hear her favourite, John Henry, with his wife Blossom, a popular comedy act. In his lugubrious voice he told stories abut married life. And the audience laughed as soon as he began in a low voice, with "Hello everybody".

Married life was a regular source of fun but tonight Ada didn't smile quite as much. Married life was something she was unlikely to experience. Dorothy's spiteful words remarking on the improbability of anyone wanting to marry her had rankled ever since, and had left her with a sense of emptiness and dismay.

The restaurant where Gareth finally took Cecily was far from grand. In fact it was little more than a cafe offering only simple fare, which was a disappointment to her. Overdressed and underfed was the theme for this long-awaited date, she thought with rising irritation. Gareth seemed unperturbed by the limited choice and settled for mashed potatoes, cabbage and sausages over which he enthusiastically poured the glutinous gravy the waitress supplied.

"Nice, this," he said cheerfully. "Sort of home cooking."

Cecily picked at a greasy omelette and was glad when Gareth had finished his disgusting meal. The waitress hovered near and would have come to the table to collect the money but Gareth elected to go to the kitchen door where he counted coins into her hand with his back to Cecily. Her irritation rose dangerously again.

He surprised her then by admitting that the food was not what he'd hoped for. "I was planning something far better," he said as they left the warm, moist air of the cafe and were walking back to the bus stop. "It was so late, see. I'd booked at a hotel but being so late I just went for the first place I saw."

"I'm relieved," Cecily said, unconvinced. "I was beginning to think I'm not worth your time or your money."

"You're worth everything I've got in the world." The statement was a surprise almost as big as the meal, but there were more surprises to come.

She didn't know Cardiff very well but enough to realize they were not heading for the bus stop. "Where are we going?" she asked, taking his arm.

"To get a drink. All right with you?"

"Of course, but I don't want to be too late. We have an early start, remember."

"That doesn't stop you when you go dancing. Not worth *your* time, am I?"

"Of course you are. I wouldn't have come otherwise."

"D'you still see Danny Preston?" he asked. "All the gang thought, even after the wedding was cancelled, that you and he would eventually marry."

"So did I for a while, but we were like hot fat and water, spitting and fussing all the time. Better off apart. Anyway, he's married to Jessie, isn't he?"

He didn't answer as he guided her across the road. It was a clear, frosty night and there were plenty of people about so he held her close as they pushed their way past others on the narrow pavements. Cecily felt warmth for him swell as his hand tightened on hers. Could she learn to love Gareth? she wondered as he led her towards the lighted doorway of a public house.

"Willing to go in there or shall we find another cafe?"

"Not another cafe!"

He looked in then frowned. "This place is crowded." They tried five. Some too crowded, some too seedy and others he declared too swanky. Cecily longed to get back to the bus stop. Her feet were cold, and wandering around searching for a place to have a drink she didn't want was not her idea of a good evening out. What on earth was the matter with him?

When they finally went inside one, there was the usual raising of heads and faces showing disapproval of the woman's presence. Two men walked out muttering complaints of the intrusion. Other faces just held curiosity and were lowered immediately on seeing that the new arrivals were not known to them.

Cecily was defiantly bold. She walked in and glared around as though those already seated were the intruders. But she was ill at ease. A public house was not the place she expected Gareth to take her. Why was he treating her this way?

He found them a corner seat and went to fetch the drinks. He didn't ask what she wanted, returning with a small glass of beer for himself and an orangeade for her.

"I would have preferred a port and lemon," she told him coldly. "Aren't I allowed a choice?"

"I don't like to see women drinking," he said. "Different if we're home."

"Thank you for taking such good care of my morals, Gareth!" She poured the drink into a convenient ash tray and stood up. "I'm going home."

Walking briskly away from the public house, she heard him running after her. She had no idea where she was, or even if she was walking in the right direction. Gareth caught up with her and dragged on her arm. "Stop, Cecily, please."

"If I ever see you again, please don't expect me to speak to you. Now, where's the nearest bus stop?"

"Please, Cecily. I'm sorry."

"How lovely it will be never to hear you say that stupid word again!"

To her alarm he dragged her around to face him then, with eyes lowered, he said in a rush, "Mam found out I was seeing you and she hid my money. There. Now you have it. I'm a weak bullied idiot, scared of my mam. That's why the evening was such a disaster." He slowed down and explained more calmly but still unable to look at her. "I spent an hour trying to find it and another half hour searching for the shop keys so I could borrow from the till, but she'd hidden them too."

Cecily felt the tickle of laughter touch her cheeks.

"In the end I went to the tobacconist in The Wedge and borrowed from him, but it was all in threepenny pieces." He pulled out a handful to show her, the coins glinting mockingly in the light of a street lamp. "The larger the bill the dafter I looked, see. They've been frowning at me convinced I'd robbed a child's money box."

Cecily began to make strange noises and Gareth was alarmed until he realized she was choking back laughter. He grinned, his face losing its glumness, laughter lighting up his face and making him once again the attractive companion Cecily knew. Their laughter rang out as they walked, arm in arm, back to the bus stop.

Cecily was still smiling when she went back into the shop and again Ada felt the prickle of jealousy but she greeted her sister with a smile, demanding to know all about the evening, and when she was told the tale, she laughed with genuine enjoyment.

Cecily and Gareth went out together several times in the following weeks and gradually he became less embarrassed at the prospect of teasing and began taking her to local places. When they went dancing, Ada always went too. Van would stay with Bertie and Beryl, or occasionally stayed overnight with Waldo and Melanie. Cecily and Gareth were accepted as a couple.

Mrs Price-Jones was not thrilled with the development although less against it now it was common knowledge that the girls had their father's money.

"Find out what their long-term plans are, mind, before you say something you'll regret," she warned her son. "I wouldn't put it past that Dorothy Owen to make them promise to leave it to her son one day. You don't want to marry an heiress and find she's given it all away."

"Hardly an heiress, Mam. Besides, if I can buy the two shops in The Wedge and take on an apprentice, I won't be exactly poor, will I?"

"If and buts won't feed the baby!"

"Too early to talk about weddings and babies," he replied. But not too soon to think of it, he added silently.

Somehow, the disastrous evening with Gareth had changed Cecily's attitude of him. She smiled affectionately at the memory of his huddled attempt to pay without her seeing the small coins he was using. He really was rather a dear, and when she saw him talking animatedly to one of the girls at the dance she felt a surge of dismay. She knew at that moment that thoughts of Danny were fading and Gareth was finding a place in her heart.

The shop was busy, business growing all the time. They began to stock the many items their father would never allow. Paraffin, cleaning equipment, household dyes, washing powder, blacking for grates, soda to soften the water, and barrels of vinegar sold by the pint into customers' own bottles. They increased their stock by vast amounts, storing it in the cellar below the stable, ready for the new orders they hoped to get from the beach traders.

Cecily had begun to discard any stock that was not completely fresh, selling it cheaply at the end of each day with a final clear out on Saturdays. This had created a small band of customers looking for bargains to feed their families and resulted in the shop getting a reputation for selling only the best.

Ada was worried about the extravagance. It did cost a lot of money at first but it was now beginning to show results in extra trade and the stuff they sold cheaply was never a complete loss. Both girls were beginning to feel optimistic about the way their lives were shaping.

Because they were tied up in the shop for so much of each day, they decided to employ a servant to look after the house and prepare their evening meal. Gaynor, the Richards' maid, had a sister and it was she whom they agreed on after a series of interviews at which both Melanie Watkins and Beryl Richards were present to give the girls the benefit of their experience. So Winifred Rees came to work for them one sunny day in April.

"She's like a little mouse about the place," Cecily reported when Melanie asked about the girl's progress. "She scuttles through the door when we open it each morning and we hardly see her after that, but the place is clean and she seems quite happy with us."

"She spends some time making 'sheep's eyes' at our Willie," Ada chuckled, "but I don't think it's getting her very far."

108

After a week, they had to admit that Winifred was a terrible cook. Besides ruining quite a lot of perfectly good food, she had broken three cups, four plates and destroyed a saucepan. She resigned and they settled for a once-a-week cleaner.

The business was growing and the beach orders, although the season hadn't begun, were already keeping them busy with finding suppliers. Orders for the shop were increasing all the time and Willie was rushed, going out several times each day with deliveries on the horse and cart. One day, the sisters asked him to come and see them when he'd finished for the day.

"Willie," Ada began. But she was stopped by Cecily.

"Hush, Ada, love. I'll tell him. You go all round the world sometimes and Gareth is calling for me in an hour."

Ada sat back and waited for Cecily to speak. She was smarting with the reproach. Everything these days was how Cecily wanted it. The risks they had taken buying in all that extra stock, widening their ranges to include lines they rarely sold: she was like a runaway train and without a moment to listen to her opinion.

"Willie, love, we have to find some help for you," Cecily said. "What d'you think of having an assistant to deliver some of the local orders? We thought of getting him a bike. You'll still have the horse and cart and of course take the important beach orders. You'll be responsible for training the newcomer too."

"I think that's a good idea," Willie replied. "And while you're thinking of it, why don't you get a phone? It's daft, me trotting all the way to the beach and coming back to find another order waiting for me. It would save a lot of my time and yours. What do you think, Miss Ada?"

Ada just nodded noncommittally. Even the stable boy thought more of her opinion than her sister, her so called partner.

"Do you know anyone. A relation, perhaps?" Cecily asked.

"What about one of our relations," Ada gave a wicked smile, good nature returning. "What would Dorothy say if we invited Owen-Owen-named-for-his-grandfather to be our errand boy?"

"We daren't!" Cecily said with a laugh. "But wouldn't it be fun to ask!"

"Mrs Dorothy isn't fussed about Annette, is she?" Willie said slowly. "I mean, she doesn't think she has a right to the shop. What about asking her? She only works occasionally over the beach serving in a cafe. She stays home most of the time, seeing to things while her mother works. She'd be glad to get out for a few hours each day, for sure."

"A girl couldn't be an errand boy!"

"What if she puts up the orders, to take some of the work off you two and only delivers the very local ones that she can easily carry?"

The sisters looked at each other, nodded and agreed to talk first to Annette then Dorothy.

"Go and fetch her now, shall I?" Willie offered. "It's half day but I haven't taken the horse out of the cart yet, in case you wanted to go to the beach. Annette won't mind that it's not the trap."

110

"I'm going out in less than an hour," Cecily said hesitantly. "D'you think you can see her and explain?"

"Of course!" Ada's voice was sharp. "I'm not exactly second in command here, am I?"

"Of course not, you silly ha'porth. But we usually do things together, don't we?"

Ada turned to Willie. "I'll go with you and we'll call on Annette, unless you have something you have to do?"

"I'll just change my coat," he said, hiding a smile of delight.

"You'll be back in time for Van?"

"When am I not?" Ada said the words quietly but in her eyes was a hint of censure. Every day it was she who was tied to meeting Van from school. No taking turns these days. Cecily sensed rather than saw the expression and added, "Oh, Ada, love. If you have time, will you call and collect the new price lists from Phil Spencer? We'll take them to the beach next week. If we both keep next Wednesday free we can meet Van from school and all go."

Slightly mollified at the thought of seeing Phil Spencer and his lovely mother, she began to set the table for their meal. The slightest of nervous glances passed between the sisters, each aware that a difficult moment had arisen.

Cecily called goodbye as she went out to join Gareth and for the first time there was no cheery response from Ada. But it was irritation Cecily felt as she slammed the shop door, making the bell jangle in reproof, not guilt.

★ ★ ★

111

The day was a blustery one. Clouds raced across the leaden sky, roof-tops reflecting the dull colour. Trees swayed in leisurely dance; the grass rippled like a gaudy sea. The horse objected to the gusts which brought dust to irritate his eyes and nostrils and he snorted and shook his head as he trotted along the road.

Ada rode with Willie, a big scarf wrapped around her hat to hold her hair neatly in place. They tied the horse to a convenient lamppost near Dorothy's house and knocked on the door. Dorothy Owen wasn't the type to approve of visitors calling and walking in. There was no response so they went around to what Dorothy called the tradesmen's entrance and walked in.

They found Annette busily scrubbing out the big larder cupboard under the stairs. She was flushed with her efforts and the colour deepened when Willie walked in behind her aunt. She dried her rounded arms and quickly removed the sacking apron she had been wearing to protect her clothes.

When they explained the reason for their visit, she was delighted at the suggestion she helped at the shop.

"Mam works all week at the department store now and uses her half day to visit friends," she explained. "Apart from occasional days at the beach helping with trays, I stay home. Mam thought it best I manage the house — she can earn more than me, after all. It makes sense and . . . I like housework," she added firmly as though to convince herself.

"But you'd prefer to help us?" Ada coaxed. "See a bit of life rather than be stuck here on your own?"

Willie stood just inside the door, cap in hand, his best coat worn over an old white shirt and a brown tie. The grey pin-striped trousers were clean and neatly pressed. Ada saw the girl's eyes dart to him before she replied.

"Yes, Auntie Ada. I'd love that. I expect Mam and I will manage the work between us."

"Pity she doesn't make your Owen help."

Annette laughed. "But he's a boy!"

"The coal and sticks for the fire? He could see to that." Ada picked up one of Annette's hands and looked at the redness and the damaged nails. "Beautiful you are, and you should be showing a healthy vanity about your hands as well as the rest of you at your age. Don't you agree, Willie?"

Embarrassed, Willie stuttered then managed to say, "Yes, Miss Ada. Beautiful, yes."

Ada smiled. It was unkind to tease them, but irresistible.

After a cup of tea and some biscuits made by Annette, they left her to discuss their proposal with her mother and set off again. They had to be at school to meet Van but first they went to the old village where Willie lived, and called on Phil Spencer, the printer.

Phil worked from the small cottage he shared with his mother. He had been knocked over by one of the charabancs that took trippers on days out a few years previously and walked with a serious limp. One leg was permanently twisted and bent awkwardly at the knee. He was a popular and cheerful man although few would trust him with either their money or their daughters.

He was in the garden when the cart stopped outside his gate and he waved and came to meet them. "Well, well. There's a lovely sight! Ada Owen in her best bib and tucker and arriving on a delivery cart! Bringing her for me, are you, Willie?" Phil was pale with a face many described as weaselly, and his fingers were constantly engrained with black ink, but his light-hearted manner always brought a smile. "Did you dress up special for me, then, Ada?"

"I wouldn't dream of coming to see Phil Spencer in anything but my best," Ada said, patting the frilly hat she wore.

"Come on in, both of you, I'll just wash my hands." He darted in his ungainly way into the house and came out a moment later, drying hands that looked the same as when he went in on a grubby towel.

"Mam's putting the kettle over the fire, come in, come in." He stepped forward to help her down, his movements jerky, his manner enthusiastic.

There was a sharp intelligence about his face with its shrewd blue eyes, but Willie, through various rumours and his own instinct, saw greed; an impression that he was counting values and costs even through his smile. Willie saw Phil Spencer as a man who loved money and didn't care how he got it. Ada saw a man who was a flatterer, a flirt and someone ready for fun.

She was genuinely disappointed that they couldn't stay for tea. "I just want to pick up the price lists we ordered. We need them for next week and you know how reliable you are at getting them to us on time!" She smiled to soften the criticism.

"Cup of tea! Now that won't take a moment," Phil insisted. "You too, Willie Morgan. Tie the horse to the gate. It's a bit loose, mind, that gate. I hope he doesn't fancy a walk!" Chattering non-stop, ignoring Ada's plea that they couldn't spare the time, he escorted them inside to where his mother was already pouring out teas. Before she spoke to them, she snatched the stained towel from her son.

"Fancy taking that outside! I don't want this lady to think I'm a slummock!" She turned to her visitors, bright blue eyes so like those of her son. "Give him rags for the workshop. Dirty *mochyn* he is, showing it outside for the neighbours to see." She pulled chairs out from the table and gestured for them to sit. "*Teisen lap?*" she asked and Willie nodded enthusiastically.

"Yes please, Mrs Spencer. No one makes that like you do."

"You must take some home with you, Willie. Poor boy, too, without his mam." Willie stopped her mentioning the absence of his mother and sisters with a shake of his head.

"Seen the paper today?" Phil asked quickly. "That Amy Johnson has flown all the way to Australia. There's a woman for you, eh?"

"Arrived in Darwin, she did." Mrs Spencer showed them the piece in the paper. "Took twenty days in her plane, called Gypsy Moth. Funny name, isn't it?" She put down the paper, which she couldn't read, but by

115

having memorized all her son told her she convinced most that she could.

It was difficult to get away. Ada felt she had been caught in a hurricane. Both Phil and his mother talked fast and continuously. When they came out, Willie clutching half of a loaf-cake Mrs Spencer had insisted on giving him, and Ada carrying the sheaf of neatly printed lists, Ada was reeling, but both were full of laughter.

"Take me home, Willie," Ada said with a chuckle. "I'm exhausted."

"We must hurry, or we'll be late for Van." He looked at Owen Owen's watch, which he had been allowed to keep. He needed a watch with so many things to remember and him not always within the sound of the town clock.

"Unless the horse wants to take the gate with him, we should do it with minutes to spare." He clicked to the horse and they hurried on their way, still smiling after the visit.

CHAPTER
SIX

Dorothy did not give her permission for Annette to work in the shop. She wrote a note explaining that when her daughter decided to take a job it would be a family decision and discussed fully by herself, Annette and Owen, who, young as he was, was the head of the family. The sisters were the least surprised and Willie the most disappointed.

A few days after the note was shown to him, Willie saw Annette crossing the main road, having done her mother's shopping not at Owen's shop but at Waldo Watkins' more expensive store. He pulled up the horse, ignoring the abuse he received from other road users, and offered her a lift. She glanced nervously around her before climbing up to sit beside Willie, placing her basket at her feet.

"You'll have to hold my arm as we turn the corner in case you fall," he teased. She waited until they had left the busy main thoroughfare and put an arm tentatively on the rough sleeve of his jacket. "Shame on your mother for not letting you work with your aunties," he said.

"It would have been nice, Willie, you teaching me things."

"There's a lot I'd like to teach you, Miss Annette."
He laughed, his dark eyes shining in the bronzed face.
"Look, what about coming with me now, over to the
beach?" He gestured back to the cargo of boxes, each
labelled with the customer's name and containing the
account. "Got some money to collect. I need some
protection I do."

"I can't!" She was shocked at the idea. "I've got to
get the meal ready for six and it's already late."

"Tell your mam the gas went out and you couldn't
find a shilling."

He was looking down at her and, warming in the
glow of his dark eyes, she relented. "All right, but what
will I say if Mam finds out?"

"Tell her you were kidnapped." He clicked to the
horse to move faster and they trotted along the road to
the beach, arm in arm, enjoying the freedom and the
fresh warm sun of early summer.

The sky was deliciously blue and small flat-bottomed
cumulus clouds were throwing an occasional shadow
on a calm sea. The golden sand was sea washed and
clean, ready for the season about to swell into full
holiday mood. A few people could be seen braving the
chilly water, paddling along the cream-curled edge of
the waves.

"Better than being home cooking for your mam, eh?"

"D'you think we have time for a cup of tea? It'll be a
real outing then," she suggested.

"Come and meet Mr Marshall." Turning the horse
around near the cricket ground, he headed for the
green painted stall.

They sat and sipped the tea Peter Marshall made and ate a freshly cooked scone. Annette's eyes shone with happiness as she sat close to Willie and watched passers-by. For a while she was one of the early summer visitors, admiring the friendly town for the first time, pointing to the island far out in the channel that had once been a fever hospital and was now inhabited only by sea birds. She saw the sandy bay as though for the first time, the figure of eight in the fairground, high about the rest, the promenade and the cafe jutting out precariously from the cliffs, where trays for the sands could be hired complete with cups and saucers, a filled teapot and food.

"Nice people, nice town," she said, adding to the illusion of being a first-time visitor. It was the first time, seeing it with Willie.

"What do you say we do this every week?" Willie asked as they prepared to leave the cafe and finish his deliveries. "I could meet you at the end of town. I have a watch," he added proudly. "Belonged to your grandfather it did."

And so it was arranged. Every Monday afternoon, Willie would load the cart and set off on the afternoon's deliveries. Annette would be waiting with her basket of groceries and they would call at Peter Marshall's stall to take tea in the open air, breathing in the sweet sea breezes and nurturing their growing friendship.

Peter Marshall took pleasure in their company and often sat with them for a few moments and asked about Cecily and Ada. "I don't see them often now the season's begun," he explained. "They're too busy I expect."

"Are you here every day then?" Annette asked.

He didn't explain how frequently he stayed in the hope of a visit from the Misses Owen. "Not every day. I have a garage to run. This little cafe is an excuse to escape and let the petrol and oil fumes blow away."

"A garage?" Willie's eyes lit up. "Love to drive a car, I would."

"It wouldn't take me long to teach you. So don't forget, if you can persuade the sisters they need a car, come and see me, all right?"

Bertie owned a number of houses in the town and several blocks of cottages in the old part of the town. He paid collectors to call each week for the rents, but during the first week of June both were taken ill. Knowing the risk that missing a week caused some to slip into arrears, he decided he'd better do the rounds himself. It was a good idea to show himself to his tenants occasionally so he could see how well his properties were being cared for.

He drove his Ford car down to the village and parked it near the stream, intending to walk to the various houses he owned. His first call was at Phil Spencer's and as usual he was there longer than he'd intended, being offered cakes and tea and becoming involved in a two-way blast of conversation between Phil and his mother.

His next call was at the thatched, white-painted cottage of Gladys Davies, who did washing and maintained the fire for Willie Morgan. He didn't intend to do more than hold out his hand for the book and money, but once again he was delayed.

"I've got Willie's rent here too." Mrs Davies handed him both books.

"Thank you. Mrs Morgan out, is she?"

"Out? She's gone. She took the daughters and went to live in Cardiff."

"You mean she just left Willie here?" Bertie frowned.

"Indeed, gone this ages. She married, so I heard, a —" She wrinkled her face in concentration. "Derek Camborne. Yes, a railwayman she told me."

When he had asked a few more questions, Bertie went on to finish his round but he determined to see Willie and make sure everything was all right with the boy. He'd been good to the sisters, loyal, and not afraid to work extra hours when necessary.

Returning to the car he stopped for another look at Willie's house. The door had been recently repaired and when he checked his book there was no record of a complaint or a request for the work to be done. The boy must have dealt with it himself. Neatly too. The thatch was patched where the straw was beginning to rot but that was not satisfactory and he made a note to get it fixed. He went closer and saw that the windows were shining clean and the wood newly painted. His estimation of Willie increased. "A tidy lad," he muttered to himself. "A boy worth encouraging."

His opportunity to talk to Willie came on the following Saturday when Willie brought Van to stay with them while the sisters went dancing. Willie carried

121

the little leather suitcase that Van used on her regular visits to the large, richly furnished house with its view over the distant sea. Willie usually left her at the door, in the care of Gaynor, but this Saturday Bertie told the servant to invite him in.

"Come in, boy, I want a word."

"Will it take long, sir?" Willie asked politely. "I have to get home sharpish as I'm back at eleven to see Miss Cecily and Miss Ada home from the dance."

"Still do that, do you?" Bertie was surprised. "I thought, with Gareth keeping company with Cecily, he'd walk the ladies home."

"No, sir, that's my responsibility."

"Well, I won't keep you long." He ushered the boy into the drawing room and Willie felt uncomfortable, aware of his dirty clothes.

"Sorry, Mr Richards, I'd have changed if I'd known. It's the stable work, see."

"I should have invited you round the back, I suppose — Beryl's always on." He smiled. "Well, you're here now. It's about your house."

"Nothing wrong, is there? I mean I pay my rent regular."

"You're doing work on it."

"Not as much as I'd like, but the long hours and —"

"Why don't you buy it?"

Willie looked at the large man, chewing on his fat cigar, in utter disbelief. "I couldn't afford to buy a house."

"Neither could I when I bought my first one, but I bought it just the same."

122

"I don't understand." Willie waited, his face a mask of misery. Was he being thrown out? What chance then for him and Annette?

"I'll lend you the money and you'll be paying me little more than you're paying me rent."

"But, Mr Richards, I don't know anything about buying houses."

"I'll put that thatch right and a few other things before we see a solicitor."

"But why, sir?"

"You've been very good to friends of mine. I want to help you as a sort of thank you. I've talked it over with my wife and she agrees. You're a good man, Willie. Stay with the Owens and continue to look after their interests as you are now and I'll help you. The re-thatching is the first thing, I'll get that sorted, then I'll sell it to you for sixty pound. That seem fair?"

"Well, yes, but —"

"Don't be frightened by the long term. Just see each week as a small step."

"Well, yes, but —"

"I won't press you, but if you agree, we'll go together to a bank and let the manager look at what I'm offering, so you are absolutely certain there are no catches."

"No need for that, Mr Richards."

"I insist." Patiently Bertie went over the arrangements — time allowed to pay, the advantages of being a property owner — and Willie began to see it was possible.

A bemused Willie walked back to the shop and brushed out the stable in a dream. He, Willie Morgan, would be a house owner! He'd work on the place and make it as he wanted it. Improve the ceilings which were at present only rotten, torn calico. He'd put a proper floor in the kitchen where there was only stamped earth and a few flagstones. He'd might even buy a rug. Or make one. Gladys Davies was sure to know how. Happy and full of plans, he counted the hours before he would see Annette and tell her his stupendous news. And it was something to discuss with Mam on his next visit to Cardiff.

It was from Bertie that Ada learned that Willie's family had left him.

"Why didn't you tell us?" Ada asked when he reported for work the following Monday morning. "Talk about feeling a fool. Fancy you going through all that and us not knowing."

"I didn't want to bother you. Anyway I managed all right. Gladys Davies is great. Does my washing and sees to the fire, cooks a meal for me now and then, too."

"Well, it's good news Mr Richards is going to help you buy your house. He's a fine man and you can trust him completely. He told us how impressed he is with you and knows you will benefit from a bit of help, as he did when he was young. Nice way of looking at things, giving something back."

"Only if it's good that you're giving back, miss." Willie's proposed new status gave him the confidence to speak out. "No sense trying to give bad things back — that way everyone gets hurt."

Ada frowned. "Thinking of anyone in particular, Willie?"

"Can't say, miss, but there's someone in your family spitting mad about your father's will and would pay for watching."

"You've got a man's head on your young shoulders, our Willie."

"Not so young. I'm seventeen next week."

When Cecily was told, she too was surprised at not being told. "Search up in the stable loft," she told him. "There's a lot of odd chairs and the like up there. Take anything you need."

So Willie loaded up two chairs that needed re-covering and a wooden cabinet plus a few smaller items and took them to his home. He felt buoyant and confident as he placed the pieces in his room and looked about him with pleasure. Next, he would set about making that bed he'd promised himself. He could have bought an iron bedstead cheaply enough but wanted the satisfaction of making one.

He had to hurry then to collect the orders and meet Annette. He told her the news and discussed it with Peter Marshall, who seemed delighted to be included in a celebratory tea party. When he went back to the shop, he asked for a few hours off and went to the wood yard with a list of his needs. To his surprise he met Danny Preston there.

"Aren't you the boy from the Owens' shop?" Danny asked, walking towards him.

"That's right. You're the man who had his motorbike pinched."

"What are you doing here?"

"I'm going to make a bed."

"Done anything like that before?"

"No, but I've watched carpenters and I think I can do it."

"I do a bit of woodwork myself," Danny told him. "I went to sea for a few years and started it as a hobby, so if you want a hand, just ask."

"Thanks!" Willie was surprised. "There is the problem of a saw. Which one do I buy?"

"One's no good, you'll need several." Danny laughed when he saw the boy's face drop. "Come on, I'm not busy for the next hour — let's see what you need and I might be able to lend you a few."

They spent half an hour poring over the bewildering selection of saws and Willie bought two. Danny went with him as the wood was loaded on the cart borrowed from the sisters, and together they marked out the frame for the bed.

"Come and see me if you get stuck," Danny offered. "I'm living in Quarry Street."

"But I thought — didn't you get married then? I thought you moved to Foxhole Street?"

Danny looked away. "No. Me and Jessie, we sort of changed our mind. Still with Mam I am. So," he said brightly, "I work for the post, delivering letters. I'm free after the second round and at your service."

Willie looked at the powerfully built, black-haired man whose eyes were darker than his own. Was he still fancying Miss Cecily? If so, why didn't he call? They had become so friendly over the past couple of hours he almost asked, but stopped himself in time. No point risking a snub and spoiling things. He wondered whether he should mention Danny's help to the sisters but decided against it. Best to let things work out on their own. That way, no trouble could bounce back on you.

He gave Danny a lift back into town before returning to the shop, very much later than he'd intended. It was closed. The girls had taken Van, straight after closing, for a bus ride and a walk on the sands. He took his time with the horses, thinking about his meeting with Danny.

They hadn't arranged to meet again but he knew they would. There was a big difference in their ages, he seventeen and Danny about ten years older, but they seemed to blend well. He felt a surge of happiness as he thought how his luck was changing. With his family gone he had been lonely, but now life was opening up and with good wages, the opportunity to buy his own house and learn to make furniture to fill it, life stretched excitingly before him.

If only he could win Annette his world would be perfect. Perhaps that was too much to hope for. But still, they met often and in recent days he had learned most clearly that nothing stayed the same. Who knew what the coming months would bring?

On the rare occasions when the sisters went out together and joined their friends at the dance, Gareth danced with them both, but on one night, instead of rushing out before the last dance was played, he stayed and danced the last waltz with Cecily — a tacit declaration that he would take her home.

Their friends accepted that Cecily and Gareth were courting, albeit a slow process, and thought it a foregone conclusion the couple would eventually marry. The waltz caused heads to turn and people to nod and point fingers as another step was taken towards an announcement.

Ada seemed unaffected but deep down she ached with misery when left to stand among the rest, to watch and wait until the dance ended, then hover while Gareth collected his coat and trilby and joined them at the entrance.

Willie was leaning against his usual lamppost, a cigarette in his cupped hand. It seemed to be the only time he smoked and the sisters wondered if it was more for the slight warmth rather than the need for nicotine. He stood to help them but hesitated when he recognized Gareth.

"You coming too, Mr Price-Jones?"

"No. You take Miss Ada, will you? Miss Cecily and I will walk."

Willie was about to argue; the sisters' safe return was his duty. Cecily nodded and he shrugged and helped Ada into her seat on the trap.

Back home, Ada went out into the chilly back kitchen and turned up the gas-light which had been left on low. She put the kettle to boil and, as it began to hum, she prepared a tray which Gareth and Cecily

128

might share. Her tasks done, she drooped with melancholy. Why did this have to happen? Life was not far from perfect now she and Cecily ran the shop without interference and she felt heart-aching dismay as Gareth threatened to take not her but Cecily away.

She looked into the ancient, spotted mirror above the sink. What is it that makes me less attractive than Cecily? We are so similar in many ways, yet it was Cecily who had attracted two such desirable men. First Danny, whose wild and casual air had devastated a number of hearts, whose appearance in the dance hall on New Year's Eve had caused so many heads to turn, so many faces to light up with interest. Women admired his strong features, his tanned skin and most of all the bold, blatant sexuality in his dark eyes. He had been involved with other women before Cecily but he'd never looked at me with even a hint of interest, she thought with a sigh.

Then, when Danny had tired of Cecily's refusal to conform to what he expected and demanded from a woman, she had captured Gareth. Why Cecily and not me? She wondered sadly.

She rubbed at the speckled mirror where steam from the kettle had blanked it and stared again at her reflection, all sad and misty. Then she smiled and told herself not to be a fool. "How could you want a man who prefers your sister?" she asked out loud. "Best you stop blaming Cecily for being more beautiful and get on with your own life," she told herself firmly. "You aren't a shadow of her! You're a person in your own right!" She heard Cecily and Gareth come in and

129

attended to the kettle. Singing to announce her arrival, she went in carrying the tray.

"Ada," Cecily said in a soft whisper. There was something about her voice that made Ada look up sharply. Cecily's face was flushed and her blue eyes shone in the light of the hissing gas-light. She smiled and her face was, to Ada, utterly beautiful.

"You have something to tell me?" Ada asked, forcing a smile.

"I've asked Cecily to marry me," Gareth said in a rush.

Ada dropped the tray clumsily and rushed to hug her sister. "Oh Cecily, I'm so pleased for you both." Tears of disappointment and jealousy coupled with the realization that she was destined to be the "old maid" of the family were presumed to be tears of joy and she made no effort to hide them. She hugged Gareth and it was painfully sweet to feel his arms around her at last and experience the touch of his lips on hers.

"Damn the tea," she said with a great gulp. "Wonderful news like this deserves more than tea. It deserves something stronger. What's in Dadda's cupboard?" She opened the wooden cabinet and pulled out a few bottles, dabbing her eyes as she searched. "Will port do? We don't seem to have anything else."

"Don't say anything about this yet, will you, Ada?" Gareth warned. "Not till I have the chance to tell Mam."

"Our secret." Ada held up her glass and drank to their health, their luck and their secret. Then the bottle was empty and Gareth had to go home.

130

"I wonder how long it will take him to pluck up the courage to tell her?" Ada giggled. "It took him long enough to tell you!"

"I'll give him a week, then I'll tell her!"

"Where will you live?"

"Here, of course! I don't want to leave you, and," she added with a wry smile, "I can't imagine me reigning comfortably with Mrs Long-nosed Price-Jones, can you?"

Excitement and the unaccustomed drink had tired them and it took longer than usual to get through the few chores left to do before bed. Yet Ada sat up for a while thinking about the promise she had made herself in the misty mirror. Tomorrow she'd stop mooning about Gareth and start moulding a life of her own. I'll no longer be half of a partnership, she decided, but an individual without strings. The decision cheered her momentarily but gloom had resettled before she reached the door of their bedroom.

The window was open and the curtains blew softly in the night breeze. The candle guttered and she snuffed it out. Opening the curtains she looked out into the silent street. Only circles of light from the gas lamps lit the scene like spotlights on stage; everywhere was black but a peaceful blackness, not one in which unpleasant things lurked. She wished Willie lived in. She'd love to have someone to walk with her and she needed a walk. A fresh cool night wind on her face would have calmed her.

On a corner further down the road a door opened and two figures fell out, illuminated by the splash of light from within. Their shapes were distorted by the pattern of light but she quickly realized it was two women and they were fighting. From the screams and the shouts that reached her, it was over a man.

The mood of tranquillity was shattered and she closed the sash with a gentle thump. Fighting over a man indeed! Thank goodness she and Cecily weren't like that. Gareth belonged to Cecily and she, Ada Owen, was free to enjoy a real romance of her own. But, she wondered sadly as she pulled the cool sheets over her shoulders, where would she find it?

Dorothy Owen was an aggressive character and many were afraid of offending her. Since being widowed she had received many invitations to "walk out". She was still attractive, her confidence and air of authority lifting her above the rest, and now, at forty, she was still a woman who men noticed.

She was fashion-conscious but always selected for herself clothes that flowed. Even when fashion dictates were for slinky, well-fitted dresses and coats, she wore skirts that were full and billowed out behind her. She frequently wore a couple of scarves around her shoulders like stoles with ends floating around her in layers of undulating cloth as she moved.

"Dorothy Owen makes fashion, she doesn't slavishly follow," she told her admiring friends.

She had worked for a few seasons on the beach, serving trays of food to families on the sand. As this only lasted for the few months of summer, when trippers came to fill the small, friendly town, she was forced to look for other work for the rest of the year. Standing for a friend who was ill, she found herself in the big department store, selling ladies' clothes, and she quickly realized she had found her natural place.

She was so popular with those with money to spend and a desire to be noticed, she had been invited to stay and, leaving the children with a neighbour during the school holidays, and on Saturdays, she continued to enjoy the work and the extra money.

The bonus was the opportunity to dress up instead of dress down to go to work. She loved it and spent more money on clothes to wear in the shop than she could really afford. This so impressed her employers they appointed her first sales when she had been there only two months, something unheard of. Now she helped with the buying and was considered indispensable in the smart fashion department. Miss Dorothy was a success.

So, it was no surprise when, sitting in the small room she liked to call her office, one of the trainee sales girls came and told her a customer wanted to see her. There were many people in the town who asked for her advice when buying new outfits and Mrs Price-Jones was one of them.

"Mrs Price-Jones, how nice." Dorothy was never too gushing, especially with those she considered her inferior. Just enough of a smile to set the customers at ease but not enough to suggest they might be equals. Dorothy considered herself above most of them, even those living around the park. "How can I help you today?"

"I want a dress to cheer myself up," Gareth's mother sighed. "Shocking news I've just had. Shocking." She stopped and covered her mouth and her long nose with a be-ringed hand. "Oh, I shouldn't be saying this, you being related an' all."

"My sisters-in-law misbehaving?"

"My Gareth has told me he and Cecily are to wed."

"Oh, how nice." Dorothy waited for the shock to pass before adding, "Why should that upset you? Two girls with a busy shop can't be a bad match, even if it is only a badly run grocery store."

"But they're so unsuited. Sorry to say this but Cecily is a bit . . . bold, for a woman, don't you think? For someone as sensitive as my Gareth." She leaned closer. "Did you know that on the day after their father's funeral they were laughing and singing, yes, singing, with that stable lad of theirs? Trotting over to the Pleasure Beach as if they were celebrating."

"No principle, Mrs Price-Jones. I sympathize with you. I wonder if there isn't some way we can persuade them to at least delay things? I mean, that Danny fellow is around again. I've seen Willie Morgan giving him a lift only weeks ago. She and Ada went off with him after the New Year dance. That must surely give him cause to wonder if she is being completely honest with him?"

Dorothy listened to the woman's criticism of Cecily for a while longer then, leaving her in the hands of a junior, went back to her office. Cecily must not marry. If either of the sisters had a son then Owen would never have the shop. She considered a few ideas on how to prevent Gareth making the engagement official. Danny

Preston lived in Quarry Street on the far side of town near the docks. Perhaps a visit might reveal something useful.

Waldo and Melanie Watkins came one evening to look through the books at Owen's shop. The fact that they were rivals was not any concern to either side: without Waldo's advice and assistance, the sisters would have found it difficult to take on the running of the shop without making expensive mistakes. For Waldo's part, he saw the small grocer's shop as a hobby, taking a keen interest in its changes and a pride in its success.

"The new business with the stall holders over the beach is impressive," he said as he closed the books. "You've specialized in lines your father refused to consider and it's paid off. Well done, both of you."

"Willie has been a marvellous help," Ada said. "Without him putting in the hours he has, we'd never have kept so many customers happy."

"Getting an extra boy, I hear," Melanie said. She put down the tray of tea she'd made and began to pour. "I wish you'd find a couple for us. Stuck we are now Jack Simmons has gone."

"What happened?"

"Fighting, that's what! We couldn't send him to our customers looking like the result of a heavyweight boxing bout!"

"Fighting? That isn't so terrible, is it?" Cecily defended. "In fact, our Willie came in looking like a map of a coal mine one morning back in the winter, and went through all the colours of a rainbow in the

135

days that followed. He'd obviously been fighting but we pretended to believe his story about falling down some steps."

"Once you can ignore, but when it happens several times in a month, it begins to look bad. No, Jack Simmons had to go."

"Shame. Well, if we hear of anyone we'll let you know."

"Plenty of people unemployed but not many like your Willie."

Melanie handed her husband a cup of tea. He had reopened the books and was thumbing through them, making sure all was well with the way the shop was managed, and what he saw satisfied him. Melanie watched him nod appreciatively before closing them again and taking up his tea.

Waldo was a small man, still fair although in his late forties. His blue eyes were paler than those of his wife but very bright, impish at times, but always giving a clear indication of sharp intelligence.

Waldo and Melanie had taken over an ailing business on the main road when they were newly married and worked together, a true partnership, dealing with every part of a complicated business together. They were separated only by their volunteer work. Melanie supported a charity for homeless children and Waldo a sport and exercise club for boys. Regret for their lack of children showed in the way they used their precious spare time.

"Young Van all right?" Waldo asked as he pushed aside the various files and ledgers and settled to enjoy the rest of the evening in social pleasantries.

136

"Yes, she's fine, although she still talks about Dadda quite a lot."

"Good thing, I'm sure," Melanie said.

"Bertie and Beryl are kind. She enjoys playing with their Edwin and of course their house is such a comfortable one. Van's home from home it is, their house and yours. She's so lucky."

"Edwin's only complaint is that she insists on playing shops all the time," Ada said with a smile.

"Remember, you only have to ask if there's anything you need," Waldo reminded them.

On the strength of Waldo's words of encouragement regarding the state of their finances, the sisters decided to re-paper the big sitting room above the shop. There was extra money and he recommended they use it to make the house more their own.

"It's yours now and should reflect more of your personalities."

"Know any good decorators, Melanie?" Cecily asked. "I don't think we should risk splashing about with flour and water paste ourselves, do you?" Cecily laughed but the smile was frozen when Melanie said innocently, "Why not ask Danny Preston? You and he were friends once and he's supposed to be very good."

"Danny? I thought he was a postman?" Cecily murmured after a pause.

"Oh, he is, but he's also working up a business for painting and decorating. Clever with colours I'm told."

The others went on talking and Cecily faded into a daydream of Danny. How could she invite him here, to spend days in their home discussing wallpaper, and act

137

as though he were simply a hired workman? She drifted back to the present conversation to hear Ada say, "No, perhaps we'll do it ourselves. The lighter evenings are to enjoy and it would give us something different to think about."

When their friends had gone, Ada brought up the subject of Danny again. "So, he isn't married after all."

"He isn't? What happened?" She had obviously missed that part of the conversation.

"Called it off, he did, a few days after giving Jessie his ring."

CHAPTER
SEVEN

Rhonwen Owen was eight years younger than her sister-in-law, Dorothy, and as gentle and unassuming as Dorothy was resolute. She started working on the beach during the summer at the same time as Dorothy when they were both widowed, but when Dorothy gave up the seasonal work and started working in the fashion department, Rhonwen had stayed on. She spent each summer selling trays of teas for the sands and working in a cinema during the winter.

To help Dorothy, she met Dorothy's son Owen from school at the same time as her own daughter, Marged, who at twelve was a year younger than Owen. The two children could hardly be more different.

Marged was a happy child, given to fits of giggling, much to her mother's amusement and her Aunt Dorothy's dismay. Giggling, unlike genuine laughter, Dorothy insisted, came at inopportune moments, like the day of her poor dear grandfather's funeral, and showed serious lack of control. The solemn Owen was a trial to Marged as she failed to make him smile. Rhonwen watched them walking through the school playground, Marged jumping about like a playful young colt, and the overweight Owen beside her, his head in a book, giving a false impression of studiousness. The solemnity was odd in a young boy and he was constantly teased, which bothered him not at all.

"Come on," Rhonwen called to him. "We have to get you to the barber before that hair blocks you off from the world completely."

"Oh no, Auntie Rhonwen! Not a haircut!" His face dropped in dismay, the mouth a wet oval, eyes peering over the glasses he now wore, his chin showing its double, cheeks wobbling in anticipation of the horrors to come.

"Never mind, Owen, it's sure to be, almost, painless." Marged shared a smile with her mother. Owen showed his teeth in a half-hearted snarl.

Rhonwen looked around the slowly emptying playground for either Cecily or Ada, who were usually here to meet Van. "Seen Van today?" she asked. "I must have missed them."

"Yes, she was crying," Owen reported. "Someone said she was crying because she doesn't have a father. Silly ha'porths. Lots of boys haven't got fathers. You and I haven't got a father but you don't see me, crying about it."

"But you do have a mother," Rhonwen admonished gently. "Van has only got Auntie Cecily and Auntie Ada."

"And us, Mam," Marged said, hugging her. "And old Owen-of-the-long-hair, he's a cousin and that's better than nothing."

Myfanwy had been sitting in the playground earlier that day, staring through the railings at the allotments

140

beside the school, where, until recently, her grandfather had worked and occasionally pushed a freshly pulled carrot through the railings for her.

When Gran had gone away he had stopped coming and now his plot was covered with a blanket of weeds: chickweed, groundsel, daisies, dandelions and even the larger sow thistles and nettles had infiltrated the once-clean earth where vegetables had once grown.

Now Granddad was gone too and from what she had gathered would never come back. Not like Gran, who was only as far away as the railway station but who never came to see her, to hug her and tell her lovely stories. Now she had to sit in the back room and play shops all alone until the real shop closed. Then it was supper and bed.

Tears welled in her eyes and slid down her rose-red cheeks. Some of her friends came to comfort her.

"I miss my granddad," she sobbed. "No mam, no dad, no gran and now no grandfather either."

Tears flowed and sobs heaved in her chest. Then, among the sympathetic murmurs that she was beginning to enjoy, a voice said, "Illegitimate, that's what you are, Myfanwy Owen. You might as well face it."

"What does that mean?" she demanded, her mouth a pout of held-back sobs.

"It means you haven't got no father and you never had no father!"

"That's nothing. All my uncles were killed fighting in the war and my dad was too, so there. We're all the same, we're all ill — whatever you called it."

141

"Illegitimate," the boy repeated slowly. "And it isn't everybody, it's just you, Myfanwy Owen. Only you!"

Van said the word silently, syllable by syllable, learning it and hating the sound, knowing it was something unpleasant. The malicious look on the boy's face was enough to tell her that, and the way he slowed his voice and repeated it, time and again.

Soon, all the children, including those who had recently tried to comfort her, were chanting it, leaning towards her, drumming the strange word into her brain until she screamed and hit out at her tormentors. Then she saw Edwin Richards and knew things would soon be all right again.

His powerfully built body pushed through the taunting children, his arms impatiently forcing aside those foolish enough to resist and soon he stood in front of her, glaring at the slowly quietening crowd. His dark eyes flashed and his face was tight with anger. No one would cause Van a moment's distress while he was there to speak for her. He had no idea of the reason for the argument but was instinctively on Van's side.

"They're saying I never had a dad," she sobbed, dirt streaking her face with the constant rubbing of her small hand.

"Van's mam and dad were heroes in the war, that's right, isn't it, Van? Her dad was a soldier like her uncles, and he died a hero, saving dozens of lives."

"What about her mam then?" one of the braver boys demanded. "You don't get women heroes."

"Van's mam was a nurse," Edwin invented, "and she helped the heroes."

142

Van flashed him a grateful smile for his inventiveness and the crowd dispersed, the fun already forgotten, on their way to find someone else to tease. Edwin gave Van his handkerchief and waited while she dried her eyes.

Rhonwen walked with Marged and Owen to The Wedge and went into the half that was Gareth's shop. There were two men waiting and Owen and Marged sat looking at comics.

"Mrs Owen. How are you?" Gareth gestured to a chair. "We don't see you in here often. You not having a boy I don't expect to, of course," he added with a smile. "Nice to be lucky enough to get a pretty lady like your Marged in here."

"Dorothy's busy and I'm here with Owen. His hair is very long."

"Soon put that right, won't we, boy?"

Owen glared at Gareth over his glasses but made no comment.

As he finished the customers before them he chatted easily to Rhonwen and when it was time for them to leave he felt surprisingly disappointed.

"Such a quiet, pleasant young lady," he said to his mother later. "It'll be nice having her in the family, when Cecily and I are married."

Throughout the evening, his mind constantly returned to the gentle Rhonwen and he found himself comparing her to Cecily.

"She's nowhere as beautiful or as lively as Cecily," he told his mother. "Cecily's the perfect choice for someone as quiet and settled as me. She's resourceful

143

and clever too. Just look how she's pulled that shop from the ordinary little grocers to the thriving place it is now." He shook his head. "No, Rhonwen would be too calm for me, nice as she undoubtedly is, mind. She'd be there, a part of the scenery but without me being aware of her most of the time. I'd just drift along the way I do now with no excitement." The thought, spoken aloud, didn't sound dull at all.

His mother was staring up at him from her chair close to the fire, a thoughtful expression on her face. "Who are you trying to convince, Gareth?"

"Cecily makes me proud, see," he said, pretending not to hear. "She's clever and beautiful and she turns heads wherever we go. When I walk with her on my arm she makes me feel great, Mam, just great."

When Rhonwen eventually arrived home with Owen neatly shorn, his sister was putting the final touches to a casserole. Marged sniffed appreciation. "Can I have some, Annette? Please? Starving I am!"

"Marged!" Rhonwen said, then laughed. "Don't take any notice of her, Annette. Starving she is from the moment she wakes till the first snore."

Annette went to the pottery bread bin and began cutting a very thick slice, locally called a *cwlff*. "Eat this — it will give you the strength to walk home."

"It's faggots and peas night, but I'd rather have some of that casserole," Marged sighed as she took her first bite.

Dorothy returned from work before they left and over a cup of tea Rhonwen told her about Van being

144

teased at school. "They called her illegitimate, would you believe? Where do children pick up these words? Shame on them for upsetting the child and her grieving for her grandfather. An orphan she is, poor love."

"Is she? I think they're right — she is illegitimate."

"Adopted," Rhonwen said firmly. "Her mother was a friend of Cecily and Ada and married to a soldier, who died before the baby was born, and the mother died in childbirth."

"There's a bit of a *tawch* about the whole thing if you ask me," Dorothy said. "Something not clear."

"Well, I think it's a shame and the teacher should be told. I'll suggest to Ada and Cecily that they sort it out."

"I wouldn't," Dorothy advised. "To have it talked about could make things worse for the child. Best you let it go. There'll be someone else to torment tomorrow, you know what children are like. Forget it — that's best."

"Perhaps," Rhonwen agreed. "Least said and all that."

Dorothy looked thoughtful for a while, then she stood up, a hint for Rhonwen and Marged to leave. "Now, Annette, that food smells good. Oh, and by the way, I'm going into Cardiff tomorrow. Is there anything you need?"

"Some ribbons, please, Mam."

"Going shopping?" Rhonwen asked.

"No," Dorothy said seriously. "Business. Important business."

Summer was filling the town with visitors and a number of private houses advertised rooms to let and were kept busy washing bedding and providing big breakfasts for their guests, mostly bread and potatoes to fill the plates.

This increased the trade at Owen's shop and Willie was run off his feet going to and from the wholesalers topping up stock. He still delivered to the beach customers and still managed to meet Annette every Monday afternoon to take tea with Peter Marshall. They didn't attempt to hide from passers-by, thinking that, should they be seen, it would be simple to explain that they met by accident and decided to share a pot of tea.

They loved the stolen hour of freedom, sitting watching the trippers parading past with new buckets and spades, the parents loaded with bags containing an assortment of food, fruit and the inevitable bottle of "pop" to quench the children's thirst.

Families staked their claim to an area of the golden sands and removed as much of their clothing as they dared. Dads wore their suits; the only concession to it being their annual holiday was the removal of their jackets and sometimes their waistcoats too. They would roll up their trouser legs to mid calf, their shirt sleeves as high as they would go, place a knotted handkerchief on their head and set to work building a sandcastle of turreted splendour.

In the background, they heard the rattling and the screams coming from the figure of eight, and the klaxons and horns and wails coming from the more sedate assortment of rides in the amusement park. The air smelled deliciously of seaweed, moist sand and chips. Whatever the weather, for Willie and Annette, each Monday was a perfect day.

Crowds increased towards the middle of August and so did the couple's feeling of anonymity as hordes of strangers filled the cafes, rides and shops. Willie was well known to most of the business people but no one mentioned seeing him with Annette.

Peter Marshall usually managed to be there each Monday for part of the time they were there. The only comment he made on their using his cafe as a meeting place was to suggest to Willie that he should persuade the sisters to buy a van for when the weather was less kind, and winter saw the closing of the cafes.

"Annette," Willie said one day as they walked back to where they had left the horse and cart. "Would you like to come and see my house? Worked on it for months I have and it's looking smart. But I want a woman's opinion on curtains and things."

"Willie, I don't think I should. What if Mam found out? Or someone saw us coming out together? What would people think?"

"I'll ask Gladys Davies to come in with us and we'll only stay for a minute or two. Like for you to see it, I would."

"All right then. But we'll make it early so I can get home in plenty of time to get the meal ready for Mam and Owen."

"No later than usual, that's a promise."

Monday was a fairly quiet day at the shop and the sisters used it as an opportunity to clean windows and scrub beneath the counters. When Willie returned from the beach and his meeting with Annette, Cecily asked, "Will you call at Phil Spencer's for the bill-heads we've ordered? If you collect them tonight you can bring them in the morning."

"That's no trouble," Willie said amiably as he carried in the last of the boxes from the display outside the shop.

"No, I'll walk down after I've met Van," Ada said. "The shop's quiet and you can manage for a while, can't you?"

"Walk?" Cecily was surprised. "All the way to the village?"

"It's such a lovely day and I'll get a bus for part of the way. I never seem to get any sun on my face."

It was after four when Ada set out in a new suit of lightweight wool in lime green with a navy blouse showing its frill down the front opening. She wore a pair of high-heeled shoes that certainly weren't meant for walking.

She had taken a lot of care with her appearance, having set her hair in kiss-curls around her face, similar to those Cecily wore. Waves made a rigid pattern, tight against her scalp, and the back was cut tightly into her neck in a semi shingle. She loosened the waves slightly with a comb and felt the wind lifting them as she went for the bus, causing her to wish she had brought a scarf. Artistically sculpted from stone was the image she had tried to create.

She alighted from the bus at the small park where Danny Preston had found his motorbike months ago, and walked down the green lane to the old part of the town, where Phil Spencer ran his printing business near where Willie lived.

Her knock on Phil's door was answered promptly. He wiped his stained hands down his overall before offering her one. "Come in, come in!" he said, opening the door wide. "Business, is it? Or am I lucky enough to have a social visit from the prettiest lady in town?"

"Don't talk daft, Phil Spencer," Ada laughed. "Come for the bill-heads I have."

Mrs Spencer came out of the living room and smiled a welcome. "Lovely it is to see you again, Miss Owen. Phil's been so hoping you'd call."

"Mam!"

"Well, the truth won't harm anyone." She picked up the local paper and tapped her finger on the relevant place. "Seen this, have you? A road race on roller skates in fancy dress. There's fun that'll be and there's going to be a Grand Fete with a carnival queen an' all, an end-of-season spectacular with summer nearly over. Lots will be going, won't they? Holiday-makers and locals alike. You taking your Myfanwy?"

She didn't need or expect answers as she went back to the fire which burned dully in the sunshine streaming through the window, busying herself with kettle and teapot.

"Sit down," Phil fussed, plumping up cushions in the most comfortable chair. "I'll just get your order." In his

149

ungainly manner he went through to the workshop-cum-office and returned with a neatly parcelled box.

"How did you come?" he asked.

"I walked down from the park. The bus dropped me there. I didn't have time to walk all the way after meeting Van."

"I'll take you back in style if you like. I've bought a van. What d'you think of that, then?"

Ada looked out of the window, stretching up to see past the wide window sill in the two-feet-thick wall. A van stood outside and painted on the side in beautiful scroll work was the legend "Phil Spencer, Master Printer and Sign Writer".

"I bought it from a man called Peter Marshall and he gave me ten minutes' instruction and left me to drive it home. Damn me! I never had such a hair-raising ride in all my life. Talk about chaos! A policeman saw my erratic progress and thought I was trying to end it all, in the dock! Came with me he did, walking and running alongside, shouting instructions through the window and him never even been in a car before!"

He went on describing the journey home and the subsequent trips he had made since as he slowly became more proficient. Ada drank tea, ate cake and laughed and forgot about time. When she heard the clock in the corner rumble and strike five thirty, she stood up, wiping tears of laughter from her eyes and insisted it was time she left.

"I don't know whether I should trust myself to you and your van, though," she said, "after all the disasters you've told me about."

150

"Safe as houses you'll be with me. I'd never let anything harm you, I can promise that." He stared at her for a moment, his merry eyes in the sharply featured face very intense. He helped her into her jacket and Ada thanked Mrs Spencer for the tea and cakes, then he bustled her out into the still warm evening. She sat in the van that smelled pleasantly of polished leather, Phil still chattering.

"Caught the button of my sleeve in the steering wheel, see, and there was this bloke trying to get away and every way he turned so did I as I struggled to release the button. Damn, it was funny. Like a flaming rabbit he was. Young Jack Simmons. Know him, do you?"

Ada hardly said a word until they stopped outside the shop and Cecily and Myfanwy came out to meet her.

"Well," Cecily teased. "Walking indeed!"

"You want to get one of these for your Willie, for delivering orders. Save a lot of time it will and it looks good to the customers, don't you think?"

Phil held out the package for which Ada had called, hoping she would come back to him for one final word. All the way to the shop he had filled the air with words while trying to pluck up the courage to invite her out. Unless she came back to collect the package he had left it too late.

He watched the doorway and just as he'd decided he must take it to her, she came back. He held it towards her but when she grasped it he didn't let go. "Meet me on Sunday for a drive down the coast?" he asked in his

151

fast, anxious way. "Please," he added, staring at her, blue eyes laughing, his expression as eager as a child's.

"Yes, Phil. I'd like that. About two o'clock?"

"I'll be here, tooting my horn with impatience."

He was sick with excitement as he released the brake and moved away. He hoped she wasn't watching as he mounted the pavement and almost ran over a cat.

"I think there's something worrying our Van," Ada said one evening as they wearily packed away the last of the goods from the porch and windows. "She hasn't said anything to you, has she?"

"No. Perhaps she's still grieving for Dadda. Or it might be something to do with my plan to marry Gareth. I've tried to involve her in all the preparations and talked about everything openly, but she might still be afraid of being left alone. She was only seven last April and it's not easy for her to explain what's worrying her. I could have said too much or not enough."

"I asked Beryl and Bertie but they don't know. And I asked Waldo. He and Melanie have taken her out a few times but they can't help. She seemed perfectly at ease with them."

"Don't let's cook tonight. We'll go for some fish and chips and try to get her to talk."

It wasn't difficult. As soon as they sat down to eat, Cecily shut off the wireless, which was giving a news report and weather for the following day, and asked softly, "What is it, Van, lovely? What's bothering you? Tell your aunties and we'll soon put it right."

152

"What's ill-e-giti-mate?" The little girl said the word as she had learned it, syllable by horrible syllable, repeating the word and forcing herself to remember it, chanting it like a litany. Illegitimate. Something very bad, something wicked.

The sisters looked at each other in surprise. Whatever they had expected, it wasn't this.

"Where did you hear that word?" Ada asked.

"In school. The boys were calling me that, said it meant I didn't have a father. But Marged and Owen don't have a father and they weren't called that."

"Your mother was our best friend," Cecily told her. "Your father was a kind, loving and brave man."

"Who died in the war like Uncle John and Uncle Victor?"

"No, lovey. He died around the time you were born and the war was over by then."

"Tell me about them."

Gradually they reassured the anxious little girl and built a picture of her parents. They had done this many times but, as before, memory faded and she needed reminders of the story they told her. They talked until she seemed content and when she went to bed, they both stayed with her, one each side of the bed, until she slept.

On Sunday, Annette made an excuse to her mother and went for a walk. She set off through the town, up the hill, on past the shops until the houses became fewer and fewer and there were fields on either side of the road. Then houses appeared again, each with its own

153

colourful garden where Phlox, lupins and tall daisies nodded their heads lazily in the warm sunshine. Wallflowers jutted out precariously from crevices in garden walls, slow and small but determined to add to summer's show. One day, she thought, I'd like a garden where I can grow flowers.

Some gardens were large and she saw rows of vegetables neatly tended and coops where chickens chortled and clucked. There was even, on occasions, the unmistakable and powerful smell of a pig sty, its occupants sprawled contentedly on the warm earth. Other cottages had small plots but these had been used to full effect and flowers crept up walls and over fences to make use of every inch of soil and were masses of rich texture and colour.

For a while her path followed the brook, as it worked its convoluted way between the higgledy-piggledy arrangement of odd cottages. It widened in places and ducks made use of its shallows to find food. A heron flew across her path to settle in a tree beside a bedraggled and now empty nest.

Annette didn't know the area well, but from the instructions Willie had given her she found his cottage easily. It was the most recently painted and shone in the August sun, dazzling her eyes as she paused to admire it.

As she looked, the door opened and Willie came out, strangely unfamiliar in shirt sleeves and the trousers of a navy suit. She had never seen him in anything but a jacket and shirt, collar and tie. Today he looked a different man. He ran to meet her and took her at once to his neighbour, Gladys Davies.

"Mrs Davies, this is Annette," he said proudly as the woman opened her door. "Will you come with us while I show her my home?"

"Now in a minute," Gladys said. "I'll have to take my potatoes off the boil or they'll be a mish-mash — no good for the pasties I'm making." She disappeared inside and Annette and Willie looked around self-consciously, unable to look at each other although that was what they both wanted. "You look nice," he said eventually.

Annette stroked the skirt of the blue dress she wore, its gathered waist accentuating her rather full hips. "Thank you."

Annette wondered why they were so different today. Usually they began talking the moment they met and were still thinking of things to say long after they parted. They were beginning a new stage of their relationship, no longer two separate people but a couple, with nothing they didn't share. Both were silently, almost unconsciously accepting the fact.

Mrs Davies walked with them the short distance across the unmade road and Willie ushered them both inside, and leaving the door open, followed them in. He showed them around with modest pride, pointing out the things he had changed since his family had left.

"You made this table?" Annette said admiringly. "But you're very clever to do that."

"Danny Preston helped."

"You wait till you see the bed he made." Mrs Davies's pride in her neighbour was apparent. It was she who pointed out the painting and the renewing of floorboards and the cupboard with its shining hinges which she polished every week, and the oven range that Willie had dragged back from a rubbish dump and spent many evenings polishing. It gleamed dully in the light from the fire.

"It's a beautiful home, Willie." Annette's cheeks reddened as they climbed the stairs to see the bed. There was a patchwork quilt over it and the wooden frame was well made and firm. As she suddenly thought of lying there beside Willie, her blushes increased alarmingly. She went out of the room hoping Willie hadn't guessed the reason.

"I want you to tell me about curtains," Willie said when they were back in the living room. "I've started making a rag rug and Mrs Davies is helping, so it won't be long before it's finished. Then the curtains are the final thing. Will you help? I want something really nice. Thick and cosy."

"It will be expensive," Annette warned.

"I'll have the money in a week or two."

They arranged to meet at a small drapers on the following Thursday between his deliveries. "If we see Mam we can pretend we met by accident." Annette was smiling happily. Seeing his home, helping him choose curtains: what an exciting day.

Gladys Davies loved being involved in the secret meeting. She could have helped Willie choose curtains but seeing the young couple together, knew this was one time when it was better not to offer.

"I'll walk with you to the bus," Willie said as Annette prepared to leave. They waved to Mrs Davies as they set off up the green lane to the park.

As they approached the park gates they could hear the sound of a brass band and soon saw a small crowd, listening to hymns and occasionally joining in with the well-known words. Willie led her past and when they were out of sight, he leaned forward and kissed her.

Startled at first, she soon warmed to the new sensation. Her arms, from hanging limply at her sides, moved slowly up and around him, feeling his lean frame pressed against hers until the kiss filled her entire body. They walked closer together when they broke away and their pace slowed even more as they were reluctant to reach the end of the tree-lined path and face strangers once again.

"I'll see you tomorrow." Willie's voice was hardly a whisper and her own sounded freakishly low as she replied, "Yes, Willie. Tomorrow."

The bus came too soon and she turned in her seat to watch until he was no more than a memory, before facing the front and wondering what would happen when her mother found out. She relaxed, thinking of the kiss and decided that Willie was resourceful enough to cope. She could rely on him completely.

Phil Spencer's van was passing the bus as Willie and Annette were saying goodbye. Ada saw they were holding hands and from their expressions, in the brief glimpse she had, they were not meeting for the first time. She'd better have a word with Willie. There was no possibility of Dorothy allowing a romance to develop between her daughter and an errand boy. When she explained to Phil he laughed.

"Spoilsport you are, Ada Owen! Leave them be. If they love each other nothing will stop them getting together and if they don't, well, there's no point in you messing up their fun, now is there?"

"It won't hurt to have a word with him," she protested.

"It'll do less harm to say nothing. Thinking no one knows is part of the magic. Love is wonderful and it enhances every sight and sound, every moment of every day. Leave them be."

"You're very poetic today." Ada glanced at her companion, who seemed to have his eyes everywhere except the road.

"Love does that. I should know, I'm in love myself." As Ada turned and looked at him, he grinned, winked broadly and added quietly, "With you, Ada Owen, soon to be Ada Spencer, with you."

"You're daft! I don't know you well enough to call you a friend, let alone consider marrying you!"

"What's taking you so long? I knew ages ago!" He began to whistle merrily and when there was a verge suitable for parking, he stopped the van and turned in his seat to face her. "Well? Will you marry me?" His thin face and bright eyes staring at her in such concentration made laughter threaten. "I promise I'll give you all you need and most of all you want. And plenty of laughter too. What more can you want?"

"No, Phil. I can't marry you." Then the laughter died in her and she saw only a man who wanted her and was offering to share the rest of his life with her. But it was ridiculous. "I don't love you, and —"

"Not this week perhaps, or even next week, but soon you will, although tomorrow wouldn't be too soon for me." He still spoke in his nervous chatter as if they were discussing nothing more exciting than where to drive next. "We'll let Cecily get her 'do' over first, I suppose, then we'll plan ours." He moved closer to the stiff, startled Ada and kissed her. First on the cheek then, as she turned to protest, he held her head in gentle hands and kissed her lips. A low moan escaped him and she felt moved and in moments had fallen under the spell of his urgent caresses. They didn't drive for several minutes and when they did she was limp with shock and confusion.

When she walked into the shop, Cecily looked alarmed, seeing the bright glow on her sister's face. "Ada? What's happened? Are you ill?"

"Nothing terrible." Ada's lips broke into a smile so devastatingly lovely that her eyes seemed lit from within. "I'll tell you later," she said, and ran from the room.

Phil Spencer had ideas far above his ability to earn. The need for money was a constant problem and never as much as now, when he knew he wanted Ada for his wife. Ada's family were hardly rich but they were used to having all they wanted and they only wanted the best. How could he expect to win her if he couldn't compete financially?

Phil had always cheated, both in his limited school career and in the small business he had built for himself after a brief apprenticeship with an old man called Prosser. When old man Prosser died, Phil had muddled through, managing to hang on to the business, through many mistakes and disasters, learning as he went, and the only way he survived was by cheating.

He charged for less than he gave, giving the impression he was woolly minded about money and prone to mistakes. That way any complaints could be put down to absentmindedness rather than dishonesty. He sometimes asked for and got a second payment for some distant and half-forgotten order. He also stole on occasions when calling at houses for settlement of an account; a small item here and there, selling to a jeweller who was even more dishonest than he.

All this was not for personal greed — for himself he needed little to be content — but the conviction that his role was that of breadwinner for his mother and, hopefully in the future, a wife. If he married Ada he wanted to provide everything. That was the man's role. He encouraged his mother to be generous in everything, and to keep a "good table". He made it clear that she only had to ask and he would provide. He would do the same for Ada. She would want for nothing while he was responsible for her welfare.

He felt a glow of pride as he imagined how he would feel when she walked down the aisle to where he waited, and in an ancient and beautiful ceremony changed her name from Owen to Spencer.

"Lovely girl, always ready to laugh," his mother said as he went back into the house.

"I'm going to marry her," he replied. "Whatever I have to do to win her, Ada Owen will one day be my wife."

CHAPTER
EIGHT

Waldo's Grocery store was larger and more important than the one owned by Cecily and Ada. The smells were different too. Lacking the smell of fresh fish and kippers and the salt fish that appeared on many breakfast tables, the strongest smells were those of delicious, freshly ground coffee and the appetizing smell of smoked bacon, which the girls didn't stock. Cheese, too, because of the larger amounts sold, filled the busy shop with mouth-watering aromas.

Waldo's customers had a far greater choice than Cecily could provide and would wander from the provisions side to the grocery, pausing to examine the displays of new items. A new biscuit one week, offers of exotic tinned fruit another, or even a table filled with several cheeses from which bite-sized tasters were offered.

There were two bent-wood chairs close to the two counters and these were used by those intending to recite a long list of requirements to be delivered later in the day. The seats were well polished and Waldo was frequently asked to provide more, but he declined. Two chairs close together would encourage people to stay and chatter and once they had given their order he wanted them out and on their way to make room for others.

The shop was quite noisy. The machine for grinding coffee was a frequent rumble as customers bought the beans from the sacks on display and waited while they were ground. The raisin-stoner was another grinding rumble that the assistants hated, the machine being a tedious one to clean but which was in frequent use. Knives being sharpened and the whirring of the overhead wires sending money across to the cash desk near the door, together with the hum of a dozen conversations, gave the shop a special symphony of its own.

Waldo loved it. He worked in an office through the window of which he could look down on the shop floor, but he frequently left the paperwork in the capable hands of his two clerks and walked around his empire, as he jokingly called it, talking to customers and encouraging the busy assistants with a kind word.

Below the shop were other rooms, sparsely fitted out but a hive of activity. Down there grey-coated figures kept the shop supplied, boning bacon and hams, preparing the large blocks of butter and removing the hard, encrusted muslin from the huge rounds of cheese. Two boys spent a part of each day cutting sugar paper to wrap dried fruit or rice or dried peas, which were sold with a steeping tablet and the muslin bag in which to cook them.

Foodstuffs were weighed and placed in the centre of the piece of paper and carefully folded with the ends tucked in. Then they were carried up to the shop to replenish the shelves, each product in a different colour so needing no labelling.

One morning, Waldo had just returned from the bank when he was greeted by a voice he always tried to ignore. He quickly hid the scowl that threatened and said, politely, "Hello, Dorothy." He gestured towards the counter. "Is someone looking after you?"

"Oh, yes, thank you, Waldo. I only want some decent bacon for Owen's breakfast. I have to do some shopping at Cecily's, being family, but Owen is very fussy about his bacon and there's none as excellent as yours."

Waldo smiled inwardly. Considering he supplied Cecily and Ada with their bacon, he could hardly agree, but he nodded politely. "Not at work today?" he asked. "Not ill, I hope?" He began to move away, tactfully suggesting he had things to do, but something made him stay.

"A day off," she explained. "I've been into Cardiff to check on something. Something personal." Lowering her voice she added, "It was about a birth certificate."

"A birth certificate?"

"Yes, Waldo. I couldn't find out what I want to know and now I have to write to London."

"Well, good luck with whatever you're doing." He frowned as he moved away, then braced himself for another of his least favourite customers. "Mrs Price-Jones, how nice to see you. How are you?" he asked, hoping she wouldn't tell him.

"Worried, Mr Watkins. I'm worried."

He only half listened, trying to edge away from her as she explained about her son's intention to marry Cecily.

"I admire the woman, Mr Watkins, but Gareth and she aren't suited. A mother knows these things."

Dorothy hadn't left the shop and she heard the words, eavesdropping without difficulty in spite of the general hubbub. She waited for Gareth's mother and Waldo watched then as Dorothy led the woman out to have a cup of tea and discuss it. He was frowning, wondering uneasily what Dorothy was planning.

He spent the rest of the day in his office but did little work. When he left at closing time he was still anxious and two spots of colour on his cheeks made him look almost feverish. He drove slowly to his house overlooking the sea and, after greeting Melanie, went into his study and poured himself a whisky. "Damn Dorothy and Mrs Price-Jones with their long, quivering noses," he muttered angrily.

"Ada," Cecily said one morning, "we are going to buy a van."

"Are we? Is this something to discuss or have you already decided?"

"What d'you mean?" Cecily looked startled seeing the tightness of her sister's lips and the warning glitter in the grey eyes. "Of course we'll discuss it. I only said it that way thinking aloud."

"Oh, I see. So you meant what do I think of the idea of buying a van?"

Cecily put a hand on her sister's arm and looked at her apologetically. "It came out wrong, that's all. I saw Waldo yesterday when you were out. He and Melanie came to take Myfanwy to the park. He suggested we buy a van to save Willie's time and provide a better service."

"Who will drive it?" Ada sounded slightly mollified.

"Willie."

"Perhaps Phil could teach him? They live near each other and Phil has been driving for a while."

"Yes, we'll ask him." Cecily had already asked Peter Marshall to both sell them a van and teach Willie to drive it, but she thought this wasn't the time to mention either. She felt guilty. She should have discussed it with Ada before telling Peter to go ahead and get a vehicle. "Is it all right, then? Shall I ask Peter to find a good van for us?"

"If Waldo thinks our finances are secure, I agree we should. But I want to drive too. We could use it on Wednesdays and Sundays sometimes to take Myfanwy out. She loves the beach and trips out into the country and we rarely take her."

"She has plenty of trips with Waldo and Melanie as well as Bertie and Beryl. We shouldn't feel guilty at not taking her ourselves. We work long hours and trying to fit in more outings would make it harder to manage it all."

"You're right, we do work hard. It seems an age since we had a really good night out. What d'you say we ask Beryl and Bertie to have Van on Wednesday? Not a night out, but there's a tea dance and they can be fun."

"Oh yes! We'll go! Just the two of us."

"Won't Gareth mind?" Ada asked.

"Of course not. He isn't jealous like — some would be." She was thinking of Danny and felt a stab of pain. "Gareth will be pleased I'm having some fun."

"We do need a change," Ada said excitedly, "and we won't be late back."

"And first we can talk to Peter Marshall and see about us buying a van!"

In many ways it was the wrong time to buy a van. Willie was constantly busy as trade on the beach was working up to its height and it was enough for him to do to keep their customers supplied and manage the routine work around the yard and the shop. He finished very late most days, then went with either Peter or Waldo and occasionally Phil Spencer for instruction on driving. To add to his problems, Waldo and Peter agreed on the way the vehicle should be driven but Phil confused him with advice. He began to accept most of Waldo and Peter's teaching but with a few of Phil's tricks for getting through a congested area.

"If you shout and sound the horn, and look scared stiff as though your brakes have failed, and drive an erratic course threatening to slice off a few legs with your mudguards, it usually results in people forgetting any arguments about who has right of way and make room for you — fast!" Phil advised with a laugh.

They still kept the horses, and were looking for a field in which they could spend their days. Willie, as a very young man, had started by using a bicycle to deliver locally and then been promoted to the horse and cart. Now he was driving a motor vehicle. He loved it, although he missed the warm friendly animals, and was soon confident to drive on his own. Their customers now had an excellent service with phoned orders delivered in minutes. Peter Marshall seemed pleased to help too and even delivered a few orders to rival cafe owners in his Riley. It was a summer they all enjoyed.

Peter had become very friendly with the sisters but had not let slip about the regular meetings between Willie and Annette. One day, when he called to pay his account, he told them he'd bought a second cafe at the other side of the beach.

"Extra business is fine but it's damned hard work." He smiled at Cecily, who he thought looked tired. "You look as if you could do with a day out. What about me taking you to Porthcawl? I want to size up the beach trade there to see if it's worth me renting a place next year. What about next Sunday? And young Myfanwy, of course."

"I'm going out next Sunday," Ada said. "I've been invited out to tea."

"Oh? And what lucky man would that be?" It was a demonstration of his acceptance as their friend that she told him.

"It's that daft Phil Spencer. He's only gone and told his mother I'm coming, so she's bought lots of food and made some of her special butter cake. I can't disappoint her, can I?"

Peter smiled, his loose cheeks quivering as he pursed his lips and said, "By the look on your face, Miss Ada Owen, it's you who'd be disappointed."

"Go on. That's enough cheek from you!" Smiling and with a blush enhancing her cheeks, she went into the back kitchen to start preparing food. It had become more and more her job to cook the evening meal and for once she was glad to get away from Peter's teasing.

She was excited about visiting Phil and his mother. He was such good fun and always in a good humour. Their occasional meetings had increased until now it was a regular thing for him to pull up outside the shop and whisk her off somewhere for the evening. She hoped Peter would leave before Phil came to collect her tonight. Teasing still made her tense. Although Phil repeated his offer of marriage often, she was not yet certain of her feelings and raillery was difficult to cope with.

Peter waited until Ada was in the kitchen then asked, "What about it, then, Cecily? Oh, it's all right, I know about Gareth, the dancing barber. This is just a friendly invitation and I'd be glad of your opinion of the place that's for rent. You've got a good business head on your shoulders —"

"For a woman?" she finished for him.

"I wouldn't be so condescending! You could teach a few local businessmen a thing or two. You have a flare for forgetting traditional ways and going for something fresh and unusual. I haven't forgotten how we moved my cafe a little to improve its site. Remember?"

"Thank you, Peter. Van and I will love it."

"I know, I'll ask Gareth myself. I'm going there now for a trim. Got to look my best if I'm escorting a couple of beautiful ladies." He patted his greying head. "I'm not too old to enjoy that."

"You don't have to ask Gareth. Thank you for inviting us." The thought of having to ask Gareth touched something inside her and made her feel rebellious. Ask Gareth indeed!

"We aren't married yet!" she said to Ada when she mentioned her acceptance.

Peter Marshall left the Riley outside the shop and walked up to the main road. He had been shaken by Cecily's willingness to go out with him. He had hoped both sisters would accompany him but it was more than he'd dreamed of for Cecily to come on her own. The Wedge was closing for the day and the tobacconist's half already had blinds pulled down. He went into the barbers and waited for Gareth to be free. Fortunately, when the customer Gareth was dealing with had paid, no one else entered.

"Just a trim, if you please. And I would like a word." He thought for a moment that it might have been wiser to wait until his hair had been cut before telling the man with the scissors that he wanted to take his girl out! He was polite and cautious with his explanations. "I'm a customer of the Owens," he began, "and they've been helpful in increasing my business over at the Pleasure Beach."

"Cafe, is it, Mr . . . er . . ." Gareth looked at the short nails, the workstained hands and wondered how he could possibly serve teas.

"Yes, among other things. The sisters are very good about delivering, on occasions making special trips to bring me something I urgently need."

"Wonderful thing, the telephone," Gareth said vaguely. His mind was already on the meal waiting for him. Lovely cook Mam was. He hoped she'd give Cecily some lessons one day soon.

"So, I'd like to take Cecily with me when I go to Porthcawl on Sunday. Just for a look around, see what the competition is. You know, get the feel of the place. Cecily would be a great asset while I'm thinking of a possible business there."

"Cecily go with you? Why?" The scissors stopped their snapping, and leaning towards him, Gareth stared at the man and demanded, "What's Cecily got to do with you?"

"As I've just explained, I value her advice."

"No, no, we've made arrangements for Sunday."

"That's funny, she told me you'd be busy decorating this place."

"That's right, yes, then I was going there for dinner."

Peter wasn't the kind to argue but in this instance he looked at the petulant expression on the man's face and said, "Sorry, but she's accepted my invitation, her and Myfanwy. You'll have to find food somewhere else." He sat nervously as the scissors continued their snipping and hoped Gareth was serious enough about his reputation to do a neat job. He paid, gave a generous tip and left, still making reassuring noises to an irate Gareth.

171

"I'm beginning to see what Danny had to put up with," Gareth muttered darkly. It was liver and onions tonight, his favourite, but instead of going straight home, he went to see Cecily.

She was contrite and submissive and he forgave her impulsive agreement to help a fellow businessman, and gave gracious permission for her to go. Cecily turned and gave Ada a wide wink.

"But," Gareth said importantly, fear of losing her overcoming his nerves for once, "this shilly-shallying must stop. I want us to name a day for our wedding and decide where we're going to live. Now, Mam would be willing for us to live there and —"

"Gareth, love, I have to stay here. There's Van and Ada and the business. No, we'll get the top rooms decorated and start our home there. Come on, let's go and see what alterations are needed."

By the time Gareth left, they had decided on a Christmas wedding and Cecily promised to go on the first free afternoon to choose a wedding dress and begin the arrangements.

He told his mother the news in great excitement as he began to eat his shrivelled-up food, but was soon holding smelling salts under her long nose. When she had recovered sufficiently her first words were, "You don't have to get married, do you?"

"No Mam!"

"Thank goodness for that. There's no telling with a woman like that, seeing Danny Preston one week and accepting you the next."

"What does that mean?"

"Dorothy Owen. I met her in Waldo Watkins' and she was saying how Cecily has seen Danny twice recently."

"Damn it all! And now she's off to Porthcawl on Sunday with some man with dirty fingernails called Peter Marshall!"

"What?"

Gareth passed her the sal volatile.

The month of August was always frantically busy, the town heaving with so many visitors it was hard to imagine where they all ate and slept. Towards the end of the month, the sisters and Gareth, sometimes with Van, managed to enjoy several of the entertainments arranged for the busy holiday period. Dancing On The Green, listening to the town's silver band in the parks, racing and crazy sports at the beach one afternoon, and even a few evening dances when they weren't too tied up with extra work. Everywhere they went, they met Danny.

He greeted Cecily like an old friend, patted Gareth on the shoulder and, if Van was with them, found her some sweets from his pocket or bought her an ice cream and a balloon. He would discuss in a relaxed manner what they had all been doing during the day and seemed not to notice the way Gareth's cheeks puffed out in anger at his constant intrusions.

Cecily wondered how he knew exactly where they would be. Even when they made some last change of plan, he would be there. But she didn't ask. She was going to marry Gareth.

There was the road race on roller skates that Mrs Spencer had told Ada about and they all went to see the fun. Cecily stood at the side of the road to wait for the competitors to pass and found herself looking into the sea of faces, certain that somewhere among them would be Danny's. To her surprise, he was competing, dressed in the costume of a gypsy fiddler. As he passed her he slowed down and waved, again knowing exactly where they would be standing.

There was community singing in the large park, polo to watch in the swimming pool and fashion shows organized by Dorothy's department store. Firework displays delighted the children and there was a choral singing competition, in which Van took part, dressed in a very warm Welsh costume. Danny was there to cheer her on.

One Sunday, Gareth was finishing off the decoration of his shop and Cecily and Van were invited to join Ada for tea with Phil and Mrs Spencer.

"Looking forward to seeing you all," Phil said, bouncing around as he settled the three of them in the temporary seats in the van. "Sorry it isn't more comfortable. Getting a car soon, I am." He limped around to the driving seat and they set off with a series of jerks.

He chattered non-stop all the way through the town and Cecily was struck by the happy, relaxed relationship between him and her sister. Phil was not a handsome man and rumours abounded suggesting he was not exactly honest, but there was something about him that made criticism or censure impossible — with the exception of his driving!

He looked at the passengers and pointed out people and places he thought would interest them, like a courier on a grand tour, but he seemed happily unaware of other vehicles, driving furiously ahead and leaving it to others to swerve and avoid a collision in a cavalier way that gave Cecily a taste of sheer panic. Ada seemed unaware of the risks he took and even pulled on the steering wheel on occasions to attract his attention to something she wanted him to see.

Mrs Spencer was at the gate. She was dressed in a long, dark blue dress over which she wore a snow-white apron, its wide ties in a large bow at the back. She ushered them inside, remarking on Cecily's paleness, told Van she was beautiful, and told Phil to hurry himself and get to the table before everything was cold. Ada she hugged with great affection. Cecily gave her flowers and some cordial which came in a pretty flower vase, a special offer from Corona, both of which delighted her.

The food was wonderful. Hot pancakes and syrup, toast spread with a homemade paste of chicken and herbs, an assortment of cakes and sandwiches and plenty of hot tea. After they had eaten, they were invited to sit near the fire, which, in the thick-walled cottage was necessary as the room was constantly cool.

Mrs Spencer stacked the dishes on the scrubbed table in the back kitchen and said, "I'll see to them later. Have you seen the paper, then? Wonderful to know the Queen has had her second daughter safely.

175

The little Princess Margaret Rose has made history, too. Hers will be the last birth at which the Secretary of State is present. Best for them too! Who wants a man about at a time like that? Terrible, I think, him a stranger and only there to make sure there's no mistake about who is the mother." She handed the paper to Cecily and ran her finger down to the relevant place. Ada smiled, knowing the woman's secret and admiring the panache with which she hid it.

"What d'you think of your sister and my son, then?" Mrs Spencer asked Cecily as they were taking their coats to leave. "Happy they are and that's what counts, isn't it?"

Cecily didn't get the chance to reply. Phil came limping in and calling them. Outside the engine purred and Cecily tensed herself for the maniacal drive home.

Cecily felt she had been fed through a mangle. She felt giggly and a sudden sympathy for her niece Marged, who was constantly reprimanded for showing unexplained hilarity.

"Your Willie lives over there." Phil turned, pointed and narrowly missed a stone wall. "Not there at the moment. Out with Danny I expect. Making a wireless they are now. Always making something or the other. I bought a table from them last week."

So that's how Danny knows my movements, Cecily thought. Her reaction might have resulted in anger against Willie but the visit to Phil's home had left her in the mood to chuckle instead. She sobered then, and felt a niggle of envy. The family her sister was soon to belong to was so happy and uncomplicated, and compared to Mrs Price-Jones, Mrs Spencer was the perfect mother-in-law.

When Phil left them, breathless and laughing, outside the shop, Dorothy was waiting for them.

"Dorothy? Is something wrong?" Cecily asked as Ada unlocked the shop door. The bell tinkled its welcome as they walked inside and Dorothy glared at it as if offended by its pleasantry.

When it had stopped, she said, "Only that I'm about to lose my home, thanks to your friend Bertie Richards!"

"What are you talking about?" Cecily slipped off her coat and handed it unthinkingly to Ada. "Take this up for me, will you, love?"

Ada took the coat and her lips tightened as she said, "All right, but don't start talking until I get back. Right?"

Cecily went to where the kettle was standing and after stirring the coals swivelled it around to the heat. It began to murmur almost immediately and before Ada had returned, minus the coats and hats, Cecily had the teapot ready to receive the boiling water.

"Well?" Ada asked her sister-in-law. "What's happened?"

"Bertie Richards has given me notice. The whole row of cottages is going to be knocked down."

"But why?"

"He says they're condemned. Nice little places like that? Never! Knowing him, it's sure to be money. Tidy them a bit he will, then find new tenants willing to pay a better rent, that's it for sure."

"When were you told?"

"A letter yesterday, telling me I have to vacate the property at the end of September. Well? Are you going to talk him out of it? Persuade him to change his mind? Or are you going to watch as I and my children are thrown into the street? Robbed of this shop, and now this!"

"We'll go this evening and talk to Bertie, find out exactly what is happening." Cecily poured a cup of tea for Dorothy. The look on her sister-in-law's face was fear. She was frightened at the prospect of searching for a new home. If only our family had more men, Cecily thought angrily. Women were at a disadvantage at times like this, no matter how she tried to believe differently.

Ada's thoughts were similar. "We'll help if it does come to a move," she promised. "And there's Uncle Ben and Johnny Fowler, they'll give a hand. The twins, Tomos and Trefor too, if Uncle Ben can persuade them."

"I don't *want* to move! I've just spent money buying new linoleum for the kitchen and I've papered two bedrooms. I want some use of it before men come and smash it all to dust!"

"You go home and we'll talk to him," Cecily said.

"If we learn anything we'll call on the way home to tell you," Ada added.

"Do what you can, will you? It's been so hard getting everything together since Victor died, and to start again —"

"We'll do everything we can." Ada ushered her out into the dusty summer evening. She frowned at her sister on her return. "What she expects us to do I don't know. If Bertie wants to sell, how can we stop him?"

They went to the big house overlooking the sea and Van ran at once into the garden with Edwin. A few words were exchanged, the sisters telling them about their happy visit to the Spencers' home. Then without explaining the reason for their visit, they followed the children out into the wide expanse of lawns and shrubbery.

Van had dragged out their pretend shop made from empty boxes and Cecily saw the pebbles in what was their till. But the shop was empty and there was no sign of the children until a muffled laugh gave away their hiding place.

They all pretended to search for them and even showed concern for their safety, then, laughing, first Van then Edwin slithered down from an apple tree into Bertie's arms. He carried Van inside, Edwin following close behind. Like a great bear with his cubs, Cecily thought affectionately. Bertie loved children and it was sad they had only managed to have one.

They were offered refreshments but refused, wanting to get home and settled down with the books to up date.

"Before we go, can we ask you something, Bertie?" Cecily said quietly.

"Of course. Beryl and I want to help with any problem. Marvels you two have been. Such a business brain, Cecily, and you, Ada, well, I don't know how Cecily would manage without you."

Ada smiled but the smile was sour. She was always referred to as Cecily's assistant. Couldn't people see she was as capable as her sister? That they were equal partners?

"Everything is fine with us," Cecily assured him. "It's Dorothy. She's been told you're selling her house."

"She's right. I am, forced to by the council. Condemned it they have. The drains need replacing, the roof is in danger of collapse, and one of the walls is bowing out with the window unsafe."

"Can't it be repaired?"

"It would cost too much, and I'd have to spend a lot more than the places would be worth. I'd lose a lot of money. You'll understand that, Cecily."

There he goes again! Ada thought angrily. Cecily understands but not me. I'm just the dogsbody! "Come on, Cecily, it's time we left." Her voice was so sharp the others looked at her in surprise. In a quieter tone she added, "It's been an exciting day and none of us will get any sleep tonight if we don't get this child home soon."

"You're right." Cecily stood and smiled at Ada. "Come on, young Van. Find your hat and coat. Monday tomorrow and we've all got a lot to do, haven't we, Ada, love?"

As they left, Cecily stopped for a moment and spoke to Bertie and Beryl and Ada waited. Cut off from important things again, she decided.

"Did Bertie tell you anything Dorothy should be told?" she asked.

"Nothing you need to be told, Ada, love. As for Dorothy, I think we'll wait till tomorrow and think up the best way of telling her we failed, don't you?"

"Nothing about the business then?"

"Nothing important."

Another decision made without consulting me, Ada fumed silently.

Cecily didn't tell her sister that Bertie had not been discussing Dorothy, but warning her about a series of burglaries that had taken place locally and reminding her to make sure the doors were firmly locked and bolted. Cecily didn't see the point of worrying Ada, who was so particular about locking doors anyway. It was a big house and the normal sounds would be misinterpreted if her mind was on someone breaking in.

Her silence just added to Ada's resentment.

CHAPTER
NINE

When Cecily and Ada had gone, taking Van home to bed, Bertie went into his study and called Beryl to join him. He set out the map showing the area of the proposed demolition site. Was there anything he could do to avoid putting Dorothy out of her home?

They discussed the situation for a while, but with the properties condemned and there being no possibility of Dorothy's, being in the middle of the terrace, being exempted from the order, her house would have to be demolished with the rest.

"I'll ask around and try to find her a place," he decided. "There is a place soon to be vacated in Slope Street."

"Oh, dear. Dorothy wouldn't like that," Beryl said. "Too near the docks."

"It's clean and it's cheap. I don't think she can refuse, do you?"

"It's a long way from the shop and that might be a good thing. It might stop her pestering Cecily. I'll make enquiries tomorrow," Beryl promised.

At the beginning of September there was a special entertainments day in the large park. Ada and Cecily were going with Gareth. Van and Edwin had been invited too, although it was likely to end rather late.

"I'll come away early with them if they're tired," Ada offered. "Without Phil there it won't be as much fun for me. He won't come, he's too conscious of his limp, silly man."

"Can Marged and Annette come too?" an excited Van asked when she was told of the treat. Eventually it was a party of seven setting off to walk through the town, among the crowds heading for a day of fun.

There was a gymkhana and a flower show, then as evening approached there was dancing on the green and Edwin danced with Van in a corner set aside for children. Illuminations were added as daylight faded and to end it all, a display of fireworks.

As Cecily and Gareth danced a quickstep, Cecily saw in the shadows at the edge of the area a figure she recognized: Danny Preston. When she looked again he had gone and she searched the crowd, desperate for another glimpse of him.

She felt the usual fluttering confusion of her senses even though she was not certain it had been he, but anger with herself swiftly took over and she pressed herself closer to Gareth, looking up at him, smiling in her provocative way.

"Gareth, I want you. I can't wait for us to be married," she whispered against his cheek.

"Hush, girl! Someone will hear you," he hissed back, whisking her away in a fishtail, their feet in perfect unison, to where the crowd was thinner.

"What does it matter if they do?" She laughed at his agitation. "Really, Gareth, love, you shouldn't be so easily embarrassed."

"You do embarrass me, Cecily, and I won't pretend otherwise."

"I want to sleep with you," she said, raising her voice so his eyes revealed his alarm. She loved to tease him and Danny's presence was an added thrill. "I want to wake in your arms. There! What would your mam think of that?"

"Stop it, Cecily. You know I can't cope with your tormenting."

"Tormenting you, am I? Tormenting you with desire?" She hugged him close and he stopped and led her off the dancing arena and back to Ada and the children. Standing next to Ada was Danny. Gareth saw him as he approached Ada and he pulled Cecily back into the dancing.

"For a moment there, I thought you were going to give me back to Danny." She laughed, her head back, her mouth temptingly close, but it was Danny she was aware of, not her stiff-faced partner.

"There are times when I sympathize with Danny. He called you a tart, didn't he?"

"I am a tart, Gareth, but only for you." She touched her lips against his tight jaw and he pulled away angrily.

"All right. I'll be chaste and well behaved, but only till we're married. Then," she whispered into his reddening ear, "then look out. I'm going to be a demon in our bedroom!"

"I think it's time we went home."

184

She looked at him as they moved back once more from the dancers, feeling guilty for teasing him, but in his face, strange in the gaudy coloured lights, she saw an expression she hadn't seen before. Desire was there and she knew her tormenting had aroused him. "Tiger!" she whispered and this time he was unable to hide a smile. He pulled her into a pool of darkness and kissed her more fiercely than he'd ever kissed her before, his face hungry with longing. But for her, the kiss had been as disappointing as everything else in their courtship.

As they strolled back to the others there was no sign of Danny and she began to wonder if she had imagined his presence. She was melancholy, alone among the crowd. She wished for the magic of the late summer evening to transport her to some place where she could be free, abandoned, without restrictions, where she was not committed to this marriage and where she and — She stopped her wild thoughts as Danny's face swam into her vision; as if the magic was working, as if she had created his image out of passionate memory and subconscious longing. But Danny's face was real, and frowning with disapproval.

He had approached them by pushing his way through the dancers and now held her, his face only inches from hers. "Van is tired and wants to go home," he said harshly. "In case you've forgotten, she's the little six-year-old you and Ada promised to care for!"

"I'm seven!" Van said promptly, before being dragged away by Ada.

"What business is it of yours?" Cecily demanded, shaken by his appearance out of her imaginings, shocked at the shattering of her dream. She looked to Gareth for support against Danny's rudeness but he had bent his head and walked to where Ada waited with the children.

She felt ridiculously close to tears, wanting to display the stamping rage of a child. She was let down so badly, both by Gareth's kiss, which failed to arouse the passion she longed to feel, and by his lack of concern when she had been accused of neglecting Van. She pushed Danny aside and ran to where Ada and Van had been joined by Annette, Marged and Owen. The children were playing ring-o-roses, falling down like idiots and having a happy time just being young and free from parental restraints.

"Ready to go home, are you?" she asked brightly.

"Oh, no, Auntie Cecily," they chorused. "Please, not yet!"

Cecily didn't dance any more, refusing invitations, although the band continued to play. Danny had disappeared and Gareth sat near her on the yellow, straw-like grass, his shoulders a hunched barrier, and did not speak. Cecily watched the youngsters, wishing she was as carefree and not facing a marriage she didn't want and a future that looked loveless and bleak. "Thank you Danny Preston!" she muttered.

The season was almost over but Annette and Willie still met on Mondays and had tea with Peter Marshall. He had become a friend and confidant and they discussed with him all the daily happenings as though he were a favourite uncle. Willie told him about the wireless he had made and the programmes he enjoyed.

"Wireless Willie Mam used to call me," he chuckled, "after the comedian Willie Rouse."

Annette explained about the demolition of their house and the planned move to Slope Street, and of Bertie's kindness in finding the house for them.

Peter was also informed of their plan to marry one day. He wished them luck and offered to help in any way he could. He always walked with them now, to where they had parked the van, and seemed reluctant for them to go. "You're like a family to me," he told them once. "The wonderful youngsters I never had. God bless you both." He always waited, waving a work-stained hand until the van was out of sight.

As he set off back to the garage, where he spent most of his days, he sighed deeply. If only he were younger, and Cecily were free. He sighed again. Things were never well timed in his life. He could only to continue to watch her and enjoy vicariously her successes and joys.

Annette and Willie had a second unexpected meeting that week. Cecily had asked the new boy, David, to take a box of groceries to Dorothy's home.

"A big order for Miss Dorothy, isn't it?" Willie said with a smile, his forthright comments accepted by the sisters, as he was a very important part of their success. "Wants a favour, does she? Buying from us instead of Waldo Watkins?" He knew all about Dorothy's move to a new house from his discussions with Annette, and since from the sisters themselves. They chuckled at his remarks and told him he was right. She wanted them to ask Bertie if he would compensate her for having to move, but that they would not do.

"I'll take the order," Willie offered. "Leave the boy, he's sorting out boxes in the stable loft. Van is down below helping him so he'll be busy for a while."

When Annette opened the door to him his heart lifted with joy. She was flushed, having just taken some small cakes out of the oven, a few touches of flour on her face.

"Willie!" She opened her arms and hugged the box of groceries as well as him.

"Annette." He bent to kiss her soft, warm cheek. "I had the chance to deliver these and thought I'd surprise you."

"Come in. Sit down. Owen won't be home for ages yet. He's gone to play with Marged and Auntie Rhonwen is sure to offer him tea."

Willie kissed her again and the warmth of his greeting melted her. She relaxed into his caress and seemed to float on air. To Willie, her skin, hot and moist from the baking, felt like swansdown.

"Annette, love, I ought to go," he groaned as she pulled him close and kissed him again and again. This unexpected moment of privacy was a dream come true.

She sat then and he stood, looking down at her. For the first time since they had become friends, he was at a loss for words. Wanting her was so painful he couldn't think of anything except her loveliness and his own desire. She slowly removed her apron and although there was no intention of being seductive, the movement added to her allure in a way that was almost wanton.

"Annette, show me your room," he murmured huskily.

"No, Willie, I shouldn't." Then she slipped off her cardigan, revealing plump pale arms and he lifted her from the chair. "Please," he whispered. "No one will be back for ages yet. Oh, Annette, love, it seems so right for us."

He carried her upstairs and she pointed to the back room overlooking the small back yard. He placed her gently on the bed and stared into her eyes. The answer to his unspoken question was reflected there.

She was limp like a doll as he slowly removed her clothes, then she turned to him and soon they were both naked. When they came together, there was never a moment in his life so perfect.

They lay together for a while, smiling at each other, marvelling at the wonder of it, kissing gently, relaxed and content in their love.

"What time is it?" Annette asked when the aftermath of their loving had subsided. "We don't want Mam to catch us, do we?"

"Plenty of time." He reached on the floor for his waistcoat and pulled out Owen Owen's watch. "Not half past one yet. We've time to do it again." He began stroking her round, rosy cheek and her neck and shoulders, but she became impatient and guided his hands, then her own exploring awakened his body with wonder and exquisite joy.

Willie knew he would never forget that room, wherever life took them. He would only have to close his eyes to see his beloved Annette lying on the bed with the blue covers and the white sheets framing her beauty. He would see the marble wash-stand with its bowl and jug, the polished floorboards and the small blue rug at the side of the bed. And the long wardrobe mirror in which they stared at their reflections, his long and thin, covered with dark curling hair, Annette's small and rounded and as feminine and perfect as any dream.

Dorothy was restless and unable to concentrate on her work. She had been waiting for weeks for a reply to the letter she had sent to London and had become almost obsessed with the need for a response. The wedding of Cecily and Gareth was two and a half months away and time was passing so quickly. If Cecily married, then the birth of a son would add to the difficulties of gaining the grocer's shop for Owen. With both sisters past their youth it was so unfair that they should marry now and produce an heir to thwart Owen's right to inherit.

At lunchtime she planned to go home to see if the second post had brought the letter. Two reps delayed her but finally she could bear it no longer and, complaining of a headache, she went home.

She stepped inside and saw the freshly made cakes and smiled proudly. Annette was a dream of a daughter. Apart from her unfortunate shyness, she was everything a mother could want. One day, she thought, her daughter would make someone a very good wife, but not for a long time yet. Annette was needed until Owen was old enough to manage without her.

Seeing the order still in its box, she wondered why it hadn't been packed away but thought that Annette, with her recent liking for walking, and probably gone to stroll through the park in the centre of the town.

On the mantelpiece, tucked behind the tea-tin with its picture of Queen Mary and King George, was the post. Eagerly she tore open the one with the London postmark, reading it with her green eyes open wide. Tucking it into her handbag, she prepared to leave. There were a few people who should see this.

She was pulling the door shut behind her when she heard something, and stopped. She was about to call her daughter's name but something held her tongue. There were voices. Surely Annette couldn't be talking to herself? She climbed the stairs softly, expecting to find that Owen had not gone to his Auntie Rhonwen as arranged. Avoiding the creaking stairs by walking at the edge, she looked into Annette's room first.

Annette had not dressed. She and Willie stood admiring each other in the long mirror. They heard the wail of dismay and at once covered their important parts in the classical pose beloved by sculptors. Open-mouthed, they stared towards the door.

"Annette! I can't believe what I'm seeing!" Dorothy began to wail then she turned on Willie and the wail became a scream of shouting in a babble of angry words. Willie couldn't understand any of it but from the look on her face and the position in which they still stood, he needed no translation.

"It's all right," he said stupidly, "we're getting married."

"Oh no you're not! Get out of here and never come back, d'you hear? When I see my sister-in-law you won't have a place there either! No one will employ you, Willie Morgan. No one! After this no one will trust you near a decent girl." She picked up his abandoned clothes and threw them down the stairs. Willie refused to move. He took Annette's hand and waited until all his clothes had disappeared over the banister.

"We love each other and we're getting married." He spoke calmly, although he was trembling with shock and the embarrassing vulnerability of being without clothes. It was difficult to stand his ground in the face of his nakedness and Dorothy's fury, but one hand gripping Annette's hand, the other covering as much as he could with the other, he waited until the first wave of Dorothy's anger subsided.

"If you aren't out of here in two seconds, you disgusting animal, I'll go and call the police. Get out! My son will be home soon and I don't want him mixed up with this —" She searched for a suitable word but found none.

"Go now, Willie," Annette said quietly. "I'll talk to Mam when she's over the shock. Best you go now. I'll be all right."

"Are you sure? I'd rather stay and talk this through. I don't want you facing it alone."

"I'll be all right. Go, and we'll make our plans later. Don't be anxious for me, Willie. Mam won't hurt me and I can explain better if you aren't here."

"There'll be no explanations from you, young lady!" Dorothy shouted. "All you'll do is listen! You are never to see this — this — person again. D'you understand? And you, Willie Morgan, get out of my sight before I kill you." She picked up the china jug from the dressing table and threatened him with it.

He didn't flinch but moved when he saw the fear in Annette's eyes. "Please, Willie, it's best you go, love."

He sidled over to the door trying to avoid Dorothy's wildly flailing arms as she waved him away as though dealing with a bad-tempered goose. As he reached the comparative safety of the landing, she threw the jug, which smashed against the wall, the pieces chasing him down the stairs. He grabbed his clothes and stood outside the back door and hurriedly dressed, darting glances at the windows overlooking this and other yards, then went back to the shop.

Dorothy went back to her daughter, trying to calm her racing heart and holding back tears of dismay and shame and disappointment. That this should happen to her and with Annette, whom she had always considered the last person to give trouble of this sort. Shy Annette! It was unbelievable! She stood for a moment on the landing and looked into the room where her daughter was dressing in fresh clothes. A lump of love and sympathy overcame her and she ran in and hugged the now tearful girl.

"Please, Annette, let's forget this happened. We'll hush it up. I doubt Willie will talk about it and no one else will know. But promise me you'll never see him again, never give in to temptation again."

"Only with Willie, Mam." Annette was unrepentant, unaffected by her mother's rare demonstration of love. "Only with Willie. There'll never be anyone else."

"You will never see that stable boy again, d'you hear me?"

"You won't stop me. Short of locking me up and throwing away the key, you'll never stop me."

Dorothy stared at her daughter, alarmed at the change in her. She had never dreamed that the quiet, obedient child could harbour such defiance.

"You're still a child. I'll do whatever's necessary. You and Willie are forbidden to meet. Do you understand?" She said the last word slowly and with emphasis but as she looked at the coldness in Annette's eyes she knew she had lost her daughter and a stranger stood before her.

Dorothy had forgotten the long-awaited letter and it was much later, when it was almost time to put Owen to bed, that it came back to her mind. With pain and anger boiling inside, believing she could lay all her troubles at Cecily and Ada's door, she told Owen to re-dress and put on his coat.

"You too, Annette. You're both coming with me." She threw on her own coat and sent Owen to the stand beside the picture house to get a taxi. They set off in silence, Dorothy looking strained, Annette convinced the journey was to do with her and Willie, Owen wondering if he could persuade his mam to buy him some chips.

Their first call was on Gareth's mother who fortunately was alone. Leaving the children in the taxi, Dorothy opened the letter and handed it to the woman.

"But this means — oh, my poor boy!"

"You agree he must be told?"

"There's no other way. I'll come with you now. Wait while I get my coat." The shocked expression left her face as she raced up the stairs in a way that would have amazed her son, who thought her frail. She smiled in satisfaction as she collected her coat and jammed a felt hat on her head.

At the shop, arrangements for the forthcoming wedding were being discussed. The wedding dress had been tried on and was now carefully wrapped in blue tissue paper and hanging outside the wardrobe, in their parents' room. Now, Cecily, Gareth and Ada were discussing lists of guests, and the sisters' suggestions for the meal were resulting in long columns of ideas, crossed out, added, then crossed out again as they struggled to plan the best menu.

"Can I try on my dress again?" Van pleaded.

Ada laughed. "Not while Gareth is here. He mustn't see how beautiful you are until the wedding day."

"Or I might change my mind and marry you instead," Gareth said, picking her up and dancing with her round the chenille-covered table.

There was a knock at the door and Cecily looked at Ada. "Go, will you, love? I expect it's someone wanting serving. Honestly, I think some people use us as their pantry!" She put down the pencil she was using and hardly stifled a groan as Ada returned with Dorothy and Mrs Price-Jones. This would probably mean even more changes in the guest list. Not that she minded. They could afford it and she wanted it to be a memorable day. She stood up and found seats for Owen and Annette, and only when the silence penetrated did she look up and see the grim expression on her future mother-in-law's face. The long thin nose looked more sharp, the eyes showed undisguised dislike. What have I done now, she wondered irritably, but she asked politely, "Is something wrong, Mother-in-law?"

"Your mother-in-law I am not! Nor will I ever be!"

Dorothy thrust the letter that was shaking in her tight grip and both women watched Cecily's face pale as she read it.

"Mam? What is it?" Gareth looked from one face to another, stepping towards Cecily, and Van, aware of the atmosphere of suppressed anger, sidled closer to Ada.

Dorothy snatched the letter and waved it. "It's about Cecily, your intended. Did you know she's Myfanwy's mother?"

When the mists of pain, shock and disbelief had cleared, Cecily looked at Gareth and knew he would never forgive her. His eyes were wide as he stared at her but there was no disbelief. He hadn't, even for a

196

moment, doubted what had been said. Thoughts tumbled through her brain. To deny was useless, to defend even less likely to wipe the look of horror off the faces of Gareth and his mother — suddenly so alike with their pursed mouths and the raised, tilted heads as they looked down their long noses.

Her confused mind wrestled firmly with the need to make Gareth understand, but with his mother standing close to him, like a lioness protecting her young, there was little chance of that. Oh, why hadn't she told him long ago? She had intended to so many times. Now, as she looked at his closed expression, she knew there was no chance of him listening to her. "Who told you?" she asked at last. Her face was clouded as she tried to guess. Who knew, apart from herself and Ada? Then she remembered one other. "Danny, how could you?" she breathed. The room began to spin and waver and she felt for the edge of a chair, sensing rather than seeing Ada push it under her and guide her trembling body into it. "Gareth, I would have told you, in my own time," she whispered.

"Left it a bit late, didn't you?" Mrs Price-Jones snapped. "And it was Dorothy who found out and she felt duty bound to tell me."

"And I wish she hadn't," Gareth muttered as he stumbled from the room.

Cecily rose to follow him but his mother leaned towards her, glaring, daring her to move and she sank back into the chair, too weak to fight. "I wish Mam was here," she said to Ada.

They had forgotten the presence of Van until Cecily saw Gareth's mother turn to the child and open her mouth to speak. Then she found the strength to stand up and threaten. "Say one word to Myfanwy and I'll push you through the door so fast your feet won't touch the ground!" Mrs Price-Jones opened her mouth but didn't speak. She left the room and the sisters stood as footsteps receded across the wooden floor of the shop and ended with the shop door banging and the discordant tinkle of the bell.

Cecily looked at Van. The girl was deathly white and the flesh seemed to have left her face, enlarging her eyes. Her mouth was a disbelieving "O". Both sisters hugged her and, holding each other tight, Cecily and Ada cried.

Van didn't respond to their hug or join in their tears. She stared unseeing across the room, the hurt already growing into coldness towards them.

Dorothy and her children walked home. It was a long way but she needed the time to recover from the confrontation. She had decided to say nothing about Annette and Willie. Gossip materialized from the slightest word and Annette would recover quicker without that. Better she was sent away and that could be arranged very quickly.

Van was very late going to bed that night. Cecily tried to talk to her, explain about her denial of her daughter, her intention to tell her one day when she was old enough to understand, but the words wouldn't come. Van was too young to accept this. Besides, the memory of Gareth's face and the way he had stood beside his mother — a united front against her — made rational thought impossible. She hugged the little girl, finally telling her she loved her and had concocted the story to make things easier for her. She promised that all the explanations she needed would be given in the morning. Van went to her bed bitter and confused.

She sat up in bed watching as the light of morning touched her curtains, remembering all the teasing she had endured, which could have been avoided. She sat silently thinking of how Mrs Price-Jones and Auntie Dorothy had looked at her. The expression on those faces had frightened her.

Panic, fear and resentment grew in her like a black miasmic cloud, the centre of which was the face of Cecily. She hated her and the thought made a shiver of fear ripple down her spine. Hating someone was wicked, she knew that, but Cecily deserved it. The way Gareth and his mother had looked at her had made that clear, made it all right to feel that way.

As soon as she was old enough she would leave. Then everyone would be sorry. Edwin would know what to do. She'd go with him and find a place where she'd never see Auntie Cecily and Auntie Ada ever again.

Downstairs, Ada and Cecily talked until morning. Ada announced that she would cancel her plans to marry Phil. "It wasn't official, anyway," she said.

"But you can't do that!" Cecily pleaded. "Dorothy will have succeeded in ruining both our lives if you change your plans. She'd be in her cups! Happy, like she hasn't been for years! Please, Ada, love. Don't cancel your wedding. I'll be all right. I've coped with only you for support for so long, and you'll still be there, won't you? I've lost Gareth but things here will go on just the same. Who knows, perhaps Van and I will be even closer now she knows I'm her mother. Why spoil your life for no purpose? I'll soon get over this, see if I don't."

"No, I'll talk to Phil tomorrow — I think I mean today," Ada said tearfully, lifting the curtain aside. "He'll see it's for the best. We couldn't be happy thinking of you and Van suffering the humiliation of people knowing. We agreed more than seven years ago that Van would be our shared responsibility and that will never change."

Van enjoyed a certain notoriety which she didn't really understand and she soaked up the sympathy she enjoyed when news leaked out, and added her own criticisms of Cecily. The attacks on her mother became the only believable part of her life and Cecily saw her daughter moving further and further away from her, affection gone, replaced by resentment eagerly fuelled by others.

It was this as much as Gareth's defection that made Cecily spend even more of her considerable energies in building up the business. Time passed and the business grew, but Van and Gareth remained cold and accusing.

For Willie, too, it was a difficult time. Annette had vanished almost overnight and he couldn't find out where she had gone. Eventually it was Marged, Rhonwen's giggly daughter, who told him a part of the story, and he spent hours driving around searching for her. He was kept very busy with the shop and his growing carpentry business with Danny Preston but every moment he could spare was spent asking, seeking the slightest clue to her whereabouts. He knew he would find her. He would never give up.

Life for the Owen sisters became a round of shop and sleep, ·with only the occasional evening out for relaxation as they both felt unable to leave Van. They were afraid the slightest sign of indifference would add to the child's unhappiness.

Van wasn't unhappy. She enjoyed the way she had the sisters running about trying to please her and soon discovered that, however she behaved, disobedience was met with soothing understanding. She rarely smiled at them and it was only when she was with Edwin, who refused to listen to her tales of largely imagined anguish, that she acted normally. Edwin was her strength and his acceptance of Cecily's deceit almost persuaded her she was wrong to harbour bitterness and hatred. Almost, but not quite. She derived too much pleasure from it to give it up. Forgiving her mother would never, ever happen. She dreamed in her child's mind of some distant day when she would take her revenge. Revenge — that was a word she liked.

CHAPTER
TEN

New Year 1935 was a sober affair for Cecily and Ada. In five years so many dreams had been lost. Since both Cecily and Ada had cancelled their wedding plans, they had found little time for dancing and having fun. Instead all their energies had been spent building their business. Cecily had heard, through friends, that Danny and Jessie had finally married after several cancellations. She wondered vaguely whether they were happy.

This year, the sisters dressed warmly in the swagger coats they had recently bought, and took Van, now eleven, to the square outside the town hall to join the crowd waiting there for the clock to announce the arrival of the New Year. The streets leading to the square were packed with people heading for the point at which they hoped to join up with friends.

Arms rose in a forest and shouts echoed across the street as friends called to friends, laughing, jostling each other in almost impossible attempts to gather in groups of families or friends. Van walked between Cecily and Ada, looking for Edwin Richards, who had promised to try and find them by the large Christmas tree near the steps.

Cecily was quiet. She disliked New Year. It was a time when, instead of looking forward, she looked back at all the disappointments and missed opportunities. Rich they might be, by their parents' standards, but happy they were not. Since everyone had learned that Van was Cecily's daughter, things had been difficult, Van the most difficult of them all.

Cecily looked at her now. Taller than her friends, slim and already showing signs of the beauty to come. Her features were small with a tilt to her nose that gave her an elfin attractiveness. But there was a hardness in her and it showed in the firmness of her mouth, the hint of disapproval in her blue eyes, and the almost constant frown on her brow.

Cecily had long given up trying to explain her reasons for behaving as she had, but continued to hope that one day she would be able to make her daughter see how it had been for her in 1924, when adoption had been the only alternative: an option she hadn't for a moment considered. Although Van's accusation that she had been protecting herself had been partly true, the invention of a friend had been a convenient cover story.

"There he is!" Van jumped up and down, waving excitedly towards the tree, where Edwin was waving a large flag. "He said I'd see him easily, he's so big!"

She dragged the sisters in her wake as she ploughed through the good-natured crowd and reached Edwin, flushed and glowing with the cold and the exhilaration of the occasion. She took his arm and said to Cecily,

"You two can find your friends. Edwin will make sure I get home safe, as soon as midnight has struck."

"No, lovey, I think we'll all stay together." Ada was struggling to stay with them.

"Don't worry," a familiar voice said, "Beryl and I will stay with them. Go and have fun, you two."

"Beryl! Bertie! Happy New Year!" the sisters chorused. "And to you, Edwin, dear." They shared kisses all round then left Van in their friends' care and pushed back into the sea of people, holding hands for fear of losing each other, to look for more familiar faces with whom to share greetings.

They were looking for Phil Spencer among others and he, being much shorter than most, was difficult to spot.

"Silly old fool," Ada said, shaking her head in bemused affection as she said it. "I told him it would be impossible to meet in this crush."

"He should have come to the shop and walked up with us," Cecily shouted above the roar of voices.

"I asked but he wouldn't. Said something about having a important job to do first. Wouldn't tell me what. You know him, he likes to keep secrets and squeeze every last ounce of fun from an occasion. I wonder what he's up to this time?"

A few people began to sing, old favourites that everyone knew, and soon the air was filled with voices; some beautiful, some discordant but all enthusiastic. Cecily stood for a moment and joined in, then they started to move again, slowly threading their way to the far side of the square.

"Don't go too far over," Ada shouted. "We don't want to stand outside the men's lavatories!"

Unbelievably Phil found them. In a gathering of at least 2,000 merrymakers he spotted their hats and, bending forward and burrowing through like a ferret, he surfaced beside Ada. "Happy New Year, ladies," he said, kissing them both. "And where is young Van?"

Ada pointed to the Christmas tree. "Over by there with the Richards."

He stood with them and joined in the singing, his voice a pleasant tenor. After they had been singing for a while, Cecily became aware of another, beautiful bass voice close by.

"Hello, Cecily. A Happy New Year," Danny said.

"And to you, Danny. Is your wife with you?"

"No. Come on, let's have a talk, just for old times' sake."

"No. I don't think that's a good idea." She moved slightly away from him, as much as the solid mass of humanity would allow, but he moved with her and she felt the touch of his hand on her elbow.

"Cecily, I must talk to you."

"Talk to your wife, Danny Preston! I thought that now you're married I wouldn't be bothered by you any more."

"You've heard, then?"

"Heard what? No, don't tell me. I'm not interested."

"Go on, let him tell us," Phil said enthusiastically. "Go on. I won't sleep tonight if I don't find out what he wants to say."

"Stop eavesdropping." There was a hint of laughter in Ada's voice, amused as always by Phil's irrepressible nosiness. "Old woman you are."

"Jessie has left me," Danny told them. "She says I'm too cold and also that I'm a bore. What d'you think of that, then?"

"She's probably right!" Cecily again tried to move away.

The clock began its rumble on the way towards striking the hour of midnight and miraculously the crowd was hushed. The chimes began and a cheer rose into the sky and everyone turned to kiss partners and anyone near. Some swayed and tried to hold hands for the traditional Auld Lang Syne.

Cecily felt a lump in her throat as her sister moved away from her to be held in an enthusiastic hug by Phil, leaving her stranded and alone in the middle of the crowd. Then Danny held her and his kiss was as wildly exciting as the chimes and the shouting and the magic that was part of the first moments of 1935. It wasn't until the echoes of the final chime had died away that he let her go.

Since 1930, when she had met him after a gap of seven years, Danny had appeared to share with her the first minute of each new year. She might see nothing of him during the months before, but always, as the last moments of the old ticked away, he would be there.

She wondered where Gareth was now, and who he was sharing the celebration with. She tried to force him into her mind and disassociate herself from Danny's disturbing kiss and the romantic way he appeared at midnight.

She still grieved for Gareth and knew that this sensation Danny aroused was not love as she had known love with Gareth, which would have been an all-encompassing love on which a lifetime could have been built. It included the calm, easy companionship she had rarely enjoyed with Danny. He disturbed and confused her. Gareth would have given her a life of unexciting contentment.

"Cecily?" Danny's voice forced her back to the present. "Come with me. Ada and Phil don't want you around, do they?"

"Go away."

She made her way through the laughing crowd, hoping to lose him in the confusion of the people moving about, many trying to leave. Some held balloons which they suddenly released to soar up into the night sky. The sound of fireworks banging and hissing was accompanied by screams and hysterical laughter and dozens of enthusiastic revellers waved flags.

To the surprise of many, some used the occasion for political warnings. Voices in the mob shouted and chanted, "Hitler must go," "Murderer of the Jews," "Listen to Winston Churchill," among others. Other voices joined in insisting that Hitler was saving his nation from poverty and the world from the evil of greed. A few scuffles broke out but the ugly moments soon subsided, as laughter and good humour won the hour and the protesters gradually dispersed.

Cecily's hand was held, gripped tightly, and this time she didn't struggle to escape. She felt conspicuous walking beside Danny, unwilling to leave him yet dreading being seen by someone who would tell Gareth about her latest defiance of convention, walking hand in hand with a married man. Gareth was still important to her and his good opinion was something she hoped to rebuild.

Danny was not love but an obsession. Why was she walking away from the chance of seeing Gareth? And with him? Why couldn't she tell him to go and make him believe she meant it? It would be so easy to run back to the square and find Ada and Phil among the thinning crowd but she walked on, his hand still holding hers possessively, his warmth and power a magnet she couldn't repel.

In the silence of the small street, Danny said, "We can't let another year pass being separated from each other, can we? What are we going to do about it?"

"Nothing! You married Jessie and that ended it finally. I'm already a woman with a sordid past. Being the mistress of a married man is something I can do without! You know it would never have worked between us. It would have been nothing but fights and arguments and I couldn't face that sort of life."

"And spending your life alone? Wouldn't that be worse?"

"More peaceful. I have a busy life running a business I enjoy. It's hard in some ways but I can afford to buy what I need to make life pleasant and comfortable.

Comfort and peace don't seem that terrible a prospect."

"Without love?"

"You don't love me, Danny." She spoke scornfully. "You want to possess me and lock me away in your home so I don't look at another man. Possession isn't love, it's a sickness!"

There were lights on in many of the houses they passed and on several doorways people stood looking out into the night as though expecting it to be different from other nights. Most were still fully dressed and they looked up and down the street, greeting everyone who passed with the same words. "A Happy New Year."

"Let's make this our happiest, shall we, Cecily? It will take time to get a divorce, but it isn't impossible and people will understand our being together. We're getting older, you and I. I'm thirty-two and I've loved you since I was eighteen."

She tried to ignore his words and the way his arm was pressing her against him. What was it about New Year that weakened resolve, filled people with foolish hope? "No, Danny. You'd never cope with my involvement in the shop for one thing, or my ways. I'm so used to doing what I want without having anyone to consider, it would be even more impossible than if we'd married back in 1922. We might be attracted to each other but we'll never make a partnership. Not now. I'm too independent."

"Too selfish you mean! Unable to give any of your precious time and effort to someone else. Selfish and cold, that's what you've become. You and your damned shop!"

They both fell silent as they passed an elderly couple standing at their door. They shared greetings with them before continuing to argue as soon as they were out of the friendly couple's hearing.

"You're right. Selfish is what I am. Selfish enough to deny you the pleasure of ruining my life. Look at you now, trembling with rage and we haven't spent half an hour in each other's company. Selfish I am, but you suffer something far worse. Jealousy was always your weakness. You hated every smile I gave to anyone but you, and were angry when someone smiled at me. You'd expect me to close the shop and lock myself away, idling my time waiting for your attention. So take your sullied love and give it to the girl who was foolish enough to marry you."

"I was a fool to ever think of us making a go of things. How can you when you're so fond of making money and dressing up to show how successful you are? I forgave you for Van. Yes, *and* everyone thinks I'm her father, but we never made love, did we? Who was he? You can tell me now. Some five-minute fumble at a dance, was it?"

She raised her hand to strike him but he held her arm, gripping it fiercely, forcing her to walk beside him past an open door where they were wished another Happy New Year. They smiled artificial smiles, returned the greetings and walked past, continuing their battle.

She struggled free of him and once they were past the couple, she ran, losing a shoe like a parody of

210

Cinderella, kicking off the other, and hurried home, biting her lips to hold back the tears. She didn't wait up for Ada and Van, knowing Ada would deal with everything. "Another damned mess of a New Year," she muttered, before allowing the tears to fall.

For Ada the occasion was a happy one. Phil had the car he had recently bought parked in a side road and after collecting Van from the Richards' they drove back to the shop.

"Van," Phil said as he limped around to open the door for her. "How would you like to be a bridesmaid?"

"I'd like that. I nearly was once before, remember? I had the blue dress and all but then Auntie Dorothy told everyone about me and the shame of it stopped the wedding."

"Van, lovey, there was no shame on you for that. It was Cecily who made everyone angry, not you. No one loves you any the less." She hugged her, thinking the shock of discovering who Cecily really was would never leave her. Van had withdrawn into herself for months after and even now frequently made it clear she had not forgiven Cecily for her deceit.

"I want you to be bridesmaid for your Auntie Ada and me," Phil said. "Choose your dress and have whatever colour you like."

"Phil!" Ada protested.

"I've been messed about waiting for her to make up her mind long enough, don't you agree?" He was still talking to Van. "I've been to see the vicar and made a firm booking for the church and Mam will do the food.

Now there's only your dress and Auntie Ada's to buy and we're ready."

"Phil?" They were talking as though she were invisible.

"I think New Year's a time for getting things sorted," Phil went on. "So, if you will take her shopping, Van, I'll foot the bill and we can start thinking about who to invite."

"Phil, I don't think —"

"You don't need to, love. It's Van and me to do all the thinking. Just try this for size." He handed her a jeweller's box which he opened with a flourish, grinning at Van. Inside was a ring nestled on blue velvet. "There, that's a beauty, eh, Van? Try it on, Ada, and don't start weeping, for heaven's sake. I haven't got a hanky. Lend her yours, will you, Van, love?"

"I can't think of another person who would propose with an audience," Ada said.

Phil hugged her and Van, squeezing them both against his small body. "Asked you plenty of times when we were alone, and a fat lot of good it did me. No, with Van by my side I thought we'd surprise you into saying yes. Go on," he coaxed, "say it good and loud so Van can be my witness if you deny it."

"Yes, Phil. Oh, yes."

For Dorothy the end of 1934 and the beginning of 1935 was not a happy time. She went to bed soon after ten o'clock, refusing to treat it as other than an ordinary Tuesday evening. But she was still awake when the ships in the docks nearby began sending out their chorus of hooting and piping as 1935 dawned. Cars passing in the street sounded their horns and somewhere close she could hear singing.

Turning on her side, she covered her head with blankets and tried to blot out the celebrations. If Annette were here they would have stayed up late as always or joined others to see the New Year in but without her daughter and living in Slope Street so far from the rest of the family, it was too much of an effort.

After finding Annette with the stable boy, as she always referred to him, she had quickly arranged for her to be sent to work in service, at a town twelve miles away. At Barlow House, she would be kept busy and on a very tight rein. There was no possibility of her ever seeing Willie Morgan again. But she missed Annette dreadfully and never more than with a new year opening out before her, certain to be as gloomy as the one just passed.

Leaving Owen in the care of Annette had made it easy for her to further her career, not having to worry about anything at home, where it had all been in Annette's capable hands. Now she had to hesitate before agreeing to an out-of-town invitation that would delay her at the home of Uncle Ben Prothero and his second wife, Maggie, who rather reluctantly kept an eye on Owen when he was not at work. Owen was seventeen now and needed no one to look after him, but he hated waiting for his meals and Auntie Maggie was a good cook.

Owen worked for Waldo Watkins, Dorothy having insisted on him learning the grocery trade for the time

213

when he would inherit his grandfather's shop. Dorothy had hated him leaving school at fourteen, she had been reluctant to give up the dream of him going to one of the universities and bringing vicarious success through his brilliant career. Now, Owen's shop was her only hope and this way he would at least be expert when the time came for him to take over from Cecily and Ada. Thank goodness she had prevented Cecily and Gareth marrying. The plans for Ada and Phil had been delayed too. After all this time they must surely have abandoned the idea. No, there was no one but Owen inheriting. Van, being illegitimate, would surely have no claim.

Another change had taken place in her life besides losing Annette. When Bertie had learned of her vicious interference that had led to the cancellation of Cecily's wedding, Bertie had refused to offer any help with the move or in finding her an alternative house. She had found this smaller, less convenient house not far from one of the docks entrances where, from her windows, she could see girls walking up and down waiting for the sailors to come off the ships. "The monkey parade" the locals called it and Dorothy hated being so near. She kept the curtains permanently closed on that side of the house.

With the shortage of work in the town there were plenty of houses to rent, but only in these poorer areas, never in the better class roads where she would like to live. It angered her immensely to be told by Cecily that Willie Morgan owned his house and was buying a second. It seemed an infernal cheek on his part to be in a better position than herself, a fashion saleswoman for the largest department store in the town.

Tormented with regret and frustration, she tossed and turned and watched as a grey dawn filtered through the curtains before finally dozing, only to be woken soon after by the strident call of her alarm clock.

Another shock awaited her. Going home from work one day she found the door opened and the place ransacked. There wasn't much of any value but the treasured pieces, memories of her husband, trinkets belonging to her parents, they were irreplaceable and she cried with dismay as she cleared the mess the intruders had left, and listed those that were missing. She hid her tears from Owen, who couldn't see what the fuss was about, and asked should he go for some chips.

The burglaries on the town were regular for a while, then they stopped and everyone relaxed, then after a gap of a month or two, another spate of entries, usually during the day, would happen and the police could find no clues. Beside Dorothy's, three other houses were robbed and then, as before, the break-ins stopped, as though the perpetrator had stayed a few days then moved on. Repairs to the damaged door were carried out, Dorothy added extra locks and bolts, and told Owen how glad she was to have him there to look after her. Owen looked bored and asked what was for supper.

"We aren't selling the vegetables we used to," Cecily complained one day as she and Ada were putting the baskets out to display their goods. "I bet it's that Jack Simmons."

"I thought Willie made him promise not to trade around here?"

"He has affected us, wherever he's selling. I haven't seen him for a while though, have you?"

"I have, miss," the young red-haired David said shyly. "Goes about in the evenings he does, selling cheap from his barrow."

Jack Simmons was the small, underweight boy with a reputation for fighting, who always looked as if a good feed was his greatest need. His movements were quick and his mind equally agile and he was the kind who never complained about any unpleasant trick life threw at him, but tackled it head on and licked it. He was what he looked like: a bantam fighter who always fought to win.

When he lost the job at Waldo Watkins', he spent little time bemoaning the fact but at once borrowed a donkey and cart. He hired it by the day from a man who used it occasionally and usually at night, to assist those who needed to get their belongings out of a house during the hours of darkness, to avoid creditors and a landlord to whom they owed rent, in a moonlight flit.

Jack went to the wholesalers late in the afternoons and filled the cart with leftover poor quality fruit or vegetables or anything else he could buy cheaply and sell quickly. At the end of his rounds, he paid the wholesaler and the man who owned the donkey and what was left was profit. It was a simple business and it was only rarely that he came home without a pocket jingling with coins. One day it might be bananas, fallen from their stalks and beginning to blacken, another it might be cabbages or some potatoes starting to smell a bit sour, which he would pick over and clean up to sell at a low price to women with large families, to fill their children's bellies.

In this way he had gradually built up a small amount of cash and a few weeks before 1934 had ended, he had decided to branch out. It was his old adversary with whom he discussed his plan.

"See, Willie," he had explained, "I can see how you got to take chances in life if you want to get on, like, and get out of the hole you were born in."

"I wasn't born in a hole." There was a warning note in Willie's voice, preparing for argument if Jack uttered one word of criticism about his mother.

"Not you, boy. It's me we're talking about here. Me, who started off with the pavement rubbing my feet sore and with no arse in my pants. Me! Going to get on, I am. I'm opening a shop, see, tell my customers where to find me and how I'll be selling cheap. Want to come and have a look-see?" he invited.

The shop to which Jack led Willie was little more than a ruin. The front wall was crumbling and the window of the front room shattered, leaving a pile of jewel-like shards outside the loose bricks that had once been a wall.

"Needs a bit of sorting," Jack said cheerfully. "Soon get it tidy."

"When are you taking over this emporium?" Willie chuckled.

"Tomorrow. I've told all my customers."

"What!"

"Well, it's only a bit of tidying that's needed."

"Come on, I suppose I'd better give you a bit of a hand."

Willie picked up a shovel and a large brush, which seemed to be the only tools Jack had at his disposal, and together they swept up the worst of the mess and rubble. After visiting a builder's yard and scrounging some cement from a broken bag, they managed to re-set the bricks and arrange a counter of sorts from wood bought at the wood yard where he and Danny bought their requirements. The window would be absent for a while.

Darkness interfered with their work but they were satisfied with what they had achieved during the few hours and for the cost of ten shillings. Willie put the finishing touches to the new premises of Jack Simmons, fruit and vegetable merchant, by writing a sign and placing it neatly where the window should have been.

"Damned draughty that'll be," Willie said. "We'd better get that glass as soon as we can."

The shop which Jack was now renting was at the corner of the lane which led to Owen's stable and back entrance. The run-down area was home to a variety of characters making a precarious living from their wits. The two young men often saw Horse, so called because of the strong smell of liniment that hung around him, which he used to ease the pain of many broken and badly mended bones he had suffered during the war. With his wife he sang hymns on street corners and cheerfully admitted they were paid more often to leave than for their musical abilities. They lived in a series of places; a room when they could find the rent then moved on to whatever shelter they could find.

Willie and Jack heard them as they were packing up for the night and they crept closer to listen. Horse and his wife were always good for a laugh. On the streets where they begged pennies for survival, they conversed through their singing, sometimes arguing and all the time fitting their abusive comments about each other to the tune, so passers-by, unless particularly astute, failed to realize.

As Willie and Jack watched, some kind soul threw a couple of coins in the hat in front of the singers. Horse sang, "What did she give us?"

"Only a penny."

"Mingy old trout, she could have give more."

"Shut up you fool there's somebody coming."

Together they sang, "We are so happy, Jesus is lord."

Willie and Jack were laughing and after throwing a couple of coins, moved away from the floating miasma of liniment, wondering how anyone could get near enough to drop money into the hat. "What with the stink and their voices, it's an effort to pass even on the opposite side of the street," Jack spluttered, but they both threw a couple more coins.

"Besides the smell, the language they use when they're quarrelling would make your old granny faint."

To their dismay, the unsavoury couple followed them back to inspect the new premises. They stopped to

219

admire their work and Jack gave them a few bananas. They thanked him and promised their business to him.

Jack looked at Willie. "Best we leave the window out, if that's a sample of my new customers!"

Willie thought Jack's customers were hardly going to make him rich but Jack was confident. "Everybody's got to eat. They'll buy what's cheap and fill up on it whether it's turnips, spuds or bananas."

"Is that what happens when you eat too many bananas?" He pointed to where Horse leaned against the wall, his legs curled like the fruit, their stiffness preventing him from falling.

"I'll straighten him up later with some rhubarb," Jack promised.

Buying as before, offering low prices to clear unwanted goods from the wholesaler and bringing it back on a wheelbarrow, Jack began to attract trade. He spent a lot of time cleaning the poor quality stuff and what he put on display looked appetizing enough to convince the poorest families around the lanes to come and buy. That he succeeded was shown in the diminishing sales at Owen's, not far away in the more favourable area.

"Damn me." Peter Marshall was amused when Cecily told him about Jack Simmons's venture. "You should have employed the man yourselves. And your Willie helping him too! Fancy that. Who told on Willie?"

"Willie told us himself. There's nothing wrong with helping a friend and Jack's shop certainly helps the poorer families around the lane."

Sundays were precious to Willie. He set off very early to cycle the twelve miles to Barlow House to see Annette. It had been difficult at first as the girl was not allowed any time off except one afternoon during the week and Willie could only make the journey on Sundays. But Annette had persuaded her employers that she wished to go to Sunday school in the nearby village, and they allowed her to do so.

They met at a barn on the road reached by crossing two fields and the church she purported to attend and they both usually managed to bring food. Whatever the weather they would picnic in the shelter of the ancient walls and with the rubber-coated mackintosh Willie carried and the extra coat Annette struggled to wear, they were warm and cosy.

Making love was a continuous joy and Annette avoided pregnancy following the advice of the cook, who had seven children and insisted she might have had seventeen, and the parlour maid who'd never had a boyfriend.

"Only two months to go," Willie said as he kissed her goodbye one blustery march day. "Come May and we'll be together and no one will be able to stop us."

"Mam is expecting me home for my birthday."

"And home you'll be, love. Our home, yours and mine, and home is where you'll stay."

He stood beside his bicycle and watched as she walked back across the fields to Barlow House and the chores awaiting her. Tea on Sunday was her responsibility and she had to hurry back to make sure the cakes she had made before leaving were arranged

221

on the beautiful Ainsley china with its rich gold on the rim and handles of the cups. She loved that china and thought it compensation for being away from Willie, working with such beautiful things. In her hands she carried a black leather prayer book, which disguised the real reason for her regular walk across the wet friends. Superstition made her stop at the little church, go in and offer up a prayer, asking forgiveness for her deceit.

After the long delay, Ada and Phil's wedding was arranged for the end of May 1935 and it had been decided they would live in the rooms above the shop, where Cecily had once planned to live with Gareth.

"It was decorated but that was five years ago and you'll need to make changes."

Ada and Phil went up the stairs, Phil limping and walking more slowly by the time they had reached the top of the house. Together they examined the three rooms under the roof.

"They're small, but we don't need a lot of room, do we? You're no giant," she teased and he growled in mock anger.

"As big as you can cope with, Ada Owen soon to be Ada Spencer. Small I might be but you'll see, I'll be a giant of a man when I get you alone." He pounced on her and she laughingly led him back down the dark stairways and corridors.

"Fine they are," he told Cecily. "Sure you don't mind us using them? You decorated them for you and Gareth after all."

"That was five years ago, and no, I don't mind. Glad I am. I wouldn't manage very well without Ada here to give me a hand."

Ada's lips tightened. There it is again, the implication she was seen only as Cecily's assistant. Phil saw the brief look of displeasure.

"That's a funny way of looking at things, Cecily. You needing Ada to give you a hand? I thought you were equal partners?"

"But we are." Cecily looked at them in surprise. "Equal partners we are and always will be. I need Ada here and she'd say the same about me if it was me thinking of moving out. We understand each other, don't we, Ada?" She smiled at Ada's nod of agreement.

Phil was limping badly when he went ahead of her to open the car door.

"Your leg, Phil? Is it hurting more than usual today?"

"Them damned stairs. Play hell with me, stairs do."

"Why didn't you say? Perhaps we ought not live there after all if it makes your leg painful."

"It'll be all right, and I know how much Cecily needs you here. Leans on you she does, just like I should lean on a walking stick. Ada! That's it! I'll get a walking stick. That'll help me up the stairs a treat."

"No, Phil. We'll do what you first suggested and go and live with your mother."

"Ada, you're wonderful. What have I done to deserve you?" He offered her his hand to rise from the car seat. "Come on, let's go back and tell Cecily straightaway."

They explained that with Phil's weak leg, the stairs would be a problem. Phil was pleased with the way his bit of play-acting had succeeded, aware of Cecily's fear of being left in the rambling old building with only Van for company.

When the excited couple had gone, Cecily took a candle and climbed the stairs to the attic rooms, wandering from one to the other, remembering where she had decided to place each item of the furniture she and Gareth had chosen. She touched the wallpaper they had selected together and disconsolately straightened the pretty flowery curtains.

She had tried to hide it, but she did mind that Ada was getting married. She occasionally sensed something less than pleasant behind Phil's jokes and laughter, like when they had explained about not using these rooms. She had caught a transient look of delight on his face which made her wonder about his motives. Phil Spencer was no great catch and she shuddered at the thought of sharing a bed with him, but he made her sister happy and she had to accept that.

She wondered whether Dorothy had ever regretted spoiling her own wedding plans. Her sister-in-law was still obsessed with the conviction that Owen would one day own the shop. And Cecily was anxious that there might be a titbit of scandal attached to Phil that Dorothy could find and use to ruin that wedding too. The motivation for her son to inherit was very strong.

These rooms, where she and Gareth had planned to start their married life, seemed cold and unfriendly in the flickering light of her solitary candle. She went down the first two flights of stairs and blew out the dancing flame and the smell of hot wax filled the air. At

Van's room she stopped and went in to stand looking down at the sleeping girl. Her arms were thrown back against the thick pillows in the sleeping position of a contented child. Cecily smiled and moved the covers up near the tranquil face. The night was not cold but the need to make the caring gesture was ignorant of necessity.

Waldo and Melanie Watkins called late that evening. Waldo looked at the books. His thin face was lined but his eyes behind the wire-framed glasses were bright and alert.

"We saw old Horse and that wife of his on the corner singing while arguing about whose turn it was to fetch water to wash. They don't do much of that!"

"I don't know how they survive," Melanie said.

"People are kind and spare a few coppers and cafes sometimes give them left over meals. As long as they have their rent and enough for food they don't ask much more of life."

Waldo tapped his pencil against the paper to draw Cecily's attention to the figures he had arrived at. "For the time of the year you're doing well," he said, passing the books to Melanie for her to agree. "Down a bit on fruit and vegetables, mind. Strange that. But up on other things so altogether you're in a good position as we approach the start of the summer season. Well done."

Cecily explained about Jack Simmons taking a few customers with his cheap produce.

"Damn me, if he has customers like old Horse and his wife, he won't get rich and that's a fact!"

"They tell me the town is expecting even more visitors this year," Melanie said. "In spite of the unemployment and poverty, many still get away to give their children a breath of sea air. Sleeping on the sands they'll be, like last year. Some with babies, little bundles wrapped against the night air, their parents having barely enough food, scant clothing and with just their return tickets and a few coins in their pockets."

"They come to find work, too," Waldo added. "Walk miles they do for the slightest hope of a job, bringing the children and the wife and in some cases the dog too. It means he can survive longer if the women look for work as well, at least while the weather's kind."

"Perhaps that's why these burglaries are taking place — men desperate to feed their families."

"We forget, don't we," Cecily said. "Us with our cars and comfortable homes and full larders. It's easy to forget the thousands who aren't so lucky."

"Yet some succeed. Look at your Willie. He owns two houses and he and Danny are making a name for themselves as makers of fine furniture, although heaven knows where he finds the time."

"Willie finds more hours in the day than the rest of us," Ada agreed. "He's never idle, always potching about with something or the other, that boy."

"Not a boy — he's twenty-one next month," Waldo reminded her. "How the time flies."

"Nine he was when he started with your father." Melanie smiled. "A skinny little urchin he was too. And now he's a man. It's hard to believe."

"He's the same age as Annette," Cecily reminded her. "Their birthdays are only days apart."

"Shame about that lovely girl, being sent off to scrub floors and slave for some other family when her mother couldn't afford to keep her at home. Pity she didn't send that fat lazy Owen instead!" Melanie didn't try to hide her dislike of Dorothy. "Treating the child like that. If we'd had a child we wouldn't have treated her so harshly, no matter what the circumstances."

"Spoiled her rotten you would have," Waldo said. He kissed his wife on her cheek, smiling at her in great affection, and for a brief moment Cecily was an intruder.

Then Waldo said, "I've often wondered if lack of money was the truth. There was never a satisfactory explanation for the suddenness of Annette's disappearance, was there?"

The arrangements for the fast-approaching wedding filled every spare moment and the house was full of clutter and paraphernalia which increased by the hour. Lots of gifts arrived each day, including a fine silver cutlery set from Peter Marshall. The three attic rooms were filled with parcels and, behind doors, the dresses were hung.

Ada's dress was in white brocade, with a lace over-skirt and matching bodice and with lace sleeves which ended in a point at the back of each hand. The train was gathered lace and richly embroidered with seed pearls. It had cost the earth and had been Cecily's gift to her sister.

Two other dresses hanging in the attic room were blue. One was Van's and not dissimilar to the one she had intended to wear at Cecily and Gareth's wedding. The second was for Van's cousin, Marged, Rhonwen's seventeen-year-old daughter. The dresses fascinated Van, who spent hours admiring them and keeping guard to prevent anyone seeing them before the day.

Cecily found her up there one morning when she took up a pile of presents that had arrived by the first post. It was Saturday and Van was still in her nightdress.

"Van, lovey? Aren't you going to get dressed? Edwin will be calling for you soon and there's you still looking like an unmade bed."

Van lifted the corner of the tissue over the dresses. "They are lovely, aren't they? Specially mine."

"Beautiful. Now, come on, let's get you back to your room and find your clothes. What are you wearing today? What are you and Edwin planning to do?"

"We're walking across the docks to the Pleasure Beach."

"It's a bit chilly, you'd better put on your warm coat." Talking about the day to come, Cecily led her daughter back to her room. She could see there was something on the girl's mind and waited, hoping to be told what it was.

"Mam, who was my father?"

"Van, lovey. I've told you many times, he's been gone this long time and there's no point in me talking about him. Except, as I've said, he was a kind, gentle and loving man and you've inherited all his best qualities."

"You could have saved me a lot of teasing. You shouldn't have pretended to be my auntie when you were my mam." Van pulled away from her angrily. "You could choose not to be my mother but I can't choose not to be your daughter!"

"Would you? If you could?" Cecily regretted the words as soon as they left her mouth.

"Yes, I definitely would!"

"Van, I did what I thought was best for us all."

"For you, you mean! Because you didn't want me. You didn't love me."

"Of course I love you. From the first moment I looked at you, I loved you very much. With Auntie Ada and Gran and Granddad, you had all the love we had to give." Van allowed her mother to hold her then, but her eyes didn't lose their resentment; they remained cold and with the glitter of anger.

Cecily left her to dress and went downstairs to the ever busy shop, trembling with emotions raw from the encounter. Van stayed in her room, staring at herself in the mirror over the wash stand. She stared until her eyes watered, the image shattering like a stone thrown into a pool. She was trying to see in herself a reflection of the man she resembled and who had such a loving nature. I'm not loving or gentle like him, she told herself. At least not towards my mother, who denied me until I was seven years old.

CHAPTER
ELEVEN

Ada woke early on the morning of her wedding and jumped out of bed at once to check on the weather. It was perfect. The sky, or what she could see of it from the sitting-room window, was a clear blue and, when she opened the window wide, the air felt warm and silky on her arms and throat. Cecily's side of the bed was empty and she guessed she was downstairs making a tray of tea, and went down to join her.

Neither knew what to say. They both wanted to talk, to explain how they felt at the strong partnership and loving friendship being set aside, with a husband coming into their lives. They poured a second cup of tea before they began to speak their thoughts. Cecily thought Ada had never looked more beautiful, and she told her so.

"And just wait till you wear that dress. Phil will think himself the luckiest man in the world, and so he is." Cecily looked at Ada seriously. "Oh, Ada, love. I do wish you the very best of luck."

"Thank you. I know you do. I don't suppose this is the greatest love story ever but I do know Phil makes me laugh and I'm never happier than when I'm with him. I'd find it hard, now, to face life without him."

"Sounds like love to me." Cecily thought of Danny and how he had so often made her miserable, yet she too had dreaded a future without him. Was that love? Looking at her sister's happy expression she knew it was not. She envied her sister her love, but in an affectionate way, wishing it had been like that for her and Danny all those years ago. She had never found the happiness with Danny that Ada had found with Phil Spencer.

The wedding was arranged for eleven o'clock and from the moment they went downstairs, it was chaos. But out of the chaos, Ada appeared, dressed in her beautiful gown and with her attendants gathered around her.

Cecily was wearing a dress of palest violet, figure-hugging and with a skirt reaching halfway down to her slim ankles. Her hat was pillbox style, still popular after being made fashionable by Princess Marina in 1934. It had been specially made to match the dress. She knew she looked elegant. She felt elegant, but almost spoilt the whole thing by crying when she saw her sister in the dress and veil, with Van and Marged beside her.

Waldo was giving the bride away and he arrived looking very smart in a grey suit. He hugged Ada carefully and told her she was beautiful, and kissed Van and Marged and told them the same. Then Cecily and the others left, with Melanie staying to see the bridesmaids on their way. Bertie and Beryl were to take Melanie when the rest were gone.

Johnny Fowler drove the wedding car. He worked for a taxi firm and did many of the special services like weddings and even drove the twenty-eight-seater charabanc on day trips to Porthcawl and along the Pembrokeshire coast to Tenby. He was grinning widely as he helped his cousin Ada into the be-ribboned and highly polished car.

"Should have been a pony and trap, really, Ada," he said as he helped her straighten her skirts. "You look a real treat and it's a pity that you're hidden, and on a day like this too."

Ada sat beside a proud Waldo and stared through the window, smiling at people they knew, who had lined the pavements to see her pass. She waved excitedly at special friends and teased Waldo, who sat stony-faced.

"Smile," she said with a laugh. "It's me who's supposed to be nervous, not you!"

At the church the roads were full of well-wishers, many dressed in their best and wearing flowers in their hats and on their lapels. There was a policeman on duty to ensure that the roads weren't blocked, but the crowd moved without his instruction, automatically forming a double line for Johnny to drive through and stop at the lych gate.

Beyond the lych gate, more people were lining the path and at her feet, masses of flowers were spread, a carpet of every hue. The sight took her breath away and she stopped for a moment to admire them. Along the path flowers stood in every imaginable container from buckets and bowls to jars and even saucers with small daisies and tom-thumbs floating in them. It was so perfect. Ada felt tears brimming in her eyes. She knew without doubt that this wonderful display was the patient and loving work of Phil's mother.

The church was dark and cold after the warmth of the sun and she shivered slightly and felt Waldo's hand tighten on her arm to encourage her.

"I'm all right," she whispered. "I just felt a sudden chill."

Phil stood with young Willie, his best man. He turned and smiled widely at his first sight of his bride. Then he nudged Willie for him to turn and look too. He was obviously not overawed by the place or the occasion. Ada smiled back happily.

The organist saw her in his mirror and began the music she had often heard in her dreams and she glided slowly down the aisle to stand beside her groom. She looked at his cheeky smile and the look of pride that made his face that of the schoolboy who had eyes for no one else.

They repeated the words with all seriousness but when they went into the vestry, Phil burst out, "Ada! You're so beautiful! I can't believe my luck. Pinch me someone, tell me I'm not dreaming!"

The signing was a blur of faces, talk she didn't hear, comments she wouldn't remember. There was just herself and Phil, wearing a smart grey suit and an expensive tie, with chamois leather gloves hiding his ink-stained hands and spats covering the shaped boots he wore to compensate for his twisted limbs and feet. The smart clothes she remembered, and his smile and the love and pride in his eyes. The rest just floated, unformed, out of her memory in a haze of happiness.

Her veil was lifted and as they went to the door to begin their procession through the church, Phil gripped her arm tightly as if afraid she would run away. Walking through the sea of faces, Ada was aware of something different. Almost at once she realized that Phil was not limping.

"Phil, your leg. You aren't limping."

"I'm walking straight for you today if I never do again," he whispered back and she glanced at him and saw the strain on his face and felt such a rush of love for him. He was forcing himself to walk without a limp that was so much a part of him she forgot until it wasn't there. "Oh, Phil, I love you very much."

They walked out into the sunshine and the beautiful array of flowers where hordes of friends, relations and customers were standing preparing to throw confetti and hand her horseshoes supposed to bring good luck. There was a photographer and he seemed to take an age, insisting they all stood utterly still, but she found a moment to thank Mrs Spencer for the wonderful surprise of the flower-strewn path.

"Raided every garden in the village I did," her mother-in-law whispered, her dimpled face under the fancy hat breaking into the irresistible smile that was so like her son's.

Among the people come to see them, Ada spotted Willie's mother with her daughters and her new husband. How perfect this would be if her own mother had appeared. She allowed thoughts to drift momentarily from the happy, noisy scene to wonder where her mother had gone. In spite of constant efforts over a long time, they had never heard from her since the moment she had left them, apart from a few brief notes posted in Cardiff during the first month. How could she have missed her own daughter's wedding?

She was brought back to the present by a concerned-looking Mrs Spencer asking, "All right, are you? Not upset about anything? Is there anything I forgot that I should have done? We tried to think of everything, me and Phil. We want today to be perfect."

"Perfect it is." Ada smiled affectionately. "Everything is perfection. Are we going back to your house now, for the wedding breakfast?" Ada spread her arms to the ever-growing crowd. "Where will you put us all?"

"Surprise, daughter mine," Mrs Spencer said, tapping the side of her nose with a finger. "Don't ask, just wait."

The cottage was not far from the church so Ada didn't expect to get back into the carriage, but Phil and Waldo called her and led her to the lych gate.

"Time to go," Phil told her, his eyes bright with excitement. He beckoned to Van and Marged and they followed him through the gateway. Outside was Willie, still in his best suit, driving the two-horse carriage. The Owens had sold their horses and Willie couldn't contain his delight at handling horses again.

White ribbons were draped over the horses' backs and each had a bow of ribbon at the side of their necks and white covers over their ears. White ear-muffs for weddings, black for funerals was the tradition. A plume on each proud head had bells attached that jingled as the animals nodded, impatient to be off.

For Ada, the ride through the town was like seeing everything for the first time. She waved gaily to passers-by who shouted good wishes, and Phil threw money for groups of children to scramble for as they passed.

"Damn me," Phil sighed. "I'm glad that part is over. I felt like an actor on stage, not knowing his lines."

"Your leg, Phil. It was wonderful of you to make such an effort on our wedding day but promise you'll never do it again. I could see how much pain it gave you."

"Do anything for you, Mrs Spencer, but all right, I'll use a stick and be damned with pride. I wanted you to know I could do it — for you."

Holding hands and smiling at each other and at the world around them, they travelled on through the town in the direction of the beach.

"When are we turning back?" Ada asked. "Your mam will be anxious for us to start on the food she's prepared."

"What say we go down Hafod Street, Willie?" Phil called.

At the Sea View Hotel the horses stopped and Phil and Ada were helped out by a jubilant Willie. "There, then! Who says we can't keep secrets, eh?"

Beryl and Bertie had hurried from the church by car and were waiting to welcome them to the surprise reception. The hotel had been arranged for the largest wedding they had ever hosted.

236

Cecily waited behind her chair to see who would be sitting next to her. Waldo and Melanie were close by, with Bertie and Beryl. The one unmarked chair remained empty until all the others were filled and to her dismay it was Danny who came to claim it.

"I sneaked in earlier and changed a few cards," he whispered. "Cecily, I have to talk to you."

"Go away. Please don't spoil today."

"I've tried to make it work with Jessie and me but it's no use. It's you I love."

She looked around to see if there was another seat she could use.

"She's hateful to me, says I bore her, that I don't give her enough attention."

"I'm sorry but it's none of my business." Cecily guessed there was more to it than quiet boredom. Indifference, unexplained absences and angry scenes were more likely. She leaned forward and began a conversation with Uncle Ben, who sat opposite with his sharp-faced wife, Maggie. Maggie disapproved of her, being a close friend of Dorothy, and made no secret of the fact so Cecily found it difficult to keep a conversation going. Sitting next to Danny would give her plenty of opinions to share with Dorothy. Cecily knew Uncle Ben enjoyed nothing more than talking about himself, and by asking a few questions about his solos with the choir and his garden, she managed to keep his words coming and avoided talking to Danny throughout the meal.

Willie was ready with the horses and carriage to take the bride and groom back to the shop to change out of their wedding clothes. He was loath to part with the horses. He had not realized how much he had missed driving the cart and the trap until he touched the reins and set out for the church. Still, the car was the important transport of the future and he was not a man to waste time looking back. But he went very slowly back to the stables, savouring the joy of managing the beautiful animals until the last moment, and staying to take them out of harness and spending time rubbing them down.

Ada and Phil were not going away but, as they set off in Phil's car to the Spencers' home, boots were tied to the bumper and they were given a noisy send-off by the crowds still gathered. Cecily went back into the shop feeling deflated and inexplicably sad. Danny was with the rest of the relations who were unwilling to leave. No one had invited him but he was perfectly at ease.

"Better get some sandwiches made, this lot are here for the night," he said. He ushered her through the passageway to the back kitchen and handed her an apron. Then he took her in his arms without warning and kissed her. "I've been wanting to do that all day."

Breathless with shock, and anger, she said, "Go away! I don't want you here!"

"All right. But first I'll help you with the food." In a silence tense with unspoken words, they prepared platefuls of sandwiches and cakes. The bread was filled with cheese and meats provided by Waldo, which she and Ada had prepared in readiness. Pickles were opened, freshly laundered serviettes piled up and eventually the loaded trays were carried up to the big

238

sitting room above the shop, where groups of people waited, hungry despite the meal so recently eaten.

"Where's Willie?" Cecily asked, stretching to look around the room filled with smartly dressed people.

"He's taking the carriage and pair back and Johnny's gone to return the car," Uncle Ben announced in his ponderous bass voice. "That Peter Marshall fellow has followed to bring them back here."

Cecily and Danny worked as a team, almost unnoticed, as they brought food and drinks to the guests and Cecily felt anger threatening to develop into a row when she heard Dorothy telling others loudly that Ada should not consider having a child. "I know he tried to hide it today but the fact remains he's a cripple and shouldn't risk having a child born with the same affliction."

Cecily slammed down a tray she was carrying and said loudly, "Phil was hit by a car! His weak leg muscles are the result of an accident. The problem is neither hereditary nor congenital!"

Dorothy shook her head but didn't reply.

"She doesn't know what you mean and is afraid it might be something rude!" Danny whispered.

Danny stayed after everyone else had gone. The piano tinkled its last tune at 12.30 when Uncle Ben sang a hymn to finish the day in proper mood, and people at last began to drift away.

Van had fallen asleep and Cecily put her to bed. Marged was sleeping too, sitting in the small armchair near the dying fire, and Peter Marshall offered to drive

Rhonwen and Marged home. He collected their coats and before leaving found Cecily for a final word.

"Don't ever feel you're alone, Cecily," he said, squeezing her shoulders affectionately. "I know how close you and Ada are and it will be strange for you to have to share her with Phil. If ever there's a time when you want company, just pick up the phone and say 'Peter', and I'll stop whatever I'm doing and come."

"Thank you. But I have to face the changes and accept them or I'll be months before I start living again. Life's too short to waste it wishing for something that can't be altered. Best to accept and go on from there, don't you think?"

"You'll do," he said approvingly, "but my offer remains. Call me and I'll come."

Cecily was surprised to realize that although she had met Peter years before, she knew very little about him. He fitted in so easily it was difficult to think back to when he wasn't there. A day out in Porthcawl, or a long discussion on some aspect of her business, they all seemed as relaxed and easy with Peter as with Waldo or Bertie. Peter Marshall, she thought with comforting warmth, was a good friend to have.

He had sold her a car and a van and looked after both vehicles with a thoroughness she admired. He ran his beach stall, where she often called during the summer months and from where he had on several occasions taken her and Van out for a meal. She looked at him with new interest. He was more than a casual acquaintance; he was someone who really cared.

240

Danny had disappeared into the back kitchen while she saw the last few guests on their way. The doorbell shook at each departure and played its busy, silvery ditty, and Cecily sighed and leaned back against the door as it closed for the penultimate time. "Now there's only you, Danny Preston," she muttered.

He stepped out of the shadows and opened his arms. She shook her head.

"I was only going to invite you to sit while I get you a drink," he said softly.

"Sorry, Danny. Yes, I haven't had a drink all evening. Too busy, but I need one now."

"How d'you feel? Apart from needing a drink?" He searched through the bottles and picked up an empty glass. "Worried about Ada not being here tonight?"

"It's funny, but all these weeks I've thought of how I'll miss her and it's only now, with the house suddenly so empty after all those people, that I've thought of sleeping in this rambling old building with only Van for company. I think I'll get a dog. And another cat. And maybe a parrot."

"You are nervous then?"

"A little. I think I'll go in with Van, just for tonight."

"No, it'll be worse tomorrow if you do that."

"Part of my nervousness is for Van. She seems so vulnerable on the floor below me and the place is a mass of empty rooms and long dark passages; ghosts and shadows and no living person within call."

"I could stay —"

"No!"

"I mean just stay. I'll sleep down here in the armchair. Your father slept there many times."

"No."

"Tie my hands and feet if you don't trust me — or yourself."

"Don't be stupid."

"Just for tonight. Tomorrow you'll have had time to get used to the idea and tomorrow is Sunday, a quiet day. You and Van can relax and get the feel of the house in its new mood. For tonight I think I should stay." He glanced at the clock on the wall ticking away the hours. "There isn't much of the night left, anyway."

"All right. You can sleep in Mam and Dad's room."

"Fine. You'll sleep well, knowing there's someone else near you." He picked up his coat and hung it on the hook in the passage. "I'll just make sure all the doors are locked."

"Ada always did that," she said sadly. She ran upstairs then, trying to fight off the excitement that was making her breathless. She knew she should have insisted he went but there was a difference about the house with one less occupant. Although, knowing Danny was so near would hardly make her more inclined to sleep.

She looked in on Van who was fast asleep in her usual position, arms thrown back in contented abandon as she had as a child, then went to her parents' room and found a clean towel and a pair of her father's pyjamas for Danny. She paused in the cold empty room for a moment, shivering in the unused feel of the place, redolent of lavender polish and clean linen and half remembered past times. She contemplated on how the absence of her parents had changed it from a well loved and welcoming room to one that was alien and unfriendly.

Why had Mam abandoned them so completely? She touched the smooth counterpane and wondered if perhaps she was unhappy and regretting her action and was too proud to return. If only they could find her, talk to her, but the fact remained that she had appeared neither at Dadda's funeral nor Ada's wedding and that seemed utterly final. If there were to be a softening of her resolve it would have been at one of these important occasions.

She put the towel and pyjamas on the bed and went back down. Danny was waiting at the bend of the first landing. He reached out and pulled at the gas-light chain and the staircase was enveloped in darkness in which their breathing seemed inordinately loud. He leaned towards her so she could feel each breath on her cheek and she said warningly, "Danny, no." She struck a match and re-lit the hissing gas.

"Good night. Sleep well."

"Thank you."

She didn't bother to explain exactly where he was sleeping. He'd been a regular visitor once and nothing much had changed. She heard him open the door and strike a match to light a candle. The door complained slightly as it was pushed shut.

It was exciting, stripping off her clothes knowing he was near. There was something sensual in the silk of her nightdress slipping so easily over her slim figure. The sheets were cool and caressing as she stretched her legs slowly down. The bedroom light was still on and she was reluctant to turn it off. The day had been long and full and she needed time to unwind before accepting that it was over. After a few minutes she reached up and turned off the gas-light but she was far from drowsy. She stood for a moment looking over the roof tops at the stars showing faintly in the navy blue sky. A slight movement caught her eye and she turned to see the door slowly opening.

"Danny. Go away!"

"I thought you'd like to see this." He stepped into her room and in the light of his candle she saw he was wearing the pyjamas she had left for him. They were crazily tight. About three sizes too small, she assessed pointlessly. She began to chuckle, trying to muffle it and prevent it exploding into laughter. He bulged everywhere. The pyjama legs ended a little below the knees, the cord fastened but the gap was a huge V. His body refused to fit into the jacket; the place for his shoulders was lower than his shoulder blades. Sleeves strained across his muscular arms and the one solitary button he'd managed to fasten was making the straining jacket look like a pleated brassiere.

Laughter was impossible to contain and he struggled out of the jacket with Cecily's help in spluttering giggles. Then he pulled the cord holding up the trousers and suddenly it was no longer funny, but serious and urgent and they fell onto the bed with the hunger of lovers after a long agonizing absence.

Cecily woke the following morning with a languid dreamy floating sensation. The only sound was the gentle flapping of the curtains in the breeze. The air smelled sweet and clean and only of the sea. There was a startled moment of realization, then a moment to savour, watching Danny breathing lightly beside her, his arms still holding her, the sight as fresh and intoxicating as the morning. In sleep his face had lost its habitual frown and with the lids closed over the intense eyes he looked so calm and beautiful she felt a lump fill her throat. Gently she kissed his cheek, already prickling with the need for a shave, the dark hairs forming a shadow on his cheeks and on the slightly thrusting chin.

The eyes snapped open then, wickedly full of laughter.

"Cecily, it was those stupid pyjamas that did it. I really did intend to stay in my room like a good boy. Really I did. But you looked so lovely and I looked so ridiculous and —" His hands began to move over her skin, deliciously sensual, and her resolve was not strong. Soon they were kissing and murmuring endearments and, as passion grew, the bed became too small and they fell to the floor, pulling the blankets with them so they were cocooned, held captive, neither wanting to be free.

Street noises grew and slipped through the curtains; the sun moved up until the light washed the walls in a glowing light.

"We have to move. If Van should come and see us —" Cecily reluctantly crawled out from the imprisoning sheets and searched for her nightgown. Danny left the room and they both stifled laughter as he tiptoed along the passage.

He dressed quickly and after a brief kiss and a promise to come back later, he went down to the shop. He held the doorbell silent while he slipped out and as he did so, a voice asked, "Hello, Danny. Are you my father?"

Sick at the thought that the child might have seen him with Cecily, he decided to presume she hadn't. "No, my lovely girl, I wish I were. It would be great to have a daughter as beautiful as you, young Van. Indeed it would."

Cecily appeared then and looked with startled eyes from one to the other. Van was staring up at Danny. "No," she said solemnly. "I don't look like you."

"Ugly old thing I am, and you as fair as a summer's day." He glanced at Cecily and said, casually, "That's the crates sorted. I'll come back later and we'll pack the empties for Willie to return in the morning, right?"

"Yes, thanks for coming so early," Cecily said, following his line. "Nice to get the muddle out of the way quickly."

Van said nothing. She and Edwin had discussed what men and women did in bed and what she had seen in Cecily's room confirmed it. She glared at her mother and went to the kitchen to prepare breakfast. She cooked only for herself and ate it without a word.

CHAPTER
TWELVE

Willie rose early the day after Ada and Phil's wedding and, thankful that the weather was dry, began his long cycle ride to Barlow House to see Annette. She was waiting for him in the barn and greeted him with affection.

"Just think, the next time we meet it will be to go away together," Willie said as he hugged her. "Only a week and I'll be here with the van to take you to Mam's in Cardiff."

"Pity there'll be none of the family there to wish us luck," Annette said wistfully. "A wedding day is so special it should be shared with all the people you love. But never mind," she added quickly when she saw her words were upsetting Willie, "the one I love best in the whole world will be there and the rest of the family will soon know, won't they? What fun it will be to tell them!"

It had been arranged well in advance of Annette's twenty-first birthday that she should go to Willie's mother to wait out the necessary period before the wedding could take place. It was to be in a register office with Willie's mother, sisters and stepfather present. He wished he could have made the wedding a huge affair with her family joining in the celebration alongside his, but they both knew that was impossible. Annette's mother had showed clearly what she thought of Willie as a suitor for her daughter when she had sent her daughter away to Barlow House. The wedding would be a small one but he would make it up to her. He'd be a good husband and provider and show Dorothy she was wrong.

"Don't look so sad, love." Annette smiled. "I don't think any wedding has been as exciting as ours will be. Imagine telling our children about how we defied everyone and you did it on your own. Booked the wedding, built up our home, planned my escape. It's been wonderful, Willie. I wouldn't change a thing."

"All that's left for me to do is ask Cecily for the loan of the van. If she refuses, and I think that's unlikely, I'll borrow one from Peter Marshall. Nothing will stop me getting my lovely bride away and safely hidden. No one will stop me marrying you."

"My clever and brave Willie," she murmured happily. "How lucky I am."

"Don't forget to tell your mother you can't get home for your birthday," he reminded her later as they parted for the last time. "Not too soon, mind. We don't want her writing to Barlow House to plead for them to let you to come. If we time it right no one will miss you for a while. Barlow House will think you're home and your Mam'll think you're at Barlow House." He kissed her and watched as she ran across the fields, clutching the prayer book that always accompanied her to "Sunday school".

248

On the following Sunday Willie again left early but this time in more comfort. The van was as familiar to him as the horses had once been, although he still missed the company of the animals. You couldn't talk to an engine, he thought as the miles passed under the wheels and signposts told of his progress.

When he reached the barn Annette wasn't there. He left the van doors open to cool the interior and lay on the grass, chewing a stalk and waiting without alarm as the day grew steadily hotter. Then after half an hour had passed he began to worry. He stood up and stared across the fields as if seeing further would make her come more quickly. The horizon and sky and grass remained empty.

As he watched with growing fear, the skies began to darken, the heat became more oppressive and soon, large rain spots wet the ground, raising the scents of dried grass and dust, redolent of long hot summer days. He sheltered in the barn for a while, then, wondering if Annette was on her way and needing help with her bag, he ignored the downpour that was increasing in intensity and set off over the field to Barlow House.

He had been to the house before, accompanying her back regularly until they were almost seen by the lady of the house on a casual walk through her grounds. He knew which window was hers, too. Right at the top of the building over-shadowed by the jutting roof.

Stepping out from the shrubbery surrounding the back lawn he saw a face at the window and a hand, waving furiously. The window opened and a note fluttered down. He caught it and opened it, his heart thumping with anxiety. Surely she wouldn't change her mind? Not now? Rain dribbled over the scrap of paper. Thank goodness she had used a black lead and not ink or it would have been illegible.

"I have hurt my knee and can't walk far. What shall we do?"

Taking a chance on being heard he shouted up, "Come down here. I'm coming back with the van. Get in while I'm knocking the front door. Right?" He waited for her to nod agreement then ran back through the lashing rain and the distant growls of thunder, to the barn.

He drove carefully back through the increasingly violent storm and approached the main door of the house. He stepped out as lightning filled the air, which was quickly followed by a crash of thunder. It was dark. More like a winter evening than a May day. As the doorbell echoed through the house, a flash of lightning heralded another loud roll; fast, brilliant and close. The door opened and a young man asked him his business.

"I'm lost, sir," Willie said. "Making for Brecon I am and without an idea of where I am. Can you help me, please?"

Willie moved closer to the door as the young man attempted to step out to direct him. Willie didn't want him to see the small figure creeping around the corner, half carrying, half dragging a heavy bag. When the van door opened and closed and he knew Annette was safely inside, he suddenly understood the instructions the man had repeated several times. As lightning flickered and another roll of thunder rumbled around the house, he ran back, pausing only to shout his thanks, and drove away.

"We've done it!" he shouted jubilantly. "We're on our way! No more partings, no more uncomfortable barns. You'll soon be Mrs William Morgan and used to nothing but the best. How does that sound?"

"Willie, it's marvellous, and just in time too." She patted her stomach and smiled at him, her eyes glowing with happiness. "You're going to be a daddy!"

"What timing! What a clever baby he's going to be!"

Singing, and laughing at everything and anything, they planned the next stage of their adventure as the little van bowled along the road to Cardiff.

"Annette is missing!" Dorothy burst into the shop one morning waving a letter. "She isn't at Barlow House and she lied about coming home for her birthday."

As Ada ran to get brandy for the distraught woman, Cecily hurriedly served the few customers waiting, hurrying them out and ignoring their curious questions.

"Dorothy, haven't you any idea where she might be?"

"All I know is that she wrote telling me she couldn't get home for her birthday, when I promised to talk to her about coming back for good. She told them she *was* coming home." She handed Cecily the letter and took the glass Ada was offering. "What shall I do?"

"The police? Have you told them?"

"Of course. They think she planned it."

"It does seem that way," Cecily said hesitantly. "Is there a boyfriend?"

"No, indeed there is not! I told them to keep a strict eye on her. She never went out alone."

"Poor girl," Ada muttered.

"Never?" Cecily asked.

"Well, only to church. I was glad of that, but she was never home a minute later than promised."

"Every week?"

"Not at first. She's been going regularly since."

Ada and Cecily looked at each other. They went into the shop to serve, leaving Dorothy sitting in the room behind the shop.

"You thinking what I'm thinking?" Cecily whispered.

"That our Willie goes out every Sunday and last week he borrowed the van."

"He wouldn't! She wouldn't!"

"What shall we do? Tell Dorothy our suspicions?"

"Best not. We'll wait and see. We don't want to get our Willie into trouble." Neither admitted it aloud but they both hoped Willie and Annette were together. They winked at each other, silently wishing the couple all the luck they needed.

They jumped with guilt as Dorothy called plaintively, "Where's that stable boy, Willie Morgan?"

"Delivering orders over the beach."

"He might know something. He once had high-faluting ideas above his station and thought he could marry Annette."

"Go home, and we'll ask him when he gets back," Ada said, her tone suggesting it would be a waste of time, but Dorothy didn't move.

When Willie returned, whistling cheerfully, Dorothy was still there. "Good morning, Mrs Owen."

"You haven't heard from Annette, I suppose?" Dorothy asked, then she looked at his clothes and his grubby hands and shook her head. "No, of course you haven't, what was I thinking about." So he was saved the problem of lying.

"Willie, come in here, will you?" Ada asked. "There's a problem you might be able to help us with." She followed him through the shop and closed the door. "Annette is missing and her mother is worried frantic. I don't suppose you know something about it?"

"I only know she shouldn't have been sent away. Unhappy she'd be up there, far away from her family and friends. If anything's happened to her it will be her mother's fault." He stalked out of the shop and into the yard without further comment. But when Ada went to see if he had loaded the second delivery, he was whistling cheerfully, and she frowned.

Over the following days, more news filtered through. A van driver had stopped at Barlow House to ask directions for Brecon on that afternoon. There had been a heavy thunderstorm at the time and the man-servant was unable to tell the police the make of van or give a useful description of the driver. The search spread to Brecon and the villages around but no trace of the van or its driver were found.

"Does Willie ever use the van?" Dorothy asked one day.

"Sometimes, not often. Only when he has to buy wood for his furniture-making. The wood yards don't open on Sundays, do they?" she added innocently.

The sisters were not certain if Willie was involved. They preferred not to know, so they didn't ask. They decided that it was unlikely, as he would have surely put

Dorothy out of her misery by at least telling her Annette was safe.

The police asked Willie a few questions and he admitted to taking the van out for a joy-ride sometimes.

"To Barlow House?"

"Where's it to?" Willie asked vaguely.

"Fond of cycling, are you?"

"Now and then, like. It's a need to get out of town and find a bit of peace and quiet, more than the effort of pushing the pedals around. I don't go far, just for some quiet." Willie seemed open and honest, if slightly less bright and well spoken than usual, and unperturbed by the questions. He did feel guilty about Dorothy's worries but he couldn't risk her finding out where Annette was, and ruining their happiness a second time.

It was Dorothy's idea that they should call on Willie's mother and her new husband. She forced the address out of Gladys Davies, who tearfully told Ada what she had done. This was a Friday evening and Willie was on his bike as soon as the news reached him, via Ada. It was late at night when he reached his mother's house and the place was in darkness. His legs were trembling with the effort of the fast journey when he dismounted at the gate.

The back door was never locked and he went in and straight up to where Annette was curled up fast asleep.

"Wake up, love, they've guessed where you are." He threw her things into a bag and together they crept down the stairs and out of the house. As they turned the corner, pushing the bike which was loaded with her belongings, a van pulled up outside the house.

They stayed the night at a boarding house, a small, insignificant place in the poorer part of the town and the following morning arrived, rather more bedraggled than either had hoped, at the register office for their appointment to become man and wife.

Willie's family were there and, as a surprise for Annette, the tall, sturdy figure of Peter Marshall was beside them. He opened his arms wide and hugged them both.

"Thank you for inviting me to share this joyful occasion with you. I'm standing proxy for the many others who'd be here to wish you luck if things had allowed." He handed them an envelope containing two five pound notes and insisted that today he had the right to kiss the most beautiful and radiant bride he'd seen in years. "Can I ask what your plans are for the rest of the day?" he asked when the brief ceremony was over.

"Home. I'm taking Annette to our home."

"Then let me drive you."

They sat in the back of Peter's car and smiled at each other, holding hands, as the houses of Cardiff made way for fields and occasional villages, then the outskirts of their home town as they headed for the neat, white cottage and the beginning of a life together.

They stepped inside, where everything was neat and orderly, with the new curtains, chosen by Annette so long ago. The fire was lit and the heavy black kettle was humming a welcome. Willie took her upstairs to where he had already started making the second bedroom into a room for the baby, due in the autumn.

An hour later, Willie left her to examine everything and admire the furniture he and Danny had made. Having discarded his bicycle in Cardiff, he walked to the shop to explain his absence.

Dorothy was there discussing the latest news with Cecily. Willie was whistling as he walked through to the yard and stables and into the house.

"Willie, at last. Where have you been? We were beginning to think you'd disappeared, like Annette."

"Annette? She hasn't disappeared, she's home, where she belongs."

Dorothy jumped up. "What have you been doing to her? I must get home to her. The police will hear about this — this — kidnap!"

"Not your home, Mother-in-law, our home. Annette and I are married and she's expecting our first baby."

Willie stood smiling as the three women began talking at once. Ignoring their questions and looking from one to the other as if they were specimens from a strange race, he walked to the door. "Better get on then, these orders will be late and I don't expect young David has dealt with many."

"Willie!", Cecily said in exasperation.

"Oh," he said, turning back to face them again. "You're all invited to tea on Sunday. Right?"

"I'll give you tea! I'm telling the police," Dorothy shouted.

"I've already told them you knew all about it and they might be questioning you about wasting their time," was his parting shot.

Dorothy soon accepted the situation, although she found it impossible to be civil to Willie. She gave out news of her daughter's wedding as if she had been the confidant of the couple's need for a ceremony and by twisting the facts implied that the whole romantic affair had been stage managed by her. Willie called her Mother-in-law and treated her with respect but with an attitude of superiority that infuriated her.

"A stable boy," she wailed. "After all my dreams of a good match for her, she marries a stable boy."

Ada lost her temper. They had put up with this for long enough. "Stop calling him a stable boy!" she shouted and Dorothy looked at her in alarm. "We haven't had horses for ages, so how can he be? And besides, don't you realize what a remarkable man he is? He owns his house and another, and he's buying a third."

"A *twll* of a place this latest one is too."

"It's in need of repairs that he can do with ease," Cecily interrupted. "He also spends his spare time — and we don't give him much — making furniture with Danny Preston. Furniture the best shops are glad to sell for them. How can you pretend to be better than him? What have you done, compared with that boy?"

"Except complain about your lot!" Ada added, her face red with anger. She warned her sister to stop then. She was right, and needed telling, but she didn't want Dorothy to walk out and be unable to return. Proud and prickly, a difficult combination, that was Dorothy, but she was family. "Come on, Dorothy, you know how much we think of Willie. Let's leave it now and have a cup of tea, shall we?" Ada guided her out of the room. "Watch the shop, will you, Cecily?"

When Dorothy tried to discuss Willie again, hoping to regain Ada as an ally, Ada stopped her and eventually she calmed down. But not before one more criticism. "You think more of Willie than my Owen."

Ada was tempted to agree but held her tongue for the sake of peace.

The white-painted cottage was busy during the first weeks of Willie and Annette's marriage. First the family filtered through the little house and took tea in the neat living room where Annette cooked a variety of cakes to satisfy the demand. Their friends began to call and were made welcome, although Willie spent as much time as he could in the shed behind the house, working on the tables and occasional furniture he and Danny designed and made.

Annette and her mother had greeted each other affectionately and with guilt on both sides. Annette, seeing the effect of the weeks of worry on her mother's face, regretted the anxiety she had caused. Dorothy wished she had accepted the love of her daughter for Willie before sending her so far away.

Knitting went on at a remarkable rate as Annette was taught by Gladys Davies to make the small garments needed for the baby. Rhonwen and Marged called regularly and always brought the tapestry bags containing wool and needles, with which they were patiently making a shawl and a pram cover, proudly showing their progress at each visit.

In another cottage only a few minutes away, Ada's marriage was a happy one, but in many ways not a fulfilled one. She continued to work at the shop from eight every morning, when Phil would deliver her in the car, until half past six in the evening when Phil would collect her to take her home where Mrs Spencer would have a meal ready for them. Ada never had the opportunity to cook for her husband or to feel married, in the sense of caring for him.

She was very happy with Phil and the standard of living at the spotlessly clean cottage was very high. Phil was an attentive husband and she would watch him occasionally and notice that his limp was barely showing. She was flattered at the effort he made to please her, although she pleaded with him not to suffer pain because of it. The limp was so much a part of him she had no desire for him to lose it, especially when she saw the lines of discomfort on his thin face.

The shop was building up to its busiest time and as Ada entered each morning, she felt she had two hats. One worn at the busy shop with a thousand things to remember, the other that of pampered and adored wife.

"Thank goodness I have the meats for the shop to cook each Tuesday and Saturday," she said to Cecily one morning. "I'd forget how to cook altogether if it wasn't for that."

Living away from the shop had meant few changes but Ada knew the responsibilities were slipping away from her. Decisions, like being extra fussy about selling only the freshest and best vegetables and fruit to compare favourably with Jack Simmons' cheap shop on the corner, were made without her being asked for an opinion. It rankled more than a little that her disagreement, when Cecily mentioned it, did not change a thing.

Not being there in the evenings meant that all the books were attended to by Cecily, with Waldo and Melanie coming in regularly to check that all was well. Bertie and Beryl called often too but she was excluded from their chatter and became less au fait with how the shop was run. She belonged nowhere and was important neither at the shop nor at home with Phil and his mother.

One evening each week she and Phil stayed for a meal and on these evenings, little shop business was discussed. They would generally stay after they had eaten, to play cards or listen to the wireless, sometimes staying with Van while Cecily went out. Neither sister mentioned him but Ada guessed Cecily was seeing Danny again. Early in July, Cecily asked if they could come again on the following Saturday. Ada looked at Phil for agreement then nodded.

"Going somewhere special?" Ada asked, thinking how strange it was not to know the moment Cecily knew of anything exciting happening in her life. The marriage had changed their relationship considerably and yet in ways so subtle she had hardly been aware of them. She waited, guessing Cecily's reply would be vague.

"Pictures."

"Who with?" Ada coaxed.

"Oh, a couple of friends from the dance. They came into the shop and invited me."

"What friends? Come on, I'd know them too if they're from the dance crowd."

Cecily looked pained as she tried to think of a reply to satisfy her sister and yet avoid the truth. Phil saved her.

"Leave the girl alone, woman," he said with a laugh. "Damn me, you don't live in each other's pocket any more. She can go out without an inquisition." He leaned closer to Cecily and in a loud whisper asked, "If it's something exciting, I'll go out for a while. Tell her before we go, for heaven's sake. Never sleep, she won't, not knowing the ins and outs."

"Right, then," Cecily said, joining in the teasing. "Make you both wait before telling you, that's what I'll do."

Ada looked serious. She has no intention of telling me, she thought sadly. Danny Preston's married and if they're meeting in secret, then it's obvious why she won't tell me. She knows I'd do my damnedest to stop her.

Danny and Jessie lived — between quarrels and frequent separations — in two small rooms not far from the Pleasure Beach. Jessie had a meal ready to serve and she glanced at the clock and sighed. It was almost time for Danny to come home. He usually finished the post around this time. Not that she would see much of him. He'd go straight down the garden to the shed as soon as he had eaten. She would hear the tools and that was as much of her husband's company as she could expect.

Saws buzzing and chisels chipping away in a rhythm of almost metronome regularity. Then the sound of the lathe as he shaped the legs for the piece currently in the making. The softer scratching and smoothing then as he rubbed patiently and without pause in the rhythm, with emery cloth and sandpaper.

Jessie never went out there to watch him any more but knew from the various sounds to reach her what he was doing. Their lavatory was adjoining the shed and even when she went there she didn't disturb him. There was no point. He would hardly look up and rarely spoke to her. Only in bed would he sometimes acknowledge her presence and even those times had all but faded away. She heard the front door opening and took his meal off the saucepan of hot water, wiped the bottom of the plate and placed it on the table.

"Thanks, Jessie, that looks good," he said as he did every day. She looked at him preparing to eat, washing his hands at the sink and staring down the garden as he dried them. He's already thinking of the work waiting for him down there, she thought as he pulled out a chair and sat down. I'm not important for longer than it takes him to eat my food. On an impulse, she plucked the hot plate from the table in front of him and threw it on the floor. Her voice was calm as she said, "I'm leaving you, Danny, and this time you won't talk me into coming back." It was a sentence she had rehearsed for days.

"Don't be a fool." Anger glittered in his dark eyes as he surveyed the mess on the floor. "You're too comfortable to leave me. I don't keep you short of anything, do I?" He hardly looked at her, still staring at the mess on the floor. "You should see some of the places I deliver to, then you'd realize how lucky you are, woman. Living on fresh air, some families around Felwell Street and Grange Court. And there are a lot of people like Horse and his missus sleeping in nothing more than an old stable. So just get me some food and I'll be off down the shed and out from under your feet."

Still speaking calmly she said, "I'm going back to live with Mam. My job at the factory is still open for me and I'd rather work in the noise and smell for ten hours a day than sit here talking to the walls."

"Visit your mother if you want, but get my food first."

"You aren't listening. I'm going and I'm not coming back." Her usually pale face with its setting of rich red hair was flushed with the frustration of not being about to get her words through to him. Neither of them had even raised their voice.

She left the kitchen-cum-living room, which was packed with furniture and a collection of cupboards where she had tried to make a home, and went into the tiny bedroom. Danny didn't follow her; he stood looking around him. One cupboard held a supply of dried food, a loaf and a few tins. He selected a tin of corned beef, which he opened and tipped out onto a plate.

He ate while Jessie came from the bedroom with a cane suitcase, the leather straps stretched to their fullest extent to accommodate the dresses and underwear it held. Her voice was breathlessly quiet as she said a prim "Goodbye". She would have been surprised if she had seen the smile on Danny's face as her footsteps echoed down the street.

He ate a few slices of the meat with some bread, then, putting the remainder in the gauze-covered meat safe to protect it from flies, he went to see Willie. He found him searching through the drawers of the sideboard he had recently made.

"Lost something, Willie?" he asked, stepping into the living room.

"Yes, a pocket watch I've had for years. Cecily and Ada gave it to me when the old man died. Funny, I'd have sworn I left it here."

"A burglary?"

"He wouldn't have taken just the watch, there are other things he'd find easy to sell. I can't have lost it."

"I've lost something too," Danny said, his smile widening as he explained. "Jessie left me at last and gone back to her mother. She means it this time; taken all her clothes an' all."

"You didn't cut up rough, did you?"

"No, man! I've never hit a woman yet and never will. No need. I just ignored her till she couldn't stand it any longer. Threw my dinner on the floor, she did, mind. There's a waste."

"What will you do now?"

264

"Use some of the money I've been putting in the bank. It isn't much but I'm going to take a chance and give up the post and start making furniture full-time. More satisfaction." He looked at his friend, younger in years but with a maturity that shamed him at times. "What about you? You ready to give up the shop and take a chance too?"

Willie shook his head. "No, I can't. Got a wife to support and a baby on the way. I'm not free to do that now."

"Fool you were to get married."

"No, I'm not the fool, you were, marrying Jessie when you loved someone else. That's what I call being a fool."

"You're right. And Annette is the one for you. But perhaps, now Jessie's gone, things will start working out for me. But first," he said, "I'll concentrate in expanding the business. Know of a barn we can rent, do you?"

"Yes, I do. But keep your job a bit longer. Money's scarce and jobs are harder to find. The two pounds eighteen shillings you earn is important. You'll have to support Jessie and there are weeks when the money is slow to come in, and weeks while we're working on a big project when there's nothing to sell. Times are hard and not many are prepared to spend on quality and luxury items."

"All right, I'll keep the job for a while longer. I want us to concentrate on the simple stuff for a while — good tables and practical things that working people

265

need and can afford. With a decent lathe we could double our output in no time."

Not far from Willie's house was a neglected brick and wood barn, once used as a hay store. It suited them for situation and size and they went at once to talk to the farmer who owned it. The farmer agreed to sell them the place and they walked back jubilant with the prospect of the surge in work they would achieve now they had proper premises.

"Should have done this years ago," Danny said. Then he stopped and pulled Willie out of sight behind a thick hawthorn. "Look who's coming."

It was Phil Spencer, and he was running. There was no hint of his familiar limp and he was startled when Willie and Danny suddenly stepped out in front of him.

"Don't tell Ada," Phil pleaded, his face falling with the urgency of his appeal, so he looked thinner and smaller than ever. "Surprise it is for her, see, me running straight. Takes it out of me, mind. Can't do it for long."

Danny laughed. "Why bother? You've got your woman, haven't you?"

"Shamed I am, by the limp. I try to walk proper but it pulls on the wrong muscles, see, and it's too much. I'll have to go slow from here."

"Go on, then. Don't let us stop you." Danny laughed again. "Unless you want a piggy back?"

"That was unkind," Willie said as the small man, limping painfully, hobbled across the uneven grass.

"Can't stand the man, with his rat's face and his whining voice." Danny kicked a tuft of grass and walked on. "And I don't trust him either," he called back. Willie glared his disapproval at the broad back and followed.

A few weeks later, Danny and Willie had repaired the barn, installed a large lathe and painted a sign advertising their business as Makers of Fine Furniture. Danny left Foxhole Street, telling Jessie via her mother that she could stay there if she wished and he would pay the rent. Willie's quiet criticism had made him feel guilty enough to make the gesture. He had been wrong to marry her while loving Cecily. He found himself a room with meals and laundry included in a house near Gladys Davies, who had looked after Willie so well.

CHAPTER
THIRTEEN

Since Ada's marriage, the sisters had agreed that, with Willie's help, they would each have an afternoon off every week. Ada imagined she would find plenty to do in her new home, sewing, cleaning and cooking. Cecily looked forward to getting out on her own and enjoying a few hours of complete freedom. Neither achieved what they hoped.

Ada was living "through and through" in her mother-in-law's house, not having rooms of her own but sharing as one of the family. Only the bedroom was hers and Phil's and even that was cleaned and cared for by Mrs Spencer and was not the private place she had presumed it would be. Mrs Spencer would walk in while they were in there, talking non-stop, or asking for a piece to be read to her from the newspaper before she went visiting, so she could continue with the illusion she could read.

The house was run efficiently. Mrs Spencer was always up early and most of the dusting and polishing and even the scrubbing of the back kitchen floor was done long before Ada and Phil rose, to eat the breakfast waiting for them. It was like living in a hotel, with even the simple tasks of clearing the table or washing the dishes denied her.

They would eat their food and before they had finished the second cup of tea they both indulged in, the rest of the dishes would be washed and back on their correct shelves. When they left for the shop, Mrs Spencer would be sitting near the immaculately clean fireplace, sewing or knitting, the house as neat as it could be.

The one thing her mother-in-law wouldn't allow was for Ada to carry water up to her bedroom so she could wash in private. She didn't actually complain, but would always bring the offending bowl down the moment Ada had finished, tutting in mild disapproval. Even when Ada took it up as she went to bed, Mrs Spencer would come into the bedroom and take it back down. Ada thought longingly of the bathroom she had enjoyed in the rooms behind the shop. Eventually she accepted the rule and washed in the back kitchen.

So Ada's half day was spent sitting with her mother-in-law discussing the local gossip, of which the lady was an expert. She rarely saw Phil on these afternoons. He spent them travelling around the town collecting his debts. Gradually she began to forget her hours off and stayed on at the shop. She used Willie as an excuse.

"Go on, Willie, you have a few hours off, there's nothing important for me at home and I know you can use the time."

After a few weeks it was usual for Cecily to take a half day but for Ada to work the full week. She was pleased to be working the extra hours; it brought her close to the amount of time Cecily worked and made her feel less of an assistant to her sister's role of manager.

Cecily didn't ask her sister why, but guessed the reason from the few remarks Ada made about the efficiency of her mother-in-law and the joy the woman found in spoiling her son's wife. Cecily knew how much Ada had been looking forward to showing her own skills in looking after a home and husband, and the dismay was written on her face when she said how wonderful it was to be so cared for. It was a symptom of the growing gap between them that neither could fully discuss their thoughts.

Cecily used her half day to meet Danny. Ada said nothing about this for several weeks but finally warned, "People love to talk and several of our customers have seen you and Danny Preston meeting outside the town. D'you want to end up in court? Imagine the delight Dorothy would have telling Jessie she has grounds for divorce."

On her next half day, Cecily didn't meet Danny as arranged but went instead over to Peter Marshall's garage. Wind was gusting, threatening to steal her hat, and the day was gloomy. She filled the car with petrol, then began talking about her dilemma. It was he who started the conversation with a gentle, "What's wrong?"

"Danny!" she said succinctly.

"You're meeting him and he's a married man." There was the slightest hint of censure in his voice.

"After Ada's wedding he stayed and for a while we met almost daily. He'd come after Van was asleep. Then I told him goodbye, urged him to try and repair his marriage. We didn't meet for several weeks and I believed he and Jessie were back together and all was well."

"And then?"

"It happened by accident really. I came to see you on my half day several times, remember?"

"I remember very well."

"One day Danny was waiting at the corner of the road and he got into the car. We drove to the marsh and sat there in the weak sunshine and watched the marsh birds. It was so good, just sitting and talking and sharing the pleasures of that lovely place."

"Then you stopped coming to see me."

"We met every week and I'd count the days. I know I'm a fool. He and I could never settle down in harmony. It only takes a suspicion that I'm being over-friendly with another man for him to start on again about my flirting ways and my desire for the attention of men. Then we'll be shouting at each other and storming off in opposite directions swearing never to speak to each other again. He'll never change. Most of the time it's wonderful, then a kind word or a smile from a stranger and the wrong response from me and anger explodes."

They were sitting in Peter's shabby office and he suggested she might like to go somewhere more comfortable. He hesitated at first, afraid any distraction would discourage her from confiding to him her concerns. He wanted to be the one she could trust.

They drove to a small beach about four miles away and stayed in the car, watching the sea, dark, pulsing, powerful, being pushed by the incoming tide and a strong wind. Clouds raced across the sky which was darkening by the minute, giving the place a menacing aura.

"Danny doesn't object to you coming to see me?" Peter asked.

"Of course not. You're a friend of long standing, like Waldo and Bertie. Even he couldn't see you as a threat. Thank goodness I have a few good friends who don't cause rows." She was looking out at the approaching storm and missed the frown and hurt expression which made his face as grey as the rest of the afternoon.

"I look forward very much to your visits," he said.

"Why don't you come to lunch on Sunday?" she asked on impulse. "Van will love to see you, and Beryl and Bertie will be there. Waldo and Melanie too. Please come."

"Thank you. I'd love to." Momentarily the frown left his face. "Will Danny be there?"

"No!"

"But you will go on meeting, and people will talk and that could lead you into trouble you'll find it hard to take. Being the other woman and facing a divorce court isn't fun, Cecily."

She didn't reply but looked down at her hands fingering the lacy gloves she had worn and which now lay like two exotic insects resting in the contours of her lap.

"Is it a special occasion, this lunch?" he asked.

"Well — yes. It's my birthday and I'm thirty."

"And I'm thirty-seven."

They were silent for a while, looking across at the pulsating sea where clouds blotted out the horizon, but nearby visibility had improved and they were able to see a pilot boat which engaged their interest, guiding a cargo boat into the docks entrance, bobbing about like a toy.

"Come on, let's go back to the beach and get some tea and sticky buns." Peter started the car and drove back along the quiet roads to the cafe.

Although rain threatened, the beach was full of late summer visitors. The gentle murmur of their chatter was interrupted occasionally by the tannoy, reporting a child found and wanting his mam, or shouting at boys for misbehaving in the sands and disturbing others.

Red-skinned bathers walked up from the sand to find cool drinks or an ice cream, and some, who during their short stay had become regulars at the green-painted stall, would chat to the girl selling teas as if she were an old friend.

The clatter of dishes told of the success of the day despite the doubtful weather as picnickers returned trays to regain their deposits or order fresh supplies. Peter left her occasionally to help the girl to clear the counter. She watched him with real affection. Such a kindly man.

Wasps were a constant hazard and they saw several children hurried along by anxious parents to the First Aid hut on the parade, to return later, still with mouths pouting in dismay but soothed and comforted. Cecily looked at Peter and they shared a look, telling each other how they felt for the injured child.

The wind had dropped as the storm had raced past and the moist heat drew smells from the wet sand and warm paving. The seas, still rough and now high on the beach, brought the smell of seaweed and Cecily tasted the salt on her lips. At each side of the bay, the tide smashed over the rocky headlands throwing plumes of white spray high in the air. The plumes were a dazzling fluorescent white in contrast to the grey rocks, sea and sky.

Cecily felt close to Peter, as if they were separate from the hubbub going on around them, invisible and unheard. She looked at him with genuine affection and touched his arm as a gesture of it. He patted her hand and held it there.

Behind them were the more mundane sounds of lively humanity, deriving the most from the last of the precious days of summer. The everpresent smell of fish and chips, the delicious smell of hot bread as a baker's boy delivered fresh supplies on a shallow board balanced on his shoulder. She soaked up the sights and sounds, aware of Peter's relaxed company and knowing it was a day to remember.

"I'm hungry," she announced and they sat like thousands of summer visitors and ate sandwiches and drank tea, which Peter poured from one of the cafe's

274

white china pots. The high tide was cooling the air and she was glad of his offer of his jacket.

The roads were filling up when they set off back to the garage to collect her car. It seemed that most of the bathers and picnickers had made the decision to leave at the same time. The car nosed its way through the jay-walking families heading for the trains and buses, and approached the edge of the town at little more than a walking pace.

Hot and tetchy children clung to their fathers' shoulders. "Like limpets with legs," Peter said with a laugh. "Sticky with ice cream and jam and smelling of the sea. A lovely cargo to carry home on a summer's evening."

"You're very poetic today, Peter." He shook his head deprecatingly.

"How is your sister-in-law Dorothy these days?" he asked as they finally picked up speed and drove past a small row of shops where shutters were being put up for the night.

"She still hints regularly that I won't marry and have children so I should make out a will in favour of Owen-Owen-named-for-his-grandfather."

"After what she did to you on the eve of your wedding?"

"She says she bitterly regrets that. But I don't," she confessed. "I was only marrying Gareth to be safe."

"Safe? Safe from whom? Danny?"

"I don't know. Just — safe."

"Perhaps Gareth isn't finished with the Owen family yet. I've seen him out several times with your other sister-in-law, Rhonwen, and her daughter, Marged."

"You have?"

"I see many people when I'm sitting in my tea stall and I'm so often there few notice me."

She was ashamed. After a niggle of jealousy. "That doesn't mean anything, going out together sometimes. After all, I've been with you for hours."

"No, us being together doesn't mean anything, being together and enjoying each other's company."

She looked at him, aware of the strangeness in his voice, but he was staring straight ahead. She couldn't see the greyness in his heart, only the defiant laughter — like the determination of the revellers earlier, to pretend the sun was still shining — showing stiffly on his face.

On Sunday, at Cecily's birthday luncheon, Bertie and Peter talked business.

"Young Edwin will be helping in the business before too long," Bertie said proudly.

"I can already read a balance sheet," Edwin said.

"And damned good he is too. Sharp as a nagging woman's elbow, our Edwin."

"I wish I could do something useful," Van sighed.

"Hark at you," Cecily said with a smile. "All you want to do after school is skip, play whip and top, or torment the boys next door."

"Only because you never give me anything interesting to do!" Van complained. "First I'm a nobody and now I'm useless. What a life to be born to. Nobody's bothered with me since Gran went away."

"Aw. Poor thing you," Edwin teased.

276

"I'm considering taking on an assistant soon," Peter told them. "The garage is quite busy and I've bought the piece of ground around it so I can take in more cars to sell, leaving the workshop free for repairs."

They discussed this for a while, then Melanie said, "Tell them, Waldo. They'll know soon anyway."

"Good news?" Cecily asked, then she saw from their faces that was not so.

"We weren't going to mention it, this being a party," Melanie said, looking at Waldo.

"We were burgled last night," Waldo said. "Jewellery, money, silver, enough to ruin our pleasure in the lovely home we have built up over the years."

"It was such a shock. Sleeping peacefully in our home, while someone came inside and —" Melanie was dry-eyed but her voice revealed the distress the thief had caused. Waldo looked angry, his cheeks bright red with the emotion he felt.

"Oh, Melanie, Waldo, I'm so sorry. When will the police catch this man!" Ada was shocked and upset.

"Your staff?" Cecily suggested. "Do you trust them?"

"Completely. I'd never believe them capable of this. The handyman was there early and he found the door wide open and I was already reaching for my dressing gown when Melanie cried out that her jewellery was gone." He sighed. "A lot of money too, I discovered later. I foolishly keep some at home for emergencies — nearly one hundred pounds."

"What can we do?" Cecily asked, hugging Melanie. "Would you like to stay here for a few days? After such an experience you must both feel too upset to sleep there."

"No, we won't be driven out of our home. It's the jewellery itself, specially chosen for special events. Its value isn't measured by the cost of replacing it."

"It charted our progress," Waldo explained. "Each piece was bought to celebrate a new success or stage in our lives."

On the following day there was more bad news. Waldo was ill. The doctor warned Melanie that it was his heart.

"He said Waldo must take things quietly for a while," Melanie sobbed. "And how can I make him do that? Loves that store he does and would die anyway if he couldn't go there every day. Oh Cecily, I'm so afraid. What will I do if he dies?"

"Tell him that. Tell him how much you need and love him. You're more important to him than the store. Just remind him — if he needs reminding. Take him on holiday, persuade him the doctor is right and make him hand over the reins to a manager. And whatever Ada and I can do, you know you only have to ask. We're so very fond of you both and we'd love the chance to help you for a change."

When Cecily and Ada took Van to see the invalid, they were relieved to find him well enough to be out of bed and already feeling stronger. He sat and listened with amusement as the four women discussed him as if he were a child, deciding for him what he must do to lighten his workload.

"I feel like the proverbial fly on the wall, sitting here learning what you think of me. Stubborn, am I? Don't know when I'm well off, don't I? Well, let me tell you this, you find me someone to run things the way they should be run and I'll gladly half — no, quarter — my working day."

"What about Owen?" Ada asked." Surely he's been with you long enough to help?"

"Confidentially, your Owen is a liability. I'd do better to trust old Zacharia Daniels, who collects other people's rubbish and sells it to people almost as badly off as he is. At least he shows some business acumen! Owen-Owen-named-for-his-grandfather, as Dorothy keeps reminding us, isn't interested in increasing his responsibilities. Give him something extra to do and he forgets all the rest! We've only kept him on because we didn't want to embarrass you two."

"Sack him, Uncle Waldo, and I'll help," Van offered. "I can serve, when these two let me!" she glared at Cecily and Ada. "And my teacher says I'm a genius at arithmetic."

"As soon as you're old enough, Van, love." Melanie gave her a hug. "Until then, I'm afraid we have to put up with your cousin Owen."

"A real pain that boy," Waldo muttered. "Fat and idle. You're worth ten of him, young Van."

"Last to arrive in the morning and first through the door when we close." Melanie sighed. "Fat he is but he slips through the door when six o'clock chimes before it's properly open!"

"What we'd give for a man like your Willie," Waldo added.

"You can't have Willie! Lost we'd be without him." Cecily turned to her sister in mock alarm. "Perhaps we'd better increase his wages again before the opposition steals him!"

"Whatever you're paying him," Waldo said, even though he knew exactly, as he dealt with their accounts, "Willie Morgan's worth double."

They didn't stay long for fear of tiring Waldo and besides, Ada wanted to get home to the meal waiting for her. Cecily was anxious to close the shop, which Willie and young David were minding, deliver Van to Beryl and Bertie and go to meet Danny.

Cecily and Van walked with Ada to her bus stop then walked down the hill past the shop and along the road with its view of the docks, to Beryl and Bertie's house.

"Edwin's got a new bike. Can I have one?" Van asked.

"No, lovey, I don't think so. It's far too dangerous for you to be on the roads."

"I could come on my own then. You wouldn't have to bring me."

"I want to come with you or at least see you off with Auntie Ada or Willie. I like to know you're safe in Auntie Beryl's care."

"I ride Edwin's bike even though it's too big for me."

"I'd rather you didn't. There are cars along the road every few minutes and it isn't safe. You're too young."

"Too young for this, too young for that," Van moaned rebelliously. She pointed to the corner of the road where Horse's wife was standing offering a cap to

280

passers-by in the hope of a few coins. "She's got more freedom than me!"

"And she begs for enough to buy food for the day and sleeps in a dirty room in a derelict house in a field!"

"I'd love it. I could do whatever I wanted. Stay up all night, eat jam sandwiches instead of the boring food you make me eat."

Cecily stopped listening and watched the woman who was usually accompanied by her husband. Strange for them not to be together. The woman wasn't singing, she just offered the hat to anyone who came near, most of whom stepped aside.

"Where's Horse?" Cecily asked as she approached. "You aren't usually out on your own." She glanced at the hat and saw that the three coins inside were foreign, obviously put there to make a jingle and encourage people to contribute. She searched in her pocket and offered some coins to Van to place in the hat but Van was stepping aside, holding her nose against the smell coming from the woman's clothes.

"Ill he is. Pneumonia so the chemist thinks. He needs some mixture to help his cough but I haven't had a penny given me today. I can't sing see, not without Horse I can't."

Cecily opened her purse and put a shilling in the woman's hand. "Use it for medicine, mind, and come to the back lane at seven and I'll find you some leftovers for your supper," she said as they walked away. She rang Willie and asked him to leave a parcel of food out in the lane for the old lady to collect.

"What about a bike?" Van asked when they were near their destination.

"No. Definitely not until you're older. Go on in, lovey, Edwin will be waiting for you."

Cecily didn't stay. She waited until Gaynor had helped Van out of her coat and scarf, then, after kissing her daughter and having a brief word with Beryl, she hurried to the bus stop. It was irritating not using the car but they hoped to avoid prying eyes by not being seen together in the well-known vehicle. The bus, taken from a distant stop, seemed a wiser plan.

Danny was waiting at the prearranged place and they sat separately on the bus which took them to a small village. They planned to go for a walk. It was all they ever did. Afraid of being seen together, the quiet village where neither was known was a haven where they could relax and forget Jessie, and the gossip their meeting would engender.

Trees were shedding their leaves, crunchy underfoot, and the wind, though not cold, made Cecily thankful she had worn her woollen coat and her brown felt hat. Danny was in brown too. A trilby worn at a rakish angle, an overcoat too large and with a belt tied without using the buckle, and tied in an untidy knot.

There was always an air of devil-may-care about Danny. The earring he wore glinted in the light from street lamps which had just had the attention of the lamp-lighter doing his round on a bicycle, his long pole balanced with practised ease as he rode past them onto the next.

282

She went into his arms as soon as they found a quiet place and felt the warmth of him flooding through her as he held her tight, reassuring her with a kiss that all was well. She was always nervous when they met, dreading the suspicion in his eyes that began many of their evenings together. It might be a chance remark about a customer, or even the way she thanked the conductor as he helped her off the bus. The innocent words would have apparently passed without trouble but the time between parting and meeting again would allow suspicion to incubate and produce that monster of jealousy that so often ruined their time together. Tonight, as she studied his waywardly handsome face, everything was perfect.

The man in the almost deserted bar room obviously wanted to talk. He tried several times to include himself in their conversation but Danny blocked him. Then he came and sat beside them, a small man, dressed in a navy suit with a white muffler around his neck. He was clearly impressed with Cecily's figure in the soft blue woollen jumper.

"Haven't I seen you here before?" he asked.

"I don't think so." She smiled as she spoke, leaning towards him slightly to avoid having to speak loudly. It was a friendly, automatic smile as she would use to customers in the shop but one to which Danny, returning from the bar, took offence.

Before she could say anything, the innocent man was hauled to his feet, his startled face turning red above the white scarf.

"Come on, Danny! We're leaving!" She stood up, abandoning their untouched drinks and walked out into the darkness. To her relief, Danny followed, leaving the man shaken and angry. She walked swiftly in the direction of the bus stop.

"Where are you going?" Danny called, running after her, pulling her back.

"Home! I can't stand any more of this. A word to someone, a polite word, and that look is back on your face. I can't stand it any longer."

"But why? I didn't say anything! I just helped him back to his own seat. I ignored it. Although I could see how you were egging him on. I was going to suggest we finished our drinks and leave."

"You think I was leading him on?" She stopped and glared at him.

"Of course you were. Just like you always do. You don't know when you're doing it."

Through the darkness she saw the lights of a bus approaching and she was glad. The longer this went on the worse she would feel.

"Don't get on the bus," he pleaded. "I'm sorry you're upset but after all it is your fault. Blame me if you must, but it isn't me who starts it. Did you see me flirting with the woman behind the bar? Did you? She was worth a wink if anyone was."

Cecily couldn't trust herself to speak. It had always been like this. As soon as she began to relax and believe that things would change, out would come stupid accusations like this. She was a fool to be standing here listening to it. After all the years she'd known Danny she had to be crazy to be still taking this abuse. Because, she told herself, abuse was what it was, even though said in such reasonable tones.

"We've been getting on so well, Cecily. If only you'd stop leading men on. I really thought you were trying to change. I love you. Isn't my love enough? See how much happier we've been since you gave up dancing. That proves the fault for our quarrelling is with you, doesn't it?"

He tried to hold her as the bus slowed and stopped for her but she shook him off angrily and stepped on. She saw him standing there, watching the bus fade from his sight.

"I hope I never see him again," she muttered.

The man sitting next to her smiled politely and asked her to speak up.

"I hate him!" she said vehemently, and the man looked startled and turned his head. He didn't glance her way again and when a seat became vacant further down the aisle he scuttled thankfully into it.

CHAPTER
FOURTEEN

Willie was excited as he parked the shop van at the lower end of town and went to the expensive china shop. The windows were full of tea and dinner services as well as ornaments in fine china and glass. He merely glanced at the tempting array. He knew what he wanted. He had been saving for this special gift since before he and Annette had married. Her dream, and his task to bring it to fruition.

The young lady assistant came up to him and asked how she might help and he handed her the piece of paper that had been in his pocket for more than a week.

"It's the china I ordered for my wife," he said. "Green, best china with lots of gold on the rims and handles."

She brought out a sample. "Here we are. Ainsley and very expensive, sir. It's so beautiful, your wife will be delighted. A surprise gift, is it?"

He nodded. "She worked in service for a while and always talked about this china. So as soon as I'd saved enough I ordered it for her. I'll be in later to order more. I'm going to keep adding to it, see, so she has plenty no matter how many friends come calling."

The assistant gazed longingly after the tall, handsome man as he left, clutching the long-awaited china. If only, she dreamed, if only I could meet someone as gorgeous and generous. She heard the intake of breath behind her that she knew would be followed by the reminder that she was there to work and not daydream. She picked up her duster to make sure not a speck of dust would blemish the treasures the shop contained.

Willie drove slowly, his cargo so special he felt like shouting complaints to all the drivers who overtook him and to the woman who stepped out uncaring into the road and made him stand on the brakes. He had seen every item of the tea set wrapped and packed and he knew that if there was a crack or a chip, he would be to blame. It had to be perfect, like Annette.

It was because he was driving slowly that he noticed Jessie Preston. He slowed even more, wondering whether he should drive past or speak to her. But the decision was made for him as he saw her stop and knock at the door of number seven Slate Street, where his mother-in-law Dorothy lived. Gently he pressed the accelerator and glided past unnoticed. I wonder what Jessie wants with her, he mused idly. Then he concentrated on getting the china safely home and forgot all about her.

Dorothy was bored. There was only Owen for company and when he wasn't at Waldo Watkins' store he had his face in a comic, only surfacing for food. So when she had an occasional day off, she spent it doing nothing more interesting than housework and cooking, at which she did not excel, or listening to the wireless.

The knock, when it came just after two o'clock, had her jumping from her chair in excitement at the prospect of someone calling for a chat. She glanced quickly around the room to check for neatness, hid her knitting under a cushion and opened the door.

"Mrs Owen? Remember me? I'm Jessie, Mrs Danny Preston. D'you think we might have a word?"

Dorothy ushered the small red-haired woman into the living room, her mind whirling with curiosity, her tongue twisting with the effort to control the questions lining up to be asked. In a display of patience which surprised herself, she waited until they had tea and biscuits in front of them, the kettle singing with the prospect of a second cup, before tilting her head to one side in silent request for Jessie to explain the reason for her visit.

"Danny and I are separated," Jessie began nervously. "I know it's a cheek, me coming here to worry you, almost a stranger, for help, but —"

"Nonsense. How can I help you, dear? You only have to ask." She smiled encouragingly. If this was anything to do with Cecily, she very much wanted to "help"! "Don't worry about mentioning my sister-in-law," she said. "I do know about her — seeing — your husband." She whispered the final words behind a hand.

"You do?" Jessie visibly relaxed. "That's a relief. I didn't know where to start."

"Seen together often," Dorothy whispered even though the house was empty apart from themselves.

288

"Terrible for you, and —" The hand came up again. "And you pregnant, is it?"

"You're right. It's a miracle though. Danny hardly bothered me in that way. He treated me more like a housekeeper than a wife."

"A housekeeper? You poor girl." Dorothy looked at Jessie with deep concern, as if that was the worst fate a woman could suffer.

"Danny doesn't know. He wouldn't want me to have it. I was pregnant once before and he pleaded and even threatened to leave me if I didn't go to someone and get rid of it as he put it. I didn't, of course, but I lost it anyway a few weeks later. I haven't told anyone about this and I don't want anyone to know." She looked down at her lap where her thin hands held her empty cup. "There's something else, you see."

Dorothy refilled their cups and looked at her visitor expectantly.

Cecily fumed through the days that followed the latest row with Danny. Breaking the silence of weeks, she blurted it out to Ada, expecting nothing more than criticism, but needing to talk about it if only to clarify the situation in her own mind.

"All he wants is to have me under lock and key so only he can see me. I'd be nothing more than a possession. Ada, I've been such a fool, I really have. Loving him, letting life slip past, wasting all these precious years. I must be insane."

"The saddest thing is, you were saying this more than fifteen years ago. All this precious time you've

289

wasted on Danny and all the time you knew it wouldn't work."

"I believed that if his love grew so he really cared for me, for the person I am, it would come right. I've never met anyone else I could love as I loved Danny."

"What about Gareth?"

"I loved him, in a way, but not with the passion Danny arouses in me."

"I thought I loved Gareth for a while. I really believed it was me he wanted to take out."

"You never said."

"There's a lot I never said," Ada replied.

"You're happy now, though, with Phil?"

"Oh, yes. He's fun and so caring. D'you know he's trying to reduce his limp to please me? He practises and thinks I don't know. Remember how he walked down the aisle for me? His leg was agony for days. The other night," she went on, "I woke and found his side of the bed empty so I went down to see where he was and saw a light in his shed. He's got electricity now. He doesn't like me going down there, what with the inks and the machinery he's afraid I'll hurt myself. So I looked through the window and he was walking up and down, to and from the bench, walking as straight as you and me!"

"But that's amazing, Ada."

"He often can't sleep, you know. I think it's the pain. He goes down there and works at improving his walk. Yes," she said, reverting to the question, "I'm very happy."

290

"I'm glad, Ada love. At least one of us has found the right one."

"There is one disappointment and it isn't a great problem. I feel guilty telling you, but I don't do anything to look after Phil, his mother does it all. She still runs the house and chooses the meals. I feel like a spare part. All our wedding gifts are wrapped up and packed in the attic. I don't feel I'm properly married, more of a lodger in Mrs Spencer's house. But, as for Phil and me, it couldn't be better."

"How is Mrs Spencer with you? She isn't resentful, is she?"

"No, never. But Cecily, she's so funny. She asks me to read bits out of the paper then goes across to chat to her friends about it as if she's reading it herself. Even finding the place for them if they have the same newspaper. I've offered to teach her to read but she refuses. She's a lovely lady and I think she enjoys the fun of it.

"Yesterday she was telling Gladys Davies how shocked she was about the Prince of Wales and the American divorcee. 'And her admiring Hitler too,' she was saying. It's clever, the way she does it. And all these burglaries; remembering names, addresses and everything. Her memory is fantastic."

After the months during which they hardly revealed a single thought to each other, both sisters were happy to return to their former closeness. Cecily talked for a long time about her feelings for Danny and how ashamed she was that she had been prepared to marry Gareth without loving him in the same way.

Ada made Cecily laugh at the antics of Phil and his mother whose capacity for fun seemed endless. Laughter released tension between them and refreshed them, and they were reminded of the misplaced close friendship they had almost lost.

"Danny said he thought we'd got on better since I gave up dancing. That has made me determined to start again. I was a fool to give up, although it did seem strange, going without you."

"Tell you what, I'll ask Phil if he would mind me going with you, just for the first few times. You'll soon meet up with the usual crowd. Beryl and Bertie will have our Van, won't they?"

Phil raised no objection and the sisters agreed to go the following Saturday. Cecily treated herself to a permanent wave and bought a dress that swung from her hips in a shimmer of silver blue. The neckline was daringly low, revealing the rise of her breasts in a V of sequinned trim. She was excited as she and Ada set off, Willie having stayed late to take them in Cecily's car.

"Take it home with you, Willie," Cecily offered. "Take Annette somewhere nice tomorrow. Thanks for staying late."

"Sure you don't want me to meet you?" he offered but they promised to get a taxi.

For the sisters, the evening was a mixed success. It was a happy time renewing old acquaintances but sad to realize how few there were. Most had married and given up the regular evenings out, staying at home to mind babies instead. Unemployment too had reduced numbers. The resulting poverty had brought an end to the carefree days of their youth.

They had ordered a taxi for eleven o'clock and Cecily — and, she suspected, Ada as well — felt relief when they could leave, in a wave of promises to keep in touch. She knew the moment had gone and she couldn't go back.

"Perhaps we'll start again when the babies are grown up and the work comes back to the town," Ada said, guessing her thoughts. "It's no good trying to recreate something that's gone, is it?"

"Not even Gareth was there. Unless he saw me and remembered his mother's warning that I am a dangerous woman!" She laughed but there was little humour in it.

"He doesn't go very often, so I hear. His mother is his problem — what's new! Every time he plans to go out she flops a fit and he has to fetch the doctor and stay with her until she recovers."

"Old witch!"

When the taxi arrived Cecily was pleased to see it was their cousin, Johnny Fowler, driving. "Glad to see you're working, Johnny," she said as he opened the door for them.

"Only just," he told her. "I only work at weekends. It isn't much but with the occasional day in the week, Mam manages somehow. Several of my friends have moved to London looking for better prospects." He tucked a rug around their feet. "Terrible being poor. When you're a child and there's always food when you want it, you can't imagine it ever being different. Not that we go short. Not like some. Mam's a good manager."

Cecily decided she'd send a box of groceries each week to the Fowlers. His father had been on the sick for months and it must be a nightmare for his mother to feed them all. Ada gave him a generous tip, which he refused.

"Come off it, Ada. I can't take that from you."

"Sorry, Johnny, I wasn't thinking."

They dropped Ada off first and as he helped Cecily out at the shop, he asked, "Be all right, will you? I mean, is there anyone waiting up for you?"

"Not any more, Johnny, love. I'm on my own now."

"Shall I come in for a minute?"

"No need, honestly. I'll be all right. Lovely to see you. Give our love to your mam and dad." She waited until the sound of the engine had faded completely and there was no further excuse to delay. She didn't want to go in. The dance had been more than a disappointment, it had made her face the realization that a stage of her life was over.

The key in the lock sounded extra loud and as she closed the door the bell sent its echoes around the empty rooms; a lonely mocking ghost. The light in the living room was low but the curtains between the room and the shop were drawn and little light showed through. Shadows grew as she stood there, her eyes becoming accustomed to the gloom, separating positive and negative, the substantial from the phantom. Shapes sprawled and moved towards her and still she didn't move.

294

Here, in the dark shop, she could still pretend there was someone waiting for her, and here, there was only a glass door separating her from people in the street. Once through the dark shop and into the living room she would be engulfed by emptiness, only cold rooms on all sides.

The living room was chilled and unwelcoming, the fire grey and lifeless. She coaxed it with some wood, took off her coat and sat waiting for the kettle to boil, feeling more dejected than at any time in her life. There was nowhere she belonged anymore, except here in the shop that had once been a joy and now was a prison. As she reached to lift the kettle, she saw years ahead of her, sitting here night after night alone and with no prospect of a change.

In a few years Van would leave. And anyway, because of the situation, they had failed to build a good relationship. It's all because of my obsession with Danny, she thought, pouring tea from a teapot ridiculously large for her solitary cup. If it hadn't been for Danny, I'd have accepted many invitations over the years. If it hadn't been for him, I wouldn't have an illegitimate daughter and a reputation that scares people away.

"Damn you, Danny Preston!" She said the words aloud, her fists clenched, wanting to hit him, pummel him for ruining her life.

She cursed Dorothy too, for the cancellation of her marriage to Gareth. It wouldn't have been perfect, being Gareth's wife, but once his mother had been sorted, a good life. And Danny's fascination would have faded. As she sat there, staring into the fire, she finally faced the fact that she was the one who was truly to blame. Why couldn't she be strong? But she could change, couldn't she? Starting from today? Perhaps the dance was more than a disappointment; it was a catalyst for her facing her demons and driving them away.

The teapot grew cold and she made fresh tea, brightened the fire, doing anything to avoid the moment when she'd have to undress in the cold lonely dark and try to sleep. She put down her cup and closed her eyes. She stayed there, her coat across her, until a cockerel crowed in a nearby yard, then changed out of the shimmering dress into a jumper and skirt, ready to begin another day.

"Damn Danny, damn Danny Preston," was her morning chant as she set breakfast for herself. "Damn Danny and damn Dorothy with her evil mischief over such a small inheritance."

Dorothy said nothing to the sisters about Jessie Preston's visit, but when she visited her daughter, she couldn't resist talking around the edges of the new development.

"There's wicked of Cecily, going out with that Danny Preston, knowing he's a married man."

"Best not to gossip over something we know nothing about." Willie spoke with such censure, protective as always of the sisters, that Dorothy felt unable to continue. She sat knitting, discussing clothes for the new arrival with Annette.

Willie sat in the back kitchen, where the sink and boiler half filled the small room. He was at the table, sacking spread around his feet to catch the scrolls of wood as he planed the top of a stool. He worked rhythmically and without pause, except to occasionally hold it aloft to make sure the shape was perfect.

The planing finished, he began rubbing with a sheet of sandpaper before placing the finished piece with the others, ready to be varnished.

"Time you were in bed, Annette love," he said as the big wall-clock struck ten. "You mustn't tire yourself."

"Yes, I must go." Dorothy stood up, packed away her knitting and kissed her daughter.

"I'll walk with you as far as the bus stop, Mother-in-law." Willie reached for his coat and cap.

"No need." Dorothy did not feel at ease with Willie, although she had to admit he cared for Annette admirably. "I'll only be a minute walking to the church corner."

It was dry and bitterly cold, with a wind rustling the leaves along the gutters as she hurried to the bus stop outside the walls of the ancient churchyard. A public house was almost joined to the church and she watched in disgust as two men tumbled, laughing, out of its doorway, helped on their way by the toe of the landlord's boot. Such a wicked waste of money, she thought with a curl of her lip. They probably had children at home, trying to sleep with empty bellies. She didn't recognize them or she'd have told their wives to be more firm.

One of the drunken men stumbled and lurched towards her and she quickly darted into the shadow of the wall. She waited, holding her breath as he approached a nearby tree and peed noisily close to her, his eyes not seeing her stiffened shape as she turned her head in embarrassment. He stood for a while as if unsure which direction led to home, and all the time Dorothy crouched, hardly daring to breathe. People on the street dwindled to none before he lurched away.

As she was about to leave her hiding place another shadow appeared. She stayed hidden and waited. She wished she had accepted Willie's offer to walk with her. You never knew who you'd meet in this area. To her surprise she recognized Phil Spencer walking towards her.

He climbed the stone wall, hardly visible in the meagre light from a lamp outside the public house and slithered like an eel over the top, to drop with hardly a sound on the other side. She found a jutting stone and risked a look over the wall to see him leaving the churchyard by the gate on the opposite side and disappearing into the lane beyond.

She was thankful when the bus came but she didn't go straight home. She alighted at the police station to report what she had seen.

"Supposed to be a cripple he is, but he can't fool me," she told the sergeant. "I saw no sign of a limp. He's that burglar the papers are full of for sure."

Ada was startled by the late-night knock at the door. She peered down at the policemen standing outside and hurriedly dressed before going down. She looked anxious as she explained, "My mother-in-law is in bed but my husband is still in his workshop if you want to talk to him."

"If you please, Mrs Spencer. Sorry about the lateness of the call."

With a curious look at the solemn-faced young men in their tall, silver-trimmed helmets, she went down to the workshop, knocking before opening the door and calling, "Phil, love, it's the police. They want to talk to you."

"Me? Whatever for? Not wanting tickets at this time of night, are they?" He limped through to the living room and leaned heavily on the table to ease his aching leg. Ada noticed he was sweating slightly and thought she would persuade him to visit the doctor again. His leg seemed worse lately. He must be straining it trying to walk without a limp.

"Phil, sit down and rest that leg. You've overdone the exercises again, haven't you?"

The police asked him to explain his movements that evening and he told them that, apart from going out to post a letter, he'd been working on Christmas orders for dances and raffles.

"One of my busiest times, it is, see," he said, and went on, refusing to be interrupted, to explain how important it was for him to work late. "I daren't refuse work. January and February are pretty lean and I need all I can get now. Printing is spasmodic, see — weddings in May, June and July, of course — but real printing is less easy to come by and —" He went on until the constables, having partaken of tea and cakes, thankfully left, their heads reeling with the lecture on the problems of the small printer.

"What was all that about?" Ada asked.

"I don't know but it's nothing for us to worry about. They wondered if I had seen anything suspicious. At least I think that's what they said." He winked and went on, "I didn't give them a chance to say much, did I?" He hugged her. "Come on, Mrs Spencer, let's go to bed."

Outside the policemen agreed there was little doubt about the man being a cripple. "The woman made a mistake."

"A relation, wasn't she? The informant? Terrible rows there are in some families. I bet that's what it was here. Still, we'll report it and let others decide whether he needs watching or not."

"That cup of tea was welcome, though." They continued their round, having written up the relevant details in their notebooks and, out of sight, finished off the cakes Ada had insisted they took with them, with relish.

Owen's shop was filled to overflowing with the extra needs of the Christmas season. With only ten days to go, the sacks of nuts and crates of oranges and boxes of apples were being constantly replenished. Figs, dates and tangerines added to the displays. Willie took the sack truck and walked to the wholesalers except when the load was large, then he took the van.

300

The extra scents of fruit and spices filled the air with the subtle reminders of the approaching season. Van had decorated the shop with greenery gathered by herself and Edwin in the fields outside the town. Holly and mistletoe hung in corners, garlands draped the walls. Bolder colour was added with balloons blown up by Van and Edwin, with an air of contagious fun.

The stables with their cellar and loft were now extra storage and sacks of potatoes and corn and other dried goods were kept there. Willie set dozens of mousetraps to prevent the stock being spoilt and used everything in strict rotation to ensure they sold only the best. Any fruit and vegetables past their prime were still given to Jack Simmons to sell to those unable to afford better.

It was a busy time and for Willie, an anxious one. Their baby was due any day and although he knew Gladys Davies wouldn't leave Annette's side, he didn't like leaving her all day.

"The baby will probably come in the middle of the night," Cecily said. "They usually do. Everyone I ask says the same. You're busy all day then you settle to sleep and they announce their imminent arrival."

"What time was Van born?" he asked.

"Midday! But she was bound to be awkward. Don't worry, you'll be there when Annette needs you."

"I'll go home at midday, though, just in case."

Every day he'd dash home when the shop was reasonably quiet and the sisters didn't need anything urgently, and spend a while with Annette. Now her time was near Willie thought her more beautiful than ever. Her face was rounded, her arms deliciously plump and her eyes glowed with happiness.

"I can't believe my luck," he murmured as he settled her into a chair to rest when he went back to the shop. "Luckiest man in the whole of Wales I am, for sure."

It did happen at night. Willie heard the slightest of sighs from her and was awake in a moment, reaching out and holding her.

"What is it, love? The baby is it? Oh, damn me, I'll go and knock up Gladys this minute."

"No, Willie, not yet. Stay with me and hold me. I don't want you to go from me yet."

He settled back on the pillow but his eyes were wide open, staring up at the ceiling as though gripped in terror. Every time she moved or made the slightest sound he started up, only to be calmed by Annette.

"Not yet, love," she whispered. "Try to rest. I'll tell you when it's time to fetch Gladys and phone the doctor. I don't want any false alarms and have them calling me a sissy. And it costs money to get the doctor out."

"This is daft beyond," he said with a groan. "Me lying here being comforted by you! I'm supposed to be the strong one."

"You are, Willie. Strong and caring and a giant among men."

It was a little after two when a gasp and a shout made him insist on fetching help.

"All right, go, you. Nothing will happen in the few minutes you'll take to call Gladys."

"I'm calling the doctor too," he said, jumping into his trousers. "No arguments, right?"

Gladys came at once and waited with Annette while Willie ran up the green lane, jumped the railings, raced through the park and down to the doctor's house. He didn't wait for a lift back but ran home the way he had come. He saw the doctor's car approaching as he reached the bottom of the green lane.

He raised his hand to wave to the doctor and at that moment saw a figure break out of the shadows at the bottom of the road. He gasped with horror as the doctor's car hit the indistinct figure and threw it like a pile of rags, into the air. It seemed to hover for a moment suspended by an invisible hand, before dropping onto the car and sliding down to the ground.

He felt no sympathy for the injured man; only fury that he had delayed the doctor from reaching his beloved wife. He ran to the spot where the doctor was kneeling beside the fallen man and said, "Go, man. My wife needs you." Willie was in a panic of fear at the thought of Annette needing help and his voice was high and loud. "I'll see to him. I'll knock someone up and send him for the police. Just go, will you?" He began tugging at the doctor's coat.

"I can't leave the scene of an accident," the doctor said calmly.

"What accident? There never was no accident." The injured man stood up, stiff but apparently without serious injury. Willie recognized the voice of Phil Spencer.

"Phil? What the hell are you doing out at this time? My wife needs this doctor so tell him you're all right and let him go, will you?"

"No need to call the police. I'm only bruised. I couldn't sleep, that's all. Let me get away from your fussing!"

"He does appear to have avoided any serious damage," the doctor said.

"Then bugger off and leave me go home," Phil whined.

"Come on, Doctor! Get to my wife. She's having a baby, now this minute!"

Up and down the road doors were opening and a crowd soon gathered to see what had happened. Phil moved with a pronounced limp to lean on the wall of a house, pushing the doctor away as he tried to continue his examination.

Someone had gone for the policeman who lived nearby and someone else brought out a chair for Phil to sit on. Many shouted about the stupidity of using cars at night and one old man insisted they should run on rails like trains do, "not run as wild as they like on roads, bumping into people," he insisted loudly, creating laughter in the group of curious bystanders.

"If you'll give me a hand, and a shoulder to lean on, I'll get myself home," Phil insisted. He was clutching his coat tightly around him with one hand. The other he waved hopefully at Willie.

"Hurt your chest, have you?" Willie asked, pointing to the doctor then at his home where the door was open and the house well lit. "I'll see to him, you go to my wife."

"Your chest?" the doctor asked.

"Not hurt at all, I keep telling you. I want to go home!"

Willie began to walk with him, while the crowd shouted encouragement and the doctor tried in vain to make him stay, following them with the chair and pleading for Phil to be sensible.

"*You* be sensible and get to my wife!" Willie shouted back. He ushered the man away like a mad dog. He glared at Phil, who was limping along beside him, still holding his chest. "You pick your moments, don't you! Why choose tonight of all nights to go wandering in front of cars?"

They were in sight of the church when a car entered the road.

"Hang about," someone called, "it's the police."

Willie hurried Phil unceremoniously back across the road. "Damn me, I want to get back to Annette. Having a baby she is." He pulled Phil roughly and turned him to face the policeman now running towards them. "Take him, somebody. Let me and the doctor see to my wife!"

"Just one minute, sir, I'll be as quick as I can, seeing your predicament. Now, what damage did you sustain from the vehicle?" he asked Phil, who was struggling to get away and was being held by one shoulder by Willie, who handed him to the policeman like a parcel.

"Fine, I am. Just fine."

"Looks like he's hurt his chest," someone said. The crowd had regrouped around them and was growing by the minute as more neighbours were woken by the voices.

"Best you take a look, Doctor." The constable ignored Phil's continuing pleas that he was "just fine" and his protests turned to a wail of dismay as, after another push from the impatient Willie, several silver items fell from his coat and landed on the ground with a musical clatter.

"It looks to me, sir, that we might have found our burglar."

The shock passed through Willie almost without giving a thought to the repercussions. He could think only of Annette and her need of him. He was letting her down. Grabbing the doctor's arm, he pointed again to his house. "Look, Constable, that's where we'll be, all right? Come on, Doc, we've got to go. My wife is more important that all this." Dragging the bemused doctor and still shouting explanations to the policeman, Willie ran across the road and sighed with relief when the doctor finally climbed the stairs.

He was shaking as he handed Gladys a kettle of hot water and the clothes Annette had put ready, then he waited, walking around the room like a caged animal, still not giving a thought to Ada and what she would be dealing with. His ears were tuned to hear the slightest sound from above and at last came the kitten-like wail followed by the doctor saying, "Well done, Mrs Morgan. Congratulations on the birth of a fine healthy son."

Standing at the foot of the stairs, one foot on the second step ready to bound up the moment he was allowed, he waited again. Gladys's head appeared and she smiled. "It's a boy, Willie. A beautiful boy!"

Willie contained his patience a little longer, until the doctor called him. "Come on up. She won't settle to sleep until you've seen her and this wonderful son of yours."

Willie was up the stairs two at a time and into the bedroom before he'd finished speaking. He was trembling as he went across to the bed. Annette was sitting smiling at him, her face red from her exertions but with hair neatly combed and wearing a pretty nightdress specially bought for after the birth. "Was it very bad, love?"

"It's over now, and look, Willie, look at our son."

He kissed her gently before looking at the bundled little person lying beside her. Tears filled his eyes for the first time since he'd left school. The wrinkled old/new face was not that of a stranger, but of a long-awaited loved one. "He's perfect," he sobbed, "and so are you, my lovely, clever Annette."

He stayed with Annette, knowing he wouldn't be able to sleep. Gladys stayed until morning. "Only a few hours," she told him, "just in case you have to go again for the doctor." Like Willie, she was too exhilarated by the drama and the wonder of it all to sleep.

Willie went outside before dawn, looking up at the stars, breathing the sweet night air, reliving the wonder of that first sight of his son. It was a while before he noticed there were still lights on at the Spencers' house.

He thought he'd go and tell Ada the wonderful news and only then did the memory of Phil's disgrace come back to him and the realization that Ada was in real trouble. He checked for the twentieth time that Annette was sleeping and Gladys was not, and went out.

Ada answered his first hesitant knock. She had been crying, her face was swollen and her hair untidy. She was fully dressed and held a coat over her arm. "Oh, it's you, Willie," she spoke dully as if his calling so early was a normal event. "I thought it was the police. They've taken him and —" She broke down and Willie guided her into the living room where Mrs Spencer sat, rocking in a chair and staring into a blazing fire. She didn't look up when Willie spoke to her.

"Sorry I am for what happened. I hope you don't think it was me who caused it."

"No. Phil insisted you weren't to blame. It was misfortune that you called the doctor at that time. How is Annette?" she forced herself to ask.

"Lovely thanks. We have a son and we're going to call him Victor, after your brother, Annette's father."

"I'm glad." She began to cry again. "It's just a pity that the doctor came at that moment and hit Phil." She poured a cup of tea and handed it to him. "I knew nothing of all this. You do believe that?" Willie nodded. "If I had, I'd have stopped it before he was caught, and made him give it all back. We didn't need it!"

"I'm sure you would." He sipped the tea and asked, "Does Cecily know yet?" He had been referring to them by their Christian names in private for a long time and tonight, fatherhood had made him brave. "I'll go over and tell her, shall I? Now Annette's safe and sleeping, Gladys won't mind staying a while longer. Grinning down at the baby, she is, as if he's her achievement. She certainly played a part and we're very grateful."

"Glad I am for you and Annette, such wonderful news. No, I don't think there's any point waking Cecily. There's nothing she can do. Let her sleep."

"I'll drive you to work at the usual time, then? Bring you back as soon as you've talked to her."

"Thanks." She smiled then, the swollen face contorting itself into more of a grimace than the kindly expression she hoped. "You won't want to stay long either, will you?"

"No, not long."

"Young David will have to cope for a few days." She turned from him, fingers twisting in her sodden handkerchief. "Willie, they found Dadda's watch, the one we gave you and which was lost. Hidden in his workshop, smashed to pieces it was. I can't think how it happened. Fell probably and got something dropped on it. Sorry."

"Don't be. It was Phil, remember, not you."

Willie glanced at the figure near the fire. Mrs Spencer hadn't moved since he had arrived and he didn't know whether to touch her, say a few words of comfort, but Ada guessed his thought as he began to rise and she shook her head.

"I've often wondered about cash," she said. "I'm not a complete fool. I've tried to persuade him to talk about our finances but he never would. He's refused to take a penny from me since we were married, insisting it's the man's job to provide for his family. Pride, you see, but I did wonder. He never seems that busy, yet we never go short of a thing."

Willie touched her shoulder, gesturing towards the door and said he had to go. She merely nodded in reply. Then he went back to Annette, promising to call for Ada at 7.30.

The first thing he did when he had greeted Annette and gently kissed their son was to give her the parcel from the china shop. "My gift for you, my lovely, wonderful wife, to thank you for all the happiness you give." Opening and unwrapping the Ainsley china was a joy for them both, she because it was such a wonderful surprise and he for the delight she showed.

Cecily woke at 6.30 and began her day. She prepared breakfast, attended to the fire and wrote out the list of goods needed from the wholesalers. She didn't worry too much when Willie was later than usual but she wondered whether Annette's baby had arrived. Such a pity neither Willie nor Dorothy were on the phone.

She opened the door as Phil's car stopped outside and was surprised to see Willie driving. Thinking about the baby, she was smiling as she greeted him. As soon as Ada turned to face her she knew that something was wrong. Not the baby, she pleaded silently. But it was Ada who showed distress. She ran out and with an arm around Ada, asked what had happened.

In the room behind the shop, with the shop door still closed and in semi darkness, Ada told her. About the

310

birth of Annette's baby causing Phil to be caught with stolen silver under his coat.

"All those burglaries, the police say it was Phil. Been watching him they have, after someone reported that he wasn't the cripple he pretended to be and was often out at night. Oh, Cecily, I thought he was trying to lose his limp to please me and all the time it wasn't true."

"Best you go home, love, Mrs Spencer needs you now. And what about you, Willie? With the new baby you'll want to be with Annette. Go on, the pair of you. I'll manage all right with young David."

The post flopped through the letterbox when she went to see them off and she picked it up and tucked it in her pocket.

"Give Annette my love, Willie. Does Dorothy know she's a grandmother yet?"

"I'll call there on my way home. I should catch her before she leaves for work."

Cecily got through the morning like an automaton. She hardly heard the friendly chatter of her customers, dreading the first remark telling her the news was out. But when she closed the shop at lunchtime no one had mentioned Phil being connected with the burglaries. Perhaps it was a mistake, she hoped foolishly.

She was starting to prepare her lunch when she remembered the letters. She picked up a coat, intending to visit Ada, then her fingers touched the envelopes. She put them on the counter, deciding to read them later, but one caught her eye, large and official, and she slid her thumb under the seal and opened it. When she read the contents she gave a little scream of dismay. Discarding her coat and hat, she ran to the phone and dialled Peter Marshall.

"It's me, Cecily. Can you come straightaway?"

He arrived in minutes, alarmed by the hysteria in her voice.

First of all she told him about the arrest of Phil then she handed him the letter with a shaking hand. "Ada in serious trouble, and now this," she said with a sob.

Peter read the letter and looked at her, his hands holding her shoulders. "So," he said quietly, "Jessie Preston is suing for divorce. I wonder who gave her the idea of citing you, my dear?" He held her against him and waited for the sobs to subside. "Don't worry, Cecily, you aren't alone. We'll deal with this together. Whatever happens, I will always be here."

CHAPTER
FIFTEEN

The shop opened later than usual and Cecily was unaware of the voices outside demanding to be served, or the bangs on the glass shop door by the more impatient. She and Peter stood discussing the implications of the solicitor's letter telling her she would be cited in the divorce proceedings between Danny and Jessie.

"I'd never dreamed Jessie would do such a thing. A divorce? Isn't separation enough? She surely doesn't want to remarry? What other reason can there be?"

"Humiliating me, changing the focus from her maybe. Knowing people are talking about her and perhaps laughing at her? An immoral woman is more exciting gossip than a foolish one."

"People aren't always sympathetic or kind," Peter said sadly.

"Don't I know it! When the truth came out about Myfanwy I experienced plenty of gossip, the conversations that suddenly stopped when I appeared, and the knowing looks and the half smiles that didn't reach the eyes. But Jessie? I can't believe she'd do this."

"Someone must have encouraged her. I agree it doesn't seem to be in her nature to make you face this.

Not from any affection for you," he interrupted as Cecily began to speak, "but facing the humiliation of standing up in court and telling the world that her husband had been unfaithful, and having people remarking that some of the fault must be hers. She doesn't seem brave enough for all that."

"I feel ashamed, and very sorry for Jessie. Whatever I feel for Danny, and how I feel about this," she said, waving the letter, "she's suffering and she's done nothing to deserve it apart from — like me — loving Danny who doesn't deserve her love."

"How d'you feel about him now?" he asked, holding his breath as he waited for her reply. "However guilty you feel, most of the blame is his, surely?"

"I think —" There was a sudden increased banging on the door and she pulled away from his comforting arms. "I think I'd better open the shop before someone breaks the door down."

"Will you be all right?"

She straightened up, brushed her hair back over her shoulders with an impatient hand and forced a smile. "Of course I will."

He went through and opened the door, hoping none of the impatient customers would have heard the news about Phil. Brave as she was, Cecily needed at least a little time to prepare for the gossip with the exaggerations and inventions of a new source of excitement. When he left an hour later, she was busy dealing with the early morning rush and smiling and laughing with her customers as though she hadn't a care in the world.

314

The morning seemed neverending. The clock on the living-room wall and visible from the shop seemed hardly to move between her glances, and the customers more anxious to chat than usual making the time drag even more. Her thoughts were on Ada and she was impatient to go and see what she could do to help her cope with the arrest of Phil. She had never really liked Phil, had found him a bit edgy, unable to meet her eye and relax with her. She had begun to think the fault was with her, that her mistrust of him as a husband for Ada had created his uneasiness, but now all her mistrust returned. Ada had deserved someone better. Anger grew as she thought of him causing such anguish for Ada and between such thoughts were panics of her own, with the threat of a court case hovering over her. Why was life so difficult for them? She and Ada did nothing out of the ordinary, apart from her stupid infatuation with Danny. Few people were completely innocent of misdeeds and nothing disturbed the run of their day-to-day lives, but she and Ada faced problem after problem.

The minutes passed and no one mentioned the arrest of her brother-in-law and she began to think it had been a mistake and he had been released — but Willie would have let her know.

When at last the hands of the clock moved to one o'clock, she ushered out the last few customers and grabbed her coat. As she drove to her sister's home she tried to rehearse what she would say. She parked the car and ran in, hardly waiting for the door to open on her sister's stricken face before pushing in and holding Ada and allowing her tears to fall.

They stood for a long time, neither speaking, just holding each other until Ada's sobs ceased. Then they went into the room where Cecily saw Mrs Spencer sitting like a statue, staring into the fire. She didn't react to Cecily's greeting or her words of sympathy, just stared at the fire, unaware of its need for coals, or the ash spilled onto the hearth. It was the first time Cecily had ever seen anything out of place in the normally neat room and as Ada sat down, she went to the fire and piled on some coal and brushed the hearth as though that insult to Mrs Spencer's house was the most important thing.

"What d'you want me to do, love?" she asked. Ada shook her head.

"I'll get us something to eat, shall I? That's the first thing. I'm starving. What would you like? Poached eggs? Or a sandwich?" Again Ada shook her head. Cecily looked at Mrs Spencer, who still hadn't moved on acknowledged her presence. "Right, then, eggs it is."

She went into the back kitchen and searched through cupboards to find what she needed and began to prepare the meal, chatting as she did so, not expecting or needing a response. She set the table then changed her mind and put three plates on separate trays and took them in. First to Mrs Spencer, who made it difficult for her to place the tray conveniently but who eventually began to eat, then Ada and finally herself.

They ate in silence and when it was time to go back and open the shop, she asked Ada what she should bring for their supper. Ada shook her head indifferently so Cecily announced that she would bring fish and chips.

"Don't bring Van," Ada whispered.

Cecily didn't reply. She fully intended to bring her daughter. Van had always got on well with Mrs Spencer and a young, bright young girl might be just what was needed in the gloomy, sad house.

Ada went with her to the door and explained briefly what had happened, repeating what Cecily had already learnt from Willie. "Tonight we'll talk about it properly," she said. "I can't explain now, there isn't time." She hugged Cecily and added, "There'll be plenty coming to the shop with the gossip this afternoon."

"I'll ignore them. That'll shut them up."

The shop was filled from the moment it reopened after lunch to the final minutes as people heard about the arrest of Phil. To all questions and comments, Cecily gave the same answer. "I know nothing about it."

Willie came during the afternoon and, although it was never his job, he served a few customers, ignoring the questions and comments completely. Some discussed it among themselves as though Cecily couldn't hear, and when it was time to close Cecily was exhausted. "I feel like I've been pushed through the mangle," she said. "Now I must go and see Ada, and, if I may, I first want to see this handsome son of yours and congratulate Annette."

Peter came as she was about to close the shop door and followed her into the living room. "I came at lunchtime," he said, "but guessed you were with Ada. I won't stay but if you need company when you get back, phone me and I'll come."

"I didn't tell her about the divorce. She has enough to deal with at present. It will keep. Sadly, it won't go away."

"Don't leave it too long or she'll hear about it from others."

Dorothy was sitting with Annette and the baby in the pleasant home she had made in Willie's small house, and as the time for Owen's shop to close drew near she looked anxiously out of the window, dreading to see her sister-in-law, afraid her face would show the guilt she felt at the complaint to the police about Phil. Although, she reassured herself, she wasn't responsible for him carrying stolen silver and being knocked over by the doctor's car. That made her feel a little better but the guilt remained; she had reported her suspicions and made them take more notice of him. They would have watched him and eventually caught him, without the intervention of the doctor's car.

She heard the car stop outside and looked up. "Annette, dear, this is Cecily come to see our darling baby so I'll slip out of the back door. You don't want too many people crowding you." She picked up her knitting and reached for her coat and with a kiss for her daughter, she slipped away.

318

Cecily smelt her perfume when she went in. California Poppy. "Is your mother here?" she asked, after admiring the baby and picking him up for a cuddle, and taking the tea Willie had made.

"Yes, she just went home to get Owen's meal. Spoilt he is and hates to be kept waiting."

Cecily didn't mention the arrest of Phil; all the talk was about the baby and their plans for him. She saw the room they had made ready and the gifts he had received but afterwards she couldn't remember a word of what had been said or anything she had seen. Her thoughts were on her sister, and the letter from the solicitor and wondering how they would cope with it all.

She and Van went that evening and collected fish and chips for their supper. Cecily was proud of the way Van sat near Mrs Spencer and talked to her, told her how she loved the pretty room, shining with polish and with bowls and vases of flowers on every surface. Gradually the young girl, with her bright and cheerful presence, eased away Mrs Spencer's pain. She relaxed her deep frown and answered Van's many questions.

Telling Ada about the divorce was hard. Distressed as she was, she hated adding to Ada's worries but, as Peter had reminded her, she had to be told before someone else happily gave her the details of her sister's latest disaster. She took the news calmly, her senses dulled by her own situation. "I'm sorry, Cecily, but you can understand poor Jessie's need for revenge, can't you? Danny is her husband."

"But they are separated. Although I was partly the cause of that, so it makes me guilty and angry with my own stupidity. Angry with Danny too for — I don't know, for not being strong, faithful, honest, I suppose. I didn't chase him. He came to me."

"And you never could resist him, could you? Even with a wife you couldn't tell him to stay away. You were a fool and you know it."

Cecily was shocked by Ada's words. She expected sympathy.

"But having to stand up in court and be named as the other woman in a divorce. That's something I'll never live down."

"What does Peter say?" Ada asked.

"He's promised to help. There's nothing he can do to make this easier but he'll be there, and his friendship will give me strength. He came at once when I phoned and told him I was in trouble. He didn't ask what had happened, he just came."

"He's the one you should have married."

"Peter? But he's just a friend and besides, he's too old." But she frowned as she said the words. Peter was a loyal friend, never critical, always listening but rarely offering advice, but there when she needed him. "He's just a very kind friend," she repeated.

The next time she called, Cecily was glad to see that Mrs Spencer was in the back kitchen setting the table for hers and Ada's supper. Ada told her that Van had called twice and sat with Mrs Spencer and asked her to show her how to make a cake. "She was wonderful,"

Ada said. "She coaxed her out of her deep shock just by talking to her and presuming that she would do what she asked. I even heard laughter as the cake making didn't go quite to plan. She's a remarkable girl, our Van."

"Yes, she is, but since the news of Jessie's divorce came out and my part in it, she hasn't spoken a single word to me. She acts as though I simply don't exist."

"You can understand that. The shame of it. It can't be much less for her than for you."

"Don't say that!" Cecily was horrified at the harsh voice and the accusing words.

"It's true. When you went out with Danny, knowing he was married, your actions affected more than you and Jessie. You've never considered Van when you do these things."

"I'd never do anything to upset her!"

Ada tilted her head and stared at her. "Wouldn't you? Haven't you already given her unpleasant things to deal with, and her only a child?"

Cecily was upset when she left the house and got into the car. Luckily Van wasn't with her, she was with Edwin. So instead of going back to the shop she drove to the beach and called on Peter. Without a word he got into the car and directed her to a small public house a little distance from the town. He hadn't said a word, afraid — from the expression on her face — that she would burst into tears if he were sympathetic. He found them a table and went to order drinks. It wasn't until they were settled that he asked, "Do you want to talk about it, or just sit for a while?"

"It's Ada, she's so unkind. I feel I've lost my sister, who's my best friend, and a stranger is living in her house and wearing her clothes."

"With the shock of Phil's arrest I don't think she has the heart for anyone else's problems, even yours, but it will pass. Like most things it will sort itself out. The important thing is not to make things worse by making an issue out of what's a temporary problem."

"Temporary?"

"Everything passes."

"You're so wise, Peter. I'm so glad to have you as my friend."

"A loving friend," he said quietly. "Nothing that happens will change that."

She dropped him off at his house and as he stepped out of the car he asked, "Would you be willing for me to talk to Jessie on your behalf? I'd be very careful in what I say, but I might find out how determined she is about going to court and perhaps who gave her the courage to start proceedings. I strongly believe that the idea was not her own."

Cecily's first instinct was to say no, that she could manage, that she'd face it alone. She had no one, even Ada had let her down and she hadn't ever felt so alone as she did at this time. The whole town was against her, she had offended everyone, no one saw her as anything other than an outrageously behaved woman. Every face she saw showed disapproval and dislike. She had no one. Then Peter reached out and held her hand.

She stared at him in the darkness, his face barely visible, but she saw him smile. She wasn't alone, she had friends who wanted to help. There was no need to fight this on her own. Ada had let her down but Peter hadn't.

"Thank you, Peter, you might just have saved my sanity."

Christmas was approaching but it seemed to Cecily like something happening in another country. She didn't see the decorations in the shop windows, or hear the carol singers or the Salvation Army playing on the corner of the main road. None of it was a part of her world. Apart from the customers in the shop, whom she served like an automaton, her world was the living room where she spent most of her days and nights.

Dorothy didn't go near the shop. As usual she did most of her shopping in Waldo Watkins' store but she managed to gather all the gossip via her group of friends. Gleefully she told her daughter all she had learned, but Annette refused to discuss what had happened to Ada and Cecily; Willie's loyalties were hers too. Disappointed, she went to join some of her friends in the cafe, where she often met them during the half-day closing. There she felt very important, and shared all she had gleaned with added opinions of her own. But she wasn't happy. Somehow the situation hadn't given the spiteful satisfaction she had expected. Ada and Cecily were her sisters-in-law and a feeling of guilt at her lack of support reminded her of that fact. If her husband had lived, he would have been supportive, not spiteful. She made a cake, and sent Owen to deliver it, with a note stating her regret at their time of trouble.

It sounded pompous but she didn't feel able to send her love or some affectionate words of comfort.

Cecily looked at it and showed it to Willie, who said, "My Annette is a better cook than her mother." Which made them both laugh.

Peter found Jessie at home when he called a day later. Recognizing him, she smiled and invited him in. There were the usual offerings of tea and cake then she said, "I suppose you've come to talk about Danny and Cecily?"

Peter nodded. "I wondered whether you are still determined to take this to court."

She didn't answer and Peter added, "Can you cope with standing up in court and telling people about your marriage? It will be hard for you and I was going to suggest that you have your family there to support you. Cecily will have her sister, and several friends. You must do the same."

"I don't think I can do it," Jessie whispered.

Peter was silent for a moment then asked, "What gave you the idea of suing for divorce? It doesn't seem the kind of thing you'd want to do. Quiet and gentle is how I'd describe you, not bold and —"

"Brave?" she offered.

"All right, brave. It takes a lot of nerve to do something like this."

She leaned towards him confidentially, "I was persuaded by Mrs Owen. Mrs Dorothy Owen," she confided. "Mrs Owen and Gareth's mother, Mrs Price-Jones."

324

"Dorothy isn't the one to have to face it, is she?"

"What d'you think I should do?"

"You must do what you think is right, no one can decide for you. Now, if I could have another slice of that delicious cake, please, we'll talk about more pleasant things."

Two days later, Cecily heard that the decision to sue for divorce citing herself for adultery was changed and the client would go by the more usual route and wait the relevant time. Peter was pleased when she phoned to tell him and he suggested a celebration.

"No. It isn't a cause for celebration, Peter. I've been a fool and I've had a lucky escape, what's there to celebrate about that?"

Strangely, there was more talk when the court case was no longer facing her. Cecily heard remarks like wriggling out of responsibilities, luck of the devil, people like her never getting what they deserve, and Ada marrying a criminal. There were many references to their mother leaving them to live with another man, remarking that the family had bad blood. Gareth's mother was the one who spoke loudest, grateful her son had the sense to walk away from Cecily just before they were married. Dorothy was uncharacteristically quiet.

Phil had made his appearance in court and was remanded in custody. Ada was in court but she forbade Cecily from being there. The newspapers wrote an article about the sisters, and even though the news was out of date, mentioned the divorce and the name of the co-respondent, as well as the suspicion of Phil's involvement in the local burglaries. Van picked up the paper someone had shown her and ran out of the house, unaware of where she was going. She eventually went to Beryl and Bertie and Edwin, but said nothing about how she was feeling. She stayed a while. Beryl rang Cecily to tell her where she was, guessing Van hadn't told her.

She went home eventually, hardly speaking to Cecily apart from telling her she was going to stay with Auntie Beryl and Uncle Bertie and Cecily agreed, although she always hated sleeping in the empty house. She watched as Van packed a bag, gave her some money in case she needed something and made her promise to go to school without fuss the following day. Van nodded, shook her head, uttering a word only when necessary.

While Cecily was in the back kitchen preparing food, Van packed a second bag and put it outside the shop. Not waiting for food, she dressed in her best clothes and opened the shop door. A protesting Cecily asked her to at least eat before she went, pleading to no avail.

"And don't leave any presents out for me, *Mother*. I'll put them in the bin!" her daughter shouted as she ran out. Van was upset and Cecily wanted to talk to her, find out what was worrying her, half afraid she had seen the article in the paper, needing to convince her that the divorce story was incorrect and it would all soon be forgotten. Van slammed the shop door behind her and the bell tinkled angrily.

Cecily didn't bother to phone Beryl. Her daughter had just come from there so it must have been arranged. She put aside the food she had cooked and turned on the wireless, the sounds filling the room with a false company, and it was late before she went to bed.

The next morning she looked into Van's room wishing she and her daughter were better able to communicate. She wanted to phone Beryl to ask if Van had slept well or talk to the school later, to ask if she was all right, but she did neither. Van would not be pleased. She wondered if anything she did would please her and sadly thought not.

At four she expected her home and when she didn't arrive, rang Beryl and Bertie to ask if she was coming home or staying an extra day.

"Van? No, dear, we haven't seen since her Bertie took her home at about five yesterday."

"But she packed her clothes, said you'd agreed to her staying the night, something about a new game Edwin had been given?" She felt a chill that seemed to melt her bones and sank into a chair. "Oh, Beryl! Where is she? It was that damned article. She read that and she's gone. But where? What's happened to her?"

Bertie came on the phone, having heard the conversation plus explanations from Beryl. "Cecily, call the police. We're on our way. Now don't panic, she'll be safe. Sensible she is, our Van. She must have known what she was doing and planned a fright for us all." The phone went down and, fighting off the need to scream in terror, Cecily called the police station to tell them her daughter was missing. Then she rang Peter.

Van had set off on the Cardiff bus with her plans clear in her head. She knew which bus stop to ask for and defiantly demanded a single ticket. She was never going back. The streets were crowded, the bus was uncomfortably full and she was pushed here and there by the excited passengers. The lively shoppers annoyed her; she resented the atmosphere of fun. The anger was really for her mother who had ruined everything. Everyone was happy except her.

Too late she realized she was on the wrong bus and got off. She was cold, the bags were heavier than she'd imagined and she began to feel nervous. What if they weren't there? People do go away for holidays, even at this time of year. Then she saw the bus coming and confidence returned. She bought another ticket and travelled on.

Night was approaching and she began to feel afraid. She imagined knocking on the door and finding the place empty. What would she do then? If that happened, she decided, I'll go back home, tell them I wanted to give them a fright, and try again another day. Her bus stop was reached and she stepped off, and didn't recognize a thing. Wasn't there a shop on the corner, selling newspapers and sweets? She was hungry and badly needed some sweets. The houses looked different. The park railings weren't where she'd expected to see them, the bags were heavy and she was so cold.

At Owen's shop people were milling around and stupidly Cecily was standing in the back kitchen making tea for them all. She had spoken to the police and explained everything with complete honesty. This was no time to hide her embarrassment. They smiled reassuringly, and told her that runaway children almost always came home safely. "There has been no accident reported, so put those negative thoughts out of your mind, Miss Owen. She's run away angry with you, upset by the newspaper report."

"Someone could have taken her. She was alone and she's only a child. You do hear about such things."

"Not around here," the policeman said firmly.

Neighbours from the local shops came and were involved in the local searches, the voices of several nationalities filling the room as everyone wanted to show their concern and willingness to help. Some brought food, which was placed on the shop counter with the trays of tea brought in by Beryl and Melanie. Dorothy came with Gareth. Uncle Ben of the booming voice announced his opinion that she was a badly behaved child who should be punished for frightening her mother.

Spanish, French, Indians from the local shops came as did a couple of Norwegian sailors. All the neighbours came and mingled then went out to search. Cecily was offered worry beads by the Greek family and in a corner a lady was moving her rosary through her fingers, praying for help: Our Father followed by ten Hail Marys then offering it up to Our Lady with a request for help. She put her hand in her pocket still turning the rosary and assured Cecily that all would be well. Cecily was grateful to them all.

Peter helped with the search and told the police all the most likely places Van would visit. "She has plenty of friends. Cecily and I have written down all we can remember." He handed over a list. Men were sent to enquire at them all as Cecily tried to remember others.

A constable came in holding Horse's wife's arm.

"I seen her, I did!" the thin old lady said excitedly. "I seen her getting on the Cardiff bus. Struggling with two bags she was."

She was questioned and Cardiff police were told to look out for a little girl travelling alone.

"Could she be trying to find Mam?" Cecily said. "She loved her grandmother." She felt a surge of hope. "I don't know where she lives; we've heard nothing since she disappeared six years ago. But perhaps someone did and Van was told?"

As she had no address for her runaway mother and the likelihood was that she had changed her name, the suggestion was of little use.

"If she has found your mother, she would surely let you know the child was safe?"

Van kept walking around the streets, not going far from where she stepped off the bus, returning to that point twice, then three times. It was the right place, it had to be. Darkness was falling and she began to feel despair. She would have to go back home. Find out the exact address then come again. She mustn't tell them where she planned to stay. Reluctant to see the end of her adventure and her escape, she turned towards the place where she had left the bus. Unable to stand still, she wandered a little way down a street she had walked before and heard laughter. The lamp lighter had passed on his rounds, lighting the street lamps, and in the garden of a neat terraced house she saw the girls. She waved and, dragging her bags, reached the gate as their mother saw her and waved.

"I'm coming to stay. There's a note from Mam in my pocket," she shouted in excitement. "Terrible trouble they're in and Mam wanted me out of it for a while. Is it all right?"

Then she saw the cause of the girls' laughter. They had a kitten which was playing with a ball and piece of wool being swung in front of its paws and performing as only kittens can with agility and boundless enthusiasm as it attacked the toys.

"She's got two sisters and two brothers," the girls told her proudly. "Beautiful they are."

Jack Simmons offered to shut his shop and mind theirs if they needed to go and search for Van. Instead, Cecily sent him to tell Ada. She didn't want to worry her but she should be told.

Dorothy came and offered her sympathy, reminding them about her own daughter's disappearance when she had run away to marry Willie. "I remember just how frightened I was," she said. Then she listed all the most frightening scenarios that could possibly befall Van, and all the time explaining how much harder it had been for her, knowing Willie was involved. Willie who was the kindest and most hardworking son-in-law anyone could wish for! Cecily, in her stressed state, could hardly contain her anger. Dorothy was an unpleasant person and her words were tearing at her heart.

Rhonwen, her other sister-in-law, was different. She came and without adding to her fears, stayed, and helped when something needed doing. Her daughter, the giggly Marged, helped. Cecily thought it impossible not to smile when Marged was there.

Ada arrived, demanding to know what had happened and why she hadn't been told before. In the middle of all the chaos, young David their assistant came.

"I've got something to say," he said to Cecily and Ada, standing together to tearfully comfort each other.

"Something about Van?" Cecily asked hopefully.

"No." He frowned in a puzzled way. "It's about me."

"Tell me, but hurry up, I'm waiting for news about my daughter," she snapped.

"I have to give notice," he said.

"Now?" Ada said, "with all this going on?"

"Mam says I mustn't stay with divorce and criminals and all sorts of carrying on, and your mam running off with some man and — and so I have to give my notice."

He wasn't sure what reception his words would provoke but he didn't expect them to burst out laughing.

"It was just too stupid for words," they said to Peter. "To tell us he's leaving because of all that had gone on."

"His red-faced self-consciousness as he repeated the words given to him by his mother, it sounded so daft."

"They were too much," they spluttered with laughter, then they cried again.

News of Van's disappearance spread in the mysterious way that could never be explained. Beside the

332

immediate neighbours, the news travelled far beyond with first one or two calling, then dozens asking how they could help. Peter said he was going to find Willie. Cecily pleaded that he shouldn't be disturbed but Peter insisted. "He might know places and friends we haven't thought of."

Willie immediately reached for his coat as soon as he was told what had happened and went with Peter to the shop. He went straight to Cecily and asked where they had looked for her. "I don't suppose it's as simple as her hiding in the stables?" he asked the constable.

The man shook his head. "We've searched the house and knocked on the neighbours and searched all the yards around. We woke up Horse and his missus and she was able to tell us the little girl caught a Cardiff bus."

"We wondered if she was going to look for her granny," Peter said. "You don't know where she is living, do you?"

"Van wouldn't know if you don't," Willie said.

Peter looked at him, curious that his question hadn't been answered.

He looked at the list of places that had been searched, then asked, "Can I borrow the car? I can't say I have any bright ideas, but there are one or two places I could try. Nothing definite but any idea is worth considering." He refused to tell the searchers where he planned to go, insisting he was going to drive around and perhaps an idea would come.

He set off for Cardiff, planning to look at the house where the sisters' mother now lived. He had always known but had promised never to tell, but this was an emergency. He didn't reach there. Puzzled by how Van would have found the place if she had known, he remembered once taking Van to visit his mother and her new husband Derek Camborne. Would she have remembered how to get there? They had gone on the bus so it was just possible.

Willie's mother had welcomed Van even though the visit was a surprise. Van pretended to search for the non-existent note from her mother, and she was settled into bed with the teddy she had brought, after playing with the kitten until the little creature was exhausted, and having eaten a huge supper.

Willie's mother was a little curious. She had read the report of the arrest of Phil Spencer and the threat of divorce citing Cecily so she could understand the need to get Van away from all the gossip. But sending her on her own to a place she had only visited once? Why hadn't Cecily asked Willie to bring her? Van was fast asleep so she would phone the shop. She would tell them how pleased they were to have her and ask how long Van was staying.

It was answered swiftly and the voice was that of a man. Her immediate thought was, Surely not that Danny! He's caused enough trouble. She was surprised to learn it was a policeman.

Explanations were brief, before the message went through to Cardiff to pick up the child, but Cecily said at once, "No need. Willie is on his way, I'm sure of it."

People began to disperse, all murmuring words of relief. The lady with the rosary hugged them and smiled happily. One of the policemen stayed and Peter went out to make yet more tea, and set a tray for Van who, like all twelve year olds, was sure to be hungry even at such an unlikely hour.

Van insisted on staying the night with the Cambornes. Messages between Cecily and the various agencies went on but with Cecily's agreement, she was allowed to stay. It was late and Van was in bed and safe. Better to let her rest, Cecily thought. She won't thank me for dragging her back in a police car.

The next morning she was brought home by Willie, refusing to allow her mother to fetch her, and she travelled with two suitcases and two kittens, which, she told them, were called Penny and Pip.

She came into the living room, a kitten tucked under each arm and glared at Cecily. "They're mine," she said, tight lipped and defiant.

Cecily didn't dare hug her or scold her, nor could she tell her how frightened she had been not knowing where she had gone. After hesitating for a few moments, she knelt down and asked, "Which one is Penny?"

Van tilted her head to the right.

"Would they like a drink of milk, d'you think? And you can cook some fish for them."

"Fresh fish, not stuff left from yesterday."

"Of course. Willie has brought fish straight from the docks. Now, will you take off your coat, freshen up and put on some clean clothes?" She helped the prickly little girl out of her coat and took the opportunity to hug her and then tell her how frightened she had been and how much she loved her. Then she led her up to her room and helped her unpack.

The next morning, Ada came to open the shop.

"Ada! What are you doing here?" Cecily couldn't hide her delight at her sister's appearance. "You're needed at home, looking after Mrs Spencer."

"You need to spend a day with Van," Ada argued. "She needs to know how much she's loved. I think she is doubting it at present, don't you?"

Van was in her room, refusing to go to school, so the idea seemed a good one. "I want to go first to see Horse's wife and thank her for telling the police she saw Van on the Cardiff bus. It hadn't occurred to us before that."

She found Horse sitting up against some hay-filled sacks in a room in a sad boarding house. There was a bed and a couple of chairs, but Horse insisted he was more comfortable lying against the sacks. His wife was cooking some oats on a paraffin stove in a corner, where there were some foul-smelling bags of clothes. They both seemed pleased to see her and after thanking Horses's wife, Cecily gave them some soup and a bag of fruit before hurrying back.

They didn't spend the day together as Cecily hoped. Every suggestion was turned down and eventually Van went to see Edwin and his parents, who listened with less than approval to her description of her adventure. Even Edwin seemed displeased with her and she went home, miserable, and went straight to bed.

The kittens were put in the stable but when Cecily went up the next morning, they were on either side of her on the bed. Van opened her eyes and said, "I'm so stiff. I'm afraid to move in case I disturb them and they think I don't love them."

"I'll take them down for some milk. You can stretch out and rest a while longer."

"I want to give them their breakfast!"

"Of course, lovey," Cecily said, carrying the miaowing kittens out, talking to them, kissing their tiny round heads.

The days seemed a blur as Cecily tried to persuade Van to talk to her and promise she would never run away again. "Tell me what's worrying you, and what you want to do and we'll deal with it," she promised her stony-faced daughter.

Thankfully, Ada continued to stay at the shop, dashing home every lunchtime and at several other times during the day to check on her mother-in-law and make sure she was eating.

"She won't let me read the paper to her any more," she told her sister. "She never leaves the house so doesn't need to convince anyone she can read. I do the cooking, which she hardly touches, and I try to do the housework, but I know she does it all again when I'm out."

"Is there anything I can do?"

Again Ada shook her head. "She runs upstairs when anyone comes, apart from Van. Our Van is the only person she'll talk to. I feel so useless, and let down by

Phil's refusal to see me. What sort of wife have I been? I've never been anything more than a visitor there."

One evening, Ada stayed when the shop closed. Cecily guessed she had something to tell her. When she spoke it was the very last thing she would have expected to hear.

"I want to come back here to live."

"But what about Mrs Spencer? You can't leave her on her own."

"Phil still won't let me see him," she said. "And now his mother tells me she would rather be on her own."

"She doesn't mean it. She's trying to do what she thinks you want, surely?"

Ada shook her head. "She is determined to cope without me. She says I make it worse, knowing how her son ruined my life; that I'm a constant reminder of his guilt and every time she looks at me she thinks of Phil in that dreadful place."

Christmas came and went, parcels were left unopened, special treats hadn't been touched. The pantry was full of cakes and mince pies and pudding that no one had even thought of eating. Sweets and chocolates and nuts filled dishes and were left undisturbed.

Cecily met Jessie Preston unexpectedly in a lane behind the shops. Too late to turn away, they stopped and stared at each other. Cecily began to thank her for not going on with the divorce proceedings but Jessie put up her small hand and stopped her.

"I didn't do it for you. Besides, I could have chosen from several women. Don't think you are Danny's only 'bit on the side'," she said calmly. "You are just the most well known."

"Is that why you chose to involve me?" Cecily asked.

"There are plenty of people that are only too pleased to offer advice to someone like me. Pretending concern for the wronged wife."

"And you were — advised — to use me to divorce him?"

Jessie didn't reply.

"Did you change your mind because of the baby you carry? A divorce in these circumstances might not have been very convincing, would it?"

"There are explanations. Someone explained it to me."

"Whatever the reason, I'm grateful." Cecily hurried on. Dorothy again. What was the matter with the woman? Didn't she have any thought for Van if not for the shame on her own family?

She was distracted from her thoughts by noticing that Jack Simmons's shop was shut and boarded up. Curious, she asked Willie later if he knew where Jack was.

"I haven't seen him all day. The place has been closed and the shutters pulled down. Perhaps I'd better give him a knock." He went out then hurried back to call Cecily. "It's Jack, he's hurt."

Cecily finished serving the customer then went out with Willie. Ada followed.

They found Jack in the shop, a bloodied nose, cuts on his face, and a huge bruise on his forehead made him almost unrecognizable.

"It's difficult to understand what he's saying. He's talking as though his nose was blocked and his mouth full of marbles," Willie said cheerfully. "Been fighting again."

They took him into the back kitchen and Ada carefully bathed his wounds.

"That Danny Preston was told that I'd been seeing Jessie and he took offence. He can do what he likes but no one else can. The hooligan!"

"And were you?"

"No fear! She's the last one I'd take out with him on the loose! All I did was fix a broken shelf and stay for a cup of tea. That's all. And the shelf wasn't finished and will probably fall down and hurt her and her expecting too," he wailed.

Willie promised to fix the shelf and explain to Danny that Jack was only helping.

"Too late now," Jack moaned, holding a wet cloth to his bruises.

A few days later, Cecily filled the back of the car with her sister's clothes and personal items and drove back to the shop in a painful silence. She helped get Ada's things out of the car and carry them up to the bedroom, then left her alone.

They ate, with Van telling Ada how pleased she was to have her back, but could she still go and see Mrs Spencer. Ada said she could go as often as she wished.

When Van was asleep, both sisters got on with their routine jobs ready for the following day in the shop. Cecily looked around the familiar room, and the shadowy shop beyond. "Here we are, sitting here, with Van asleep upstairs, angry about Danny, just as it's always been."

"You doing the accounts, me planning our meals for tomorrow. It's as though your near marriage to Gareth and my failed marriage to Phil have never happened."

"We've come full circle," Cecily said with a sigh, "and we're back where we started."

CHAPTER
SIXTEEN

When Cecily stepped out of the shop and saw Uncle Ben and Auntie Maggie approaching, she smiled and waited for them to reach her. Their expressions were frosty, disapproval written large on their faces. They were about to walk on but Cecily touched her uncle's arm and asked, "Will you come in for a coffee? Ada and I are just having one, and there's some cake too. Seed cake, your favourite, Uncle Ben."

Maggie shook her head and Ben said, "Some other time. We're in a bit of a hurry." Then, as though conscience had struck, he asked, "All right, are you?"

"We're fine. Van is settled after the fright she gave us and Ada and I are busy cleaning and decorating, as we don't have time once the season starts."

Ben nodded and they walked on. It was one of those questions to which no one wanted or expected an answer, Cecily thought sadly.

They had seen nothing of Dorothy or Rhonwen, or Johnny Fowler. The only family member who called was Van's cousin, Marged, who called regularly to see the kittens and laugh at their antics. She wondered whether there was some way of getting the family back together. An excuse for a party, that was what was needed. She decided to talk to Ada about it.

The weeks after Christmas were quiet. There was no trade at the beach, everything was closed down and would remain so until Whitsun. Most of the local customers were plentifully stocked with the excesses from their Christmas stock-piling as well as being short of money from the over-spending. So apart from the basic perishables, trade was slow.

Cecily and Ada thoroughly scrubbed every shelf and cupboard, then began to decorate the living room behind the shop, taking away the smoke-stained, dull colours of their mother's time and brightening it with a fresh coat of paint and some subdued but less melancholy wallpaper. It wasn't work they enjoyed and they would normally have employed a tradesman but they needed something to fill the lonely hours, the cold, dark hours that seemed endless.

Both were trying to forget their loneliness. Cecily thought often of Gareth and how different life would be if she had married him. They would have been happy, she believed that, and any thoughts of Danny would have been relegated to the distant, barely remembered past. She tried to stop herself thinking about Danny, who had caused so much unhappiness, their love even affecting her relationship with Van, who still hardly addressed a word to her. When her difficult daughter needed something, she would ask Ada, or Willie. Never her mother.

Ada still visited her mother-in-law each day and usually took food. She would ask about Phil, grateful for any crumbs of information, although there was very little. Each time she asked if she could visit, she was told no, Phil wouldn't let her see him in that place. After the trial, when he knew how long he would be imprisoned, he told his mother that she and Ada could count the days with him but he wouldn't see his wife until he was home. So far he hadn't even written, he just sent the same message via his mother, that he hoped Ada would be there when he walked back into their home. Unless I'm told exactly when he'll be released, I might not even be able to do that, Ada thought sadly. She wondered whether he knew his mother lived alone, having sent her away.

For Phil, every morning was like the first day of his imprisonment. The noises that went on all day and night were the worst. The banging, the cries, the shouts and wailing. Then there were the hours of soulless routine and worst of all, the realization that this would go on and on, for months. Looking up at the sky on the brief exercise minutes, aware at that time most of all, of the freedom he had lost, he felt a dread of going back inside. He wondered how he could cope and come out anything like the man Ada had married. He cried a lot.

When Ada walked up to the main road one morning to give some accounts to Waldo, she heard the unmistakable voice of Horse accompanied by the tinny voice of his wife. Today he was ruining "Ding Dong Merrily On High". It didn't have to be Christmas for Horse to sing one of his favourite carols, although the words had changed and the tune was a bit confusing for anyone trying to join in. His wife stood rattling coins in his hat and as usual they were having a conversation.

"We've got the rent and-shillings-more."

"Some fish and chips for supper."

"Hide it then so we'll get-some-more."

"Will we have bread and butter?"

"Glad to see-e-e you're back on for-or-or-m —" Ada sang, joining in as she passed, making passers-by laugh, and more money rattled into the cap.

"We have to try and do something for Horse and his wife," she said to Cecily when she got back to the shop.

"We can try, but when I ask, they insist they don't want more possessions than they can carry on their backs."

"That's in case they don't have the rent and have to do a moonlight flit!" Ada said with a smile.

"Still, we could offer them a couple of spare blankets. The ones they are using are a disgrace."

"Where's Van? I thought I'd take her when I go to see Mother-in-law. She's always pleased to see Van."

"Has she any news of Phil?"

"He still won't let me visit him. I write, of course, but he never replies, he just tells his mother he hopes I'll be there when he comes back home."

"Not lucky in love, are we?" Cecily said sadly. "I saw Danny yesterday. He and Jessie were quarrelling. Nothing changes."

"I hope your involvement has!" Ada spoke sharply and Cecily stared at her. "Well, more gossip is something Van can't cope with. How can she? She's only a child. Your affair with Danny, and my Phil being arrested and found guilty of burglaries, it upset her so badly she ran away from us. You can't risk that again."

"She's hardly spoken to me since the night she ran off to Cardiff."

"I'll see if she'll come with me. She talks to Mother-in-law and cheers her no end."

"She'll be in the stables with the kittens."

Willie came back from a delivery and stood slightly embarrassed in front of them.

"Baby Victor all right?" Ada asked. "I'll call and see Annette when I go to Mother-in-law at lunchtime."

"She'll have some news for you." Willie looked unusually embarrassed.

"Good news I hope?"

"The best. We're going to have a second child. It's sooner than we'd hoped but we're both delighted."

Congratulations were offered and the sisters were cheered by the happy news. If it wasn't their happiness, it was at least theirs to share.

When Ada went to find Van, she found her nursing the kittens and talking to Edwin.

"Edwin! We didn't know you were here. Do your parents know?"

"Yes, Auntie Ada, they're shopping at Uncle Waldo's, then coming here to see you and take me home."

"But how did you get in without us seeing you?" She was smiling. "Did you crawl past the counter? Come down the chimney? Hide in the animal food delivery?"

"No, I knocked on the stable door and Van let me in!"

"I'm off to see Mrs Spencer. Would you like to come, Van? I'll wait till Edwin leaves. I don't want to miss his mam and dad."

Leaving the kittens in their specially made bed, they went through to the shop. Cecily too was amused at Edwin's appearance and explanations were repeated.

"Make sure the stable door is locked, mind," she said. "Willie's very fussy over that door."

"Me too," Van said, and she and Edwin began to laugh. Ada was curious about the laughter and the confidential glances but said nothing. She was relieved to see Van laughing, and children loved secrets.

Jack Simmons had reopened his shop and called each evening to see what stale fruit and vegetables he might get cheaply to offer his customers. He told the sisters that his fighting days were over. He wouldn't get involved in anything that would make him angry enough to fight. "Mind you," he told them. "That has to mean avoiding Danny Preston. He gets fighting mad about nothing at all. I spoke to his wife, that's all, and you saw the result of that!" Muttering about the unfairness of life when friendly greetings lead to a good thumping, he went back to his shop where patient customers waited to see what they could buy to feed their families.

So many men were out of work and neighbours shared the caring of children while mothers worked when they could find a vacancy. They all looked forward to the start of the summer season. Now, in the winter months when jobs were fewer and regular wages little more than a dream, life was even more of a

347

struggle for many families. On good weeks, tinned food was bought and hidden in readiness for a lean time. Allotments flourished where men were fit enough to work them and even there, the usual place reserved for men to chat without the interference of their wives, women added to the busy community, often with their youngest children. They would leave the men as school ended to meet the older children and get a meal while the men sat in the pub and made a drink last for as long as possible. Apart from a few leeks and some Brussels sprouts, there wasn't much to harvest. The earth was turned and cleaned ready for the start of the season. Men browsed over seed catalogues and decided what to grow, each growing more than needed so they could exchange plants with friends later.

Many people helped where they could and it had been a regular habit for some weeks for Ada and Cecily to fill a box with food and leave it in the lane for Horse to collect. There was usually enough to provide a reasonable meal for the two people. The odd couple always called on the way back from their regular spot in the town to thank them.

Horse was back to full health and Cecily wondered how he had survived the winter living as they did. The blankets were delivered by Willie, who reported that they were received with delight, Horse's wife declaring she had never owned anything more beautiful. So their gift was followed by a pillow, old but surely better than a hay-filled sack. Their business was thriving and they were glad to be helping the two homeless old people.

348

"We've known them for years but do you know their real names?" Ada asked, "because I don't." Ada was packing their evening's food.

"I think he's called Horse because of always smelling of horse liniment," Cecily chuckled. "What is even more odd is that we don't know his wife's name either. He always calls her Wife."

"Let's ask!"

Van was out so they locked the shop door after them and went to the place where Horse and Wife lived. The landlord answered the door.

"We've called to see Horse and his wife," Ada explained, about to walk in.

"Sorry, but they've gone."

"Where?"

The man shrugged.

"Why did they leave here?" Ada asked.

"If they don't have the rent they don't have the room. I've got plenty of people waiting to move in here, more respectable people too," the man blustered.

"How much did they owe?" Cecily asked.

"Eight shillings and that's before this week. Come Saturday and all I'll get are more excuses and you can't expect me to go on giving them a room with nothing but promises."

"You made an ex-soldier, wounded for his country, homeless for eight shillings?"

"More than that come Saturday!"

They walked away sadly, wondering where the two people were sleeping that night.

"We'll ask Willie to keep his eyes open."

"His ears as well! He's sure to hear him singing from streets away!"

Later that evening, Willie stood just inside the stable on the lane and waited for Horse to pick up the box of food. Wherever they slept, the food would be collected, he was certain of that.

Ada sent Van out at half past eight to tell him to go home. As soon as he left, Horse slipped around the corner where he had been waiting and picked up the box and hurried to the barn where they were sleeping, without the farmer being aware of his unpaying guests. Horses shared their accommodation and made it warm and cosy. They would stay for as long as the farmer was unaware of their presence. It meant getting up very early but they didn't mind that. The nights were the most important. Pity they couldn't heat food, but something would turn up, like it always did. Most days they could afford some soup, and cups of tea were often on offer, usually by shopkeepers as a bribe to make them move away.

His wife's only worry was his cough. She was afraid he might be heard and then they'd be sent on their way. She fingered the coins in her pocket. Tomorrow she would buy some more cough mixture. That always helped.

It was after the trial that had sentenced Phil to nine months in prison that Ada finally had a letter from him. She had been told nothing about the trial, Phil insisting that his mother didn't tell her when it took place. He couldn't stand in court and listen to his crimes and hear the sentence knowing she was there, watching him, listening to it all.

But she was there. The case was in the local paper and if she hadn't read it herself there were plenty to tell her when and where, some with sympathy, others with a less than kindly interest. Dressed in less than her usual style, she had shuffled in with the other curious members of the public, hoping Phil wouldn't see her and cry out, tell her to go away as she feared he might. Huddled in heavy winter coats she was anonymous among the similarly dressed strangers.

She was upset when she got back to the shop and went straight into the living room and sat crouched in their father's old armchair and stared into the fire. Cecily came as soon as the shop emptied and put her arms around her. They didn't talk for a long time. Cecily went in and out of the shop to serve and in between made tea and sat with her sister.

All Ada said about the afternoon was, "He looked so small, so defenceless."

"Will you try again to see if Mrs Spencer will agree to your going home?"

Ada shook her head. "I have tried but she insists she copes better on her own, although I don't think she leaves the house. Neighbours shop for her and she spends her time rearranging the furniture to decide which way it looks best, for when he comes home."

It was after the shop closed one evening when there was a knock at the shop door. Cecily went to open it, saw Mrs Spencer and called Ada.

"Mother-in-law, what a lovely surprise, come in, come and sit by the fire, it's so cold for you to be out."

Mrs Spencer held up a letter but didn't step into the shop. "No, I won't stay, I've brought you this." She put the letter into Ada's hand and hurried off, ignoring the pleas for her to come in and warm herself. Ada watched her until she disappeared in the darkness then went into the living room and threw the letter onto the table. It would only be the account from the coal man, which she had paid ever since Phil had been arrested. It was as they began to clear the table after their meal that Van picked up the letter, saw the envelope and threw it towards Ada. "A letter from your criminal, Auntie Ada," she said dismissively.

It was then that Ada recognized the large scrawling writing and knew that at last Phil had written. Grasping the envelope, she ran up to the bedroom, sat on the bed in the icy cold room and opened it. Unfolding it was almost frightening. What would he say to her after all this time? Would he ask her to visit at last? Foolishly she sat with the single page folded as though the imagination of his words were sufficient for her and the real thing would be a disappointment. She pulled the chain to increase the gaslight and opened it. It was disappointingly short.

I'm sorry. I hope you will forgive me.
Nothing like this will happen again.
Knowing you'll be there for me is my strength.
Fear that you'll walk away is a nightmare
that makes me afraid to sleep.

All my love,
Phil.

She went at once to the cottage where her mother-in-law lived alone and read it to her. Although she pleaded, Mrs Spencer still refused to let her come home.

Cecily heard little about Danny. She knew he was working part of the time with Willie and together they were making and selling small pieces of furniture. She often glanced at men who resembled him and felt both relief and disappointment when she was mistaken. So it was a shock to hear his voice behind her as she stood outside the shop putting the sacks of bird seed and corn in the shop porch.

"What are you doing heaving those sacks about, Cecily?"

She turned, saw him and afraid he would see the confusion in her eyes, the longing and the dread, she turned quickly away. "Willie is having a few days off. He and Annette are going to take little Victor to visit his mother and stepfather."

"I know that, I work with Willie every day. Haven't you got someone else to do the heavy lifting?"

"We manage fine."

"I'll come and help put it back in, when you close tonight."

"No. Thanks, Danny, but no." She went back into the shop and closed the door firmly.

That evening she brought the display from the porch in much earlier than usual.

"I'll do that for the next few days too, in case Danny isn't easily discouraged," she told Ada.

"Gareth hasn't been in recently," Ada said, one thought jumping to another. "He's stopped calling in for fruit each week."

"His mother insists he buys it in Waldo's. Ours isn't as good apparently, even though we buy from the same wholesaler and give any past its best on to Jack Simmons."

"We don't see much of our Dorothy either, not that I'm complaining about that!"

"We're dangerous women, Ada, love. You with Phil in prison and me, well, every mother dreads having someone like me as a daughter-in-law." They smiled but there was no humour in their eyes.

"I've been thinking. Would it be a good idea to invite them all for some sort of family party? We can think of some excuse, can't we?"

"Ada! I've had the same thought! Yes, we'll get it sorted and Van can go around with invitations. They won't refuse if Van asks."

They began making notes of who to invite and what food to prepare and for a while at least they felt less isolated from them all.

That night, they heard a commotion outside and when they opened the door, footsteps ran off and they found Jack Simmons with blood running down his face, his clothes torn.

"I thought you promised no more fighting," Ada said, guiding him into the shop.

"They were tormenting poor old Horse. I tried to stop them," he said, a blocked nose making his voice sound strange.

Cecily rang the police station and made a complaint. Jack knew who the men were and the police took a statement and went in search of them. Justice would be done via their fathers; the constable knew there was no need for a court case. Their parents would make sure they apologized and they knew that if it did happen again, there would be no leniency.

For a while Jack was a star. People called to tell him how brave he was, and gifts were given — many of which he took to Horse and his wife, who also gloried in his fame. A room was offered to them and they stayed for two nights before — afraid of not finding the rent — they left. Jack took the sister of one of the hooligans to the pictures and her brother nodded approval. Things were looking up for Jack Simmons.

On Wednesday afternoon, when the shop closed for half day, Ada went to see Mrs Spencer and Cecily decided to go to see Peter. The day was cold but dry and the garage was in the hands of Peter's apprentice, so they went for a walk. They set off in Cecily's car and drove to Dinas Powys to walk across the common and down the green lane where few people went, enjoying the quiet, appreciating the lack of people. It was a change from talking to customers all day and they were both content to walk and allow their thoughts to wander over previous places they had seen, and times they had shared.

They found a place to sit and enjoy the flask of tea Cecily had brought and eat the sandwiches and cakes. It was chilly but they sat close, sharing each other's warmth. Peter smiled. "I'll be glad when summer comes and the life at the beach starts again. I love to watch the families having fun. Not having much money doesn't affect their enjoyment. Mam fills a basket with food and some pop; children only want a bucket and spade and a picnic to be happy all day long."

"Van missed out on all that," Cecily said. "When Mam was here she used to take her sometimes, but Ada and I have been too busy, especially since Dadda died."

"Don't feel guilty. You and Ada have given her a happy childhood. Don't think she has suffered from deprivation; she's always known she is loved. That's more important than picnics."

As usual, a few hours with Peter made her feel more cheerful and confident. It was with regret she parted from him and began to drive home after returning him to his house. Loneliness hit her as a corner was turned and he was lost to her sight.

She was taking a short cut along country lanes when the car began to splutter and finally stop. There were no houses near and she was blocking the lane for anyone who drove along it. What could it be? She took out the starting handle and tried ineffectually to restart it but achieved only a groan from the engine. She stepped out and began to walk. She had no idea where she would find the nearest house but decided that as she hadn't remembered passing one recently she would walk in the direction she had been travelling. She walked a long way, then disheartened turned and walked back to the car. She had no idea what to do. Leaving it where it was wasn't a choice but what could she do? She couldn't push it. She just hoped that another car would come and be able to help. The lane was twisted and had high hedges on both sides so she came back to the car suddenly and there, standing beside it, was Danny.

"Run out of petrol, have you? The efficient Miss Owen forgetting something as basic as petrol?" He was laughing.

"Danny! Where did you come from?"

"I saw you turning into the lane and followed. I'm repairing a farm gate a bit further on."

"How much further? I walked for about ten minutes but didn't see a house."

"I'll drive around to get in front of you and tow you to a garage, how's that?" He was laughing again. "Running out of petrol! Dear me, I'd never have believed it!"

Angry now, she said, "It's Willie's job every week to fill up the car and the van. He's away and he forgot. Right?"

"Tut tut. Blaming poor Willie Morgan now. Really, Miss Owen the cold, efficient business woman, forgetting petrol. Tut tut. I'll have to tell Peter how I rescued you." Still laughing, he reversed his van away and she heard him turn into a gateway and drive off. A few minutes later she heard him coming back, this time in front of her and he took out a rope and tackle and fastened it to the front of her car.

"I'll drive slowly. Just steer carefully and we'll soon get you to a garage," he said.

The car seemed slow to move and he shouted, "The brake, woman! Take the brake off."

"I have! I'm not stupid!" she lied. "It must have been stuck on a stone or something!" She released the brake, hoping he hadn't seen, and they began to move along the lane. To her alarm he towed her back to Peter's garage. Then with a laugh he drove on again, this time to Peter's house. He stopped outside, came to the window of her car and sounded the horn. He waited until he saw Peter's face looking out of the window, then waved, the face disappeared and they drove on. When the car was filled, Cecily couldn't find the starting handle. Danny held it up and smiled at her.

"Come and have something to eat first," he said, approaching the car door. "There's a little place not far away. I'll drive you there."

"I want to go home. If you don't give me the starting handle I'll get on a bus."

His voice changed and he said, "Come on, Cecily. Friends we are, and I did rescue you from a difficult situation, didn't I? You can spare me an hour."

She opened the car door and he helped her up and hugged her briefly before setting off for the cafe he'd mentioned.

As usual they talked easily and slipped into their longstanding friendship with ease. They talked about Ada and Phil, and Willie and Annette and how happy they were. They even talked about Jessie, whom he admitted loving but was treating badly. "She doesn't understand that I can't sit and talk to her in the evenings, I have to be doing something. She hates it when I spend my time in the shed. Willie and I are trying to build a business and that's what I want to do. She'd benefit once we get the business underway but she can't, or won't, see that."

"Now there's going to be a baby," she said softly.

"I should have been more careful."

"Jessie wants this baby. But she'll need help to bring it up."

"She'll get that. But I won't be there hour by hour to see her grow."

"I think Ada would have liked a child."

"And you? D'you think of Gareth and what might have been?" She was about to speak when he added, "No point regretting anything now, mind. He's out and about with your sister-in-law Rhonwen. Lovely girl she is. Gentle and kindly and surprisingly, his mother approves. Serious they are, according to Jessie."

It was a shock for Cecily to realize that somewhere deep in her heart she had hoped that, one day, she and Gareth might have found each other again.

The day had been full of twists and turns emotionally and she was happy to have met and talked to Danny, a reminder of how well they got on, but there was Peter too, and the way Danny had made sure they had been seen together. Then being told that she and Gareth were over. Never to revive their love affair had been a final disappointment. Forcing a smile, she went in to tell her sister about the events of her afternoon off.

"I went to see Mother-in-law," Ada told her. "I read Phil's letter to her again and pointed out that he believed and hoped that I was at home, waiting for him. I pleaded but as usual she refuses to let me return."

Cecily's attempt to make her sister laugh with exaggerated details about her afternoon failed and both were subdued when they went to bed.

Peter had been upset at seeing Danny and Cecily together. There was little hope of her loving him and making his remaining years happy, but putting aside his own regrets, he was worried about her continuing to be seen with Danny. There was no happiness for her there. He banked up the fire but didn't go to bed. Midnight passed and still he sat, emptying a bottle of beer, something he rarely did, and stopping once to make sandwiches which he couldn't eat as they reminded him of the picnic he and Cecily had shared.

At five in the morning he had made a decision. He packed a small suitcase and left notes for the baker and milkman. He emptied the larder and put the perishable food outside for the birds to finish. At eight he drove to the garage and arranged for the apprentice and a retired mechanic to look after the place for a week or so and drove to Owen's shop.

Ada was putting out the barrels and sacks of animal feed and he helped her. Then he shook his head when she offered him breakfast.

"No, I'm going away for a while," he told her.

"Going away? Where?"

"I'm not sure. I'll just drive where the fancy takes me."

Willie came in then and overheard him. "If you're passing through Cardiff, call on Mam and the girls. They love visitors." He reached into his pocket for his order book and wrote out her address. Peter took it, thanked him and was leaving when Cecily appeared.

"Peter? Did I hear you say you're leaving?"

"Just a little break before the season starts."

"Why didn't you tell me?"

"I'm telling you now." He smiled and turned to go.

"Come on, Peter, you haven't just thought of this. You must have known for ages so why didn't you say anything?"

"It was a sudden decision."

"How sudden? You saw me." She looked at him curiously. "Was that when you decided? When you saw me with Danny?"

"It isn't my business."

"I ran out of petrol and Danny was passing and —"

"Danny told me what happened," Willie said. "How embarrassing, you forgetting to lift the brake and pretending you hadn't an' all!"

"Willie, he shouldn't have told you that." Willie and Ada were laughing and Peter hurried away.

"I'll check on the places from time to time to make sure all is well," Willie promised, shouting after his departing figure.

Cecily was upset and shocked by the suddenness of Peter's departure. He must have presumed she and Danny were seeing each other and although he was right and it wasn't his business, she wanted it to be. She wanted him to be a friend who cared; cared a lot.

Van and Edwin had a secret. They had escaped from parental care and gone out at night and wandered around the lanes looking for Horse and his wife. They found them hiding in a corner of a yard not far from the docks road. It was Horse's cough that helped them to locate him and while they talked to him, his wife returned with a meal of sausages which they cooked on a paraffin stove. The smell of them cooking made the children hungry but they refused a share.

"What will you do if you're thrown out of here?" Edwin asked. "I wouldn't know what to do if I didn't have Mam and Dad to run home to."

"There's always a place to sleep. Some better than this, others a lot worse."

Horse entertained them with stories of the various nights they had spent sleeping in rooms and sheds and barns and being chased off by landlords, farmers and shopkeepers. He made it sound like fun. Van laughed but Edwin, always more serious, wanted to know more about how they survived.

"The thing is," he told them, "Myfanwy and I worry about you both and we want you to know —" He stopped to allow Van to finish.

"We'll unlock the stable door every night and you can go in if you haven't anywhere better."

"But your aunties won't like that."

"They won't know. It's just an emergency, for when you have to sleep in places like this." Van's face curled with disapproval. "As long as you don't stay too late in the morning and Willie finds you, you'll be safe and you can go there any time."

Edwin saw Van safely back to the stable and watched her go in, giggling and blowing him a kiss. Then he went home and slipped through the hedge and in through the back door and up the stairs without his parents being aware of his absence. He didn't quite approve of what they had done, but Van's enthusiasm was sometimes impossible to resist.

The stable with its assortment of filled and empty boxes was a palace compared with many of the places Horse and his wife had used in the past and after one night, it was unthinkable of moving to a place with less comfort. They made their way there every evening, making sure they were out with all their bedraggled belongings before Willie arrived at eight.

Sometimes Van crept down to see them, opening the door from the yard and calling to let them know it was she and not one of the aunties. Sometimes she brought food and stayed to have a midnight picnic even though it was only nine o'clock and the gas-light was still showing from the living room behind the shop. Her secret made her smile a lot and if Cecily and Ada noticed her improved humour they didn't ask themselves why, but just hoped it would continue.

At night, once the sisters were in bed, Horse lit a fire. He built it from the paper, cardboard and wood lying around, close to the small exit door where the smoke would escape into the lane.

Steam rose from their damp clothes and the warmth gave them a joy that few would understand. It was sheer luxury; the warmth, the heat, the cheerful glow, flickering flames and fascinating shadows. Things they hadn't seen, apart from in their dreams, for many years.

After a week, Horse's wife dared to light the paraffin cooker which they carried in one of their bags, and warmed a tin of soup, and as they became braver they cooked eggs or sausages and put some for the kittens to find in the morning.

Gareth's mother was a constant irritation to him but this was too much. She was constantly asking if it was his intention to marry Rhonwen, reminding him that she was a widow and had a daughter who might not like having a stepfather. Many times he had explained that at present and in the near future he wasn't in a position to marry anyone and that he and Rhonwen were good friends. She still continued to ask. Her friends were questioning her and she wanted to be able to tell them the news and enjoy the congratulations, boast about the wonderful plans for a high-class wedding. For Gareth it had reached the stage when he simply refused to answer her repeated questions.

He and Rhonwen were meeting regularly, usually with Rhonwen's daughter Marged too. They went to the pictures, for walks and bus rides and on the train into Cardiff where they visited the museum and the parks. One day after another argument with his mother he closed the shop without telling her — although he hoped she wouldn't find out — then took Rhonwen and Marged to Cardiff for the day, filled with proud defiance. They had lunch at Marged's favourite cafe out of doors near the Cardiff market then to the market itself. After looking around the busy colourful stalls they went upstairs where pets were sold and Marged stared longingly at the kittens.

Gareth looked questioningly at Rhonwen, who sadly shook her head. She promised her daughter that one day they would have a kitten, but not yet. "Not while I'm working," she explained. "It wouldn't be fair on the little creature."

Gareth thought it might be the day to ask or at least hint about asking Rhonwen to marry him, but he put the thought aside. He was saving for something very important, something that would improve their future. Best he didn't discuss it, though, in case someone heard and ruined his plan.

Now was not the time. He wanted to buy the other side of the shop called The Wedge and extend his business, take on a second hairdresser and then he'd be financially secure. He hurried them past the jewellers to make sure Rhonwen didn't think he was showing an interest in the glittering rings on display.

A few days later he became aware of half-smiling glances and a few innuendoes about married men and engagement rings. He took the opportunity of seeing Johnny Fowler to ask if he'd heard any strange rumours. Taxi drivers heard all sorts of gossip from the driving seat of their cab.

"About what?" Johnny asked, grinning widely.

"Well," Gareth waved an arm vaguely, "there's some talk about an engagement. Definitely not mine. I just wondered if it's someone I know."

"Come on, Gareth, everyone knows you and Rhonwen are getting married. Your secret's out. Your mam told my mam and it's reported in every parlour and tea room in the town. Everyone's saying, 'Someone's caught Gareth Price-Jones at last.'"

"It isn't true! Mam's making it up. Short of gossip she is so she makes it up. Please, Johnny, tell everyone you see, tell them it's not true."

"It's a bit late for that, boy. Dates are being discussed and engagement gifts chosen."

Gareth didn't go home. He had no concern for the wasted dinner and prepared no words of apology for being late. He wasn't sure that he'd go home at all. He went to a hotel where they served meals and using the day's takings and money from his pocket he ate well and drank well and was feeling happy and defiant when he left. He still didn't go home. He had to wait until his mother was in bed or he'd completely lose his temper.

Besides making him look foolish, she had almost certainly ruined the lovely friendship between himself and Rhonwen. I would have married her, he thought, but now, with rumours and denials, she would probably avoid him. The humiliation was hers to suffer too.

He refused to speak to his mother all that day and avoided Rhonwen too. When he closed the shop he went to a restaurant for a meal, ignoring his mother's plea for him to eat the favourite meal she had made, and then went to the pictures. He stayed until the show — two films, the news and a couple of short items — had been around twice and finally, when the programme ended and "God Save The King" had been sung, he left and went over to the beach.

There were few people about. The place was silent, his footsteps echoing around the empty buildings, and the occasional bus drifted past with few passengers. Still unwilling to go home, and thinking of Rhonwen and Marged, he stood for a long time looking across the docks, lights showing the outlines of ships large and small, and wanted to leap onto one and be taken far away.

Outside Owen's shop, Gareth watched as the lights were dimmed. When all the lights were out he still stood there. He didn't want to go home. Life was such a mess and it was all due to his interfering mother. It was almost midnight, and still reluctant to reach his destination he walked away via the lanes, the longest way, and it was then that he smelled smoke. An investigation led him to the stables at the back of the shop and he ran to the front and banged on the shop door. Ada answered it, in her dressing gown and with curlers in her hair.

"Gareth! Whatever is it?"

"Grab a coat and get out — there's a fire," he shouted. He ran to the stairs and called anxiously for Cecily to wake Van and do the same.

"Where?" Ada asked. "There's no sign of it here. The living-room fire's out and the one upstairs was damped down with tea leaves."

"Don't argue! I'm going for the fire engine. Just get out and wait across the road till I get back. Wrap Van up warmly, mind, and wait there. Right?"

Cecily came down and although they couldn't see a sign of a fire they began to smell smoke. Cecily woke Jack next door and sent him to tell Danny and Willie. She didn't feel able to phone Peter since their recent uneasiness with each other. They crossed the road to where lights were appearing and neighbours were coming out onto the pavement dressed in an odd assortment of clothes and blankets. Willie came and banged on the door of the shop adjoining theirs before going to investigate. He quickly realized that the source of the fire was the stable.

Cecily and Ada hugged Van, all were shivering mainly with fright. A scream from Van chilled their blood and Cecily and Ada stared at each other for a long moment as the girl pushed herself free of them and ran across the road. They raced after her as she tried to get back into the shop and was being stopped by the couple from the shop next door.

"Horse!" she screamed. "Horse and Honoria! They're in the stable!"

"What are you talking about? Who's Honoria?" The sisters held her as she struggled to go through the door.

Willie held her shoulders and demanded, "Stop screaming and tell me what you mean? Is Horse in the stable? What's he doing there? How did he get in?"

"I left the door open for them," she sobbed.

He didn't wait for any more and as the sound of the fire engine was heard approaching, he ran through the shop and out into the yard.

Jack followed and as the first fireman entered and quickly followed, he shouted, "Give a bit of a squirt over my shop next door with them hoses, boy! All I've got is in there."

Annette sent a neighbour to tell her mother what was happening, even though it was the middle of the night. Dorothy woke Owen to tell him and he said, "Can I go there, Mam? The firemen will be there and lots will be helping, won't they?"

"You silly boy, of course you can't go. Wonderfully brave of you to want to help, but I can't let you go." Dorothy hugged him, overcome with pride at his offer of help for her sisters-in-law.

"I don't want to help," he said in surprise. "I want to see the fire engine."

She slapped him and sent him back to bed.

The firemen organized themselves with a speed that amazed those watching. As the officer was asking Willie for as much information as he could give, the hoses were already being carried through the shop. Following instructions as well as directions from Willie, some checked the house and others opened the door and hoses were dragged across the yard. Before they saw Horse and his wife, hiding in a corner behind piles of wooden boxes, the water was pouring over the middle of the room where flames were engulfing the cardboard boxes and supplies of paper bags.

The firemen went through the room swiftly and methodically, looking behind everything that could be hiding someone. They gave a shout when they found the couple cowering against the double gates that led out into the lane. They had been trying to get to the small gate set in the large ones to escape, but the fire was preventing them reaching it.

One man picked up Horse's little wife and another carried Horse and they hurried out of the burning building. Willie was told to leave but he stood outside, urging them to look to make sure there were no other uninvited guests sleeping there.

Waldo had arrived, and Bertie was there with a sleepy Edwin, having been phoned by Willie. Gareth was outside the shop, insisting that Cecily, Ada and Van were to sleep at his mother's house, assuring them that his mother would be glad to help them after such a frightening incident. They turned to look at Van but she wasn't there.

"I bet she's gone back in for the kittens!" Cecily said, and Willie went back into the house and ran up the stairs. He didn't find Van but the two kittens were sleeping peacefully on her bed. Willie carried them down, placing them in a basket usually filled with potatoes. Ada had found Van sitting in the fish and chip shop cafe drinking pop, the two owners making tea and sandwiches for others.

The sisters refused Gareth's invitation, imagining the expression of pained tolerance on his mother's face, and instead went back with Waldo and Melanie. They slept for a while but rose early and went to see what damage the shop had sustained. Apart from the smell of smoke and the mess caused by the people filling the place through the night hours there was no damage to the shop. It was too early to judge the state of the stable but Willie felt confident it was only clearing the debris and whitewash for the smoke damaged walls that was needed. The structure was unaffected.

"Thank goodness Gareth couldn't sleep," Cecily said. "We were so lucky he saw it so soon."

"He didn't come," Ada said softly. "Danny didn't bother to come. Willie told him but he didn't come to help."

"He told Willie it wasn't his problem and to ask someone else," Cecily said brightly. "Puts me in my place, doesn't it?"

They didn't open the shop that day and as soon as they could they went to the hospital to see Horse and his wife, who Van insisted was called Honoria. "She hates the silly name," Van told them, "so he just calls her Wife."

Horse was unrecognizable and they had to ask which was his bed in the long ward with two rows of patients. He was shining clean, as though he had been scrubbed and polished. He wore a pale blue nightshirt and his hair had been cut into a neat short back and sides. Honoria was sitting in a chair beside him, her hair washed and brushed, her face as clean and as wrinkle-free as that of a baby, and they looked so angelic they might have been born out of a fairy tale for children.

They were full of remorse. "Don't blame your Myfanwy," Honoria pleaded. "She was just being kind to us. We'll never go there again, we promise, but don't be cross with her, lovely girl she is, so kind."

Horse said nothing. He was breathing harshly but seemed comfortable in the unfamiliar cleanliness. Cecily decided to make some enquiries about his army service. "Perhaps he's entitled to a pension," she suggested to Bertie later. Bertie promised to find out what he could.

As the shop closed, the phone rang and Peter asked if they were all right. "I've just seen the news about the fire in the local paper. Are you all right? Is anyone hurt? Is Van safe? Is the house damaged? Why didn't you ring me?" he asked, not giving time for answers between the questions.

"Peter, we have a meal ready, please come over and share it and we'll tell you all about it."

Van began the explanation, admitting her part in the near tragedy.

"They should never have agreed to what you offered without checking with Ada or Cecily first, so the blame isn't yours," Peter told her.

She looked defiant. "I did it because I felt sorry for them. I'm glad I let them stay."

"Lucky the kittens weren't out there — they might not have survived," he told her seriously. "The smoke would have been enough to kill them. That's the risk you took. Are you sure you aren't sorry you didn't check with Cecily or Ada?"

"I wouldn't let Penny and Pip sleep in the stable," she said defiantly, "even though *she* told me to."

Glaring at her mother, she stroked the soft furry bodies purring beside her.

Ada went to bed early and Cecily stayed talking to Peter.

"I know I can't be anything more than a friend, but Cecily, my dear, I always want to be the one you turn to whenever difficulties arise. You know how fond I am of you. I want you to promise that I'll be the first person you call, every time you need help, whether it's as serious as a fire or as trivial as not being able to open a jar of pickle!"

He was smiling, but the smile didn't reach his eyes. There was something he wasn't saying. She felt uncomfortable, unsure of what was coming next. Did he want to be treated as someone for emergencies only? How ridiculous that sounded. But he couldn't be about to ask for something more of their relationship, not after all this time. She stood up and moved the kettle over the fire and said brightly, "Cocoa and toast all right? I'm starving!" They ate, and talked about many things, but she was left with the uneasy feeling that something needed to be said. But not tonight, she pleaded silently. Too much had happened, and she couldn't cope with more shocks or disappointments.

The next morning, as they began preparations for opening the shop, Willie came and told them that he'd received the first orders from the beach traders.

"Another summer begins and I hope it's a better one for you two than the last," he said.

It was unusual for Willie to make personal comments and they smiled at him. "We hope your summer is as perfect as the last one, Willie," Ada said. "For you and Annette and your son."

"I don't think you can ask for more, can you?" Cecily added. "You have a loving wife, a beautiful son and hopefully another child by the time Christmas comes again."

"And what of us?" Cecily asked, when they were alone.

"We've come full circle. The two of us here alone and neither sure how this year will end for us."

"Phil will be home. You know how it will end for you."

Ada shook her head. "Phil won't be the same person that I married. Who knows how he will feel about me, about our marriage. He can't talk to me, face me, and he might still feel that way when he comes home. I might be staying here longer than you expect. You and me running the shop just as we always dreamed. No Dadda to interfere. We had our wish there, but it hasn't been the dream we'd imagined, has it?"

"Van facing up to the truth of who we really are and our friends supporting us. We've said goodbye to many hopes and dreams. Dreams have been just that, ethereal, fanciful dreams. But we'll cope and be happy, because that's who we are: two women with a chequered past and a doubtful future, but a good business and some wonderful friends."

"True friends and that's more than many can say."

"And who knows, Phil might want our marriage to continue."

"And Peter, dear Peter, as long as he's in my life I won't complain." She was certain that Danny was no longer in her life; he was just one foolish dream. Perhaps Peter would make her forget him, make the foolish hope of a happy future with Danny Preston go away, drift into nothing more than a bad memory. She didn't discuss her dreams of a life with Peter. Dreams are ethereal things, easily shattered.

"Next New Year," she said, "we'll be laughing with the rest. Happiness is just around the corner, for us both."

The Promise

Susan Sallis

There were four of the Thorpe family in the Anderson shelter the night of the raid on Coventry. Mum and Dad, Florrie and little May. Jack was missing . . . he was one of those who did not return from Dunkirk.

When Daisy and Marcus, sixth formers in Coventry, are given a project on the bombing of the city in 1940, they go to talk to May, now living in sheltered accommodation but full of memories of the war. The two youngsters both have their problems — Marcus has to care for his alcoholic mother while Daisy's large and complicated family is full of tensions — and as their lives unfold they strike up an unlikely friendship and become involved in the strange history of May's missing brother and of a promise made all those years ago which still has its repercussions today.

ISBN 978-0-7531-8904-7 (hb)
ISBN 978-0-7531-8905-4 (pb)

Alice's Girls

Julia Stoneham

In the last months of World War II, ten Land Girls are serving at Post Stone Farm, under the watchful eye of their warden, Alice Todd. The local Land Army representative had at first been reluctant to give Alice the warden's job, and Roger Bayliss, the farm's owner seemed not to have any confidence in her at all. But she proved herself more than capable of the job and she has won the girls' admiration.

But Alice privately admits that one of the reasons she is so involved with the lives of her girls is that she has worries of her own. Recently divorced and with a ten-year-old son to bring up, she fears for the future. When peace is finally declared, and all Alice's girls make plans for their lives after the Land Army, she too has a decision to make.

ISBN 978-0-7531-8836-1 (hb)
ISBN 978-0-7531-8837-8 (pb)

Gull Island

Grace Thompson

The year is 1917, and Barbara Jones is shocked to be
told that she is carrying a child. Her boyfriend is a
soldier and there is no one to whom she can turn for
support. Indeed, her horrified father sends her away in
disgrace when he learns of her condition. Fortunately,
the generous Carey family give Barbara a home in a
derelict house on a beach near Gull Island and it is
there that her daughter Rosita is born. *Gull Island*
traces the lives of Barbara, Rosita and the Carey family
over many years — through wars, hurt, hope and
betrayal. When Rosita grows up, she must cope with
more than her share of deceit and disappointment —
but when she faces danger on Gull Island, those around
her find that they are stronger than they ever imagined.

ISBN 978-0-7531-8786-9 (hb)
ISBN 978-0-7531-8787-6 (pb)

Facing the World

Grace Thompson

Sally Travis appeared to have been badly let down by Rhys Martin, who had gone away when under suspicion of burglary. Sally knew he was at college and secretly supported him. She had faced the gossips alone when their baby was born, and ignored the worrying rumours about him.

Rhys's father, Gwilym Martin, had lost a leg in an accident but whereas Sally held her head high under difficulties, Gwilym, who had been a popular sportsman and athlete, hid away, unable to face being seen in a wheelchair. But Sally ignored unkind remarks and helped others, especially Jimmy, a young boy put in danger by his parents' neglect during their marital difficulties.

But doubts about Rhys begin to grow. When Rhys finally returned, would she still be waiting? Or had too much happened for things to be the same?

ISBN 978-0-7531-8586-5 (hb)
ISBN 978-0-7531-8587-2 (pb)